T. A Higgins

**The Life of John Mockett Cramp from 1796 to 1881**

T. A Higgins

**The Life of John Mockett Cramp from 1796 to 1881**

ISBN/EAN: 9783337333546

Printed in Europe, USA, Canada, Australia, Japan

Cover: Foto ©Raphael Reischuk / pixelio.de

More available books at **www.hansebooks.com**

# THE LIFE

OF

# JOHN MOCKETT CRAMP, D.D.

## 1796-1881.

LATE PRESIDENT OF ACADIA COLLEGE;
AUTHOR OF "THE COUNCIL OF TRENT," "BAPTIST HISTORY," ETC.

BY

## REV. T. A. HIGGINS, D.D.

MONTREAL:
W. DRYSDALE & CO.
1887.

# INTRODUCTORY REMARKS.

A word of explanation is deemed advisable. It was the hope of some members of the family that Thomas Cramp, Esq., late of Montreal, would prepare a brief sketch of his father's life for publication. So far as tender regard and needful information were concerned, no one else could hope to do it so well as he. He was old enough when the family left England in 1844, to be able, in after years, to call to mind many incidents of early life. Frequent visits were made by him, during the last few years of his life, to the home of his childhood. Correspondence was also kept up with the friends of the family in England.

Had he been permitted to undertake this work, doubtless many reminiscences, which give so much of life and interest to biography, would have been interwoven, and added great value to the record.

It required some time after his much lamented decease in 1885, before the work could be thought of or undertaken by another. This may explain why over six years have been allowed to pass without some permanent record of such a useful and instructive life, as that which is but too imperfectly exhibited in this small volume.

The work, such as it is, has necessarily been done at short intervals, as other pressing duties could be, for the moment, laid aside. If more time could have been devoted to it, the memoir might have been much more worthy of him whose record is given.

Nearly all the documents and papers left by Dr. Cramp, from which information could be derived, were in his own peculiar system of short-hand writing. This enhanced the difficulty of the work. While it was easily read by himself, it was sometimes difficult for others to decipher. And the writer wishes hereby to acknowledge his great indebtedness to Miss Cramp for her valuable assistance in this matter. Without her aid, the task, which has been an exceedingly pleasant one, would have been, to say the least, much more difficult, if, indeed, it could have been done at all.

Two chapters—the one referring to efforts in behalf of the Missionary cause, and the one headed "The last things," were furnished entire by Miss Cramp, who was the constant companion of her father, during the latter years of his life.

Valuable assistance has also been rendered by the other members of the family. If any pleasure or profit is derived from the perusal of the book, it will be largely due to the aid thus received from those who justly revere the memory of so great and good a father.

The labors, as well as the attainments of the subject of the following sketch, were so varied, and touched the world's interests at so many points, that it has been found difficult to avoid some repetition. Thoughts, and even expressions and dates already found in one connection, may appear again in another.

The hope, however, is cherished that whatever defects may be discovered in the style of the work, the unselfish life described therein, may be found stimulating and useful to some who peruse it, and especially to the young student who is looking out upon life, and anxiously enquiring in what direction success may be found.

The compiler of the following pages will have failed in one prominent aim of his endeavour, if the reader fails to see, that whatever natural endowments one may possess, work,—*honest, persistent* and *persevering* work, is the royal road to both usefulness and success.

T. A. HIGGINS.

WOLFVILLE, N. S.,
    February, 1887.

# CONTENTS.

# CHAPTER I.

" The voice of parents is the voice of God, to steer the wanton freight of youth through storms and dangers."—*Shakspeare.*

Literature has been greatly enriched by the record of devoted and useful lives. These records have often been made the stimulus to noble endeavour. By them, men " being dead yet speak," and thus continue to call to action those who might otherwise flag in the course. The material is not yet exhausted, and will not be, as long as Divine grace operates upon human hearts.

Many friends of the late Dr. Cramp have expressed the opinion, that his life and labors were too important and useful to be allowed to slip away from the memory of the young men of this generation.

In harmony with this feeling, an attempt is hereby made to rescue a few of the leading events of that life from oblivion, and to place them where they may act as " lights along the shore."

" To be useful " was the oft-repeated prayer of the subject of this memoir. And quite sure are we, that had his opinion been asked as to any account of his life that might appear, he would have had no higher ambition than that anything said or written of him, might be made useful to those left in the warfare.

He lived and worked for others while he lived, and, that his works may continue " to follow him " is the end sought in sending forth this small volume to the world.

He began early in life to use the Press as a means of usefulness. And it is thought, that by the employment of numerous extracts from his own pen, his history will be given with more accuracy than in any other way.

The following reference to his family history is taken from his account of the life and labors of Rev. Thomas Cramp, his father:—

" My father was a native of St. Peter's, Isle of Thanet, in which place he spent his whole life, and labored there in the Gospel during the long space of sixty-four years. He was born, March 25th, 1770. He died, Nov. 17th, 1851.

" At the time of his birth his parents were members of the Church of England. Martin Cramp, his father, was a strong-minded, well-informed man, accustomed to independent thinking, and therefore, not likely to submit to traditionary trammels."

The following passage from a sermon preached on the occasion of his death in 1822, refers to his religious character :

" With respect to religion, he thought for himself—he thought much—and he thought well.

" Great names never swayed him ; whenever he deemed that he discovered error, he freely animadverted upon it ;

and, if in maintaining his own sentiments, he sometimes assumed a tone nearly approaching to dogmatism, it was not because they were his sentiments, but because they appeared to him to be the sentiments of the Bible—the truth—the truth of God. He was well versed in Scripture, and would often astonish us by the length and correctness of his quotations."

Martin Cramp, becoming dissatisfied with the instructions of the Vicar of the parish of St. Peter's, united with the Congregational Church at Ramsgate, under the pastoral care of Rev. George Townsend (who died in 1837.)

Subsequently, a change of views on Baptism separated him from that community, and he became a member of the Baptist Church, of which his son was the pastor.

The anxious search for truth, which characterized the father, Martin Cramp, early manifested itself in the son. We quote again from the account referred to above.

" My father was the subject of serious impressions in his early youth. He felt deep reverence for sacred things, and was very desirous of gaining religious instruction. There was a yearning after spiritual life, which was not produced by the teachings of the parish minister, whose dry, moral essays, though listened to with utmost attention, were entirely incomprehensible, because they were destitute of heart."

In 1785, when Thomas Cramp was fifteen years of age, he heard a sermon from the Rev. Jonathan Purchis, pastor of a small Baptist Church at Shallows, half a mile from St. Peter's. That day proved to be the turning point in his life. He continued to go to Shallows, seeking for light. And sermons from the texts, " The end of all things is at hand," " Striving against sin," and "Come unto me," were made the means of great blessing. He saw the way of life through the atoning sacrifice of Christ, and yielded his heart to the Saviour.

He was baptized and became a member of the church, in March, 1787. In the autumn of the same year, he began to preach the Gospel. His occasional efforts were highly appreciated, and a room was secured at St. Peter's, where he preached every Lord's Day, morning and evening, for some time, worshipping meanwhile in the afternoons with the church at Shallows, under the pastoral care of Mr. Purchis. The room soon became too small for the congregation, and, in 1797, a chapel which had been built by the Methodists, and opened for worship by John Wesley, was secured. This building was purchased by Mr. Cramp for 100 guineas. Here the services were carried on till the year 1800. At this time, Mr. Purchis died. Then the church was divided into two : one having Margate for its centre, the other St. Peter's. The old house at Shallows remained the common property of both churches, each in turn using it on baptismal occasions, till better provision was made. Mr. Thomas Cramp was chosen as the pastor of the church at St. Peter's. His ordination took place July, 1800. For twenty-seven years he labored over this church alone, preaching three times on Sundays, once or twice during the week, besides attending prayer meetings and business meetings frequently. For about fifteen years, from 1827, Rev. J. M. Cramp was associated with his father in the pastorate of the church. In 1837, Rev. Thomas Cramp completed the 50th year of his ministry, and Jubilee services were held.

The son describes the event as follows :—

" It was truly a gladsome day. A large attendance of friends from different parts of the country were present. In the morning, after a meeting for special prayer and praise, my father praeched from Acts xx. 32-35. The sermon was one of his happiest efforts. The exposition of the text was clear and full; historical reminiscences were interwoven in the discourse with much tact and pathos ; and in adopting the language of the Apostle in reference to himself and his labors, the preacher took great pains to show that he did it not in a spirit of vain-glorious boasting, but under a deep sense of gratitude to God, through whose goodness he had been enabled to preach the Gospel without charge, as he intended to do till the day of his death."

In the evening, a public meeting was held, and an address from the Church and congregation was presented, a gift of valuable works accompanying the address. We can venture only upon one extract :

" And to you, dear sir, has fallen a rare and uncommon lot. You are a prophet receiving honor in your own native village. The companions of your childhood and youth have received from your lips the instructions of wisdom. Here, in your own home, you are accepted of God and approved of men.

" While we have no wish to use flattering words, or to

burn incense to vanity, we cannot withhold the just tribute of admiration and respect to the manner in which, by the grace of God, you have conducted your ministry among us. Your discourses have been distinguished by a transparency of meaning and a warmth of emotion which could not fail, under the Divine blessing, to instruct and edify.    To the sick and sorrowful, your attentions have been unusually prompt and exemplary; and those of us who are 'poor in this world,' have more abundant reason to cherish the most affectionate feelings towards you, and to declare in this public manner our unfeigned gratitude. We have shared in your tenderest sympathies.  Often, very often, have you strengthened the weak hands, confirmed the feeble knees, and caused the widow's heart to sing for joy.   Your life has been an extended illustration of the saying of the Lord Jesus, 'It is more blessed to give than to receive.'"

For fourteen years after this Jubilee service did the highly esteemed pastor of the Church of St. Peter's continue, without fee or reward, to labor for Christ in that neighbourhood. The Church grew. Other Churches were organized, and he had the happiness, before his departure, to witness great improvement in the religious condition of the people. Full of years, honored and beloved, he passed away to his rest, Nov. 17, 1851, in the 82nd year of his age.

The testimony of friends who were with him during his last illness, was very comforting and gratifying to the son, as it came in letters from time to time.   Many of his remarks were remembered and repeated.  Frequently did he talk on the subject of glorifying God, and lament that he had done so little, and that so little concern was manifested respecting it by professors of religion. Four months before his decease he remarked, "I have no desire to live but for the glory of God, and I don't see how I can glorify Him much now." Again, "I don't expect, nor do I wish it to be said to me, 'Well done, good and faithful servant.' If the Lord will condescend to say, 'You have been an unfaithful servant, but I have forgiven you,' that will be enough for me."

Such was the language of one who, for sixty-four years, had been engaged in preaching the glorious Gospel of the Son of God, in his own neighbourhood and entirely at his own charges, so far as remuneration was concerned.

And it can hardly be doubted that the spirit of humility and unselfish labor, so manifest in the father, had something to do in developing the same disposition in the son. Acknowledging the grace of God as the prime source of all nobility of character, we may often see the channel through which the good comes, and admire the wisdom which links causes and effects together, so that the latter are sure to come, because the former came. The devoted life of the Rev. Thomas Cramp, in the Isle of Thanet, England, from 1787 to 1851, helped to furnish a leader for the cause of religion and religious education in these Maritime Provinces, one to whom the Baptist denomination especially looked for wise counsel and warm-hearted sympathy in all times of difficulty.

The following is from the memory of one of the family :—

" My earliest recollections are connected with the little chapel which we attended at St. Peter's. My grandfather was a person of dignified and commanding appearance. His sermons were plain, doctrinal discourses thought out during the week. Study he had none, and of books a scanty supply, when judged by the needs of modern preachers, but there was a vein of originality running through his remarks which was well appreciated and generally admired. For many years he was always accompanied by his little dog, who gravely followed him up the pulpit stairs, and curled himself under the seat. He was perfectly quiet and decorous in his behaviour; but, if the sermon exceeded the usual length, he would rouse, and by moving gently about, intimate to his master that it was time to close."

Many changes have taken place in the Isle of Thanet since those days. The principles which the Rev. Thomas Cramp so long defended, have more advocates now. The church is larger and the pastors better provided for. But modern progress owes a debt of gratitude to those earnest, God-fearing men, who so faithfully laid the foundations on which we are still building. The only way to account for their self-denying efforts, in the midst of all opposition, is to acknowledge that God prepared them to do what a different class of men could not have accomplished.

The following description of the Isle of Thanet and surrounding neighborhood, may not be without interest to the readers of this memoir. Especially when it is remembered that locality has much to do in forming character. We become a part of all we see and hear and enjoy. It has been kindly furnished by Richard Smithett, Esq., of Hengrove House, near Margate, nephew of Dr. Cramp. So far as can be ascertained, this neighbourhood has been the home of the Cramp family for several generations at least.

This is certain that the three referred to in these records—Martin Cramp, Thomas Cramp, and John Mockett Cramp, were all born there.

"England has been compared by an intelligent foreigner, to a beautiful garden, its land itself looking as if, instead of the plough, it had been worked up by the pencil. In no part is this more manifest than on the southern coast. The ever varying landscape, tinted and colored, according to the period of the day, and state of the weather, the lights and shadows of the picture standing out, in consequence, in greater or less relief, the sun's rays floating over rich woodlands and pastures in the distance, the instability of an English sky, obscuring his light in the close vicinity of the spectator, or, reversing the scene, the distant and approaching shower, seen from the heights of the stern cliffs, like a straight line, separating the sunshine from the gloom, is an essential to the picturesque, which no foreign country displays in so great a perfection."

*Turner's Southern Coast of England.*

"The county of Kent, famed for its fertility, forms no exception to this charming description, and in some parts, has additional claims of interest from historic associations. The term 'Isle of Thanet,' though now strictly accurate, was in ancient times more visibly appropriate than at present. Alluvial formations have taken the place of the broad river beds, and the strait of the sea which once divided it from the mainland of Kent; vessels of large burden once sailed where flocks of sheep and herds of cattle now peacefully graze. Ships, when possible, avoided the stormy coast of the North Foreland, and, if bound for the channel, sailed round Thanet from the East, and emerged at that part of the mainland over where the twin towers of Reculver now stand. The derivation of the word 'Thanet,' has been sought in most unlikely places, and curious legends are connected with it in the chronicles of ancient writers, but on the whole, it seems probable that it was derived from fire (Saxon, Tan), since there were various beacons along the coast, intended, doubtless, rather to warn the inhabitants against hostile fleets, than to humanely point out the dangerous cliffs. Few parts of England, if any, have witnessed so many invasions as have fallen to the lot of Thanet. History is silent as to most, but the eloquent testimony of places of burial is conclusive.

" But, however obscure may be our insight into the earliest history of Thanet, that island is famed as the landing place of St. Augustine, with his forty monks, in the reign of King Ethelbert, in the year 956. The new missionaries were at first accommodated in the old British Church of St. Martin, at Canterbury, and, after overcoming many obstacles, speedily obtained a permanent footing for their faith, and by their influence, Christianity gained position and a strength which was never afterwards subverted, but rapidly increased.

" The isle of Thanet was the seat of the ancient monastery of Minster, once famed for its vast possessions which afterwards passed into the hands of the monks of St. Augustine's Abbey, at Canterbury. The abbey house still remains, and has been restored, and converted into a private residence.

" Although this island is somewhat small, containing

less than 26,000 acres, it embraces no less than nine parishes and two villes. Of the former, St. Peter's (where the father of the late Dr. Cramp was, for fifty years, a pastor beloved by the members of his own congregation, and respected by those of all other religious creeds) was one of the most important, and included the neighbouring town of Broadstairs within its limits.

" The Episcopal church, built in 1184, is a very handsome structure, with a lofty tower, from the summit of which the ordnance and other surveys of the surrounding country have been made. It appears to have been injured by an earthquake in the year 1580. This shock destroyed Saltwood Castle, near Hythe, and must have been one of unusual severity as affecting England.

" A very interesting journal was published in 1836, by the late Charles Mockett, of St. Peter's, a kinsman of the late Dr. Cramp. Therein the Cramps frequently appear, especially an ancestor whose name was Thomas Crampe, who adhered to the correct spelling of the ancient family name, from Suffolk, and various offices, and purchases of land made by members of that descent are mentioned. The island is remarkable for its fertility in most parts, and high cultivation in all.

" Enormous fortunes in the olden days were amassed by some agriculturists, when our constant and prolonged wars caused all food to command abnormal prices, and every security, Governmental and otherwise, fell in value. Two instances are known of nearly £300,000 having been computed to have been bequeathed, resulting from such sources. But those days have passed away, and the harvests of golden corn are of little pecuniary value. The days have passed when the beacon fires warned the scattered inhabitants of Thanet of the dreaded approach of ruthless Norsemen, when the subterraneous passages, now known to exist, but only very partially explored, were used as means of flight from one part to another, or as hiding-places for the weak and tender through age or sex, doubtless also, as store-houses for food, stock or moveable valuables.

" Now the invaders bring wealth and prosperity to the large and populous summer or autumn resorts, content to carry away with them no other booty than the health and vigor, so readily offered to, and gratefully received by, the peaceable hordes sent forth from the huge metropolis, and countless other parts of England. The old posting times, and the cumbrous trading hoys (often used as passenger vessels), are almost of the past, and the two railways bear their tens of thousands in search of strength, amusement, or relaxation from the iron fetters of business.

" Numerous hospitals stud the coast, churches have been restored and founded. Religious denominations work harmoniously together for the benefit of all, and though the earthly harvests may not be prosperous to the gatherers and toilers, full and abundant tithes are, doubtless, accepted and cherished in the eternal granary of Heaven."

# CHAPTER II.

## 1796—1818.

" Lord, my first fruits present themselves to Thee . . . . from Thee they came, and must return. Accept of them and me."

HERBERT.

John Mockett Cramp was born at St. Peter's, July 25th, 1796. He was, therefore, four years of age at the time his father was ordained as the pastor of the church there. According to his own amusing account of the ordination service, August 1, 1800, while the father was at the church, passing through his examination and receiving the ensignia of his office, the son was at home, vigorously pulling up the broad beans, which were at this time some inches above the ground. And so the day was well remembered by both.

What wonderful transformations time and God's grace can effect! Little would any one have supposed that in fourteen short years from that date, this father would be listening to sermons from the son, and soon after, with other grave divines in

Council met, to set apart to the Gospel ministry, this mischievous boy. And yet so it came to pass.

It was amid the scenes described in the preceding chapter, that his early days were spent. Here he received his first impressions of life. Here commenced the moulding which resulted in producing a vigorous intellect, great industry of character, and an unusual ability to perform work. The information acquired and the work done were both so great and so varied, that practical men were often astonished. While many men may have surpassed him in special departments of knowledge, few indeed could be found with such a fund of almost universal information, and largely at hand at a moment's notice, if called for.

A few extracts from his own pen in reference to early life :—

" My mother. Rebecca Gouger, was daughter of John and Mary Gouger, of Ramsgate. She died, 1803. My father married again, the year after. My grandfather, Gouger, died in 1809, aged 85. My grandmother in 1825, aged 89.

" I was sent to school at Canterbury, to a Mr. Baines, in 1806, and removed to Margate in 1808. Under Mr. Lancaster, who was usher at Mr. Lewis's, I first learned *how* to learn Latin. I left school in 1811."

We are too far removed from the scenes of these early school days, to be able to recite any incidents in connection with them. A boy's freaks of fun, idleness or industry, failures or successes, do not, except in rare cases, follow him for three thousand miles across the water. And if only half the time, forty instead of eighty years had passed since those school days, no teachers, and but few schoolmates would be found in Canterbury itself, to recall the incidents connected with them.

"Time and Tide roll on,
And bear afar our bubbles."

Submissive or wilful, at the head or at the foot of the class, we have no means of knowing. But drawing reasonable conclusions from what we do know, the presumption would be that there must have been great energy of intellect and rapid development even then.

"I first learned *how* to learn Latin," implies, to those who know his modest way always of referring to his own performances, that already the main difficulties of that language were conquered.

The foundations of many departments of learning must have been laid well at that time, for he continued to build upon them all his life; and the building became fair in its proportions and very substantial in structure.

The quantity of Latin and Greek read in the course of his life was very great, and he could read ordinary French books almost as readily as the English. The groundwork of all after development was laid in those years at Canterbury and Margate. He left those schools, however, not with the feeling that his education was finished, but that it must go on as long as there is more to be known. This conviction he acted upon till the end, and strongly urged the duty upon all young men going out from school studies to the work of life.

We quote again from the Journal :—

" My religious history began in 1812. I attended a baptism at Shallows—an old meeting-house, about half a mile from St. Peter's, where Mr. Atkinson, the officiating minister, stated that the candidate's first convictions of sin were produced by hearing a sermon on 1 Pet. iv. 18, ' If the righteous scarcely be saved,' &c. The words struck me forcibly, and led to thoughts and feelings which terminated, I trust, in conversion to God. I appeared before the Church and was accepted, Sept. 6th, and baptized by my father, Sept. 13th, 1812.

" About the same time I commenced the study of Greek, and made some progress; the first Greek Testament I had was given me by the Rev. S. Pigott, Vicar of the Parish.

" Desires for the salvation of others followed my profession of religion, and on January 31st, 1814, I addressed the people at the prayer meeting, and continued that exercise weekly, till I left home in September of that year, and engaged in theological study at Stepney Theological Institute, afterwards known as Stepney College."

The Rev. W. H. Newman was president of the institution at that time ; Rev. J. Young was classical professor, and the Rev. F. A. Cox, of Hackney, gave instruction in mathematics.

We quote again :—

" Dr. Newman was a well read man, especially in theological works, written in the Latin language, as was the custom of the Continental divines of the two preceding centuries. He was also an instructive preacher; his Sunday morning service at Bow was usually an exposition of

some portion of the New Testament, in which mode of
preaching he excelled. He resigned and was followed
by Rev. J. Young, whose tenure of office was short. He
was followed by Dr. Murch, and he by Dr. Davis. Dr.
Cramp says, 'subsequently the College was removed to
Regent's Park, under the presidency of Dr. Angus, who
enjoys a high reputation as a professor and an author,
and has been an active member of the Commission for the
Revision of the New Testament.'"

The following reference to Dr. Cramp, contained
in a letter recently received from Dr. Angus, will
be read with interest in connection with these remarks :—

. . . " Dr. Cramp was, as you know, one of our early
students ; but unhappily, the applications of students for
the first twenty years of our college life have not been
preserved. When I first settled as pastor in London, in
1837, I became personally acquainted with him; and between 1840 and 1847, I knew him and corresponded with
him on matters connected with our Mission, of which I
was then secretary. He bequeathed to our college library a collection of the works of the Fathers—a very
pleasant memorial of his good will.

" All through those years, he displayed the same admirable qualities. He was equally clear-headed and
warm-hearted, bright, unselfish, scholarly, and warmly
attached to Evangelical truth and to nonconformity ; the
friend of all good men, especially of his own brethren.

" The last time I saw him was, I think, in 1873. We
met at the Evangelical Alliance meeting at New York,
and recalled many old friends and many old incidents to
our mutual satisfaction. . . ."

From September, 1814, till May, 1818, the time
seems to have been spent in study at Stepney.

They were evidently years of great application, perseverance and growth. There were during this time many excursions into various parts of the city and surrounding country, in order to supply vacant pulpits, and do good as opportunities presented themselves. One is thus described :—

" A visit to Norwich in 1816, was very useful to me. I spent a month there, while the pastor, Rev. Mark Wilks, was absent. During that time I preached twenty sermons, and had access to the city library, where I found the works of the Rev. R. Cecil. I read them with great eagerness, and have continued their perusal ever since ; I know not how many times I have travelled through these volumes. Latterly I have read them over yearly, and always with greater thankfulness, and much reverence for the author. Young ministers of every denomination should endeavour to place Cecil's works in their libraries."

# CHAPTER III.

## 1818—1825.

"A workman that needeth not to be ashamed, rightly dividing the Word of Truth." 2 Tim. ii, 15.

In the year 1817, the church in Dean street, Southwark, invited Mr. Cramp to supply their pulpit for a time. His services proved to be acceptable to the people, and it resulted in a call to the pastorate of the church. The invitation was accepted, and on May 7, 1818, the ordination services took place.

The following account of the exercises is taken from the *Baptist Magazine* :—

" On Thursday, May 7, 1818, Mr. J. M. Cramp, late of Stepney Academy, was set apart to the pastoral office over the Church in Dean street, Southwark, where the Rev. W. Button had presided during a period of forty years. The Rev. Thomas Thomas commenced by reading the Scriptures and prayer. The Rev. T. Griffin delivered the introductory discourse describing the constitution of a Gospel Church, and asked the usual questions.

The Rev. T. Cramp, of St. Peter's, Mr. Cramp's father, offered the ordination prayer, the Rev. Dr. Newman gave the charge from 2 Tim. ii. 15. The Rev. T. Thomas addressed the Church from Rom. i. 11 and 12, and the Rev. Dr. Rippon concluded the interesting service with prayer. The hymns were read by Rev. S. Brown, of Loughton, and Messrs. Coombs, Reynolds, Green, Pope and Clarke, students of Stepney, were also present."

Some comments on this service were found among the papers of him whose ordination is thus described. He says :—

"The ministers who were engaged in this exercise were the principal ministers of our denomination at that time in the metropolis. Their gifts varied exceedingly; they were not popular men, but much esteemed in their churches. There was no laying on of hands, as Dr. Newman never practised it at ordinations. He regarded it as a Jewish custom in confirming appointments, frequently adopted in Christian Churches in imitation of the Jews, and when used by the Apostles after baptism, accompanied by the bestowment of miraculous powers, but as wanting Divine sanction in ordinary cases. It is at present an open question in the Baptist Churches in England."

The connection formed between the young pastor and the Church of Dean Street lasted for about seven years, till 1825.

They were years of great labor, of earnest prayers, some disappointments and some success. The following extract will speak for itself:—

"January 1st, 1820. Another year has begun. May it be better spent than the last; more for the glory of God, the prosperity of my soul, and the good of the

Church. Last night I set apart some time for serious reflection, and trust I found it profitable. I reviewed the events of the year, and discovered, as usual, cause for gratitude, sorrow and self-abasement. As a Christian, the retrospect is important. In my experience I cannot but think Mr. Ward's coming and addresses form a new era. It gave fresh vigor to my thoughts, directed my mind into a new channel, and was the means of a spiritual revival which lasted some time, the effects of which are not yet lost. The last part of the year has been but barren, though I hope I am returning to a better state of things. I trust I am not presumptuous in believing that I have been led into a more clear and correct view of the essentials of religion as a transaction between the soul and God. As a minister, I have had much cause for thankfulness. God has blessed my labors, has helped me in them. O for more fervor, apostolical simplicity and unction. This, I trust, I desire more than ever: to know the will of God in his Word, fully to understand and faithfully to preach it. . . . And now, O Lord God, I again give myself up to Thee. Be with me this year if I shall live. If thou shalt call for me, fit me for death. . . . Help me to be more in earnest for my own soul and for the souls of others, to forget self, to glorify Thy holy name, to live as for eternity, to pass through the world as a pilgrim. The text for my sermon to-morrow morning, 'Lord help me' (Mat. xv. 25) comprises my many feelings on this occasion."

These intense breathings after a deeper consecration of heart and life are very frequent in the somewhat imperfect journal of those times. There was an eager search for truth. References to the books read show that every effort was put forth to secure more thorough knowledge of divine things.

There were usually three services on the Lord's day and two or three during the week, and yet we find in January, 1820 :—

"I have read the 2nd volume of Milner, and nearly finished the 3rd. I have begun Robinson's works. I have read also Evans (one of the seceders) on the Trinity, and it has almost staggered me. Truth, however, is my object, and I trust I shall be able to receive it, whatever it be. I have formed a plan for reading the Scriptures critically through, a work I hope shortly to commence."

Early in February of the same year :—

"I have read the 3rd and 4th volumes of Milner, and am now reading the 5th. Have also read the 1st volume of Robinson's works and Paley's 'Horæ Paulinæ.'"

Those who knew the subject of this memoir only in his later years, and came to regard his views of Bible doctrine as always sound and reliable, may be surprised to find that he too had to pass through his struggles of uncertainty and doubt. And much of his reading, which was abundant, was nothing else but an intense earnestness to find the truth. Such expressions, for instance, as the following occasionally occur:—

"My mind is rather in an agitated, unsettled state. O Lord lead me into thy truth, and teach me. Dwell in my heart, help me to love and serve Thee, with all my powers, make me useful in Thy service."

On February 3, 1820, there is this record :—

"The times are eventful. On Sabbath day, the 23rd, the Duke of Kent died after a few days' illness, and on Saturday last, the 29th, our good old King died. On Monday I was present in the city when George IV. was proclaimed, and now I hear that he is very ill. Oh God, have mercy on Britain."

February 12: "To-morrow afternoon I am to preach a sermon on the death of the Duke of Kent.

"I have been busying myself this week in collecting materials for a sermon on the death of the King, to be preached next Wednesday, the day appointed for his funeral, which will be a day of general cessation from business."

In reference to work outside of the pastoral office, we find the following entries :—

"Soon after my ordination I began to make use of the Press as an instrument of usefulness. My first attempt in this line was a sermon entitled 'Bartholomew Day commemorated.' The reference was to the ejectment of the 2,000 from the Church of England ministry. This was followed by another discourse in commemoration of the death of King George III., in which the events of the reign were briefly related and the character of the Sovereign described. Other pamphlets appeared, among which I may mention an essay on weekly communion, advocating that practice as being universally observed by the primitive Churches. I found employment of another kind as a member of the British and Foreign Bible Society, and subsequently one of its hon. secretaries. In this connection I became acquainted with Wm. Allan, well known as a very distinguished member of the Society of Friends. Lord John Russell, afterwards Earl Russell, was a regular attendant at meetings of this committee, and frequently joined the sub-committees which were held at Mr. Allan's office in Plough Court, where he gave us tea sweetened with East India sugar, because it was not slave grown.

"I had two denominational appointments, one was a

secretaryship of the college, the other; assistant editor-ship of the *Baptist Magazine*, which was at that time conducted by a ministerial committee, who edited the publication in turn, aided by their assistants, who re-ceived £50 a year for their services."

In the year 1820, Mr. Cramp was married to Miss Maria Agate, a native of Garling, in Lancashire, a woman of superior mind and ardent piety, who read much on theological subjects in connection with independent study of the Bible. But this union was of short duration. In his own hand we find :—

"It pleased God that our union should be short. It ter-minated in 1823. Our only child became the wife of S. Selden, well known in these provinces as editor of the *Christian Messenger.*"

There were various seasons of illness during this pastorate at Dean Street, and many struggles be-tween failing health and desire for activity and usefulness are manifest in the records of the times.

March 12, 1821. "I have been very unwell lately, but am now better. I have been reading Fuller's ecclesiasti-cal history, and Hume, intending to pursue my studies in the church history of our country pretty extensively, with a view to compiling a book on the subject, chiefly for young persons."

April 12. "We can foresee scarcely anything. When I last wrote (in the journal) I was engaged in studying ecclesiastical history. I was soon obliged to desist. My sickness increased so much and so much weakened me, that I was obliged to lay aside labor and seek medical advice. I have not preached for a fortnight, nor can I even walk a mile without weariness.

"Yet I trust that this dispensation has been blessed to me. When *one* stroke will not serve, *two* must be given; first my dear wife was smitten, and now I myself am the sufferer. So be it, if the end of my trials be but accomplished in me, that I may be brought nearer to my God. I trust that this will be the case; though I need for this, as for everything else, continued communications of grace. Left one moment, I am gone. How humiliating, and yet so it is."

Because of this illness, there was a season of entire rest from public duties. A visit was paid to the old home at St. Peter's, in the Isle of Thanet, in the hope that the change of air and scenery might help to build up the constitution. The following record refers to that time :—

May 5. "Through mercy I am now returned from Thanet, better in health than when I wrote last. Hope I am now recovering. May my renewed strength be given wholly to God. Perhaps He has laid me aside awhile, because I did not do His work aright, nor aim sufficiently at His glory. Now that I am about to commence again, may I go in the strength of the Lord God, with humble, holy fervor and active diligence. I have heretofore wasted many precious hours, and sometimes exhausted my strength on pursuits scarcely worthy of it. May it never be so again. My time, my strength, my talents, are not my own, but God's. There are some things of which I see the importance more than usually great, and which I hope specially to guard should the Lord spare me and again employ me in His work. These are more personal intercourse with God, and more diligent reading of His word; a more spiritual manner of stating the whole truth, with more prayer for the Holy

Spirit on myself and the people, and a more diligent attention to my private pastoral duties."

About this time, there were some special trials for the pastor of the Dean Street Church. The Church was small. Many of the members were able to contribute but little. There was a general depression. Some were greatly disheartened. The majority of the Church were strongly attached to their pastor, but a few who were the best able to bear financial burdens were somewhat indifferent. The result was great uncertainty as to whether the cause could be sustained. We find the following reference to the case :—

" What will be the issue, I know not, things look rather gloomy. . . . I trust I can say that I only desire to know the will of God and then to do it, and that I should have grace to add, 'Thy will be done.' If He should please to direct me to stay, and still to labor under the cloud—be it so ; it will be for my good and His glory. If He should say, 'Go,' I am ready, but I wish to act towards the people as if my mind were perfectly at ease, and settled, and also to look up to the Lord for His guidance. And He *will* guide me. He has ends to answer in these trials which I shall one day know, and approve. And He has said, ' My grace is sufficient,' this is enough."

We may safely affirm upon the general principles of the Divine Word, that such prayers were answered, such strong assurance rewarded. Even if no change of condition could be noticed to warrant the assertion, still it may be asserted, that there were ends to be answered in the trials, and further results to flow from the quiet submission to the same.

But the journal that reveals the conflict followed on for a few days, records also the victory.

"June 7. Though I believe I am better in health, my strength is still more impaired than ever, owing to the very violent measures adopted. I am able now to bear but little exertion, either bodily or mental, but through mercy I have been able to go through my public work with much pleasure, and I believe with profit to the people, though at the expense of no little exhaustion. Last Lord's day, especially, my mind was impressed in a way which I wish particularly to notice. I preached from Rom. viii. 6, and Rev. v. 9 and 10. In the afternoon I was particularly elevated and animated, and continued through the whole day to preach and think with an unusually copious flow of light and energy. After the afternoon sermon and previous to the Lord's Supper, I was walking in the vestry, and my mind was powerfully impressed with this idea, that the Lord, in giving me such light and strength, was, in fact, directing me to employ my time and talents more especially in the illustration of His word and the advancement of His cause than I have hitherto done, and to renounce the idea of uniting them with anything that would entrench upon these sacred duties. I have latterly spent much time in scientific and historical pursuits, and I viewed this as a call to disengage myself more therefrom, and following the example of the apostle, to give myself unto prayer, &c.

"My mind continues to be affected in the same way, and I trust that the instruction will not be lost upon me. My own pleasure would be consulted by engaging more in the above mentioned pursuits, but our Lord saith, 'If any man serve Me, let him deny himself.' His service requires sacrifice. May I not be unwilling to give it. O Lord keep me in this mind."

A little later on, "I will just add that it appeared to

me that the reason of my not recovering was, that the Lord intended to bring me into this state of mind, and to cause me fully to acquiesce in His pleasure, and that till this was the case, I must continue to be afflicted. Blessed be His name, does He not deserve all my time, all my powers? May there never be a withdrawment or neglect on my part."

Deep regret is expressed because of heart wanderings and dullness of feeling at the Table of the Lord. "But," says the record,

"I found relief by confessing it to the Lord as my fault, and imploring mercy and grace; from which I derived this lesson—that it is in vain for us, when in a dull state of soul, to expect Divine manifestations, till we have humbled ourselves before the Lord, acknowledged our sin and entreated pardon and strength. Such has been the experience of my soul lately. May the Lord keep me in such a frame, humble, holy, watchful, prayerful, submissive. Amen."

These earnest breathings after a holier life, a deeper consecration to God, during the early years of the first pastorate, are very instructive. The record of them cannot be other than helpful to all who are longing after usefulness in the great work of proclaiming Christ; especially when it is remembered that he who penned these thoughts, thus frankly confessing that he had not yet attained, and was, therefore, far below the ideal standard, did grow in grace and knowledge, till the entire Baptist Ministry of these Maritime Provinces came to regard him both as a pattern of piety and authority in doctrine.

It may, perhaps, be as well stated here as elsewhere, that a ruling desire upon the part of the late Dr. Cramp was to be helpful to the rising ministry. He had great admiration for superior ability, and whenever men distinguished themselves in any of the honorable callings of life, his heart, so to speak, was drawn towards them. England's warriors, statesmen, philanthropists, filled a large place in his affections. But foremost of them all were the men whose learning and eloquence were employed in advancing the kingdom of Christ in the world. He admired the great and good of all callings. But he loved the men " called of God" to preach the Gospel. The name was not essential, but these belonged to the true nobility. This feeling grew with his years. And although for nearly forty years of his life he was not acting as the pastor of any church, he regarded himself so identified with the cause, that all the pastors had a prominent place in his thoughts. They were as his brothers or his sons. And not to be thinking of them and planning for their greater success, would have been to him as unnatural as for parents to cease to care for their children.

For this reason it seems all the more appropriate, that his thoughts, his resolutions, his aspirations, while in the pastorate, should be placed within the reach of that class, particularly for whose benefit he labored so much. His work as an educator would have lost more than half its charm for him only for the thought that an efficient ministry was being fitted for the supply of the churches.

Aug. 5, 1821, we find the following:—

"I have great reason to be thankful to the Lord for the mercy I have received from Him since I wrote last. I have been led to more active labour in the cause of God, in which I have found great pleasure. As to my health, it has been fluctuating. I hope soon to be entirely restored, though at present I am prohibited from preaching more than once a day. I have been led to see more clearly than ever, the need and importance of Divine influence, both as a Christian and a minister, and of prayer to obtain it. The promises on this subject have much interested me, as well as the facts contained in the Scriptures, the answers to prayer and the assurances of the connection between asking and receiving. The result has been that my own soul has been aroused to more earnest seeking the Lord ; I trust that I have enjoyed more seasons of delight in this exercise, and I feel a happy confidence that I shall be led into the truth, both in the knowledge and experience of it, and that the Church will be revived. At the same time, I have seen my own deficiencies, failings and faults. More : there has been too much independence, hastiness and self-importance in my conduct with the people; too much of the pride of talent and far too little humility before God, and earnest following after Him in private. Why have I been led to see these things? Doubtless for some good and laudable purpose. Certainly for the glory of God and my own good. How happy, how honored should I be if this be the case. O for more of the Divine Spirit, more life, fervor, energy: that my text for to-morrow, Eph. iii. 17, may be realized in my own soul, that I may be filled with all the fulness of God. How precious and how profitable has the Word of God lately been ; and in the Church some good is being done. Two persons, if not more, are about to come forward.

These are tokens for good. Oh, that I may be kept humble and prayerful.

" I have read with pleasure, Scott's 'Force of Truth,' Wilson's 'Sermon for Scott,' Jay's sermon on the words, ' Brethren pray for us,' and Ward's 'Farewell Letters.' "

A month later—"Sept. 18th. The Bible has been a precious book to my soul; the way of salvation through our Lord Jesus Christ, and wholly by grace, has appeared more glorious and suitable than ever, and the importance of an experimental acquaintance with it greater; in the exercise of faith and love, I have found unspeakable pleasure, and can truly say that my views of the Divine character, and my approaches to the divine throne have been accompanied with holy delight before unequalled. A great desire ever pervades my mind to know the will of God, especially as to the way of salvation; and to have a comprehensive idea of it; the more I think and search, the less I seem to know. May the Lord bless my public endeavours. As to the Church, the Lord is graciously remembering us. Four persons are about to come forward. The congregation has improved, a better spirit is prevalent. I have begun to act upon a plan of visiting the people by taking one day in the week for that purpose, and this also promises well; in short, I must say, ' Bless the Lord, oh, my soul.' "

The following letters to a member of the family refer in part to this period :

" My dear———

" Time rolls round, as the poets say, and brings the anniversaries with it. To-morrow will be your birthday. I wish you, according to custom, many happy returns of it. There are no new reflections to suggest. It is the old story—' goodness and mercy.' You have got through the duties and difficulties of another year, and so it will be during the whole pilgrimage: nor is·that all. It is not a mere negative. Not only is it true that nothing will harm a Christian, but even chastisements are for his profit, and ' all things work together for good.' Thus, ours is a blessed lot; the past has been mercy, and the future will be mercy. Yea, ' goodness and mercy ' will follow us all the days of our lives. So we will ' trust and not be afraid.'

" July, 25, 1873. I am this day 77 years old. As I lay in bed this morning, I thought of these words of the Psalmist: 'I am as a wonder unto many.' Those who saw my feeble infancy and my frail boyhood, and those especially who knew me fifty years ago, running the gauntlet of the physicians in London, would not have dreamed that I should be alive to-day. But here I am and still able to work, though with diminished strength. The review of the past is of the same character as on former occasions. There are mingled emotions: astonishment, —gratitude,—regret,—distrust,—hope. The best motto is Psalm xxiii. 6.

" I have been amusing myself, by noting where I was on the double figure birthdays.

" Thus—1818, when I was 22, in London.
      "   1829,    "    " 33,    Sowell Street.
      "   1840,    "    " 44,    Bromstone.
      "   1851,    "    " 55,    Wolfville.
      "   1862,    "    " 66,    College, Wolfville.
      "   1873,    "    " 77,    Wolfville.

" The next, 1884. 88 will not be seen on earth. But there is a place where anniversaries are unknown, because time will be no more. There may we all at last meet a redeemed family.

" January 5, 1822. Thus far I have been brought. The last year was an eventful one to me. What this may bring, God only knows. My times are in His hands, and He is wise and good. This is my comfort."

Following is a reference to Mrs. Cramp's failing health, and fears are expressed that there may be an incurable disease.

"If so, she cannot survive a great while: we must part. O what shall I do? In what a desolate state shall I be? a cheerless, comfortless being. Yet, it may not be for some time. God may be merciful. Let me remember that He is all sufficient, and will give grace for the trial. There I leave the matter. I have begun another year. Oh, that it may be better spent than the last. If not, I shall have had the rod in vain."

Mrs. Cramp's health failed rapidly after the records above were made, and she died, January 29, 1823.

"Dec. 31, 1823. I have reached the last day of the year. How it has been spent, I can hardly tell. I can only say, it is gone, gone like a dream. Widowed and alone my time has been much occupied in study. I have labored more in this respect than in any former year, and I hope to some good purpose. I have also opened a Lord's Day evening lecture, and have commenced with a course of sermons on the person and work of our Lord Jesus Christ, in preparing and preaching which I feel much interested. But the cause at Dean Street is very low. I am sometimes much perplexed and cast down. Whether I ought to stay or go, seems sometimes doubtful. I trust the Lord will direct me."

It appears that the principal, if not in fact, the only difficulty, in connection with the cause at the Dean Street Church, was a financial one. Those able to support became disaffected or indifferent, and the ordinary results followed.

" July, 1824. When the accounts of the church were audited, it was ascertained that a considerable deficiency existed. A special church meeting was called, when, without consulting me at all, it was resolved that for the future, I should have what was collected, without stating any fixed sum, I did not feel myself justified in making any further sacrifice, and therefore, after consulting Mr. Burls and some others, told the church my mind at another special meeting."

This action of the church led to the resignation of the pastor, and a separation, painful alike to pastor and people. There is this reference to it:—

" I much regret this event, for there are very promising indications among us: the congregation is increasing, the lecture is well attended, and several young persons wish to come forward. On the other hand, however, there seems to be a spirit of coldness and indifference upon the part of certain members, so that they will make no further effort. The bulk of the church are much grieved, but I am satisfied that I am doing right. Nevertheless, I cannot understand it. It is altogether mysterious. May I be directed."

The latter part of 1824 and the beginning of 1825, was a period of some trial. In addition to bereavement, and perplexity in reference to the affairs of the church, there was a severe attack of illness.

"Jan. 30. It is the Lord's Day, and the seventh of my confinement to my house. It has pleased the Lord to afflict me very severely. For three weeks I was considered by the physician in danger. But the Divine blessing was vouchsafed to the means employed, and I am now fast recovering, though I have not yet been out of doors.

" That this dispensation has been designed for my spiritual good, I cannot, must not doubt. I hope that I am already deriving benefit from it. I had been resting too much on official religion; there was too little *personality*, if I may so speak, in my godliness. The Lord has caused me to retire from the bustle of life, and bids me meditate and pray and turn again to himself. O that I may do it with my whole heart and serve him with more fervor and strength than ever! The consequences of this trial are likely to be very important. I am forbidden to reside in London, or to preach three times a day. I am told that I must give up some of my engagements, and make the preservation of my health my main object. So it is most likely that I shall relinquish the idea at present of taking any pastoral charge; seek some respectable employment, literary or otherwise; live a little way out of London, and preach occasionally. This will make a great change in my life, and what may be the nature of my engagements, I cannot tell. But I am enabled, in a good degree, to commit all unto the Lord, who will ' choose my inheritance ' for me. I have much pride and independence about me; perhaps it is now intended that I shall feel my dependence on the Divine care, and have my daily bread supplied as it were daily, and not with my own exertions. Well, be it so——Whatever my God ordains, will be for my good. Only this I pray, that I may be permitted still to do something for God."

The pastorate of the Dean St. Church closed with the services of Lord's day, Aug. 22, 1825. It was a day of mingled feelings. There was thankfulness, joy and sorrow. Thankfulness for the good that had been accomplished, for the advance made in knowledge, some growth in holiness. Joy in the thought that there was no break in the feelings of love and esteem between the pastor and the church. They had been seven years of honest toil.

and much good had been done. Truth had been set forth clearly, and principles boldly defended.

We have no means of giving the number of additions to the church. Although there are frequent references to persons offering themselves for membership and to baptismal occasions, the numbers are seldom given. These, of course, were kept in other records, which are not in our hands. But enough is given to show that there were seasons of refreshing, when pastor and people rejoiced together.

But there was much sorrow. Deep regret that circumstances compelled a separation. Health was much impaired. There were doubts whether it would be possible again to resume the work so congenial to the feelings. From any human standpoint there was, therefore, much of anxiety and uncertainty as to the entire future course. There had been deep grief during this first pastorate. The union formed in 1820, and which promised much comfort at the time, was broken off in 1823. The wife, and mother of the first child, was laid away to rest. The father was left with enfeebled energies to look out upon the world and face its difficulties alone. Thus, in the furnace of affliction, the Lord prepares those destined for great usefulness in the world. "To be of some service" was the constant desire, both spoken and written. And, as in many other cases, by ways that he understood not, the prayer was being answered. Great usefulness lay before him. Great perplexities and trials were the paths leading to it.

# CHAPTER IV.

## 1825-1827.

" Such let my life be here.  Not marked by noise, but by success alone.  Not known by bustle, but by useful deeds."

We have materials here for a very short chapter. Partly because the period was short, and partly because it constitutes a break in the life work. In tracing a stream, so long as the body of the water keeps together, although there may be many turnings and windings, yet the course may be followed without difficulty.  But if the obstructions become so numerous and great that the stream itself is divided, and takes divergent channels, one may be in doubt whether he is following the main branch or some smaller outlet.  Dr. Cramp's life, for two or three years just here, was in an unsettled state. His work was of various kinds, and one could hardly say which was the chief.  His residence was in or near London.  A portion of the time was given to seeking for health.  His physicians told him that he had been overworked, and that his only hope of permanent recovery was rest or an entire change of work. This period includes a portion of the time that he playfully represents himself as " running the gauntlet of the physicians." The time that no one would have dreamed that he could live to be an old man.

It was hard, however, for a man of Dr. Cramp's temperament to rest long at a time, even if the state of health demanded it. He engaged in variour literary pursuits. He examined manuscripts and reviewed books for the Tract Society of London. Large works were abridged, so as to be suitable for distribution among the masses of the people. Many efforts were put forth on behalf of popular education, a matter in which Dr. Cramp was deeply interested.

About the time of his first pastorate in London, the subject of popular education was pressing itself upon the British Government and the legislators of the kingdom. But few schools existed to supply the demands of the rapidly growing population of the laboring classes, especially in the larger cities. Lancaster had recently introduced his method of giving the masses the rudiments of learning at a cheap rate, and efforts were being made to extend the system throughout the kingdom. The British and Foreign School Society had been recently formed for the purpose of promoting this good work. Among the friends of this movement, the Rev. Mr. Cramp was recognized as one of the leading minds, and at the anniversary held in Freemason's Hall, on the 10th May, 1824, His Royal Highness, the Duke of Sussex, being in the chair, the following resolutions were unanimously adopted by the committee and the public meeting, respectively :—

"This committee having considered the importance of the openings now presenting in different parts of the world and the extensive correspondence which is likely to ensue, is of opinion that the services of two honorary secretaries will be necessary, and therefore proposes that the Rev. J. M. Cramp be united with Francis Cresswell, Esq., in that office.

"That the office of honorary secretary, which had been held from the commencement of this Society by the late, ever to be lamented, Joseph Fox, and which has continued vacant since his death, be now filled up, and that Francis Cresswell, Esq., and the Rev. J. M. Cramp be appointed honorary secretaries of this Society."

By means of this appointment, Mr. Cramp had wide scope given for extensive usefulness in the cause of popular education, and was brought into intimate relations with the more prominent friends of education and the leading politicians of the day, none of whom were warmer advocates of this Society for many years than the late Lord John Russell.

When it is borne in mind how much Great Britain was indebted to this Society for the spread of general enlightenment amongst the people at that day, before any general provision was made on behalf of its common schools, and when education depended upon the charitable bequests of benevolent persons or private adventurers, it will be seen what appropriateness there was in this appointment, and how well he was suited to such a wide field of usefulness—that he was emphatically "the right man in the right place"—which office he continued to fill for several years.

In harmony with this movement, and partly to promote its interests, a new publishing company was started in London : the object being to furnish cheap literature for the people. Dr. Cramp undertook to superintend the literary work of this company. The result may be given in his own language :—

"The interval (since the last record) has been filled with momentous events. The society for promoting general knowledge mentioned in my last, did not succeed. The publishing company engaged the premises, 24 Paternoster Row, and soon formed extensive connections. I stipulated that I should only take the literary department, such as examining manuscripts, correcting for the press, &c., &c., and should not be required to occupy myself further. I soon found, however, that more than this was necessary, and I was engaged ordinarily in business from breakfast till tea time. The effects of this occupation were most disastrous in a spiritual sense. With sorrow I must record that my soul became increasingly barren and lean during the whole of this period."

We find in the journal of these years many regrets for coldness and heart wanderings, many confessions of unworthiness, which forcibly remind one of a fact to which the Doctor, in after years, frequently called attention, that is the beautiful simplicity of the Old Testament saints, in humbly confessing their own wrongs. One said, "Few and evil have the days of the years of my life been." Another, "I am not worthy of the least of all the mercies." And again, "But, as for me, my feet were almost gone; my steps had well nigh slipped." And, David, " I acknowledge my transgressions, and my sin is ever before me." Paul, " Not meet to be called an apostle, because I persecuted the Church of God."

In addition to literary labors, and the efforts in behalf of general education, there was much preaching in supplying vacant pulpits during these years of uncertainty. An average of con-siderably over one sermon a week for the whole time. And yet, Dr. Cramp never reviewed this period of his life with satisfaction. He felt that, in a certain sense, they were lost years. He had been turned aside from the channel of his life work. And some of his own references to the time would lead to the conclusion that his connection with the short-lived publishing company, had proved disastrous to him in financial, as well as in other matters. Whatever he suffered, however, he regarded it all, in after years, as needed discip-line, and a part of the one Divine plan in working out the results of his life. He was no anti-nomian, and yet he believed that a guiding hand had been leading him all the journey through. Light and shade, rightly blended, make a pleasing picture.

One event, however, of this period stood out in strong contrast from many of the others. To this he never looked back with regret, but regarded it as a special mercy from God, and given as an off-set to much that was painful.

On February 1st, 1826, Mr. Cramp was married

again. The second Mrs. Cramp was Miss Anne
Burls, daughter of W. Burls, Esq., of Lothbury.
He regarded himself as singularly fortunate in his
choice.

And as the years rolled by, it became more evident that "fortunate" was not the word to employ,
but "providential," and that the "choice" was
less his own, than that of the One who was directing his way. A record of his own, may express
the gratitude. After a reference to his marriage,
he says :—

"Two years and a half have elapsed since that event.
Blessed be God for his goodness. My beloved is everything I could wish—pious, prudent, careful, amiable, retired, modest, most sympathizing and kind; a treasure
indeed. The providence of God singularly directed to
this union; I received her from the Lord, to Him be all
praise."

This union continued 36 years. It closed July
26th, 1862. But the opinion expressed above,
strengthened as the years passed. And all who
enjoyed the intimate acquaintance of Mrs. Cramp,
would cheerfully testify to its correctness.

Shortly after the sad separation in 1862, the bereaved husband published a small pamphlet, entitled, "A Portraiture from Life." It was a sketch
of the history of the one who had been taken away.
It was not designed for publication, but rather for
perusal by the friends of the family. The picture,
however, was so lovingly and tenderly drawn, and
the one who drew it, having now gone, we think

that there can be no impropriety in inserting a few extracts. He says:—

" Her parents were persons of eminent piety, held in high esteem by all with whom they were associated. They were members of the Baptist Church, then meeting in Carter Lane, Southwark, of which the Rev. Dr. Rippon was pastor, and which is now under' the care of the Rev. C. H. Spurgeon. Her father was one of the deacons of the church. He was also for many years London treasurer of the Baptist Missionary Society. Her religious advantages were of no common order, and were no doubt, greatly blessed to her. She was led to give herself to God early in life. The following is her own account of her conversion:—

" ' I can hardly remember the time when I did not feel *some* interest in serious subjects—a love to God's people—and a great pleasure in committing to memory, hymns, passages of Scripture, &c. Thus it was with me till 1810, when it pleased my Heavenly Father to visit me with a severe illness. I was obliged to leave school, and for some months could not leave my room. Then did I especially feel my need of an interest in Jesus, and I longed to *lay hold* of that hope which I felt I had been only *look-ing at.* My dear parents often spoke to me, but I was unable to tell any one what was passing within. Gaining some strength, change of air was desired, and Kettering was the place fixed upon. There, my dear mother placed me under the care of an old and valued friend of hers, who not only supplied her place, with respect to those attentions my situation required, but often spoke to me of the things belonging to my everlasting interests. There also I had frequent visits from Christian friends, and when able, regularly attended Mr. Fuller's ministry. About this time I was much impressed under a discourse I heard him deliver. It was an exposition on John xv.

1-5. On my return from the house of God I freely opened my mind to the friend with whom I was placed. She encouraged me to hope that I was really united to the 'living Vine;" but I felt there was something wanting, and I longed for more evidence of a renewed nature. A few days after, it pleased the wise Disposer of human events to destroy my expectations of complete restoration to health. I caught cold one evening; an inflammation of the lungs followed, and I was considered in danger. My own impressions were that I should never be raised up again. My distress, at first, was extreme: distance from my beloved friends—every circumstance added to the anguish of my mind. But God was pleased to "speak peace unto me," and enabled me to resign myself into His hands. I felt Him near to me, and could look at death without much dismay. The 276th and 277th hymns of the selection, I found contained the language of my heart, and I almost longed to be where I should grieve my best Friend no more. But God was pleased to bless the means used for my recovery, which was very rapid, so that in April, 1811, I returned home.'" After some other statements, the account proceeds:—" I then determined that, in the Lord's strength, I would avow my attachment to Him and His people. I had found I could live upon the Fountain, and that there was enough in God to make me happy. Thus, in April, 1812, I was united to the church (in Carter Lane, then under the ministry of Dr. Rippon). I cannot say I enjoyed much at that time. The adversary was permitted to harass my mind with the apprehension that I had done wrong; but I trust God accepted the surrender, and has enabled me to make it again and again. Different means have been used to show me the hidden evils of my heart. I have proved that God never inflicts a wound he could safely spare. My conquests have been slow and inconclusive; but I trust I can look forward to the period when I shall wield no more the 'warrior's sword' but 'wear the conqueror's crown.'"

"The above was written in 1824, in which year my acquaintance with the dear departed one commenced. We were married Feb. 1, 1826. Since that time I have had, of course, full opportunity of observing and knowing her manner of life. We have travelled together in sunshine and storm; we have climbed the hills and descended into the valleys; we have tasted of the "cup of salvation," and we have drank some bitter draughts: joy and grief, hope and disappointment, with other contraries, have fallen to our lot;—and now, "one is taken and the other left." The survivor is called upon to discharge the last office of friendship and love. From the baptismal vow to the departure heavenward, Christian uniformity of demeanour was observable in the lamented deceased. It was a quiet walk with God, a well sustained endeavour to exhibit, in temper and conduct, the influence of the Gospel. Her gentleness of spirit and retiring disposition shrank from the whirl and bustle in which some find themselves at home, and Christian graces shone in a limited sphere, yet not less brightly. When she entered into the marriage relation, wider scope for the manifestation of love and zeal was furnished, bringing into operation powers and qualities which had not been before developed. Nearness to God was habitual. Her times of retirement for meditation and prayer were sacredly observed. They were hallowed seasons. She came forth from her chamber refreshed, and prepared for labour or conflict. How she was occupied while there;—what Divine communings she enjoyed;—how closely and impartially she examined herself, in regard to principles, feelings, aims, and motives;—and with what earnest pleadings, she sought

God's blessing, especially on her children, cannot be
told; but enough is known to warrant the conclusion
that the hours of her withdrawment from society were
spent in heavenly exercises, the effects of which were
seen in the whole course of her life.

"These habits were conjoined with maturity of character, to which indeed, they largely contributed. Her
piety was at once intelligent and warm-hearted. Unlike
many Christian professors, who satisfy themselves with
the rudiments of religion, and are therefore ever at uncertainty respecting their state, she desired to 'comprehend, with all saints, what is the breadth, and length, and
depth, and height, and to know the love of Christ, which
passeth knowledge,' that she 'might be filled with all the
fulness of God.' . . .

"She enjoyed in a high degree the pleasures of benevolence, esteeming it an essential part of the Christian's
calling to tread in the steps of Him, who 'went about
doing good.' Her whole training, in the family and in
the church, tended to this result. She had seen bounti-
fulness at home in manifold forms, and her conduct
proved that she had learned the lesson well.

"Our denominational objects were dear to her heart;
especially the foreign mission, with which she felt particularly identified, having had frequent opportunities of
forming acquaintance with missionaries when they were
sojourning for a while under her father's hospitable roof.
Her co-operation was frequently sought and cheerfully
given in connection with the multiform plans of usefulness in which Christian females take delight. The poor
experienced her kindest sympathies, and no small amount
of relief was afforded to them both from the purse and
from the 'basket and store.' Afflictions, many and
various, were endured. Children were taken away, and
near relations removed, by death. Sickness, losses, disap-

pointed hopes contributed to swell the list of her sorrows, and sometimes the 'waves and billows' followed each other in rapid succession. She bore all with submissive patience. . . .

"Warning was given, several years before her death, when it was ascertained that she was the subject of a disease (an affection of the heart), the final blow of which might be parried for a while, but would at length fall fatally, and might come on a sudden. She received the warning with composure, and was thankful for it, because it so powerfully enforced the necessity of habitual preparation. From that time, she sought to live as 'dying daily.' . . After an interval of suffering, endured with characteristic sweetness and submission, the peaceful close of the quiet life, thus described, took place at Wolfville, July 26, 1862."

The following letter was addressed to his oldest son, the late Thomas Cramp, Esq., of Montreal, shortly after his return home. It had been a very sad family gathering, but the writer of the letter could see that there had been much of mercy mingled with the bitterness of the cup:—

"August 11, 1862.

"We all felt your departure very much, but could not feel thankful enough that you had come, and that you came just when you did. It seems to have been mercifully ordered by a kind Providence.

"The recollection will be mournfully grateful to you, especially connected with the assurance that your visit contributed so materially to the relief and comfort of the dear departed. . . . Mr. de Blois preached a good funeral sermon on the Lord's day after you left, from Psalm cxvi. 15,—the funeral text for your grandfather

Gouger, fifty years ago. I have written a paper entitled, 'A portraiture from life.' It contains a sketch of your dear mother's character, and an account of her death-bed experience. . . . not meant for the public eye, but printed for circulation among our friends.

"I could not feel satisfied without doing something of the kind; for though *we* cannot forget what we have seen and heard, there is a large circle of relations and friends to whom such a document will be very acceptable, and it will tend to perpetuate your dear mother's memory in a suitable manner. I trust it will do good, as an additional testimony to the reality and power of religion; for so assuredly it must be regarded. Contrasted with the delicate reserve of former life, that death-bed freedom and fulness of communication could not but be regarded as striking. Certainly God was there, influencing and blessing the soul of the dying one. The recollection of these scenes must be instructive to us; we shall dwell upon them with deep interest, and seek to become better acquainted with that 'form of godliness' which was associated with so much power, and life, and hope. I desire to feel the quickening effect in my own soul, labouring henceforth as one who has but a short time to live, and setting before me the bliss- and purity attained by those who have gone before."

# CHAPTER V.

## *CO-PASTORATE WITH HIS FATHER.*

### 1827–1842.

"Year after year he trod the round of patient toil, plodding, preaching, praying—the lamp of his zeal was fed with 'fresh oil' from the fulness of God."

The event which changed the course of Mr. Cramp's life occurred in June, 1827, about fourteen months after his second marriage. This was the sudden and unexpected death of his only surviving brother. After explaining some of the circumstances and symptoms, he says :—

"I took my station in the room and left him not, till he breathed his last very early on Friday morning. Oh it was indeed a trying, an agonizing scene: I had not seen death before. I loved my brother. I saw him die. On the following Friday, he was buried, and on Lord's day, June 10th, a funeral sermon was preached for him to a crowded congregation from 2 Cor. v. 1–5."

The record continues :—

"This afflictive event operated in an entire change in all my prospects. My father felt his inadequacy to the cares of business, and the labors of the pulpit. After

4

mature consideration it was arranged that I should leave London, reside at St. Peters, and occupy the farm at Bromstone, lately occupied by my brother. And here I am at home. Business requires but little of my care. I share the labor of the ministry with my father, and am gratified to know that the people are pleased therewith. I think I am in my right place."

The following is from "Reminiscences of a member of the family":—

"In 1827, my father left London and went to reside at St. Peter's, where he assisted my grandfather in preaching at the Baptist Chapel of that village. Many of the people were poor, and had not been trained to give of their substance for the support of the Gospel, so that it was necessary to do something more, to aid in providing for the expenses of a growing family.

"For several years, the literary tastes formed while living in London were made to subserve this end. The Tract Society furnished him with congenial work, and was enriched by many books, compiled, abridged or otherwise prepared by his own facile pen. This was work which he loved, and for which he had great aptitude.

"In 1832, he removed to a farm in the neighborhood, but amidst all the extra care and labor, his pen was never idle, and his study was his cherished retreat. Pastoral labor he did not fully enter into, but in those days three services on the Lord's day was the rule. My grandfather always preached in the morning, leaving the other two sermons for his son; there was also a prayer meeting on Monday evening, and a short discourse was usually given on another night, later in the week, so that he had more than enough to tax his strength and energies.

"My father was very partial to singing, and as his children grew old enough to join in the exercise, they were always expected and encouraged to do so. It became a custom to employ a short time on the Lord's day morning, before starting for service, in this way. The family were brought together, and various hymns were sung. There were no Moody and Sankey books in those days, but our service of song was culled from 'Watts' or the 'Selection.' Memory recalls two of the favorites : 'Safely through another week,' and 'Sweet is the work, my God, my King.'

"Four of the loudest and sweetest voices of this family circle are now hushed in death; but the time will come when all will unite again, though in a sweeter strain.

"As we grew up to years of understanding, my dear father was anxious that the subject of personal religion should be considered."

While yet quite a child, and away from home. the following letter was received :—

"April 5th, 1834.—We were very glad to hear that you are well, and doubt not that you are very happy. But we cannot be quite happy, you know, unless we love God, and try to serve and honor Him, according to the directions of the Bible.

"Now none of us can say we have done everything that we ought to have done. We have sinned against the Lord very often, and deserved his anger. Even you, my dear child, young as you are, must confess that you are a sinner; bad thoughts, bad tempers, bad words, are sins as well as bad actions. You know this; do you feel it? Does it *grieve* you to think, that you have sinned against the Lord? Do you pray to him for forgiveness and for a new heart? Do you love to think of Jesus who came to earth to die for sinners, and do you look to him to be your Saviour? All this must be done if you wish to be saved; let it be done now, for to-morrow is not ours."

Two years later, the following was received :—

"Saturday night,
"July 16, 1826.

"MY DEAR—

"I have just finished a day's hard work and completed my preparation for to-morrow; but I cannot retire to rest, without placing on this paper the expression of my feelings respecting you at the present time.

"To-morrow your friend is to make a public profession and avow herself a lover of the Lord Jesus. She is younger than you, my child. I cannot tell you how much I feel it. You have sat together to see others baptized—but to-morrow you will be separated. You have sat together to witness the celebration of the Lord's Supper—but now she will be within, and you will be without. Oh, what delight would it give me to see you also within. But I could not consent to your admission, till I possessed satisfactory evidence of your having a new heart, hating sin and loving the Lord Jesus, and striving to be holy and like Him. You have knowledge, but this alone will not save you. You have sinned, and must repent; you are guilty, and must look to the Lord Jesus for salvation; your heart is depraved, and must be renewed by the Holy Spirit, or you cannot go to heaven. Would you go there? Then seek the Lord while He may be found.

"When you have read this, take the first opportunity of retiring, and pray earnestly to the Lord for pardon and grace."

These earnest, loving, faithful letters show that no amount of public labor could drive paternal

anxiety from the heart. But the writer was in
the habit through life of pressing personal religion upon intimate friends by the pen rather than
in conversation.

The literary labors, during the time of this co-
pastorate, were abundant. "A Text Book of Popery" was written, comprising a history of the
Council of Trent, and a translation of its canons
and decrees. Also funeral sermons were published on the death of King George IV. and
William IV. "The Reformation in Europe" was
written for the Tract Society; and articles on a
variety of subjects, from the same pen, found their
way to the magazines and weekly papers.

The journal of those days discloses an intense
desire for personal growth in holiness and usefulness in the cause of truth :—

"I hope that my labors here have been in some respects useful, especially in reviving the Sunday School
and the Auxiliary Mission Society. We have also instituted a special prayer meeting to be held monthly, for
the outpouring of the Holy Spirit.

"I have been lately reading the life of Philip Henry,
that heavenly-minded man. I feel the need of more
seriousness, more of the Spirit of God. Oh! that I may
be able to live as a redeemed one ought. With a view to
personal growth and extended usefulness, I purpose, in
the strength of the Lord, to consider the following subjects as specially to be meditated on, with prayer and
deep concern, on the days mentioned."

Then follows a plan for each day in the week,
showing that these desires for advancement were
no mere idle aspirations, but intensely practical

efforts to reach the highest possible point of attainment.

Those who, in later years, sat under the instruction of Dr. Cramp, and frequently wondered at the extent of his knowledge of the Bible, as well as the depth of his experimental acquaintance with almost everything pertaining to the Christian life, and especially the trials of the Christian ministry, would have better understood whence the power came, had they been permitted to peruse his journal in the earlier years of his life. His desires for a greater grasp of truth, and more usefulness in the Church were most intense.

There was, in fact, an intensity of earnestness that never manifested itself at all in any of his public utterances. It was a sort of reserved force, which though unseen was impelling to work, driving on to action all the time. And hence the secret of so much accomplished. The fact is there was no stopping ; there was no rest, except by constant change of occupation.

Sometimes there is a grateful acknowledgement of goodness and mercy. Again a humble confession of want of zeal and love ; a lamentation that there was so feeble a sense of the presence and power of Christ, so little earnestness in prayer, such a feeble grasp of the promises.

Then such Resolutions as the following :—

" In dependence on Divine grace (for I cannot confide in myself), I do hereby resolve :

" 1. That I will pray more.

" 2. That I will read the Scriptures more carefully, and pray over each portion read.

" 3. That I will be more observant and watchful of the state of my mind, temper, &c.

"4. That I will cultivate religious conversation, in which I have been deficient.

" 5. That I will endeavor to act in all the relations of life, more in the spirit of Christianity.

" 6. That I will earnestly labor after a tender, feeling sense of the value of souls, and the importance of truth, so as to resist shamefacedness, and not shun to speak to men of their eternal interests.

" 7. That I will, at least once a week, set apart some time for an exercise similar to this, for self-examination, abasement before God, and prayer and praise.

" Who can tell what God may be about to do? Lord help me, keep me, give me grace to fulfil these intentions. May the remainder of my life be spent for Thee."

July 25, 1831. "This is my birthday, on which I have completed my thirty-tifth year.

" I have enjoyed some degree of gratitude and chastened pleasure. Among the thoughts that occupied my mind was this, 'Where shall I be thirty-five years hence?' I could not anticipate so long a continuance on earth, but I was enabled to look forward with humble joy to the realms of bliss, and to entertain a hope that I should be there, joining the glorified in their holy and heavenly celebrations, 'Far from a world of grief and sin.' The thought was delightful. Ought it not to be stimulating, too? Time is rapidly passing away, how diligent, active, devoted, should I be. Lord help me to be so. But oh! how much cause have I for continued humiliation before God! My heart seems so dull that nothing can move or affect it. On every hand I see reasons for self-abasement. I have indeed to begin every-thing afresh. I desire to do so. May the Lord deign to begin again with me, for my salvation and His glory."

Such are the feelings, the longing aspirations of one who even then was actively engaged in suc-cessful endeavours in making known the truth, one who was regarded by his brethren as among the brightest of the saints. Doubtless, many, far inferior to him in both mental and spiritual attain-ments, regarded themselves as models of excellence, and patterns of piety. What a different estimate men put upon their lives and acts, when the grace of God operates in the heart !

These resolves and prayers were followed by re-newed consecration to the work :—the labors more abundant, the sermons more earnest, the appeals more pungent and spiritual.

Aug. 26. About a month after the last entry, we find the following, referring to seasons of medita-tion and prayer :—

" The difficulty I find in fixing my thoughts on these occasions has led me to consider the propriety of prepa-ring a series of enquiries to be instituted whenever I re-tire for special meditation and prayer. They are such as these:

" 1. How is my heart affected in prayer ? Is there the spirit of adoption ?

" 2. Do I realize the presence and the character of God ?

" 3. Do I feel a deep sense of my insignificance and vileness? Do I plead the promises? Do I believe and expect ? Am I watchful over my besetting sin ? Do I cultivate those virtues and graces in which I am most deficient? Am I daily doing something for the souls of my family—my wife—my children—my servants? Does tenderness of conscience continue and increase? Have I lively, close, realizing views of truth, especially of those truths which are immediately essential to the salvation of men?

"What have I read lately, and with what spiritual advantage? Have I had any edifying intercourse with my Christian brethren? Am I conscientious in the employment of my time? And do I preserve order in this matter, preferring supreme to subordinate objects?"

Here we have again a leading characteristic of him whose life we are studying. Comments seem needless. It might be better to say nothing, and, simply allow the reader to ponder for himself upon this wonderful record. What heart-searching enquiries! What minuteness in details! What honesty of purpose! What determination, by God's grace, to find out where the secret wrong was, if any, that might stand in the way of fuller displays of heavenly grace, so as thus to become more instrumental of good. Surely, to every earnest Christian, who knows what these struggles mean, the memory of the man, who, in his secret chamber, and in his Isle of Thanet home, recorded these solemn resolves, will become doubly dear. This is no official piety, nor any external form of godliness. These are the secret, sincere struggles of a human soul, under the stimulating influences of God's grace, panting for a divine life and closer walk with God. And yet the remark may be ventured, that not one of those most intimate with the Rev. J. M. Cramp at the time these records were made, had the slightest idea that he was thus wrestling for the victory. They thought that he had already attained.

The compiler of these records thought that he knew him tolerably well. The acquaintance commenced in 1851, and did not end till 1881. He sat under his instructions in classics and in theology. He enjoyed many of his public lectures and addresses. He listened to his sermons and went home weeping and condemned. And yet he is free to say that he never really knew Dr. Cramp, till after his decease, when the seal of secresy was removed from his private papers.

In September, among many other things, we find this record :—

"The more I look into myself, the less I think of myself. I need to be converted anew. Have pity upon me, Oh Lord, have pity, upon me. Save me. Sanctify me. Fit me to enjoy and glorify Thee, and to be useful in Thy cause, whatever it may cost me.

"Possibly, this may be in its results a fearful petition; for surely it will require much to make me an 'able minister of the New Testament,' and perhaps some cutting and pruning will be necessary, that will make both flesh and spirit smart. Still, if I know my heart, I do really wish to be of some service in the cause of God, as well as to make personal advance in piety. I leave myself in the hands of the Lord."

Again, a little further on—

"I have this evening resolved that I will especially consider, in my devotional exercises, the following subjects:—

"*Lord's Day*—My own soul.

" *Monday*—The Ministry.

" *Tuesday*—My family.

" *Wednesday*—My friends.

" *Thursday*—My efforts in the cause of God.

" *Friday*—The state of the Church.

" *Saturday*—The state of the world.

" May God give his blessing."

These extracts from the journal, bring us to the time already referred to, when Dr. Cramp removed to the farm at Bromstone. The immediate cause of his leaving London and coming home, was the sudden death of his brother, who had been in charge of his father's farm. The Rev. Thomas Cramp was entirely taken up with the care of the church, and needed assistance, both in preaching, and in matters of business. And so, after due deliberation, it was arranged that the son should unite with the father in the work.

But the church, for all the previous years, had been supplied without the necessity of paying a salary. This was, of course, very kind upon the part of the pastor; but it was a very bad training for the church. Dr. Cramp often spoke of it as a mistake. For it was inducing and fostering the habit of neglect of the Christian duty of giving to the Lord. And no church will be likely, under such circumstances, to become healthy, strong or progressive.

A change, however, could not be made suddenly, nor was it attempted to any great extent. The plan was for Dr. Cramp to superintend the farm, and thus secure a support for his family.

How he viewed this contemplated change may be gathered from his own record while it was still in prospect :—

" Dec. 27, 1831. My mind has been much occupied of late respecting a contemplated change of residence, and mode of life. It will not take place till Michaelmas next, but it will be important. I believe it to be the will of God. Circumstances render it imperative. My duty to my family calls me to go and reside on the farm, and undertake its practical management. This will induce considerable change. My literary purposes must be cut off. But little time will be spared for my study. I must relinquish my favorite pursuits, and engage in others less congenial to my tastes and habits. But it is the will of God, and to it I desire humbly, and even cheerfully, to bow. Important designs may be to be answered by it, mysterious as it at present seems.

" I have endeavoured this evening to surrender myself unreservedly to the Lord, in reference to the whole, that He may do with me as He pleaseth. That passage much dwelt upon my mind, ' Even Christ pleased not Himself.' My studies have pleased myself; they have been a source of enjoyment. But this was not an end for the Son of God to seek. Why should I wish to do otherwise than my Lord ? No, let me give up everything, that God may be glorified.

" Henceforth, my reading must be eminently devotional and ministerial; perhaps it may have a good effect. God grant it. It has occurred to me that my ministry has not been sufficiently doctrinal. I must direct my attention to this thought. Alas, I seem to know nothing, to have done nothing. Yet, I do read the Word of God with much more pleasure and profit than I did some time since. I am determined to read it more and more."

Following this there are expressions of thanksgiving and gratitude. A number have offered themselves to the church, and in relating their experience, stated that the sermons to which they had listened were the means of their conversion.

Mingled with this joy there is the voice of lamentation :—

" March 2, 1832. This morning it has pleased God to visit me with a new and sharp trial. After suffering about three weeks from the whooping cough, in a very violent form, my lovely babe has left this world of sorrow and entered glory. It is, indeed, a severe and heart-rending affliction. My soul is wounded to the quick. The child was greatly endeared to me; his faculties were beginning to expand, his engaging ways were attractive, and the personal attentions which my dear wife and myself rendered in his illness had drawn him closer to our hearts. But God has a prior claim. . . . Perhaps He intends to wean us much more from creature love, that we may be more fully possessed by Himself, and therefore more useful. Be it so. It is the Lord. Withered and desolate as I feel this day, surely I am bound humbly to submit, yea, acquiesce in an arrangement which has my own good ultimately in view, and may enable me to glorify God. Lord help me ! "

About this time, probably in 1835, Mr. Cramp was appointed Guardian of the Parish of St. Peters, under the Poor Law Amendment Act. England contains the two extremes of wealth and poverty. Probably, the wealthiest nation in the world, but many of the inhabitants extremely poor. Under previous laws, the support of the poor was becoming a terrible burden. There were not only those actually poor to be cared for, but hosts of worthless and idle people, well able to sustain themselves, were relying upon the public bounty. When the thing became unbearable, the law was changed. The provision made was that those asking help must give up their homes, such as they were, and go to the Poor House to be provided for. The cost of keeping the poor was reduced nearly one-half in this way.

The Guardians had charge of this matter, each in his own parish. Mr. Cramp was appointed Guardian, and soon after he was selected as chairman of the Board of that body. It was a very responsible position. The law having been recently passed, there was no precedent for action. Everything had to be taken up from the beginning. Much patient investigation into the condition and claims of the parties to be provided for, was imperative. Many references to this period in his journal, show that he was giving time, energy and thought to the duties of this office, but that there was much in connection with it far from desirable to one of Mr. Cramp's tastes and habits. It did not bring him into contact with literary or spiritual life. That the duties of the office were, however, discharged in a manner satisfactory to the parish, may be gathered from various sources.

On his retirement from the position, after three years of incessant toil, a beautiful silver salver was presented, which contains the following inscription :—

# 63

THE VICAR, CHURCHWARDENS, OVERSEER AND GENTRY,
Of the Parish of St. Peters.
—TO—
## JOHN MOCKETT CRAMP,
In testimony of eminent services rendered by him,
IN THE YEARS 1835, 1836 AND 1837,
When acting as the first elected Guardian of the Parish of St. Peter,
AND AS CHAIRMAN OF THE BOARD OF GUARDIANS OF THE
ISLE OF THANET UNION.

It will be noticed that this presentation was not from persons in sympathy with Mr. Cramp's religious views, and is, therefore, a testimonial pure and simple as to the ability and fidelity of the recipient.

The following document from the Board itself was found among some old papers. There are twenty-five names attached :—

"May 11th, 1838.

" We, whose names are undersigned, being or having been members of the Board of Guardians of the Isle of Thanet, during the last three years, feel ourselves bound in duty to Mr. John Mockett Cramp, for the important services which he has rendered to the Board as chairman, to state, in a public declaration of our sentiments, the full conviction we entertain of his eminent qualifications for the office of Auditor of the East Kent Union.

" We, therefore, take this opportunity of recording our experience of his punctuality in the fulfilment of official engagements, of his courtesy in transacting business, and his accurate perception of all particulars which may most effectually and satisfactorily accomplish the salutary purposes of the Poor Law Amendment Act."

All of which must have been eminently satisfactory to the retiring chairman. It would, probably, have convinced many persons in similar conditions, that they had been in the right place and doing the right work.

There are, however, different standpoints from which to look at things. Mr. Cramp had his own. He was not as well pleased as others seem to have been. His own record may explain :—

" This was a laborious and thankless office. The place of meeting was six miles from home, and the meetings were weekly, besides occasional duties in the interval. I was brought into connection with worldly men, and placed in a situation which exposed me to considerable obloquy. I do not know that any good whatever resulted from it. It was one of my mistakes."

The " obloquy " referred to, doubtless arose from the complaints of the undeserving and dissatisfied poor, who wished to choose their own mode of life, and yet receive constant aid from the parish. There were, doubtless, many unpleasant and even painful things, in the execution of the new law. Families were necessarily broken up. Husbands and wives, parents and children were separated. And yet the change was absolutely essential to relieve the tax-payers of the heavy burdens they had been bearing. And if all the Guardians had been as kindly disposed as the chairman, doubtless, was, perhaps the grounds for complaint might have been even less than they were.

As we gathered from the sketch of the Isle of Thanet, farming operations in that section of country were formerly very remunerative. But these were the days of good crops, little competition, and consequent high prices. England can never be again what it once was in this respect.

The world's abundant surplus is now poured too easily into London for this to be. And even at the time when Mr. Cramp shared the pastorate with his father, and undertook to relieve the latter, in his old age, from the care of the Bromston farm, the profits on farming operations were not large. In fact, the care of the farm proved to be neither congenial nor remunerative. How could they have been either the one or the other ? No business can run prosperously by itself. Mr. Cramp's tastes and habits were not in the line of this work. He was born for books, the study, the platform, the press, the pulpit. At these tasks he felt at home, and as might have been expected, he left the workmen to go on with the farm work, while he attended to his. The result was that, after sustaining considerable loss of worldly means, the farm was given up.

The lesson would seem to be: let no one undertake a business for which neither nature nor training has qualified him.

The preaching, however, was greatly enjoyed, and the literary labours were persistent. The church was stimulated and strengthened. It was the second instance in the same neighborhood in which a prophet was receiving honor in his own country. It would be gratifying if we could weave into this account some reminiscences of those days. But this is impossible, for we have no access to the records of the church. We cannot give the dates of revival times, the numbers that were added. Nor can we show by statistics what advance was made, during the fifteen years, in those

great principles of religious equality, converted
church membership, loyalty to Bible teaching,
freedom of speech, rights of the personal conscience
in all things sacred, which were so firmly held
and vigorously maintained by the co-pastor of the
Church of St. Peter's. But that all these principles
were being made known, and better and better
understood by the people generally, we can not
doubt. And among the scanty records, there are
frequent references to hopeful indications, the
special means employed to awaken a deeper interest in spiritual matters—baptismal occasions, &c.
Sometimes there are found expressions of joyful
thanksgiving for the prosperity granted to the
church. All of which shows that there was constant advancement upon the part of the church as
well as of the pastor.

The following extracts from letters written
during this period, will show the intense earnestness of the writer. They show that his methods
were most thorough, and that he had no desire to
build up the church out of any unsound materials.
With him, emotion or sentiment would not do instead of genuine piety. There must be the evidence
of thorough conversion and full consecration, otherwise parties would not be encouraged to seek admission to the church.

The letters were addressed to his oldest daughter,
afterwards the wife of S. Selden, Esq., formerly of
Hastings, England, now of Halifax, N.S., and so
well and favorably known in these provinces, as
the editor and proprietor of the *Christian Messenger*.

"Thinking that perhaps it would be easier for me to put thoughts and feelings on paper than to speak personally on the subject of religion, my dear father writes, while I was attending school:

'October 29, 1836.

'I expect that two members of my Bible class will shortly be baptized. This reminds me of my dear M—— Is she concerned about religion, and her soul? Does she seek God? Has she a new heart? Write to me, my dear child, and answer these questions. Tell me your real feelings and desires on the subject of religion. Let me know the actual state of your heart. . . .'

"Three years later he wrote again, while I was away from home :—

'April 19, 1839.

'Yesterday evening, the following persons attended our church meeting, and will be baptized next Lord's Day. . . . I think there are others ready to come, who will, probably, be baptized before the Ordinance day in May. It is on that account, desirable to know your own views and feelings on this important subject.

'If, my dear child, you have been led to see your sinful state, and to confess and hate your sin;—if you perceive and acknowledge the righteousness of God in your condemnation;—if you believe in the Lord Jesus, the all sufficient, gracious, and only Saviour, and are content to be indebted to the free grace of God in Christ for your own salvation;—if the love and service of God are your delight, and eminence therein the object of your constant prayer and effort;—and if, with these views, you are willing to commit yourself to Christ and His church, to walk in all His ways, and do His will, nothing on earth can give me greater pleasure than to place your name on the list of candidates. . . .'

" My reply elicited the next extract :—

' April 27, 1839.

' To recognize you as a subject of grace, a sister in Christ, affords me far higher pleasure than can possibly be derived from any other considerations. Persevere in your resolution to abide by the word of God, and make it your principal study. The better you become acquainted with that holy and heavenly book, the more thoroughly will you be convinced that God is its author, and that it contains truth, the whole truth, and nothing but truth. "He that believeth, hath the witness in himself." Confiding faith has its appropriate reward. It has been well said of the Bible, that no bad man *could* write it ; and that no good man *would,* unless it were true, since it would impeach his honesty, and invalidate his credit. The infidel would persuade us that all is a delusion. Be it so, it is a happy and a holy delusion, and we are the better for it, all through life, especially in our sorrows : he has nothing half so good to substitute in its place. If *he is right*, we are in no worse condition for being believers, since there is no penalty attached to our faith ; but if not, then of what vast consequence ' that we should believe.' Blessed be God, the evidence is so clear and strong, that the difficulties of infidelity are much greater than those of faith. And then, if we are satisfied that the Bible is God's word, it is of the greatest consequence that we cultivate a humble, teachable spirit—that we be willing to wait for the fuller discoveries of another world—and that we count it no strange thing if we are sometimes baffled and perplexed. The entire comprehension of all things is only possible to God. If, therefore, suspicion at any time arises in your mind, regard it as a temptation, which, if yielded to, becomes a sin, and will bring sorrow. Believe and be blessed. Your answer to my questions, my dear child, gladdens my heart. You have given yourself to Christ, and you wish to serve and honor Him, in His own ways. Come, then, and do so, and say: 'I will go in the strength of the Lord God.' I cannot recommend delay. Enter the fold, that you may partake the food of the flock, and be more secure from harm. . .'

"The next year he gives some excellent advice as to the deportment of a young convert in different surroundings from those of home life :—

'March 11th, 1840.

' Do not forget, my dear child, that temptations are linked with every mercy, and adapted by our great foe to all the situations we occupy. It is now a season of indulgence with you. Take care lest it become a time of dissipation, and your spiritual energies be thereby unnerved. Let not your soul be defrauded of its nourishment by your carelessness or neglect; you can only preserve its health by constant recurrence to the word of God and prayer, and it must be your aim to secure stated seasons for privacy, as frequently as possible, without infringing on the rules of decorum, or appearing unsocial. By this means you will be better prepared to sustain your character as a professing Christian and a member of a Christian Church. Do not forget that you have this character to sustain, and that more is expected from you in consequence.'

"In 1841, my father left St. Peter's and settled over the Baptist Church at Hastings, in Sussex. The portion of his life included in the years spent in the former place, was a most important one. He was then in the full vigor of his mental and physical powers. Full of energy and unceasing activity, few men could have gone through the work he managed to perform. Beside the supervision of the farm, he had constant and unremitting literary labour; two sermons on the Lord's Day, and one during the week, beside the constant vigilance necessary where a young family were growing up, needing a father's wise direction and judicious counsel. They were also, in many ways, years of painful and trying discipline, but the Lord, in whom he trusted, brought him through, and step by step guided his pilgrim wanderings to a peaceful close at last, honored and revered by his loving children, and held in affectionate remembrance by numerous friends.

'The memory of the just is blessed.'"

The co-pastorate at St. Peter's closed, as stated elsewhere, in 1841. The immediate cause was the invitation from the church in Hastings, Sussex, to take the charge of it. Mr. Cramp first supplied the pulpit for three months, and then assumed the pastoral charge.

The desire for thorough work noticed in the extracts above, characterized every effort in which he engaged. Work half done or carelessly done, was to him worse than not done at all. This gave to his published works a value that otherwise they could not have possessed. He must be sure of his ground before he would venture upon a declaration. He seldom had occasion to correct what once went forth from his pen.

The comprehensive means employed in order to secure accuracy, may be gathered from the following letter, written at the time he was preparing one of his published works.　It was addressed to Dr. F. Wayland, President of Brown University, Providence, R.I.

" St. Peter's, Oct. 31, 1836.

"To Rev. Dr. Wayland,

" *Rev. and Dear Sir,—*

" Although I am personally unknown to you, I feel assured that any communication from a Christian brother and fellow-labourer in the Gospel, to whatever country he may belong, will be received with your accustomed courtesy, and treated with all due respect.

" A few years ago, I published a small volume entitled, ' A Text-book of Popery :' it was favourably received here, though not extensively circulated.　My esteemed friend, the Rev. H. Malcolm, of Boston, sent me, last year, a copy of the American edition.　The manner in which it is quoted and referred to in some of your periodicals induces me to hope that its re-publication in the United States will be of some service to the great cause of Protestantism.

" The Popish controversy still engages my attention. I am now employed under the auspices of the Religious Tract Society, in preparing for the press, small works on the subject, adapted for general circulation.

" Anxious to render any historical statements I may give as perfect as possible, I find it necessary to initiate correspondence with Christian ministers in different parts of the world, whose situation and means of information are such as to enable them to assist me in the prosecation of my researches.

"With these views, I now address you, presuming that the state and progress of Popery in your western world cannot but have engaged your serious attention.

" I wish much to ascertain to what extent the reports that have reached this country, are entitled to credit.

We hear that Popery is rapidly on the increase—that its agents are indefatigable in their endeavours to subvert Protestantism and diffuse their iron tenets ;—that they are liberally aided by the Pope, and by certain funds derived from Austria ;—that their seminaries for education are of a superior kind, and offer such attractions as induce many unwary Protestants to entrust their children to the care of their bitterest theological foes ;—that many young persons, both in and out of these seminaries, have been (by sophistical reasoning, and allured by the pomp of superstition) led astray and persuaded to embrace Romanism ;—that the influence of the Papists is beginning to be felt in the elections ; and there is reason to apprehend, at no very distant interval of time, their preponderance in the valley of the Mississippi and the Western States, and, by consequence, throughout your Union, whose future condition seems likely to be considerably modified by the influence of these States.

"My inquiry is, how far are the above-mentioned statements true? If you can aid me by answering the question, by directing me to accredited sources of information, or by procuring the kind co-operation of any other brethren who may feel disposed to correspond with me on the subject, I shall be very greatly obliged. In return, I beg to say, that I will most cheerfully render you similar assistance in regard to any inquiry that you may wish to institute respecting this country.

"I have addressed this letter to you, because I conceived that the important and responsible station you occupy, necessarily brings under your notice whatever affects the religious statistics of your noble land.

"When your valuable discourse on the 'Moral Dignity of Christian Missions' was republished in this country, I embraced an early opportunity of perusing it. It appears to me that the churches of Christ in America have largely imbibed the spirit which breathes in your pages. There is a dignity in your plans and operations which betokens far-reaching views, grand designs, and heaven-inspired faith. Long may you, rev. and dear sir, be spared, to train the spiritual children of the churches for engagements in the ' enterprise,' of which you entertain such just and exalted sentiments!

" I do not know that it is needful to add that I belong to the same denomination as yourself, and have been engaged in the ministry nearly twenty years—first in London, and since 1827, in this, my native place.

" The Rev. Dr. Cox, formerly one of my tutors, and whom you know, would have added a line attesting the above, could I have met with him in time. Having no present occasion to go to London, I must waive the advantage of his introduction, and throw myself on your candour.

" I am, dear sir,

" Yours in the bonds of the Gospel,

" J. M. CRAMP."

# CHAPTER VI.

" No eye can see
The changing course which life may take."

Hastings, a favourite and beautiful watering place in the county of Sussex, was the next scene of labour, Mr. Cramp having become the pastor of the Baptist Church in that place.

His journal, from which occasional extracts have furnished information with regard to previous appointments, gives no record of the short period, about two years, spent there, and family memorials are scanty.

Some few interesting details have, however, been obtained, and are given in the following:—

" RECOLLECTIONS OF REV. DR. CRAMP.

" By S. SELDEN, Esq.

" My earliest recollections of Dr. Cramp, date back several years before I had seen him. When quite a lad of fifteen or sixteen years of age, about the year 1834, I regularly read the London *Patriot*, a weekly newspaper, ably edited by Josiah Condor, representing the Dissenters—Baptists and Independents—and the monthly *Baptist Magazine.* In these periodicals, articles and letters frequently appeared over the signature 'J. M. Cramp.' The controversy on the Bible Monopoly was one of the leading topics of that day. Previous to this, the Church of England Universities alone had permission to print Bibles, and consequently the price was much higher than if the monopoly were broken up. Whilst some of the articles and letters written on this subject were long and tedious, the occasional letters of Mr. Cramp were terse, incisive and forcible, and of course were read with avidity by all interested in the wider circulation of Gospel truth, and the progress of freedom. Sunday school teachers generally took great interest in this matter, and it was perhaps, owing to the immense petitions from them to the Parliament, that the friends of cheaper Bibles were eventually successful. The circulation of the Word of God was immediately immensely increased.

" Mr. Cramp also occasionally wrote in the *Patriot* on other subjects :—Church Rates, Tithes, Education ; and all matters relating to civil and religious liberty received his careful consideration ; and his ready pen was employed in their discussion. His letters were always readable, forcible and convincing. Those who were concerned in the removal of the disabilities under which the Dissenters were then placed—whether churchmen (of whom large numbers wished for the reform), or Dissenters—read what was written, and took an active part in seeking to get rid of the obnoxious and oppressive restrictions. It was only by slow degrees that advances were made against the power and corruption that existed. Yet, progress could be discerned, and every concession was used to hasten its course.

" Having myself become a member of the Baptist Church on its formation in my native place, Hastings, about the year 1835, I went with a friend, a few years my senior, to attend a session of the West Kent and Sussex Baptist Association, held with the Church at Bessels Green, in the county of Kent.

"During the first meeting I was much gratified by hearing it announced that the delegation from the East Kent Baptist Association—Rev. Mortlock Daniel, of Ramsgate, and Rev. John M. Cramp, St. Peter's, Isle of Thanet, had arrived. After they were introduced to the Association, they were formally addressed by the Moderator, and welcomed to a participation in the deliberations of the body. I had not then had any personal introduction to Mr. Cramp, nor had I the most remote idea that we should ever meet again. A few years after this, however, the Baptist Church at Hastings, was without a pastor. They had a handsome stone house of worship, with a minister's residence attached to it, erected principally by the beneficence of Joseph Fletcher, Esq., a wealthy shipowner of London, given by him as a thank-offering for the restoration of his daughter's health at Hastings.

" Its first pastor, Rev. P. J. Saffery, having been called to labor in London, Rev. John M. Cramp, of St. Peter's, was recommended to the church as a suitable successor. Mr. Cramp came to Hastings in January, 1840, and preached there for about three months. His ministry proved highly acceptable, and in answer to a unanimous invitation which he accepted, he removed with his family in March of that year, and labored with good success for about two years. Being one of the deacons of the church from its formation, I had intimate acquaintance with Mr. C.'s plans of church work. Whilst he was, at all times, actively seeking revival influences, he sought to make them continuous, and orderly in their operations—the development of Christian character, and the result of a reception of the truth as it is in Jesus.

" Heretofore, Mr. Cramp had defended the moderate use of alcoholic drinks, but in addition to the private and public discussion of the question, a circumstance occurred which resulted in an entire change of opinion and practice on this subject. A member of the congregation, a retired merchant, and husband of one of the most esteemed members of the church, appeared in the prayer-meeting two or three times, slightly intoxicated, and disturbed the meeting by making some incoherent remarks. I had been a total abstainer several years, and well remember the morning that Mr. Cramp came to me with a pledge of total abstinence, which we signed ; he proceeded to induce others to append their names, and succeeded in getting quite a number of persons to join us and labor in the cause of temperance.

" Whilst at Hastings, Mr. Cramp delivered, on successive week evenings, the excellent course of lectures on important subjects, subsequently published in London, in a volume of 308 pages, under the title, ' Lectures for these Times.' "

An incident of this period may here interrupt the foregoing narrative. Mr. Cramp's interest in ths Sunday school connected with his church, led him to request the favor of a hymn for an anniversary occasion, from the pen of the poet, James Montgomery. The characteristic letter in reply is subjoined, with the hymn, which does not appear in general collections, and has, probably, never been published.

"THE MOUNT, Sheffield, 1842.

" DEAR SIR,—I thank you for having given me, after the lapse of years, an opportunity of acknowledging the sin, first of procrastination, and then of omission, which

I committed against your kindness, when you sent me a copy of your valuable 'Text-Book of Popery,' and for which I now humbly ask forgiveness. In truth, however, these are such frequently besetting sins with me, and I have so repeatedly resolved and re-resolved in vain to mend, that I dare not promise never to do so again. Besides indolence habitual, and infirmity constitutional, I am so overpowered with the liberality of friends and strangers in conferring such and other tokens of goodwill upon me, that I am always in arrears of gratitude, generally the more felt the less it is expressed, because it is ten times easier to do a duty at once than to bear the rebukes of conscience for neglecting, especially neglecting so long as to be too late to do it at all, without a new and imperative call, such as you have given me, and if the foregoing verses be of no other value in your sight, I trust you will accept them as an acknowledgment, perhaps, 'better late than never,' of the old, not obsolete, obligation afore-mentioned and of my sincere repentance. You will please to use them for your benevolent, Christian purpose, or not, as you deem expedient.

" And believe me,

"Truly your obliged friend and serv't,

" J. MONTGOMERY.

" Rev. J. M. Cramp.

" *P. S.*—Thank you for your excellent initiatory address to your congregation. May they be indeed a 'Church' in the sacred sense, and you long the angel of it, and a star in your Lord's right hand."

### A HYMN FOR CHIDREN.

Lord Jesus Christ, the children's Friend
On us lift up Thy gracious hands,
And from Thy holy temple send
Blessings on our united bands.

How precious in Thy Father's sight
  Were children's souls when Thee He gave,
His only Son, his heart's delight,
  From hell to heaven those souls to save!

What love to them, what love was Thine,
  Meek Lamb of God! when Thou didst give
Thy soul, a sacrifice divine,
  Dying Thyself that they might live!

Nor less the Holy Spirit's grace,
  When by His light He Thee reveals,
As though they saw Thee face to face,
  And them as heirs of glory seals.

Are children's souls of such high price?
  With grief and gladness may we see
How sad their loss in Paradise,
  How great their gain on Calvary.

Our own no longer, Thine they are:
  In mercy bind them to Thy cross,
Safe only from the tempter there,
  From second death and final loss.

JAMES MONTGOMERY.

" Higher Collegiate Education for persons having the
Baptist ministry in view, was to Mr. Cramp a matter of
deep concern. He, about this time, entered into extensive correspondence, with the object of establishing a
plan which seemed likely to promote the best interests
of the churches. The colleges in Stepney and Bristol
were then almost the only institutions of learning belonging to the Baptists in England, and it was thought by Mr.
C. and many others, that an arrangement among the
ministers in different parts of the kingdom, might be
made, by which four or five students, after passing their
collegiate course, might spend some time with them in
further theological studies, and in preaching at mission
stations in the neighbourhood of their churches; and by

that means become familiar with church work, under the supervision and direction of these more experienced men, before entering fully upon the duties of the settled pastorate. However, whilst these projects were under consideration, and before anything practical had resulted, a communication came from the Baptist Foreign Missionary Board in London, inviting Mr. C. to the Presidency of the Baptist College at Montreal. This, after due deliberation, was accepted by him. He left Hastings, and with his family sailed from London, in April, 1844.

"The farewell meeting at Hastings was attended by a large number of ministers and other friends; the leave-taking between pastor and people being marked by many evidences of genuine affection existing between them, which continued for years afterwards, and some are still living there, who, after the lapse of nearly half a century, cherish the memory of his pastoral work among them."

An extract or two from his last addresses, or lectures rather, to his own congregation at Hastings, may illustrate the spirit in which he was going forth to the work.

"We only see now the beginning of the end. A great conflict is at hand. Church tyrants are maturing their plans, and marshalling their forces for the fight, sternly resolved to gain that ascendency over the human mind, for which the dark ages were distinguished, and to trample their opponents in the dust. But the eyes of men are opened. Knowledge is everywhere diffused. Education is all but universal. We have the Bible, the Press, and above all, a noble army of intelligent Christians in both hemispheres, who are prepared to make a bold stand for truth and primitive godliness, and to use vigorously those weapons of warfare which are not carnal,

but mighty through God, to the pulling down of strongholds. The battle will be sharp, probably long, and some
painful reverses may be experienced by the advocates of
New Testament piety. Nevertheless, let no man's heart
fail him. The cause is God's, and victory is sure. The
time is coming when the Bible shall again be the book
of the church—when personal godliness shall be regarded
as indispensable to fellowship—when the supremacy of
the Lord Jesus shall be acknowledged by all—when the
operations of the Spirit shall be unchecked—and when
the people of God shall be one—a happy, harmonious
family—one fold, under one Shepherd. The Lord hasten
it in His time."

Cheering farewell words these to his fellow-
laborers in England. Although when he uttered
them he was not aware that they were among his
last utterances in his native land.

A little nearer still to the time of his departure
he addresses them thus :—

" But whatever be the conflicts and controversies in
which we may be engaged, it should be our concern, that
all may be conducted in a religious spirit. The great
object must be to publish and defend the truth, in such a
manner that souls may be brought to God. To that, everything should be subordinate.

"How powerful are the motives by which we may be
influenced in pursuing such a course. Think of the peril
of souls, allured by the deceitfulness of sin to their own
destruction, and seek to save them from death. Think
of your obligations to the grace of God which has delivered you from the power of darkness, and translated
you into the kingdom of His dear Son. Think of the
glory which will redound to the Lord Jesus Christ, from
the successful results of his people's labors. Finally,

6

think of the prospects that are before you. . . . .
The time of our pilgrimage is short. Soon, if we are
the servants of the Saviour, shall we enter into a pure
and perfect state. There, jars, differences and conflicts,
will be unknown. There the Church will be complete in
holiness and bliss, and the fellowship of the saints will be
purified, and perpetuated. Having this hope, let us labour
diligently and perseveringly in the cause of truth.
Labour in this cause is not lost. It is an honor to take
any part, however humble, in building the Temple of
the Lord. It is a high privilege to work in the heavenly
field, though it be only to plough up the fallow ground,
or sow the seed of the kingdom. The time is coming,
when he that soweth and he that reapeth will rejoice
together."

This was the manner of his teaching in England.
And surely, no one who knows the manner of his
life in this country, will venture to affirm that his
practice did not correspond thereto. By precept
and example he taught men to live worthy their
calling.

# CHAPTER VII.

## REMOVAL TO CANADA.

### 1844.

"England, with all thy faults, I love thee still—
My country!"—*Cowper.*

It is interesting to trace events in the history of
an individual or a nation. It is more instructive
and satisfying when those events can be linked
together, as cause and effect, and then viewed as
constituting only parts of some comprehensive
scheme, by which the divine purpose is being accomplished. Many a life would furnish materials
for this kind of exercise, if we had the time and
inclination to ferret them out and put them together. We have given a brief sketch of the life
of Mr. Cramp in England. Now he is about to go
forth to new scenes and untried duties. The causes
of the removal we will find have been at work on
both continents.

The statements made in the preceding chapter,
touching the last two years in England, the pastorate at Hastings, are exceedingly valuable in this
connection. That is, they show the mental char-

acteristics of him whose life we are considering, and the channel in which his thoughts were running. They come from personal recollections, and from one intimately acquainted with Dr. Cramp, long before his name even was known in any of these Maritime Provinces of the Dominion of Canada. They show that there was deeply imbedded in his nature, the idea of equal rights and privileges for all Christian denominations ; and that he was able and willing to defend the rights of those not enjoying them. In fact, he could not help himself, for he was impelled by a righteous indignation to attack, and so far as possible destroy, all monopolies and chartered rights, which stood in the way of general progress. Liberty of speech for every man, a free press for every nation, a good school for every village, an open Bible for every family, and religious worship untrammeled by the law, for every church, or any body of people, few or many, regarding themselves as a church ; these were principles as dear to him as the right of choosing a profession or owning personal property.

And wherever legislation seemed to give one man or one party an advantage over another in any of these respects, his indignation was stirred. The kind of man needed in a new country, where things are maturing.

The remarks quoted above also show in what estimation he was held by the brethren among whom his youthful days and early manhood had been spent. He was sent as a delegate from the Association of East Kent to the West Kent and

Sussex Association. Representative men, who understood and could make known the views of their brethren on important matters, were always chosen for such offices. Dr. Cramp then must have been regarded as a representative man, and trustworthy on· points of doctrine and policy. The kind of man the churches here would be sure to welcome.

We may also gather what were his views of the Gospel ministry To whatever extent "unlearned and ignorant" men might have been instrumental of good in apostolic times (and no man had a deeper reverence for them than Dr. Cramp); to whatever extent the same class may have accomplished good since the days of primitive piety, he plainly saw that the time had gone by for piety, without learning, to hope to accomplish the grand results aimed at by the setting up of the kingdom of Christ in the world. He saw this and was working in the line of his convictions. And so, long before he had even dreamed of being personally connected with colleges or theological schools, he was endeavouring to mature methods for giving the rising ministry advantages their fathers had not enjoyed. He knew that agnosticism, infidelity, and "science falsely so-called," were all arranging their forces against the truth, and that only men of the broadest culture and deepest research would be able to cope with these forces. He was thinking of England's dangers. We can hardly doubt now, that the Great Head of the Church, with broader view and more comprehensive plans,

was providing an Angus, a Spurgeon, a Brown, a
Stanford, a Clifford, Maclaren, Landels, Chown,
and many more of like spirit, for England, but a
Cramp for this country, one of England's loyal
colonies, whose future may do more for the kingdom of Christ, than the past even dreamed of.

The plan interpreted in the light of subsequent
events, was that Dr. Cramp should cross the Atlantic, and spend the last 37 years of his life on this
side. The circumstances which led to his coming,
may be found in a brief sketch of the Montreal
Baptist College. In England, the man was being
prepared for the work. In Canada, developments
were going on, and desires deepening which would
soon make work for the man.

Many of the colonists, in what is now known
as Ontario and Quebec, had come from England
and Scotland. They had brought with them much
of the good and much of the evil of their native
land. Among the evils was that of Episcopacy,
with all its implied Church and State connection.
The successive governors sent out, after England's
supremacy in Canada was acknowledged, were
men believing in " the church," and all the advantages that could be secured for her. All legislation, therefore, was in her favor. Extensive tracts
of land were reserved for educational purposes and
glebe lots. Political influence was almost entirely
in the hands of the members of "the church." The
interpretation of the law, therefore,, was that all
this property must be managed by the church in
fostering education and religion, in this new and

undeveloped country. It is easy to see how all this would work. Education of any higher order than that of the common village school, poor enough in those days, was for those who favored the existing state of things.

The Baptists of Canada, few in numbers, and very limited at that time in worldly resources, did not so favor it, and believed that their young men, including those looking toward the ministry, must either go without education, or receive it under conditions which they did not approve. There were, however, among them, men of intelligence and energy. They enquired anxiously in what direction deliverance lay. The young men, especially the future preachers of the Gospel, must have the means of education. They could get it by going abroad, for there were excellent schools and colleges open to all, in the New England States. But, going abroad for education, frequently meant laboring abroad after the education was secured. So these men determined to have a school at home. They were willing to give, but they could not give enough. The matter was discussed and agitated until its importance became overwhelming. A society had been formed, called "The Canada Baptist Missionary Society." This society found the double duty resting upon them, viz., the raising funds to send out missionaries, and the equally important work of finding missionaries competent to be sent. Many of the active workers of those days, especially in the neighborhood of Montreal, were English and Scotch. Their thoughts naturally turned towards their native land.

The Rev. John Gilmour, who had been pastor of a Baptist church in Montreal, was sent home in 1836, to England, to raise funds for the training of a native ministry for Canada, and for carrying on home mission work in the Province, now Ontario and Quebec. His efforts were somewhat successful. A society called the "Colonial Society" in England, organized some time before this, sympathized with the work, and promised aid. These two societies,—one at home and the other in Montreal, commenced the work. The society at home engaging, at the outset, to pay the salary of a principal for the proposed college. Dr. Benjamin Davies was selected as the first principal, a building was bought near Montreal, and operations were commenced, Sept. 24, 1836. Great hopes were entertained of the good results to come from this endeavour. The men managing it were unselfish, public-spirited, large-hearted and generous. The principal was all that could be desired.

Many obstacles, however, presented themselves. The young men, looking toward the ministry, had not all caught the spirit of progress. Railroads were not in operation, and the school was 400 miles east of the principal churches belonging to the Baptists. But, worse than all this, the Baptists in the East, and those in the West, were not a united body,—the one body sympathised more with the English, the other with American views in many matters. They were agreed on all the grand essentials, but they differed on some minor points. And when it could be shown that the difference was not so great as was suspected, then they, some of them at least, chose to suspect that there were other differences hidden somewhere, and that united action in education even would imperil Baptist principles. They were all good men and true, only perhaps a little more zealous in maintaining the *faith once delivered to the saints*, than in adopting wise measures towards making that faith effectual in the saving of the lost. In many of the minor matters of life it would seem to be just as well to let the chameleon remain green or blue as each has decided, lest by the time the dispute is ended, by victory to him who can strike the hardest blows, both may be found wrong, the animal having meanwhile assumed still another colour.

For some five or six years, the college went on doing excellent work, but the attendance was not large, and the opposition, arising out of the differences referred to, did not abate.

In the summer of 1843, Dr. Davies resigned his position, and accepted the presidency of Stepney College, now presided over by Rev. Joseph Angus. For the following year, the Rev. Mr. Fyfe, afterwards Dr. Fyfe, so well known as the founder, and for many years the successful principal of Woodstock Literary Institute, presided over the Montreal College. During this year, a correspondence was opened up between the two societies, the English and Canadian, as to securing a permanent successor to Dr. Davies. The result was, the position was offered by the Colonial Society in London to the Rev. J. M. Cramp. After much consultation and prayer, he accepted the offer, resigned the charge of the church at Hastings, and made arrangements for the journey to Montreal with his family, on the 2nd April, 1844.

The voyage was long and perilous as compared with a similar journey in these days. Schooners of moderate size and uncertain speed carried freight and passengers from the Old to the New world then. Counting the parents and the children, there was a family group of nine. It required no little courage and trust, to leave the scenes of early life, and all the associations of an English home, to test the perils of the deep, and all the uncertainties that lay beyond it. But many Christian friends had committed them in earnest prayers to the care of Him who " measures the waters in the hollow of His hand." And the father of the family fully believed that he was moving in obedience to the divine command. This fact appears in the records of his own hand.

·Under ordinary circumstances, it would be enough to say of the voyage, the " Prince George" set sail from London on the 2nd of April, and reached Montreal the 29th May. But Dr. Cramp was exceedingly observant of every incident, and made a note of all.

A few extracts from the "Journal" may be given as specimens of the whole :—

"April 2, 1884, 1 P. M.—Joined the ship (the Prince

George) at Gravesend, with Mrs. C. and all the family. Opened boxes and prepared the sleeping berths. Mrs. J. Burls, Miss M. A. Burls and Mr. Selden, accompanied us. Quarter to 4, left for London, to attend the farewell service at Maze Pond in the evening. The family remained on board."

We regret that we have no records of that service.

"April 3.—Half-past 12, joined our ship, then about seven miles below Gravesend. Brother Groser, Mr. C. Burls and Mr. Selden accompanied me. Quarter to 3, passed the Nore Light; 10 minutes past 4, anchored off Whitstable and in sight of Margate.

" N. B.—My old friend, Robert Foster, of Tottenham, was in the Gravesend Packet with me this morning. At parting he said to me, 'There are two things which I commend to thy special notice,—popular education and religious liberty.'

" April 4.—Quarter to 8, weighed anchor; wind S.W. Quarter-past 10, anchored in a dead calm; cleared the cabin of superfluous boxes, and set things to rights. Half-past 12, weighed anchor; wind N.E., very light. Quarter-past 2, passed the Reculvers; came in sight of St. Peter's Church; gazed at it long, and thought of home, parents and friends, not without sadness, nor with dry eyes. Quarter-past 3, abreast of Margate. Quarter-past 7, off Broadstairs; Messrs. Hodgman (father and son) R. M. Cock and J. Jarman, with Misses S. Dawson, Johnson and Summers, came off in a boat to see us, and staid a short time. It was a kind attention, and affected me much.

"April 5.—Wind S. W. At anchor all day in the Downs. Arranged my books for use, and commenced the studies which I mean to pursue during the voyage."

And so the journal goes on with most minute

details all through the journey, perfectly wonderful to those accustomed to allow all small matters to slip by unnoticed.

"April 7.—The breeze became stronger as the night advanced, and continued till morning. We had but little sleep. Mrs. C. was very ill. Found when I rose in the morning that we had passed Beachy Head, Brighton, Portsmouth and the Isle of Wight.

"There was a heavy sea. Only Willy and myself at the breakfast table. The others were in bed. . . . . Though not actually sick, I was too unwell to do anything, and could not venture upon a public service. I gave a few tracts to the sailors. It was a melancholy, useless day. Yet it was pleasant to pray for others who were better employed, and to think at intervals on God's word.

"April 9.—A beautiful calm. The weather warm, the sky clear. The aquatic scenery truly enchanting. Only we are not getting on.

"The land scarcely visible in the distance, and in the course of the day, ceased to be seen. The sunset this evening was most beautiful. Not a cloud was to be seen. We beheld the sun sinking, and watched its descent, till it seemed to meet and combine with the wave and finally disappeared from view. It will re-appear to-morrow, and the Christian will have a bright rising again.

"April 10.—A very fine day; wind S.S.W., a gentle, pleasant breeze. We saw the Light-houses at the Lizard Point, and in the afternoon, passed the Land's End, and lost sight of England. I did not realize the emotions which Brother Harris, of Ceylon, predicted I should experience. They were not heart-breaking emotions. I felt as Mr. Hodgson told me, that I was not like Abram going out 'not knowing whither.' Neither is mine a banishment. I am going in obedience to the call of God, and in the hope of being useful. This sustains me. In addition to this I am not constituted as some are, whose attachment to place is as great as to persons.

"Nevertheless, I could not help turning towards the coast as I walked the deck to get another view. Nor was I wholly destitute of feeling. I am leaving my father-land. I may never see it again, never see again those whom I love. Can I think of this and not feel? God grant that this removal may tend to His glory, and the good of many souls. Should not that satisfy me? Lat. 49·49 ; long. 4·49.

"April 13.—. . . A homeward bound vessel passed us. She hoisted signals, showing her number to be 1723, and her name the 'Fox Hound.' We then did the same. Our number being 4563.

"The view from the deck is often truly sublime. We seem literally to mount up to the heavens and then 'to go down to the depths' and as literally we 'reel to and fro, and stagger like a drunken man.'

" I have sometimes thought that the engravings of ships in a gale must be on an exaggerated scale, but now I can believe in all that the painter has endeavoured to depict. Lat. 49.35 ; long. 8.12.

" April 15.—The wind increased last night, and the pitching and rolling were terrific. We lay uneasily, sleeping but little till about half-past 3, when it seemed to blow a gale. There was a loud knock at the door, and the steward and carpenter entered to fasten up the dead lights which had been left half closed a few days ago to let in the air. It was too late, however, for before they could accomplish their task, a wave broke in and sadly drenched us. It was then blowing a gale, and the carpenter said that the sea was one sheet of slimy foam.

"As the morning dawned, the gale abated, leaving a

tremendous swell. The ship heaved and rolled so much that I left my berth soon after 6, and went on deck, where the scenery was magnificent beyond description. The huge waves approached us, rising far higher than the vessel and threatening to engulph us all, and yet she bounded over them, or sinking into the hollow, seemed to give them an embrace as they glided away.

" The waves of the Atlantic differ much from those on the coast. They are rather heaps than waves, and though they flow in the direction of the wind, do not form continuous series, but break into lumps and commingle on all sides in inextricable confusion. Lat. 51.14; long. 11.52.

" April 19.—The wind still contrary, and the weather dull and cold. Not being very well, my rest was disturbed. When I awoke in the morning, I had been dreaming that my father was dead. I thought that affairs had gone on uncomfortably since I left him. Something had hurt his mind very much, and it affected him so powerfully that he died the following Friday. I am not inclined to superstition, and yet could not help feeling depressed and sorrowful, fearing that some such result would be one day experienced.

"April 22.—About half-past 3 this morning the wind changed to north, and carried us on in our right course at a rapid rate. In the middle of the day, it slackened, returning partially to the west, in the evening. A fine day, though rather cold.

"In the forenoon, we had service in the cabin. I read Ps. xcv. and xcvi. Prayed and read Luke xviii.; expounded verses 9-14. The captain and some of the crew attended. The whole family were at dinner and tea, being the first time we have all so met for a fortnight.

" April 29.—Saturday night, the 27th, was fearful. There was a strong wind and a heavy sea all night. Early

in the morning, the wind suddenly changed to the north
and blew with hurricane-like fury for some hours   It
was impossible to bear up against it.   All that we could
do was to bear up against the wind which carried us
along at a rapid rate.   At length, by dint of great effort,
the ship was hove to under a single sail, and so continued
till the evening.   The sea was mountainous all day, terri-
fically mountainous.   The view from the deck was awfully
grand, but the motion of the ship was uncomfortable in
the extreme.   She rolled from side to side continually, so
that it was scarcely possible to keep in one position for
a minute.   The scenes at our meals were most amusing.
No vessel with liquid in it could remain on the table.
We were obliged to hold our soup-plates in our hands and
balance them every second.   Spoons, knives, forks, plates,
and even the joints in the dishes seemed endued with life.
It was perpetual motion realized.   Lat. 48.9 ; long. 35.

" May 16.—We had an excellent run in the night.   At
eight o'clock this morning the bold coast of Cape Breton
was in sight.   The morning was fine and warmer than
usual.   The sea was calm, and our spirits buoyant under
these new circumstances, not having seen land for many
days.   We returned to the cabin for family prayer, thankful for the mercy which had been shown us in conducting us thus far in safety.   At half-past 2 this afternoon we
passed the island of St. Paul, and entered the Gulf of St.
Lawrence.   That island is about 15 miles long, is unin-
habited, save by the inmates of two light-houses.   It is a
barren rock, strewed with dead men's bones, the ship
wrecks in former years having been very numerous and
very destructive to life.

" May 20.—When I went on deck yesterday morning
before breakfast, the hills of Canada (the Gaspé district)
were just visible, about 50 miles distant.   In the forenoon
we had service; text, Ps. ciii. 1-2.   The Island of Anti-

oosti came in sight about noon. In the evening, the wind changed from S. to S.W., and compelled us to sail directly towards that island which we wished particularly to avoid, as it is a very dangerous coast.

" May 23.—Just as we were going to bed last night, we were summoned on deck by the captain to see the Aurora Borealis. It was a beautiful sight. A luminous arch stretched across the sky; its centre being at an elevation of about 45 degrees. It appeared like a bright cloud, as if it were illuminated by a concealed sun. Perpendicular rays darted up and down continually. At the east end it resembled a beautiful drapery, folding and unfolding every moment. At the same time the moon shone brightly on the water, adding greatly to the interest of the scene.

" May 25.—Great was my astonishment to learn when I arose this morning that we were within 60 miles of Quebec. Our progress during the night had been very rapid, and we were then scudding away before a strong breeze, with the advantage of a flood tide. As the river narrowed, it became more beautiful and interesting. Houses were thickly scattered on both sides of the stream, and many pretty villages were passed, each possessing its church, the roof of which was usually covered with tin. The foliage of the trees was exquisitely beautiful, much resembling the autumnal tints of our own country.

" At half-past 2, we reached Quebec, and dropped anchor amongst a crowd of vessels, having sailed from Bic, the pilot station, 180 miles from Quebec, in 21 hours, the finest run we have had since we left England. The view of Quebec from the river is very imposing, but it is impossible to form any idea of the plan of the town. All appears a confused mass of buildings. Churches abound, whose tin-covered tops glitter like polished silver.

" May 27.—Left Quebec half-past 7. A beautifully fine day. Towed up the river by a steamer. A magnificent river. It varies much. Sometimes there is a slope down to the water's edge. On the opposite side, a precipitous bank forty to fifty feet high, covered with woody foliage, in every tint of variegated green. A little further on, the bank becomes a cliff, and small streams are falling down its sides in beautiful cascades. Here the river narrows and little is seen on either hand but low forest trees. Then it expands, till it becomes almost a lake. Farm houses, cottages and small villages diversify the scene. Every village has its church; and the churches being universally adorned with light and elegant spires, are very interesting features of the landscape.

" May 29.—Soon after 7 this morning the mountain behind Montreal became visible. At a quarter-past 10 we reached the " Rapids." At half-past 12 we arrived in safety. The committee of the college were waiting to receive us, and conducted us to the house of Joseph Wenham, Esq., where we are to be entertained till we can get a house.

" Thanks be to God. Distance sailed: London to Beachy Head, 150 miles; Beachy Head to the Banks, 2,743; Banks to Cape Gaspé, 825; Gaspé to Bic, 312; Bic to Quebec, 180. Total, 4,390. The actual distance is about 3,000. Our zig-zag tacking making the difference."

# CHAPTER VIII.

## LIFE IN MONTREAL.

### 1844–1851.

" We are not to choose for ourselves what parts to act on the stage of life, but to act those well which are allotted and appointed for us."

TUCKER.

We have given somewhat extended extracts from the " Journal," (extended and yet very few as compared with the whole), partly, because they contain interesting descriptions of incidents and scenery, but much more, because they wonderfully unfold the character of the man who kept the Journal. They let out the secret of Dr. Cramp's power to do two or three men's work. The activity of his mind was such that he could not rest. The persistent energy of his nature was such that he must be busily engaged in work. He evidently gave just as much thought and attention to that whole voyage, the varying winds, the distances made each day, and all the other details, as the captain of the ship himself. How far the course of study planned for the journey was also pursued we know not. But, knowing his avidity in devouring books, we doubt not that extensive reading was carried on meanwhile.

Now he assumed the presidency of the Montreal College. It was weak and struggling. But there were noble helpers, men willing to give money, sympathy, time and thought. It was hoped and expected that all unreasonable opposition would soon be withdrawn, and that the whole body would rally around this institution. With Dr. Cramp at the head, and Mr. Bosworth, who had been associated with Dr. Davies in the work, as an assistant, it was thought that the matter was hopeful. More students began to gather around the institution. The work for which the president had been for years unconsciously preparing himself had fallen now into his hands. The committee of the "Canada Baptist Missionary Society" resolved to erect a building adapted to the wants of the institution. Montreal was selected as the place. Partly because they had already secured a considerable tract of land there, and partly because the men competent to aid in this important enterprise, were living in and near that city. We quote from an article of the late Dr. Fyfe :—

"The Montreal Committee of the 'Canada Baptist Missionary Society,' erected a fine cut-stone building upon a beautiful site which they had reserved from the land they had bought. It was a beacon which could be seen from a great distance, and brilliantly proclaimed the enterprise of the Baptists. For some time, the enterprise seemed to feel the impulse of this new departure. The attendance of students was considerably increased, and a number of those who had not the ministry in view were received into the school."

The internal working of the Institution was at this time eminently satisfactory. In fact it had been so from the first. There were drawbacks, however. Education throughout the country had been much neglected, and, as a result, many of those looking toward the ministry, were very deficient in the simplest rudiments of learning, Some, therefore, came to the Montreal college, whose proper place would have been in an elementary school. The diversified attainments made a proper classification impossible. And, young men were, therefore, compelled by the circumstances of the case, to join classes too far advanced for them. In such cases results would not always appear in proportion to the work done. And yet the teachers worked on and did the best they could, and the friends were encouraged, and convinced that a valuable impetus was being given to education generally, and to all the interests of the denomination. Young men were being taught the value of learning, and put upon the road to secure it. They were being fitted to become more instructive and useful preachers. Some of them had superior abilities, and having enjoyed the advantages of early training, were prepared to receive the full benefit of the instruction given at Montreal.

We quote again from Dr. Fyfe, who knew the whole history of the institution :—

" Some excellent men were indeed trained there, the

benefit of whose labors the whole denomination feels to
this day. I need only name Dr. Davidson, W. K. Ander-
son, J. Dempsey, A. Slaght, and others, to suggest to my
readers some of the services rendered by that college to
the Baptists of Canada. No intelligent Baptist can look
back forty years and ignore the great impulse imparted to
the Baptist cause by the Montreal society. Of the men
educated at this Montreal college, we have one in England and six in Canada, still engaged in preaching the
Gospel. There are besides, seven in Canada, who are
not engaged in the ministry. I can recall four others
who are in the United States, and several who have
finished their course and gone home. Besides there were
a number of ministers, who were induced to come to
Canada by the Montreal society, who rendered good service to the cause of the Master. From my heart I gratefully thank God for the good work done by the Montreal
society."

And yet, after a few years of heroic struggle, the
work was abandoned. Then, why did the college
fail ? Not through any defect or deficiency of the
teachers. Not through any failure of the committee who had it in charge. For, Dr. Fyfe says of
them :

" Never did a body of men labor more faithfully, or
struggle harder to succeed. I know that we have no
men now among the Baptists—and we never had any—
who would work harder, or give as liberally as the Montreal committee did, according to their means, to make
the school successful. But they were striving to make
water run up hill."

In what respect ? First, the college was too far
from the centre of the Baptist population ; secondly,
an unjust and foolish prejudice, or perhaps fear,

prevailed. I refer to the apprehension that the influence of the college would unsettle the Denomination in the Communion question; thirdly, the Baptists of Canada were not, in those days, as a body, sufficiently enlightened to appreciate and sustain such an institution as was needed; fourthly, there was not the spirit of enlightened liberality which has been awakened since, nor was there the amount of wealth which now prevails; fifthly, the society at home, which had been assisting, withdrew their aid. It had been expected that they would furnish at the least $10,000 towards the building fund. Instead of this they contributed nothing. The plan of the home society was changed, confining its efforts to mission work. A heavy debt rested upon the Montreal college. There was a general depression in business in Canada, as well as in other places, from 1846 to 1850. The burden bearers were reduced in circumstances, and the society, through sheer necessity, failed to meet their liability, and the Montreal college, in the beginning of its usefulness, ceased to be. The building was sold during the business depression at a great sacrifice, to pay the debts, and the Canada Baptist Missionary Society was disbanded.

A bitter ending to a noble, patriotic, unselfish struggle of good men to do good. What did it all mean? It may have meant many things not yet unfolded. But, among the things which the overturning of events have disclosed are these: It meant that Dr. Cramp should come to Nova Scotia and help the Baptists there to fight through similar struggles, with all the additional experience gained at Montreal. That through his aid, many men would be raised up for important work for God in these and foreign lands. That of these men so raised up, a number of them should go back to Upper Canada, and go on with the same work.

That a Fyfe, a McMaster, a Castle, and many others, should, in due time appear, and under more favorable auspices, and with all the impulse given to the cause, even by the college, which came to an untimely end, in the year 1849, carry on the work of developing intellect and preparing workers for the Lord.

" God moves in a mysterious way his wonders to perform."

But what it all meant, and other mysterious things, we shall know better when we know as we are known.

Dr. Cramp's labors in Montreal continued from 1844 till 1851. They were not years thrown away. He was, during a portion of this time, the editor of the *Register*, the *Colonial Protestant*, and then of the *Pilot*, and wrote many valuable articles for the papers of the time, both in England, Canada and Nova Scotia. He wielded a ready pen, and it was always at work, when the times seemed to demand his efforts.

Many changes have taken place in the people, the institutions and the country since Dr. Cramp reached Montreal in May, 1844. He and his family were kindly entertained for some weeks in the house of Jos. Wenham, Esq., a leading banker of the city. The banks continue their business; but the kind-hearted Wenham, and many others then actively engaged in building up the city and country, are not, for God has taken them. Montreal was then a city of 45,000. It now contains about 200,000.

The voyage across the Atlantic was a long and tempestuous one, occupying about seven weeks in "The Prince George," a barque of 400 tons, the usual size of ships then carrying freight and passengers from England to Montreal. Now steamers of from 2,000 to 5,000 tons burden, make the passage in 9 or 10 days. There are no less than ten different lines of ocean steamers. He who came as one of the passengers in the " Prince George," now the late lamented Thos. Cramp, Esq., Dr. Cramp's oldest son, was largely instrumental in organizing the company which owns and controls one of them (The Dominion Line).

There was one Baptist church in Montreal, of a little over one hundred members, worshipping in St. Helen Street, in a building that had cost about $6,000; the pastor, Rev. J. Girdwood. Long since, the pastor and most of those who then composed the church and congregation, have passed over to the other side. And yet the church has lived, and become two bands. There are now two churches, with two handsome buildings, in prominent positions in the city, erected at a cost of about $50,000 each, and a membership of over 600. There is also

in the city a French Protestant Baptist Church,
Sunday schools and missionary societies, and other
agencies of good, hardly thought of then, are now
in active operation.

Many churches in the country of 30, 50 or 75
members in 1844, have now hundreds on the roll
list. For instance :—

Chatham, J. King, pastor, membership, 1845.....92
Osgoode, J. M. Phail,     "      "       "   .....91
Stanstead, E. Mitchel,    "      "       "   .....11
Leeds, P. Schofield,    . "      "       "   .....34
Brockville, R. Boyd,      "      "       "   .....30
Brighton, J. Holman,      "      "       "   .....28
1. Hamilton, H. Brown,    "      "       "   .....33
2.    "    A. Booker,     "      "       "   .....42
St. Catherines, W.Hewson" "      "       "   .....58

The largest membership reported in those times
was that of Walsingham, 193 ; Brantford, 88 ; Paris,
10 ; Newmarket, 8. The whole membership of the
province (now two provinces) Ontario and Quebec,
could not have been much over 8,000 or 10,000.
Now, it is well up towards 30,000.

With these facts before us, we can hardly wonder that the Montreal Baptist College failed. The
wonder rather is at the courage that gave it existence, and the energy that kept it alive, till it had
convinced the Denomination "that the soul to be
without knowledge, is not good."

Among the men who welcomed Dr. Cramp and
family to their new home and sympathized with
him in his work, may be mentioned Jos. Wenham,

James Milne, James Thomson, T. M. Thomson, E. Muir, W. Muir, Rev. R. A. Fyfe, Rev. J. Gilmour, Rev. Dr. Davies, Rev. Mr. McPhail. Only one of these faithful friends now survive. The others have passed away.

In answer to enquiries as to the habit of life of Dr. Cramp in Montreal, one of the family writes :—

" When my father resided in Montreal, his duties as president of the college, gave him freedom from regular Sabbath labour. Yet, he preached almost constantly. He was often asked to occupy the pulpits of various churches. This he was always willing to do ; and at one time, during an interim of regular pastors, he frequently supplied the Presbyterian Church of St. Gabriel Street. He was also popular as a lecturer, and his sermons on special occasions were always able productions, and heard with great interest.

" More energetic than most men, and ever ready to labor for the cause to which his life was devoted, he rendered valuable service to the Canada Baptist Missionary Society, by visiting remote country churches, attending ordination services, etc. While his efforts for the Grande Ligne Mission were untiring, and resulted in effecting a union between that mission and the Baptist Denomination in Canada.

" Some of the men of like spirit with himself, and with whom he labored in various Christian enterprises were— Rev. H. Wilkes, D.D., Rev. W. Taylor, D.D., Rev. Caleb Strong, and several ministers of the Methodist Church. With these and others he worked heartily in the Evangelical Alliance, Bible, tract, Sunday school, and temperance societies, often speaking at their anniversaries.

" He also edited the Montreal *Register*, a Baptist weekly paper, and, with the Rev. W. Taylor, the *Colonial Protest-*

*ant*, and after the college was given up, he edited with Mr. Bristo, the *Pilot*, a tri-weekly paper, established by Mr., afterwards Sir Francis Hincks, now deceased.

"During Dr. Cramp's residence in Montreal, there were commotions and upheavals of various kinds; all of which helped to make his anxieties greater and his work more difficult.

"Montreal, instead of Kingston, had been made the Seat of Government. The Governor-General was Sir Charles Metcalf, a man of much ability and power. But, unfortunate differences arose between him and his responsible advisers. Some of these resigned, and the country was appealed to. The Governor was sustained with a small majority, and much trouble followed.

" Political excitement ran high. Tory was opposed to Liberal, and Loyalists were pitted against rebels. A terrible collapse in business matters occurred about the same time; the Montreal merchants alone losing some $4,000,000. Then followed the outburst against the new Government, after the appointment of Lord Elgin as Governor-General, when the mob assailed the Governor with stones and rotten eggs. In the words of another: 'The citizens were thrown into a ferment, a crowd assembled on the Champ de Mars. Violent speeches were made. The cry was raised, "To the Parliament House." The excited mob, led by men with flaming torches, went to the Parliament House, where the Assembly was in session. Suddenly, a shower of stones shattered the windows, and the rioters rushed in to the chamber. The members fled, and the work of destruction went on. The building was set on fire, and totally destroyed, with its valuable library and records. . . .' The city was in the hands of the rioters for four or five days. These were sad times for the city. For, besides the reproach brought upon the fair fame of the country

by this lawless vandalism, it caused Montreal to lose the
Seat of Government.'

" The burning questions in those times were ' Responsible Government,' 'the Clergy Reserves,' ' School Lands,'
' the right of the Cabinet to be consulted in the appointment of all Government officers,' &c., &c.

" The leaders in the discussion, and final settlement of
these questions, were such men as Baldwin, Lafontaine,
Hincks, Viger, Aylwin, Cameron, Sir Allan McNab, John
A. McDonald, George E. Cartier, A.T. Galt, L. H. Holton,
and George Brown."

With such men as these grappling with questions of vital interest to the entire Province, questions touching not only its civil interests, but its
social, educational, and religious prosperity, no one
who knew Dr. Cramp could suppose that he was
an idle spectator in it all. Not a man among them
all gave more anxious enquiry into the principles
of righteous government than he.

We quote from one well acquainted with Dr.
Cramp at the time referred to, and in fact till the
end of his life.

" The *Pilot* was the champion of the Reform party on
these and kindred questions; and its support was efficient and invaluable. It had been edited by Mr. Hincks
(the late Sir Francis Hincks), a bold and able writer.
In coming under Dr. Cramp's editorial charge, the *Pilot*
certainly did not lose in interest or influence. His profession as a Christian minister had never in the least
interfered with the keen interest he always took in politics; and in the government of the country in which his
lot was cast. In England, as a Baptist and a Dissenter,
he was naturally on the Reform side. Indeed, consider-

ing the host of legal restrictions and disabilities, which, at the time of his early manhood, were imposed by law on all outside the State Church, it would have been surprising indeed, if he had taken any other position. In Canada, the circumstances were somewhat different. Still, there was a Tory party and a Reform party—and the same difference in principle lay between the two parties. The controversies of those days have long been at an end; and it would not be interesting to submit any details as to this period of Dr. Cramp's life. He gave to the work which he then undertook, the energy and labor which he conscientiously bestowed on all his undertakings; and, looking back, we now see that the side on which he fought has prevailed; and that all the different questions so hotly contested at the time, have been long ago settled in accordance with the principles supported by Dr. Cramp in the *Pilot*."

Dr. Cramp's life then in Montreal was not that of a recluse, or simply the teacher of a few young men in the college. He had to do with all the interests of the Denomination and of the Province. He grappled with all the questions which pertained to the well-being of humanity, and did much towards effecting reforms which are now enjoyed.

Some important changes took place in his family relations during his stay there. A son dearly beloved was taken from the group in July, 1844. Two of the daughters were married and settled. One in Halifax, N. S., the other in Montreal. The two sons then living had settled down to business in Montreal,—one as a merchant, the other as a lawyer. His removal to Nova Scotia never lessened his interest or affection for the old friends of his former home. He frequently spoke of them and looked forward with great delight to anticipated visits among them. One of the family says:—

"It was a constant source of gratification to him to pay frequent visits to his children residing in Montreal. This intercourse was delightful, indeed, and is a precious remembrance to them now. The long journey, so often made, was undertaken, in spite of increasing feebleness in 1878, and was then made for the last time."

From Montreal, Dr. Cramp removed to Nova Scotia, in 1851, to assume the duties of President of Acadia College.

# CHAPTER IX.

*ACADIA COLLEGE.*

"That the soul be without knowledge, it is not good."
—Prov. xviv. 2.

Omitting for the moment all reference to Dr.
Cramp's literary works, it may be stated that the
most fruitful portion of his life was spent in connection with Acadia College, in Wolfville, N. S.

A brief sketch of the history of the educational
institutions at Horton may not be out of place
here.

At a meeting of the Baptist Association held at
Wolfville, in June, 1828, measures were adopted
for founding a school of a higher class, than the
ordinary public schools of those times. The want
had been long and deeply felt, but no public action
had been taken till the date named. A respectable
education could be secured at the academy and
college in Windsor, N. S., but it was necessary to
subscribe to the 39 articles in order to gain admission. The academy at Pictou, under the able
management of Dr. MacCulloch, was open to all
classes ; but the Baptist churches were neither

numerous nor strong in the eastern part of Nova
Scotia, and in those days of slow travelling, that
school was of little use to the denomination which
founded Acadia College. As a people then, the
Baptists were without the means of education, beyond the mere rudiments of learning, provided in
very poor common schools.

The people, as a body, were satisfied with this
provision. Some of them, in fact, opposed to anything beyond, so far as the Christian ministry was
concerned. They believed in God—ordained, not
man-made preachers. There was, however, a large
and rapidly increasing class, who recognized the
loss the denomination was sustaining for the want
of men of trained minds, and fully developed intellects. They came to the front at this first public
movement in behalf of advanced education for
Baptist young men. It would be impossible at
this date, to convey an adequate idea, of the pathos
and power of some of the addresses on that occasion. The fathers in the ministry, as they were
called, spoke from the fulness of their own bitter
experience, when they told what they had suffered,
and how they had been hampered in their great
work, by the want of training in their younger
days. Many long standing prejudices melted
away in the presence of these veterans pleading
for their sons in the faith. And from that day, a
denominational school was assured. Results followed at once. Money was raised, an education
society was organized, a property in Wolfville was
purchased, and in the following year, a school was

opened under the management of Mr. Asahel
Chapin, afterwards Dr. Chapin, from the United
States. This was the commencement of what is
still known as Horton Collegiate Academy. Rev.
John Pryor, a graduate of King's College in Windsor, was the successor of Mr. Chapin. He, with
various assistants, continued to carry on the school
successfully for about ten years. Pupils came from
all parts of the Maritime Provinces. Their mental
and spiritual interests were well provided for.
Buildings were erected. One for class-rooms, and
another for a boarding-house. The blessing of
heaven seemed to rest upon the endeavour, and
the denomination might, for many years, have
been satisfied with this provision. Some, indeed,
were looking forward to the time, in the near future, when academical training would make a
demand for a full college course, but there was no
expectation of immediate action in that direction.
Circumstances, however, sometimes compel or
prompt people to go faster and farther than they
had intended. It was so in this case.

In the year 1817, Lord Dalhousie, Governor of
the Province of Nova Scotia, had appropriated
£9,750 out of what was called the Castine fund,
toward the establishment of a provincial university at Halifax. A few years after, a building was
erected for that purpose, and funds were contributed from the provincial chest, to the amount of
£10,000. In 1838, an effort was made to commence actual operations. It was hoped and fully
expected by many at that time, that King's College,

8

Windsor, would unite its forces with Dalhousie, at Halifax, and thus form one strong metropolitan college. Dr. MacCulloch, however, of Pictou, was appointed president, and Mr. E. A. Crawley, now Dr. Crawley, a graduate of King's College, a young man of great promise and superior education, was strongly recommended to the managing board as a suitable person to fill one of the chairs as a professor. His application, however, was rejected. Not because of any suspected inability on his part, but because of his denominational views. He was, at the time, the pastor of a Baptist church in Halifax, and the decision reached by the board of management of Dalhousie was, that all the professors must be members of the Presbyterian Church.

This decision, as might have been expected, awakened very deep feelings in the Baptist denomination in the Maritime Provinces. The exclusiveness of King's College could be endured, for that was avowedly denominational, in its origin, and largely in its means of support. But Dalhousie funds were not in any sense derived from the Presbyterian body. Shut off, therefore, from all educational advantages, both in Windsor and Halifax, the question was seriously asked, "What other course is there open before the Denomination?" Many letters appeared in the papers, calling attention to the recent action. Among these a series of communications from the able pen of Rev. E. A. Crawley, in the *Nova Scotian*, showing that the duty of the hour was to push on the work commenced at Horton, to its legitimate issue. In other words, to found, equip, and sustain a college, walled around by no creed, for the benefit and training of all who might seek instruction therein, This onward movement commended itself to the intelligence of the people, and efforts were put forth at once. The Rev. J. Pryor's place in the academy was filled by the appointment of another principal, Mr. E. Blanchard, of Truro. And Dr. Crawley and Dr. Pryor were appointed to chairs in the college about to be established. Application was made to the Legislature of the province for a charter. This application, though fiercely opposed by many of the leaders in politics and religion, was finally secured. Twenty students were, upon examination, found prepared for the first-class in the college. On the 21st of January, 1839, the college was formally opened, each of the newly appointed professors delivering addresses appropriate to the occasion.

The executive committee of the education society, who assumed the responsibility of this undertaking, were as follows :—Rev. J. E. Bill, Dr. Lewis Johnston, Rev. William Chipman, Simon Fitch, Esq., Rev. John Pryor, A. M., Rev. Richard McLearn, Rev. E. A. Crawley, A.M., William Johnston and J. W. Nutting. Of these ten men, only three now survive. The others have gone to their reward.

That the circumstances recited above did not originate the idea of Acadia College, but only hastened its approach, may be gathered from various sources.

In 1836, the managing committee of the education society, urged upon the Denomination the establishment, as early as possible, of a seminary which shall become so fully possessed of the highest literary merit as to deserve every immunity that the law can grant to chartered institutions. This evidently referred to financial as well as other support. The opposition to State aid for educational purposes, had not been developed as it appeared later on.

In 1837, the managing committee's report contained the following :—

" The education of the country is at this moment in a singular condition. Windsor Academy is only beginning to revive from a long period of depression; Pictou Academy, by the unfortunate dissensions which have long agitated it, is said, even by its friends, to be hastening to decay; the college at Windsor is acknowledged to be too sectarian to allow Dissenters, with any confidence, to seek its advantages for their sons, and still suffers that depression which its contracted system inevitably involved. All efforts to open Dalhousie have hitherto failed; there is, therefore, at once a loud call and an open field for all who feel the importance of a liberal education to engage in the important work of forming and animating an enlarged system of instruction, such as the country urgently needs, and is sought in vain within its borders."

Attention was also called to the fact, that young men, of the various religious persuasions, were continually going out of the provinces to seek that mental training which should be provided at home, and that a thoroughly equipped college, open to all classes, would, therefore, be a boon to the country as well as to the Denomination which might found it. Urged on by these general considerations, and stimulated by the events referred to, Queen's College, afterwards named "Acadia," was started with only two professors, as stated above, January, 1839. In October following, an addition was made to the staff, by the appointment of Mr. Isaac Chipman, A.B., a former student of the academy and graduate of Waterville College, Me. He was selected to fill the chair of natural philosophy and mathematics. In this choice the managing committee was surely guided by something more than mere human wisdom; For Mr. Chipman was a young man, and as yet untried. He was very unassuming, and possessed no external force of character. His retiring and gentle manner, would seem almost to invite defeat in any contact with difficulty or danger. But there was a wonderful fund of talent, energy, and persistency of purpose in the man, which made him invaluable to the young college through all the years of its early struggles. It may be truthfully said, that the one aim of Professor Chipman's life, from the time of his appointment in 1839, till the sad day in Acadia's history, when the surging waters of Mines Basin swept his body from the overturned boat, was to foster the interests of higher education, through the means of the institutions at Horton. His acquaintance with the branches taught was comprehensive, and yet, simply as a teacher, in the class-room, perhaps, he would not hold the first rank. But as a man, and a Christian, as one devoted to what he believed to be his calling, his rank is among the first.

The college thus established and equipped went forward in its appointed work, The course of study embraced four years after matriculation. The first class of graduates was in 1843. Of the twenty who entered, only four continued to the end. Very similar has been the history of many classes since. But, although the work accomplished from year to year was acknowledged to be good, and although considerable enthusiasm seemed to gather around every anniversary oceasion, the one great want was money, sufficient to make provision for the work.

A small provincial grant was secured. But, even this became a bone of contention. It was easier to see the iniquity of State and Church connection, even in education, than to recognize the duty of furnishing the needful funds. Infinitely easier for those not valuing education, or perhaps, even hostile toward it, to see how the denomination would sacrifice all those great principles for which our fathers died, by allowing the boys to study Euclid or Longinus, under a professor whose daily bread came in part from the filthy lucre of the Provincial chest, than for the governors of the college to find the means to make the institution what it ought to be. So there was struggle, and effort, and appeal. With commendable liberality, some responded to the call A building of fair proportions was erected, which, together with the original building for the academy, furnished class-rooms and sleeping apartments for a considerable number of students. And the college came to be regarded as equal, if not superior, to any other in the provinces.

Agents had been sent out at different times, through the provinces, and occasionally to England and the United States, for help. · Money was collected by these means, but never sufficient to meet the demands. There were frequently large deficits when the accounts were balanced at the end of the year. Professors' salaries were small, and not promptly paid. The Hon. J. W. Johnston, the able and conscientious leader of one of the political parties in Nova Scotia, was one of the warmest friends of the college. On the floors of the house in council chamber, as well as at the public gatherings of the Baptist denomination, he had given most valued aid. But in those · days, politics was everything to a large class of the people. Every other interest, educational or religious, was looked at and judged from the standpoint of Party politics. And the simple fact that the leader of one Party was also a leader in building up and sustaining Acadia College, was quite sufficient to call out the hostility of the other. Put together the want of educational zeal in these provinces, the lack of funds, and political animosity, and it is not difficult to see that the friends of the Horton institutions had no small difficulty to cope with.

A remark may be made here, with, perhaps, a better chance of gaining credence, than if made thirty or forty years ago: Acadia College is not now, and has never been, partizan in politics. Among teachers and students, from the first, there have been varied views, full and free discussion. The writer has been personally acquainted with all the professors and teachers, with the exception of Mr. Chapin and Mr. Blanchard. He studied seven years at the institutions at Horton, and taught in the academy twice that time, and has no recollection of any influence ever being used to give a bias on any political question, either in the class-rooms, or elsewhere, by the teachers during all these years. The avowed object of the existence of the Wolfville insitutions, was education, under the guidance and fostering care of religion, and neither governors nor teachers have, as yet, turned to any inferior work.

Difficulties, however, from the first, surrounded this enterprise. Opposition of the fiercest kind was manifested. A central university at Halifax continued to be the fond dream of many of the leaders in Provincial politics. The poverty of the college was turned into an argument for its use-lessness. Again and again its friends feared that the enterprise would prove a failure in the end. Had they not been men of faith and prayer, pur-pose and perseverance, far beyond ordinary men, that must have been the result.

### FOUNDING OF A THEOLOGICAL PROFESSORSHIP.

Among other donations, £100 sterling was pro-mised in England for a limited time, toward founding a theological chair. An equal amount was pledged by the Association in 1845, and in 1846, Rev. E. A. Crawley, A.M., then made a D.D., by Brown University, was appointed to fill this chair. He, however, shortly after resigned his position at Acadia, and removed to Halifax in 1847. Mr. A. P. S. Stuart, of Brown University, was appointed professor of mental and moral philosophy, and resigned his position in a couple of years. Things were looking dark, and many of the friends of Acadia began to despair of success. We quote from the " History of Acadia College and Horton Academy," published in 1881 :—

" In the summer of 1850, the outlook was very gloomy. Prof. Stuart had left at the end of the previous year. Dr. Pryor was to leave in June. Prof. Chipman had also tendered his resignation, the Denomination was divided upon the question of Government aid, and a debt of £3,000, about $15,000, rested upon the governors. Without professors, and without resources, it seemed as though the end must soon come. It is saying much for the intelligence, piety and zealous courage of the Baptists of the Maritime Provinces, that in the face of such apparently insurmountable obstacles they did not flinch, but unhesitatingly decreed that Acadia College should live."

In July of 1850, Dr. Pryor removed to the United States. Prof. Chipman had been induced to withdraw his resignation, and remained at his post, and he, with the aid of teachers in the academy and advanced students, carried on the work of the College for the balance of the year.

Thus we have the condition of things: Only one

professor in Acadia College, and he the junior one, A heavy debt resting upon the institution, and no income to meet it. Enemies railing, old friends disheartened, the students, some of them packing their trunks for home, or for some institution in more hopeful condition. Under these circumstances it was that the managers were looking for deliverance, and finally decided to extend an invitation to the Rev. Dr. Cramp, of Montreal, to accept the presidency of Acadia College.

We quote from "The Vaughan Prize Essay," written by Alfred Coldwell, A.M., now Professor Coldwell, of Acadia College.

"Prof. Chipman was now left alone. With the aid of Mr. C. D. Randall, A.M., as classical tutor, the work of another year was performed, and the first epoch of the history of the institution finished.

"After the departure of Dr. Pryor, a year elapsed before another president was appointed. The governors were extremely desirous, at this critical juncture, of obtaining the best man possible for this important position. None seemed so likely to meet their requirements as the Rev. J. M. Cramp, D.D., President of the Baptist College, Montreal. The Baptists of the Lower Provinces had formed the personal acquaintance of this gentleman in 1846. As an author, he was favourably known many years before, his 'Text Book of Popery' and 'The Reformation in Europe' having had quite a circulation in Nova Scotia and New Brunswick. During his visit in 1846, he attended the college anniversary and associational gatherings, everywhere making a very favorable impression."

This visit in 1846 was made chiefly in behalf of

the Swiss Mission. The following extracts are taken from a record of the journey, headed :—

FIRST IMPRESSIONS OF NOVA SCOTIA. 1846.

This journey was undertaken chiefly on behalf of the Swiss Mission, and including a short visit to Boston, then seen for the first time, occupied several days before reaching Halifax. Dr. Cramp's Journal contains many descriptions of the beautiful scenery which the slow method of travelling enabled him to enjoy, and several references to ministers and other friends whom he met on the way.

Arriving at Halifax on June 2nd, the narrative proceeds as follows :—

"June 4.—A fine warm, clear day. After writing since nine in the morning, called on Mr. Ferguson, and conversed at length on the state of religion in the province. In the afternoon went across the harbour to Dartmouth. Mr. Hunt took us for a ride through a very pleasant, hilly, wooded district. The trees are small and apparently stunted, the soil covered with a thick layer of stones. Called on the Attorney-General—his country residence being beautifully situated. A very fine view of Halifax from Dartmouth, somewhat resembling that of Quebec from the Charlesvoix and Montgomery roads, but not so imposing.

"June 5.—Took a pleasant walk to the N.W. arm of the sea, which runs in above Halifax, a very rocky district with low trees. In the evening, attended the Conference meeting. Father H. Harding, 85 years old, presided."

"June 7.—A very fine day. Preached in the morning

from Rev. i. 17, 18, and in the evening from Rom. xiii. 18. The Lord's supper in the afternoon. Father Harding presided, and I assisted by taking the latter part of the service.

"June 8.—Fine day, the Nova Scotian anniversary. Flags, blue newspapers, ribbons, handkerchiefs! Went to the Province House. Externally it is neat, and even handsome. Dined at the Attorney-General's. Conversation about registering births. Attended prayer meeting in the evening.

"June 9.—Breakfasted at Dr. Sawers, saw the Mechanics' Institute, museum and lecture room. Wrote letters to the churches in Nova Scotia and New Brunswick. Conversation with Dr. Sawers and Mr Nutting on the college question.

"COLLEGES IN NOVA SCOTIA.—*Dalhousie*, with an endowment of £7500, Three per Cents, and rentals from the Post-office; neither professor nor students. *King's College*, Windsor, about 15 students. *Acadia, St. Mary's*, R.C., a mere school. *Pictou Presbyterian Academy*. The three latter receive £250 a year; King's College, £444.

"June 10.—Began collecting at Dr. Hume's. Preached in the evening.

"June 12.—Continued collecting. Went with Dr. Sawers, Mr. Barss and Mr. Selden to the twelve-mile house, a very pleasant drive on the S. side of the basin. It has all the appearance of a lake, the shores wooded, soil very rocky. Prince's Lodge, about five miles from Halifax, where the Duke of Kent used to live, all in ruins. Walked a mile or two beyond the house, the scenery quite lovely. Dined and then came back.

"CHURCHES IN HALIFAX.—Two Methodist chapels, one African do., two Scotch kirks, one Free church, one Anti-burgher, two Baptist, three Episcopalian (another

building), two R. Catholic, one Universalist, one Sande-
manian (30 to 40 of them), one Campbellite.

"June 16.—Finished collecting. At Mr. M. Black's
with Mr. Richey.

"June 17.—Left at 10 minutes past 6, and crossed the
harbour to Dartmouth, where Brother Hunt met me with
his waggon. The road along the basin .is retired, and
rather rough. Beyond, it is somewhat hilly, and the
country begins to be slightly cultivated. Stopped to
breakfast at the half-way house ; the next stage was
through a more cultivated and picturesque country.
Some parts had been evidently long settled; the trees
were larger and the soil better. Here and there a small
lake. When we passed the ridge, and began to descend
towards Windsor, about twelve miles from that place, the
view became very beautiful. Nearer Windsor, the scenery
became more English. At one time I was reminded of
the valley of the Stour between Canterbury and Ashford.
Saw Sam Slick's house, King's College Academy, etc.
Windsor is a pretty village. The prospect from Fort
Edward is very pleasing. Dined there. Left again at
half-past five. Passed through some good forest scenery
at some places, very deep ravines, several beautiful
valleys; the land about Horton is very rich dyke land.
Arrived at nine o'clock,—sixty miles.

"June 18.—Acadia College is situated on a beautiful
slope, before it the Cornwallis River, with the Bay of
Minas on the right, and a very fertile district on both
sides of the river.

"At 10 A.M., the governors met in Mr. Pryor's parlour,
and resolved to grant the degree of B.A. to five students.
The college exercises began at 12. A large attendance.
Conferring the degrees. Addresses to the students. Dined
at Dr. Crawleys. Ascended the cupola; extensive and
beautiful prospect. Spent the evening at Mr. Pryors.

"A very rainy day. Breakfasted at Dr. Johnston's. Many years ago he met with my work on Weekly Communion, and re-published it in Nova Scotia, with extracts from other works, in a pamphlet. Attended the examination of the academy, saw the philosophical apparatus, the electrical, chemical, etc.; select and good. The geological and mineralogical specimens very numerous, and as regards the Provinces, complete. Much conversation with the professors.

"ACADIA COLLEGE.—Description of the building &c.: 50 acres of upland; 14 dykeland; the building of wood, the pillars of the portico wanting; a neat cupola over the centre, with a good bell, worth £40, presented by a lady at Liverpool.

"The Academy, a separate building, also of wood, on the west side. Mr. Pryor resides at the west end of it. Dr. Crawley in the east end of the college. Mr. Chipman has apartments in it. Gardens at each end for the Professors.

" June 20.—Rose at half-past 3. Left about 5. Rode 25 miles, the road generally good: the country between Lawrencetown and Bridgetown very beautiful, the road passing over high ground with many interesting views Arrived at Bridgetown about 5, heard the conclusion of H. Harding's sermon.

"June 21.—Lord's day. A good congregation in the morning. Father Manning preached from Matt. v. 7. A fine tall benevolent looking old man, with a black silk cap on his head. I sat in the pulpit with him and gave a short address after his sermon; in the afternoon preached to a crammed congregation. In the evening, Father Magee preached a plain, useful sermon. Father Manning was in his 80th year when he began to preach 57 years ago. There were but two Baptist Churches in Nova Scotia, at Horton and Shelburne.

"June 22.—Attended the Education Society Committee at 8.30, and the service at 10; the Association was then organized. During the reading of letters from the churches, reference was made to a specially destitute region. After hearing of the need, Father H. Harding rose and said: ' If I were young, I would put on my fisher's coat, and go among them.' Father Manning added: 'And if *I* were young, I would go and help our brother here, in Canada.' I gave an account of the Swiss Mission, and the people *determined* to have a collection, though it had been resolved not to have one.

" June 24.—The Association closed at two. Just before my departure, I met Father Manning in the road, and took leave of him. ' Have you a family ?" said he. On my answering in the affirmative, he said, ' May the Lord bless you, personally—domestically—ministerially—and eternally ! ' Drove to Annapolis, about 14 miles, a pleasant ride through the valley.

"June 25.—Walked about Annapolis, a quiet, and rather desolate place, once the capital of the Province. Took a view of the neighborhood from the fort. Found some soldiers from Kent: one from Chatham, one from Dover, one from Sandwich. Left in the steamer at 12. Annapolis Bay is a very pretty sheet of water. Digby pleasantly situated. (The captain and several of the men intoxicated.) Reached St. John at 9, very tired.

"June 26.—A pleasant day; spent it chiefly in walking about and calling on friends. St. John is built on a rock, the site very uneven. It is a bustling place, much business going on. Tokens of activity and enterprise in every direction—the houses principally of wood, but the new ones of brick,—the streets wide, the harbour completely land-locked, and well defended. Almost all the places of worship are of wood, no high towers or spires."

" June 28.—A fine day. Preached in the morning at

the First Baptist Church, a long, narrow building, with galleries on three sides, it was well filled. Crossed the harbour in the steam-ferry, and preached at Carleton,—the place small and crowded. Two friends conveyed us in a boat (Mr. Duval and myself) along the harbour to a convenient spot, whence we walked over a ridge to Portland, drank tea at Mr. Seely's, and preached in the evening; the place of worship new, on an elevated site, neatly built, and commodiously fitted up. Walked home very weary. Texts: Isa. lii. 13. 2 Kings, v. 14. Rom. xiii. 11.

"June 30.—Left at 10 in the steamer. For many miles, the banks of the river rise from the water's edge, leaving an interval of land, and are but thinly covered with grass or wood.

"But 50 miles down, the scenery changes, the prospect widens, there are extensive marshes and fertile fields on each side, with the forest in the distance. The river was as smooth as a pond, the trees on the banks being reflected beneath, and the view sometimes resembling that from the Thames, on the way to Richmond. In several places there are islands on the river, furnishing very beautiful scenery. At Oromuctoo it was particularly fine. the banks are low, the land is in a good state of cultivation. The village is evidently flourishing, the farm-houses and buildings are respectable; altogether, it is an enchanting spot. Arrived at Fredericton at 8.

" July 1.—Collecting in the morning; a meeting in the evening, when I gave an account of the Mission.

"July 3.—Left at 9; reached St. John. Conference meeting in the evening, when several ministers spoke.

" July 4.—Fine day. Walked out with Mr. Duval; meeting at 2. Mr. Thompson preached; after the sermon, about twenty ministers and others gave short addresses, some of them very forcible and good.

" July 5.—Preached at Portland; the place was crammed and packed with people, and many stood at the doors.

" July 6.—Services continued; the Association constituted; Committee meetings.

" July 7.—Committee on union at 9; public business at 10. Domestic missions; an eloquent speech from Mr. Kinnear; then an account of the Swiss Mission by myself. Subscription followed; £36 paid at the meeting. A speech from Brother Cunningham, who was once a Roman Catholic.

" Business again at 3. Foreign Missions—another speech from Mr. Kinnear—much business tact, zeal and energy—the province well divided into districts for Missionary purposes.

" July 8.—Education Society at 10, and the remaining business of the Association. Then I preached to the ministers from 2 Tim. ii. 2. A ministerial conference in the afternoon.

" Left at 6. A very affectionate farewell from Father Crandall in the name of the whole, all standing.

" July 10.—Went on board the 'North America' at 7. The coast of New Brunswick is generally almost bare rock, very thinly wooded, and sometimes wearing the appearance of utter desolation. St. Andrew's Bay, a very interesting spot, from the number of islands in it.

" July 12.—Reached Boston—a very hot day. Heard Mr. Olmstead in the morning, from Rev. xiv. 6. Preached in the afternoon from Isa. xlii. 44.

" July 13.—Walked out with Mr. Colver, called on Mr. Stow and some others. Left at 5 by train, and reached Providence (45 miles) in an hour and 40 minutes. After tea, walked into the city. The upper part is like a West-end suburb: it consists of fine, wide, handsome streets, the side-walks shaded with trees, and the houses very substantial. The lower part presents an animated scene of busy bustle, betokening energy, activity, and a prosperous, thriving State.

" July 14.—Walked up to Brown University, and found Dr. Wayland disengaged. Dined, and spent the day with him, one of the pleasantest days I ever spent.

"We talked much about Jamaica; he is greatly interested in the success of emancipation, and yet puzzled by the conflicting statements. We talked of England, and of present changes. He thinks that Sir Robert Peel has done more for his country than any man since the days of Cromwell. He adverted to the treatment he had received in England, on account of his views on slavery, and remarked, to shew he was misunderstood, that most of the students who came to the University from the South, had returned home friends of abolition, and some had determined to devote themselves to the amelioration of the negro race. He made many enquiries respecting the state of religion, and general affairs in Canada. At his earnest request, I gave him an account of our theological system of training, of which he was pleased to express his entire approbation. He seemed particularly pleased with our sermonising exercises. He shewed me the library, containing 20,000 volumes, carefully selected, admirably arranged, and continually increasing, the sum of $5,000 being appropriated annually to it from a bequest. Manning Hall, comprising on the principal floor, the philosophical lecture-room and apparatus; and on the upper floor, a chapel, neatly fitted up, where the Doctor preaches every Lord's Day afternoon, to the students, and any other persons who may choose to attend; and Rhode Island Hall, the lower part of which contains the chemical lecture-room, laboratory and apparatus, and the upper part, the collection of mineralogical specimens. In the last mentioned room there is also a splendid portrait of the late Mr. Brown.

" In conversation, Dr. W. strongly urged the importance of keeping the students employed in religious exercises of a useful kind, and of inducing the churches to pay for them, as a proper check against needless or interested recommendations.

" He gave me four volumes of his works; walked part of the way with me when I left, and insisted on carrying my great coat, pleasantly remarking that he supposed that was what the Apostle meant when he spoke of ' helping them forward after a godly sort ! ' Referring to the Swiss Mission, he expressed his admiration of Madame Feller, and his conviction that the work was of God. Adverting to its success, he said that it was like the Lord slaying Sisera by the hand of a woman.

" Left at half-past 6 in the ' Rhode Island,' an immense steamer.

"July 15.—Rose at 5. The shores on both sides much resembled the banks of the Thames, between Gravesend and the Nore. Arrived at New York at a quarter before 8. Called on Messrs. Colby, Kelly and Cutting; saw Dr. Cone, &c.

" July 18.—A cool and windy day. Left at 7 in the ' Troy.' The first half of the voyage is very interesting. The banks of the river are bold and steep, and the changeful scenery often sublime. The latter half of the voyage presented fewer points of interest ; the only commanding objects were the Catskill mountains. Arrived at 7, and remained for the 'Lord's Day at Troy.

" July 20.—Left in the coach at $8\frac{1}{2}$ A.M. A very fine drive all the way. The numerous windings of the road, and the inequalities of the surface, some of the hills being of considerable height, contribute to render the journey very interesting; reached Whitehall late in the evening.

" July 21.—Arrived at home. There are reasons for gratitude:—

" 1. For *preservation*.

" 2. For *pleasure*—new acquaintances found—Christian fellowship enjoyed—much useful information obtained— assistance rendered to the cause.

" 3. For the *accomplishment* of objects—misapprehensions removed—the Swiss Mission—Union between the Provinces."

The *Christian Messenger* of May 15, 1846, then under the editorial management of Messrs. Nutting and Ferguson, refers to the visit of Mr. Cramp to Nova Scotia, as follows :—

" The Baptist Theological College at Montreal, has been founded chiefly through the aid of the English Missionary Society, and is now in active and useful operation. The name of Dr. Davies, as connected with the opening and subsequent management of the institution, is well known to most of our readers. On his having been called to preside over the Theological College at Stepney, near London, the Rev. J. M. Cramp, A. M., one of the most learned and able of our English brethren, has been chosen to supply his place. The name of Bro. Cramp is, doubtless, familiar to many, as the author of several highly useful publications, intended to counteract the influence of Puseyism and Romanism. . . .

" We shall hail with pleasure the arrival of our worthy brother, the Rev. Mr. Cramp, one of whose chief objects is, besides forming an acquaintance with his brethren in these Lower Provinces, to obtain assistance for the Swiss Mission. We shall rejoice in the opportunity which will also be afforded of furthering a union greatly to be desired between our Canadian brethren and ourselves, as well as strengthening the link that binds us to the denomination in England, of which Bro. Cramp may be said to be the chief representative on this side of the Atlantic."

In the *Christian Messenger* of May 29, a long letter appears signed "C."—probably Prof. Isaac Chipman—discussing the expected visit of Mr. Cramp, and the benefits to be derived from a further acquaintance with the Grand Ligne Mission.

The *C. M.* of June 5, 1846, contains a letter from J. M. Cramp, then in Halifax, in which he says :—

" My only object in sending you these few lines is to correct a statement in the closing paragraph of your correspondent's ('C.') letter. It is to this effect :—'Our brethren in Canada are, many of them, more open than we, in their communion practices.' Allow me to inform you that there are eight associations in Canada : seven of them comprising 106 churches, practice strict communion ; the eighth, in the Niagara district, contains but *four* churches, which are founded on the open communion principle, and the same principle is adopted by two of the churches, twenty in number, which are reported as unassociated."

The next issue of the *C. M.*, June 12th, informs us that :—

" The Rev. J. M. Cramp, the Principal of the Baptist Theological Institution at Montreal, preached to the Granville Street Church on two consecutive Lord's Days, on the latter of which he presented the object on whose behalf he had come from Montreal."

Succeeding numbers of the *C. M.* speak of Mr. C.'s presence at the Association at Bridgetown, where he met aged and younger ministers of the body. Only a few days after this, the first one of these, Father Dimock, died.

Mr. Cramp also attended the Acadia College anniversary, which was held on the 18th of June. Of the graduates of that year, but one now remains—Mr. James S. Morse. Rev. Stephen W. DeBlois was also one of that number. Mr. Cramp is said to have given—"a very interesting, highly practical, and useful address to the new graduates. . . His position, as the head of the Baptist College in Montreal, gave additional effect to his remarks, which were listened to by all present with profound attention."

Some time after this, Dr. Cramp wrote some interesting articles in the *Christian Messenger*, on "The Fathers of the Nova Scotia and New Brunswick Baptists."

# CHAPTER X.

"In labours more abundant."—2 Cor. xi. 23.

At a meeting of the Board of Governors of Acadia College held in St. John, N.B., in September 1850, a resolution was passed, inviting Dr. Cramp to come to N. S., and undertake the Presidency of Acadia College.

There had been evidently some endeavour before this, probably of a private character to induce him to make a second visit to the Province  Some friends of the College were doubtless thinking of him as the man to save the Institution, although he at the time knew it not.

The following letter addressed to Prof. Chipman in 1849, will show that he had been urged to come and that at one time he had hoped to comply with the request.

"MONTREAL, April 28, 1849.
" MY DEAR BROTHER:—

" Yours arrived yesterday, and I am very much obliged to you for the trouble you have taken in preparing the excellent suggestions contained in it.

"It is now, however, necessary to inform you that an unexpected change has taken place in my affairs here, which will deprive me of the pleasure I had anticipated.

"Mr. Campbell, the Publisher of our *Register*, has bought the *Pilot*, a liberal newspaper, now the organ of Government, and I have undertaken to manage it for him. It is a tri-weekly paper, besides a weekly edition, and is somewhat larger than the *Register*. You will at once perceive that it will be impossible, under these circumstances, to leave Montreal. I am to enter on the new duties next week, and shall have to carry them on, conjointly with my engagement here, till the end of May.

"I have been induced to enter upon this occupation, partly because I have a taste for it, and partly because it will enable me to retain my personal superintendence over my youngest son, who is about to commence active life in some department.

"Although my time will be pretty much occupied, I shall find time for certain literary enterprises, and shall endeavour to advance tho interests of our denominations in various ways.

"My excellent brother, the Rev. F. Bosworth, A.M., who was Professor of languages here, for several years, was compelled to leave us last year, and undertake a voyage for the benefit of his health. Excessive study had overpowered him. He went to Buenos Ayres, and spent several months there. He returned this week, with restored health. We have nothing here to offer him, nor is he desirous of remaining in Canada. You would find him a great acquisition. He is an excellent classical scholar, enthusiastically fond of Hebrew, and other oriental languages, and well stored with all kinds of general knowledge. He is, besides, an acceptable preacher. If you can find a niche for him, either in the College, or as

a Pastor of some Church, you will soon begin to rejoice
in having enriched Nova Scotia by transplanting him
among you. I commend him to your notice, and have
his permission to do so. Any communication to him may
be addressed to my care.

"Please to give my kind regards to Dr. Pryor, and
say that I am greatly disappointed. I had hoped to enjoy
much pleasure in attending your meetings, and conferring with you all respecting the cause of God. That hope
is now cut off. I trust that you will have a season of
holy delight, and that enlarged liberal purposes will
testify the genuineness and depth of feeling.

"In this Province, saving a few very green spots, all
is dry and barren. Oh! for a plentiful shower.

"I am obliged to conclude, or I shall lose the mail.
Every blessing rest on you.

"Yours faithfully,

"J. M. CRAMP.

"Professor Chipman."

The engagements referred to in this letter,
made it very difficult for him to decide, even after
the formal invitation of the Board reached him.
The Governors of the College, however, pressed
the claims of Acadia. The correspondence was
conducted by Prof. Chipman, who entered into
that, as into everything else which he undertook, with all his heart. The result was that,
at last, all difficulties werere moved, and Dr.
Cramp accepted the invitation. Not, however,
until he had satisfied himself by correspondence
with many of the leading men in the denomination that his appointment would be generally
acceptable to the people. When assured of this, he
wrote :—

" I respond to your call, and henceforth devote myself to the cause of education in Nova Scotia, especially as connected with Acadia College."

He came to Wolfville in May, 1851, and was installed President of the College on the 20th of June. The Hon. J. W. Johnston was President of the meeting and introduced the new President in his usual happy and eloquent style. The following years showed how true were his words when he said :—

"The acknowledged talents of Dr. Cramp, and his well-known acquirements as a Scholar and a theologian, attest the wisdom of the appointment made by the Governors of Acadia College ; and offer the surest pledge that the interests of the Institution, whose welfare lies so near our hearts, will be promoted by the selection they have made."

The Rev. Theodore Harding occupied the chair, implored the divine blessing on the exercises of the day, and presenting the right hand of fellowship to the President elect, cordially welcomed him to his new office, and assured him, in his peculiarly fervent style, that the friends of the College would give their sympathy and support.

A few extracts from the Inaugural Address which followed may be deemed appropriate here.

" I rejoice that it is not necessary on the present occasion, and before this assembly, to plead on behalf of learning. I stand in the midst of the friends of education. *You* require no convincing argument or persuasive oratory on this subject, If there were ever any doubts in your minds, those doubts have been long since removed.

The inspired sage has taught you that for the soul to be without knowledge it is not good, and that divine saying has been illustrated and confirmed by the experience of accumulated centuries.

"Instructed by the records of past ages, and contemplating the human constitution in the light in which it is presented to view by the best and holiest authors, you regard the intellectual powers of man as capable of high cultivation. You recognize also the duty of cultivating them, and of employing mind with all its acquisitions, for worthy purposes. You deem it of great importance that man should become acquainted with the works of God, and investigate the laws which He has instituted in the kingdom of nature, both animate and inanimate, and that he should know the history of his race, and be able to derive instruction and improvement from the productions which have immortalized the wise men of antiquity, and exerted a powerful influence on all successive generations . . . . . Spared then the necessity of advocating the claims of our Institution,. as a seminary of learning, it is with great satisfaction that I offer you my hearty congratulations on the success which you have already achieved in the glorious enterprize. This establishment is a splendid manifistation of Baptist energy. You have set your fellow countrymen an example of enlightened liberality, and testified before the world the deep sense which you entertain of the advantages of mental improvement. Posterity will doubtless award the due meed of praise, and bless the memory of the founders of Acadia College. . . . .

"A clear and comprehensive view of our present position and prospects will enable us to discern the path of duty. It is especially incumbent on us to bear in mind that the age is remarkably progressive, and that all institutions must keep pace with it, or sink in public estimation. The range of study is extending every year, as the boundaries of science expand, so that the instructor finds it necessary to incorporate additional branches in his course, and the student is compelled, if he would avoid the reproach of ignorance, to spend much time in making acquisitions for which there was no demand in the days of his predecessors ; while the ancient standards of learning still retain, and must continue to retain, their place and pre-eminence. . . . .

"To such considerations must be added the peculiar claims of these Provinces, now beginning to emerge into activity and enterprise. Nova Scotia and New Brunswick are shaking themselves from the dust, and rousing up the energies of their sons. They ask for railroads, and they will assuredly have them. Their agriculture is to be improved by science. Their mineral wealth is to be profitably explored. Their ships will sail all waters. Their resources and capabilities, not yet half developed, will be ascertained, and brought into useful operation. Now, in order to the accomplishment of these and other beneficial results, the talent of the Provinces must be sought out in every direction, and carefully cultivated. There will be abundant employment for men of ability and skill, both in originating improvements and directing the agencies, by which they may become available to the public; and if such men are trained in the Provinces, patriotism will inspire them with ardor, and their efforts will be carried on with zeal, which strangers would emulate in vain. It is obvious, therefore, that a solemn responsibility rests on our institutions of learning, and that such arrangements as the exigencies of the times call for, must be provided. The supporters of this College, it cannot be doubted, will duly consider these facts and expectations, and act with characteristic 'largeness of heart.' . . . .

"There are two other points to which it will be proper to advert. One is the importance of *thoroughness*. A superficial acquaintance with any subject may be easily and quickly acquired, and may excite the admiration of persons who are apt to mistake appearances for realities, and are therefore ill qualified to form a judgment; but good scholarship is the result of patient assiduity. The students of Acadia College, it is confidently hoped, will carefully avoid the danger into which those are liable to fall, who in their desire to learn everything, learn nothing well. . . . .

"The second point to which I ask attention is the importance of religious influence, pervading the whole course of study, and sanctifying, so to speak, all the arrangements. This College is open to all denominations, no religious tests being imposed either on students or Professors; nevertheless, we must claim the right of aiming to imbue literature with the spirit of religion, and of inculcating, from time to time, those principles of our common Christianity, and those moral lessons which are admitted by all who wish to shun the reproach of infidelity. Habitual recognition of God, should distinguish every seat of learning, so that while the din of controversy is never heard, and party contentions are unknown, all may be taught that 'the fear of the Lord is the beginning of wisdom.' It has been well observed, that 'it is our educated young men who will give the tone to society, and control the destiny of the generation in which they live.' How desirable, nay even necessary, it is that the education they receive, while truly liberal in its plans and provisions, should be connected with that moral conservatism, without which, the advantages of knowledge itself may prove comparatively valueless.'"

The inaugural goes on at length, pleading for progressive movements ; for liberal support ; for ample provision for imparting theological instruction to such as may need it, and concludes as follows :—

"Invited by the Governors of this College to assume the Presidency, I have responded to the invitation after much reflection and prayer, and stand this day before you in the official character which has been conferred upon me. I undertake this office with a deep conviction of the responsibilities which it involves. I should shrink from those responsibilities, and from the trial and anxiety which must unavoidably be encountered,were it not for the assurance which I entertain, that in answering this call, I have obeyed the voice of God, on whose promises of aid his servants may confidently rely, when they walk in the path of duty. The cordiality with which the invitation was extended, and the gratifying fact of the union of the Baptists in these Provinces for this object, together with the noble subscription raised for the purpose of liquidating the heavy debt on the Institution, tend still further to cheer and encourage me, showing that the interests of Acadia College have a high place in the esteem of the Denomination, with which it is especially identified, and that they will not be suffered to fall into decay.

"When I call to mind the persevering devotedness and self denial, with which my predecessors pursued their course, and the respect in which they are on that account deservedly held by the churches, I feel that I enter upon the office under far different circumstances, and that I cannot hope to reach the position to which they have attained, yet I trust that by the manifestation of sincere and ardent desires for the prosperity of the cause, and by diligent attention to the duties of the station in which I am placed, I shall succeed in gaining your confidence. I have come, therefore, believing that my brethren here will evince a generous sympathy, and heartily co-operate with me in the good work. I have come, expecting to find a chivalrous zeal for education, and determined endeavour, on your parts, by judicious and liberal arrangements, to establish and maintain a course of instruction so appropriate and comprehensive that the youth of the Provinces will feel the force of the attraction, and seek to satisfy within these walls their desire for knowledge. I shall not be disappointed. You have ventured on a bold experiment, and you will succeed. Resources will not be wanting. United as one man in the prosecution of this undertaking and constantly invoking the blessing of Almighty God, Acadia College is safe in your hands. *Esto perpetua* is the fervent prayer of her sons."

This inaugural address, fragmentary extracts of which have been given, so thoroughly prepared, so appropriate to the occasion, and so admirably delivered, showed in what spirit the new president entered upon the duties of the office. He realized that a great work lay before him. It was not Acadia College, simply as a seat of learning, that he took charge of that day. It was not to settle down among the musty books of learned lore, and starve himself and his students among the dry bones of theoretical learning. All the varied interests of the comparatively young and undeveloped Provinces, were before him. To provide for these interests was his aim. The wants of the churches, many of them soon to be left vacant by the retirement of the well tried and worthy men, who under God, had given piety a prominent place

among the people, were outstretched before his
eyes and pressing upon his heart. The college,
with all its possibilities was to him, not an end,
but only the means to an end. And that end was
the temporal and spiritual advancement of the
people among whom his lot was now cast. From
the day that Dr. Cramp assumed the management
of Acadia College, he completely identified himself
with every laudable enterprise in these Provinces.
He soon knew more about the educational wants of
the country than those who were teaching the
schools ; and more of the religious condition and
history of the churches, than those who had been
for long years preaching to them. He girded himself for a great work. And so many and so varied
were the duties undertaken, that any ordinary man
would have been bewildered and appalled thereby.
It is very difficult now to understand how he
overtook all the work which pressed upon him
day after day.

All the provincial aid had been withdrawn or
surrendered. A heavy debt rested upon the institution. The students were scattered and gone.
There was only one professor besides the president. The friends of the college were disheartened.
The appeals to the benevolence of the churches
had become stale and almost ineffectual. Drs.
Crawley and Pryor, through their personal influence, had gathered much sympathy around the
college. They were both gone, and in the estimation of many, when they were gone, all was gone.
It was very like beginning at the original founda-

tions again, with this difference—all the romance and enthusiam which gather around a new enterprise had already expended their strength. A hopeful, prosperous Baptist College for the Maritime Provinces was deemed by many as a dream of the past and a failure. These were disposed to say: It is useless to make further efforts,—and but for some faithful friend like J. W. Barss and a few others, these gloomy forebodings would have been realized.

After much prayerful deliberation by the board of governors, the meetings of which were frequently continued till after midnight, it was determined to endeavour to raise an endowment for the college. Dr. Cramp took hold of this matter with great energy. He wrote to friends of the institutions all over the Provinces. He had personal interviews with as many as possible. He attended associations and ably urged the claims of Christian education, and kept the matter before the people in the press till it became a settled conviction that Acadia College must be endowed, and that by this means only could she be equipped for the work that lay before her. In connection with the general scheme of endowment, a system of scholarships was inaugurated. By the payment of £100, into the endowment fund, the donor secured the right of free tuition in the college for all time to come.

Agents were appointed to help work out these schemes, and many friends assisted. But the one man who was the inspiring and guiding agency

10

of the whole was the president of the college. His determined energy, cheerful manner, genial spirit and stirring appeals awakened a hopefulness for the future that had not been known for years. It was at once felt that a new life had been infused into the educational work of the denomination. Old friends were encouraged, lukewarm ones were overawed, and new ones were found, many of whom are still giving their best energies to this enterprise.

The work outside, however great and important, was not allowed to encroach upon the official duties of the president. A glance at the first published programme of college work proper after Dr. Cramp's appointment will show that the internal duties were not light ones.

### FACULTY.

Rev. J. M. Cramp, D.D., President and Professor of Hebrew and Chaldee Languages, Theology and Moral Science.

—— Professor of the Greek and Latin Languages and Literature.

The President is acting Professor in this department till an appointment is made.

Isaac Chipman, Esq., A.M., Professor of Mathematics and Natural Philosophy, and acting Professor of Intellectual Philosophy, Logic and Rhetoric.

### COURSE OF INSTRUCTION.

The course of instruction comprises the following branches:—

The Greek and Latin Classes.

Mathematics, including Geometry, Algebra, Trigonometry, with their application to Mensuration of Surfaces and Solids, and to Navigation, Surveying &c., Differential and Integral Calculns, Natural Philosophy, including Mechanics, Hydrostatics, Pneumatics and Optics.

Chemistry.

Astronomy.

Intellectual Philosophy.

Moral Philosophy and the evidences of Christianity.

Logic and Rhetoric.

The French Language.

A monthly Lecture is delivered on subjects not included in the course. This lecture is open to the public at a small charge.

No small amount of work then was undertaken by the President of the College and his devoted assistant, Prof. Chipman. The educators of the present day would cry " preposterous." "No two men could over take the work," and even with an additional professor, whose appointment was expected at an early date, instruction worthy of the name could not be given in all these varied branches Each of them would require the full strength of an able man. And yet with some assistance from senior students, the work of the classes went regularly on. There are several men now filling important positions in the church and in the state who were students at Acadia at the time referred to. And it may be safely affirmed that not one of them will venture to say that he ever entered or retired from a class conducted by the President of the College without the feeling that his teacher was thoroughly master of the work in hand.

There was indeed such a fund of information, and always ready, not only on the question under discussion, but upon all kindred topics, the text book used, and other authors on the same subject, that the students soon came to regard Dr. Cramp, as a comprehensive encyclopædia of all knowledge. But his knowledge was not theoretical and speculative. For this kind of learning he had no taste, and sometimes but little patience. The facts of the case were the matters with which he loved to deal, and these were wonderfully at his command.

If the class were required to translate a difficult Latin book, it was soon found that the teacher could go minutely into the grammatical structure of the sentences and make the meaning plain, and also give the history of the author and his contemporaries, and the circumstances under which the book was written.

If it were an oration of Demosthenes, or a Greek play, not only were the Greek roots uprooted, but Grecian history, literature and mythology were all freely taxed, to make enigmatical references bear their part in the composition. If it were a lesson in moral science, not only were the thoughts of the text book thoroughly weighed, but the views of other authors on the same subject were placed side by side with them, to see how far they agreed, and where they differed. If it were a lesson in theology, for ministerial students, it was found that every doctrine of the Bible had been most deeply pondered, the circumstances of every inspired author thoroughly considered, the contemporary literature of each book gathered up, the errors or evils which needed correction, and called forth the warning, were alluded to. In fact, the entire Bible, from beginning to end, and all that pertains to a life of piety, or to the preacher's work, were so completely grappled with, that every student felt that Dr. Cramp was competent to give instruction in theology. All of which would call forth no special comment, if a specialist had been dealing with each subject. This would be nothing more than might be expected, and indeed ought to be demanded of the teacher. But the wonder was to find any one man who could act so well the part of a specialist on such a variety of dissimilar subjects. In this respect, it is doubtful if any man in these provinces at least, was the peer of the late President of Acadia College.

As already stated, in June, 1851, Dr. Cramp was installed President of Acadia College. During the year previous there had been no president. Prof. Chipman, with the aid of tutors, had kept the classes at work, with a forlorn hope on the one hand, but with wonderful trust in God on the other, that deliverance would come. If earnest prayers were ever offered, Isaac Chipman offered them, during the year that he alone kept the college alive. These petitions were answered as already shown. A great burden of anxiety was rolled off, and with a new spring, he bounded to the work. He trusted the president, and the president confided in the professor. A very superior class of students gathered around the institution, as honest, as earnest, as devoted and as sincere as any class that has ever sought instruction within her walls. Some of them, we may venture to name, for they are beyond the reach of our praise or blame: Grant, Rand, Phalen, King, Angell, etc. These and such like men, thirsting for knowledge, and competent to receive it, inspired the teachers to make ample provision for the yet undeveloped resources of mental power in these Provinces.

The endowment plan was seized upon. In April, 1852, it was resolved to raise for this purpose, £10,000. The work was in progress. Scholarships were subscribed and smaller sums contributed. Things looked hopeful. The following extracts from a report of the anniversary exercises of June 4, will show that there was life manifested :—

" The hall was crowded by an amazingly attentive and patient audience, whose repeated expressions of approbation indicated the satisfaction with which they had listened. The orations were pronounced excellent by competent judges.

" Father Harding gave vent to his kind feelings in a strain of impassioned eloquence. He was followed by Rev. Messrs. Very and Hall, who expressed their approbation in strong terms, and favored the meeting with many instructive remarks.

" The President referred to the endowment, and stated the very encouraging fact that the sum of £2,000 had been subscribed in the townships of Horton and Cornwallis. The name of J. W. Barss, Esq., stands at the head of this list: he subscribes £500. Five scholarships are subscribed for by other individuals in Horton. One is raised by the First Horton Church, and another set on foot by the students,—it will bear the name of the Rev. Theodore Harding. Four scholarships are secured by members of the First Cornwallis Church; a church scholarship is also subscribed for, and an Edward Manning scholarship. Two scholarships are connected with the Second Cornwallis Church.

"The examinations of the students occupied two days. There were classes in Latin, Greek, algebra, mental philosophy, evidences of Christanity, Hebrew, nautical astronomy, and other branches. The students acquitted themselves well. Several of the governors were present, and expressed themselves as highly gratified with all they saw and heard.

" This exhibition of life, both outside of the college and inside, shows that the touch of a master hand was being felt."

And here follows a brief outline of the class work of the President during the year :—

" *Classics.*—In Greek, the senior class have read the Medea of Euripides, from the 908th line to the end. A portion of the first book of Homer's Odyessey and 95 sections of the Oration of Demosthenes on the Crown.

"The junior class have read in the Iliad of Homer throughout the term.

" In Latin, the senior class have read the Agricola of Tacitus, from chap. xix. to the end, the whole of Germania, and chap. xiii. of Cicero de Officiis.

" The junior class have read Sallust's Catiline, from chap. xvi. to the end, and twenty of the Odes of Horace, selected from his third and fourth books. This class has also been regularly exercised in Greek and Latin composition.

" *Mental Philosophy.*—The class in Mental Philosophy

have gone through Upham's Treatise on the Intellect as a text-book, with extended comments.

"*Moral Philosophy.*—A class, chiefly composed of senior students, was formed immediately after the opening of the fall term. Dr. Wayland's Moral Philosophy was used as a text-book.

"*Evidences of Christianity.*—Having completed the course of moral philosophy, the above mentioned class proceeded to the study of the evidences of Christianity. Dr. Paley's well-known treatise was the book employed, and lectures were delivered, embracing many topics, which are but slightly touched or altogether omitted in that work.

"*Rhetoric and Elocution.*—Blair's Lectures have been the basis of the instruction in rhetoric, and once a week exercises have been conducted in reading or declamation.

"*Essays.*—The students have written essays on various subjects, literary, historical, etc., which have been examined and criticised, with a view to improvement in composition. Seventy-six essays have been prepared during the terms.

"*Theological Department.*—The President regrets that so little has been done in this department. Having been compelled to undertake the duties of the classical professor, he has been unable to give attention to theological instruction, except to a very limited extent."

"An exegetical exercise on the Greek Testament has been attended to once a week, in which all the students have shared. A Hebrew class has been formed. After studying Gesenius's Grammar, the class commenced translation, first in the reading book and then in Genesis, in which the first six chapters have been read.

"Skeletons of sermons have been prepared every week by the theological students and submitted for examination.

" Lectures on preaching and on church government, have been delivered, but theology and ecclesiastical history have been entirely neglected, for the reason above mentioned, with the exception of the delivery of " an introductory lecture."

This with a monthly public lecture on various subjects, and a sermon every Sunday evening in the church, will afford some idea of the first year's work of Dr. Cramp as the President of Acadia College.

It can only be accounted for by remembering that he had been all his life a most diligent student. He was always at work. He had a vigorous, active mind, and very retentive memory. Names, dates and incidents which might be needed, were labelled in some way, and always on hand. He was very systematic and careful in all his habits, so that neither time nor strength was wasted. And thus by using materials already collected, and persistent energy, the result of long training, he was able to accomplish the work which would seem to have required two or three men.

We have dwelt long on this first year's work at Acadia, because it may be taken as typical of all that followed. But the busy, active, hopeful year had a fearful ending.

The College closed on June 4. On June 5, the President prepared a report of the year's work for the *Christian Messenger;* extracts from which have already been given.

On June 8th, the following was sent to the same paper:—

"After sending you the telegraphic dispatch this morning, I obtained full information respecting the catastrophe which has spread mourning, lamentation and woe, throughout our Denomination in these Provinces, and now hasten to transmit it to you. Brother Very, having a taste for geological pursuits, felt desirous of obtaining specimens from Cape Blomidon, so well known as Professor Chipman's favourite resort for that purpose. They agreed to form a party for a visit to the spot. Four of the students, Benjamin Rand, Anthony E. Phalen, W. Henry King and William E. Grant consented to accompany them. There were also two boatmen, George Benjamin and Percy Caldwell. The following narration of the disaster is given substantially in the words of Benjamin, the only survivor.

"They left Wolfville yesterday morning about five o'clock. The weather was then fine. They were three hours crossing over to the Cape, where the gentlemen landed, and remained till noon. It began to blow, just before they started on their return, but became calm when they were between the Cape and Long Spell. It freshened again when they were about half way across and veered round more to the south, heading them off towards Long Island. They tacked and stood across for Cornwallis, when they came about again they stood for Long Island Creek, intending to land there, as the wind had become stronger. When they were nearly half a mile from the island, a sea struck the boat and half filled her; they succeeded however in baling out nearly all the water and put about the boat before the wind, purposing to run in at the back of the island. Just then (it was about four o'clock) they were struck by a heavy sea, which swamped the boat immediately. She went down stern first and turned bottom upwards. All, with the exception of Grant (who sunk at once) and Professor

Chipman (of whom presently) clung to the boat and endeavoured to get upon it, when it turned completely
round till it was bottom upwards again. Rand and King
were lost in this movement. The remaining four still
clung to the boat. They were washed off two or three
times, but gained it again. At length Phalen and Caldwell were washed off together and rose no more. Soon
Mr. Very was washed off, but he swam to the boat and
was assisted on it by Benjamin. He held on by the stern
for ten or fifteen minutes, when three heavy seas in succession broke over them and swept Mr. Very away.

"Professor Chipman was upon the mainsail which had
got adrift when the boat upset. He was heard to call
aloud for help, but none could be rendered. Benjamin
saw him at about twenty rods distance a few minutes
before Mr. Very sunk ; he appeared to be then dead.

"The boat dragged towards the shore till it was right
off the point of Long Island, when it held on. Benjamin
then stripped off his clothes and swam to the shore, which
he reached in a very exhausted state. The boat was
found this morning bottom upwards, but little injured.

"Benjamin adds that Messrs. Very, Phalen and Grant
had suffered much from sea-sickness ; Grant seemed to be
disabled by it, which may account for his sinking immediately.

"It is not surprising that in the confusion of such a
struggle, no words escaped them, indicating their inward
feelings. All their energies were concentrated in the
effort for self-preservation. The Lord understood the
utterances of their hearts.

"Careful search for the bodies is now going on. I hope
we shall have the melancholy satisfaction of paying them
the last tribute of affection and respect.

"I cannot attempt reflections, for I can scarcely think.
It is a stunning stroke. God have mercy on the widow

and the fatherless—on sorrowing friends—on our churches and institutions, so sorely bereft.

"J. M. Cramp."

This letter has been given in full, both for the sake of affording a permanent record of the greatest calamity that has as yet fallen upon the institutions of Horton, and also as an illustration of a leading characteristic of the writer. In all the overwhelming distress of the hour, he addressed himself to the duty which seemed to lie before him, knowing that the minutest details of the sad event would be eagerly sought after by all the mourning friends, he went directly to the only one who could give the facts. And by repeated questions on every conceivable point, secured all that ever could be found out of this sad calamity, and then hastened to place it before the public. Painstaking in research, and promptness in despatch, gave him success when another of equal ability, but lacking these elements might, have failed.

It is difficult at this date to realize how completely this event seemed to upset every plan in connection with the college. The students, whose classmates and companions had been thus swept away, felt that college life was spoiled for them. Professor Chipman, who had been a tower of strength, was gone. And it was some time before the President knew what to advise. Wisdom and strength, however, were given. The cause was too important to be abandoned. The resolve was to go on, and trust.

In January of 1853, the college was re-opened. No new appointments had been made. But the President undertook, with such assistance as he might secure from the academy, and from a senior student or two, to carry on the work. The report of the governors stated that the result was satisfactory.

Dr. Crawley was shortly after this invited to return. We quote from the history of the College published in 1881.

It was felt that the college, at this crisis in her history, needed the best men in the denomination to fill the vacant chairs, but it proved to be a somewhat difficult matter, without doing injustice to existing arrangements, to offer Dr. Crawley a position commensurate with his present standing and past services. What the governors were unable to effect, was, however, very amicably arranged by Dr. Cramp and Dr. Crawley themselves in a personal conference. Their scheme, as adopted, is embodied in the following resolution of the Board :—

" Resolved that there shall henceforth be in the University of Acadia College, an institution for literary and scientific instruction, to be called Acadia College, and also an institute for theological instruction to be called the Theological Institute. Dr. Cramp was appointed principal of the Theological Institute and professor of logic, political economy and history in the college; Dr. Crawley was made president of the arts course and professor of Hebrew in the institute. This arrangement went into effect in Sept. 1853. In Nov. Prof. Stuart returned, to fill with marked ability, for the succeeding five years, the chair of mathematics and natural science."

The following reference to this period is taken from a "Tribute In Memoriam" written by Dr. Crawley, and published in the *Acadia Athenæum*, of January, 1882 :—

"'Dr. Cramp had been comparatively but a short time President of Acadia, so fondly styled the child of Providence, when all at once Providence seemed turned against her. Then came the perhaps unwise appointment of another president, and of his own removal to the position of principal of the theological department. Dr. Cramp's demeanour at the time well deserves to be remembered ; there escaped from him no unseemly word; he met these untoward changes with calm composure. Some singular transpositions occurred then and afterwards; for the change of position made in 1853 was again reversed in 1865. The former president then took the position of professor of theology, with other branches in the art course; Dr. Cramp continuing at the head of the university.

" The eleven long years passed between 1855 and 1866, well deserve to be made the proud boast of all who honor the memory of our departed friend.

" The college was still weak and staggering at the time of Dr. Cramp's resumed presidency in 1855. In 1866 it had become well organized and flourishing. In 1869 occurred his formal resignation of the presidency.

# CHAPTER XI.

" . . . The same commit thou to faithful men who shall
be able to teach others also."—2 Tim. ii. 2.

The change referred to was mutually agreed
upon between Drs. Cramp and Crawley. It was
very gratifying to many of the old friends of Dr.
Crawley, to see him once more identified with the
institution. In fact, some supposed that, but for
his efforts at the outset, the college would never
have come into existence. Whether this were so
or not; it is true that, both by his voice and pen,
he had given a great impetus to the undertaking.
And the denomination could not easily forget the
valuable services rendered by him during all the
early years of its struggles.

This change, together with the appointment of
an additional professor, relieved Dr. Cramp of
many burdens which he had been bearing. It also
gave him work far more in the line of his own
sympathies and interests. Education he prized as

highly as any man could. But the special phase of education which tended to develop the kind of men needed by the churches, was that on which his heart was most thoroughly set. He, therefore, entered into this new work with great enthusiasm and zeal. Theological students were made to feel that a great work lay before them, and that they needed all the training of the schools, and much that the schools could not give them, before they would be prepared to perform that work aright.

The address delivered at the outset of this new phase of college work will show in what spirit and with what aims the principal of the theological department entered upon these engagements :—

"ADDRESS AT THE PUBLIC CELEBRATION, DEC. 20, 1853.

"The patrons and friends of Acadia College have good reason to rejoice that their arrangements are so far completed. Ample provision is now made for all the ordinary branches of collegiate education, and our young men have no need to go out of the country.

"Special reference is here made to candidates for the ministry, . . . that is, not those who would study for the profession, . . . but true-hearted believers . . . whose aptness to teach is perceived and acknowledged, who ' desire the office of a bishop,' because they are under a holy constraint, borne away by love to Christ and to the souls of men, and who repair hither that they may be better fitted, as far as human perception goes, for the great and good work. For them as well as for the general student, the means of instruction are supplied.

"The facilities offered to the theological student, embrace these particulars: acquaintance with the languages in which the Scriptures were written, principles and rules of Biblical interpretation, illustrated and applied in exegetical exercises; . . . . the reasons of faith, *why* they believe; . . . . the faith itself; *what* they believe, tracing the gradual development of religious truth from the patriarchal period to the Gospel dispensation, and upholding the mind of God, so far as it is revealed, respecting His own glorious character, attributes, and mode of existence; the state of man; the salvation; the Church; the invisible world, and the Divine purposes; the history of the faith, including the state and progress of religion in successive ages; the divergencies from truth, the controversies; the sects; the sufferings; the fall and the rising again, including a full history of our own denomination; the Divinely-appointed means of propagation, the manner in which ministerial and pastoral duties may be most profitably discharged.

" Such is the course. Views relating to one branch, ecclesiastical history, have been given at length in a former lecture. Present observations are confined to Biblical theology, with a design to state the thoughts, feelings, and intentions of the theological faculty."

## " BIBLICAL THEOLOGY.

" This expression is used in contradistinction from human systems. Their object is, not to collect and compare many various opinions, nor to hew and square the divine revelation by the measure of any human standard; but, first of all, to ascertain, by assiduous and reverent inquiry, the truth of God, as contained in His own word, . . that they may place before the mind of the student, the Infinite One, by Himself pourtrayed, in the splendour of His character, the harmony of His perfections,

10

the marvels of His redemption, the mysteries and mercies of His dispensations, the unsullied glory of His government, from the first promise to the fulfilment of the last prophecy, the completion of the cycle of heavenly manifestations and God-like works.

"They are deeply impressed with a sense of the dignity of their enterprise. Theology is the most sublime of all sciences. Other studies relate to combinations of matter, arrangements of words, the things and events of this passing world, or the characters and deeds of men; but here we have to do with the eternal mind, its arrangements and influences, . . . the laws of His holiness, the Gospel of His grace, . . the paths of life and death, . . and the everlasting destiny of His creatures. They know that here mistake is perilous, error may be fatal, and that it is of utmost moment that those who engage in holy ministry should ' by manifestation of the truth, commend themselves to every man's conscience.' They feel the solemn responsibilty of their position: those who train the teachers of Christianity should themselves understand, and clearly and comprehensively state before them ' all the council of God.'

"In making this attempt, they feel the necessity of constantly bearing in mind that Christian theology is pre-eminently the word of Christ—nothing more— nothing less. All perversions of the faith have arisen from neglect and forgetfulness of this fact. Men have sought to mingle the services of science, falsely so called, with God's revelation; they have grafted their own imaginations on the stock of Christian verity; they have placed over the lamp of life the dark covering of Scholasticism; they have made the Word of God of none effect through tradition. Nor were such endeavours confined to the Middle Ages—they characterise many sects and systems in these times, and hence the perpetual need of reminding the inquirer that if he would have pure theology, he must derive it from the Bible, and the Bible only, and of so ordering, so directing his studies that the holy book may be ever before him—the mine which he will ceaselessly explore—the fountain at which he will daily slake his thirst,—the authority from which there is no appeal. This will be the distinguishing feature of the instructions imparted in the Theological Institute.

"The faculty, moreover, rejoice that Christianity is the revelation of God's grace to the guilty—that it makes known the way in which He can be just, and the justifier of him which believeth in Jesus, even by sending his own Son, and that 'by grace we are saved.' As they review the history of the past, they note the strivings of men against these precious truths, because, precious though they be, they are deeply humbling to human pride; and they cannot but observe that even in countries where the true light now shines, there is, in numerous instances, a lamentable tendency to substitute 'weak and beggarly elements' for the doctrines of the Cross. Therefore, they hold it to be of immense importance that the rising ministry should be thoroughly prepared for the work which they will be called upon to do."

By this time, hopes were revived. The sum of £12,000 had been collected or pledged towards the endowment fund. The attendance was increasing, and efforts were being made to increase the endowment to £15,000, but disaster frequently follows closely upon the heels of prosperity. An unfortunate investment of college funds was made, and heavy loss followed. This not only crippled the finances for the time, and furnished an excuse for not paying in old subscriptions or pledging

new ones, but subsequently resulted in removing
Dr. Crawley from the Institution. By this means,
Dr. Cramp was left again in charge. But not now
of one department as at the first, but of the two.
The Literary and Theological departments both
fell into his care. He was made Chairman of the
society, and afterwards re-appointed President of
the entire Institution, and with marked ability,
and giving entire satisfaction to all concerned, he
continued to discharge the duties of the office till
his resignation in 1869. Some years before, feeling
the burden of years and of work pressing heavily,
he had sought release, and placed his resignation
in the hands of the Board of Governors. He was
then about seventy years of age, and used to say,
" when three-score and ten are reached, it is time
to give place to more vigorous men." The Board
however, and in fact all who came in contact with
him in public life, failed to share his feelings. It
was felt that so far as the interests of the Institu-
tution were concerned, there was no need for any
change. The following resolution of the Board,
unanimously passed in June 1866, will show how
his services in the College were regarded :—

" Resolved that this meeting has learned with deep
regret the Rev. Dr. Cramp's determination to resign the
Presidency of Acadia College. In his official position
at the head of the college, as a Governor and as connected
with our institutions and the denomination generally, no
language can express too strongly the appreciation in
which he is held. His retirement, viewed from any
standpoint, can be regarded only as a calamity. The
board cannot admit that in any respect Dr. Cramp's age

has in the slightest degree impaired his influence or efficiency."

This resolution, re-affirmed at the meeting of Convention the following August, and strengthened by many letters and personal appeals from the warmest friends of the Institution, overpowered for the time the President's détermination. He withdrew the resignation and resumed the duties. He did it, however, with the distinct understanding that the Board would at once enter upon the work of securing a successor, to whom the responsibility could be assigned at no distant date.

The resolution above, refers to Dr. Cramp's position as a member of the Board of Governors, and as connected with the denomination generally. As a member of the Board, his counsel was regarded as invaluable. And he was one of the few men who could look at a question from different standpoints. As President of the college, and very progressive in disposition and aims, he could see how far the institution fell below the requirements of the age. He knew how loudly the times were calling for improvements; for better accommodations, for apparatus, for books, for the introduction of other branches of study, and the consequent establishment of new chairs, etc. He saw all these things, and no man in his position ever saw them more clearly or felt them more keenly. But upon the other hand, he well knew the straitened circumstances in which the Board was placed. He could sympathize with the poorer churches, which were called upon to give to the cause of education, and the many under-paid pastors throughout the country, who were expected by word and deed to lead off in denominational enterprises, must share in the struggle, and be content to grow with the growth of knowledge and piety in the country. With burning desires for rapid development, he never urged advance beyond the bound of prudence. He was cautious, and would not recommend expenditure without fair prospects of the means to meet the outlay. Out of his own small salary, he contributed for some time $400 a year to the funds of the college, but seldom expended a dollar of the institution's funds, with a view to his own convenience or comfort. The Governors therefore learned to rely implicitly upon his counsel, and he seldom recommended any course that was not cheerfully adopted. He did not magnify his own toils or discomforts, but cared only for the welfare of the interests committed to his care. When new men were wanted to fill important positions in the faculty of the college, or on the teaching staff in the academy, it was only natural that the judgment of the President should be relied on. And the passing years have shown how safe it was thus to rely. With scarcely an exception, it has been found that better selections could not have been made. The record of good scholarship must always be a leading consideration in choosing teachers for an institution of learning. But Dr. Cramp made this one, and only one, of the requisites. He regarded good

moral principles and a settled conviction in matters
of religion as of equal, if not greater importance
than mere intellectual power. As a result, he had
always around him a band of workers whose influence was on the side of truth and righteousness.
Free thinking and sceptical notions never found a
congenial atmosphere in Acadia during the years
of his administration. And with all his other
labors he was prompt and regular in his attendance
in the services of the church. His place was
always filled in the prayer meeting; and a word of
encouragement, instruction or warning, was sure
to fall from his lips whenever opportunity offered,
or occasion required.

### DENOMINATIONAL.

In his unwavering attachment to the denomination with which he was identified, Dr. Cramp had no
superior, if indeed, he had an equal. The condition
of all the churches was soon before him. Their
history was studied and known. With extensive
knowledge of the leading men of all denominations,
on both sides of the Atlantic, and a very broad
sympathy for the good and the true wherever found,
he was in heart and aim a Baptist. With great
respect for men of talent in all the professions, his
warmest sympathy was ever towards those who
were engaged in preaching the Gospel. The pastors were to him as the members of his family.
The older men were indeed "the Fathers," and the
younger men were regarded as sons in the faith.

In fact, his own family had frequently occasion to feel that his " care of all the churches " was consuming all his care for his home. For when the former called for thought and care, the latter was compelled to yield the claim. And so if any church were involved in a difficulty, Dr. Cramp was looked to for counsel. If any pastor found a hard point in theology, or was in the fog in some question of church history, or found himself plunged into a controversy with some brother of another faith, Dr. Cramp was expected to furnish all needed materials for the conflict. His extensive library was always at demand. And it was fortunate for the one " contending for the faith," that the owner of the books generally knew just where to put his hand upon the right volume and the passage that was needed. But very few knew the amount of time that was consumed in this way, or the cheerfulness with which the time was given. Books were the Doctor's passion. The whereabouts of each, his delight, and the ferreting out a needed proof, sweeter to his taste than honey.

The Governors of the college learned to rely on his judgment; the students, on his instruction ; the pastors, on his sympathy ; the churches on his counsel; and both associations and conventions wonderfully looked to him for guidance in all undertakings. So much was this the case, that many came to feel, that a public gathering of the body for dealing with important questions, would be very incomplete, if not a failure, unless Dr.

Cramp's place was filled and his counsels heard.

His warm regard for the ministers of the denomination continued to the end. He planned many things for their benefit which never went beyond his own study, simply because the time of life was past for giving execution to the kindly desires of his heart. But all those who studied at the institutions during his presidency were remembered. And his executors, after his decease, had the pleasure, in obedience to written instructions, of sending his last recollections of them in carefully selected and valuable books to each ; or, at least, that was the design. If any names were omitted from the list left for guidance, it was an omission of the memory and not the intention of the heart. It would not be strange if some were forgotten. The wonder was that so many were remembered; and that the selection in each case was so thoughtly and judiciously made. Showing that the teacher had not only remembered the pupils in a general way, but carried for all the years intervening, in his own thoughts, the peculiar habits and tastes of each.

But we must return to the history of Acadia College, in order to pick up a few items to substantiate this estimate of the late President. The general inadequacy of funds, the terrible disaster of '52, the unfortunate investment of funds shortly after, had a most depressing effect. From 1851 to 1854, there was no graduating class. From sixteen to twenty students were about all that could be got together. For various reasons, many of these were unable to continue their studies through the entire course. But meanwhile the rough work was being done. Confidence, that "plant of slow growth," was increasing year by year. The young men who were going out with only a partial training, were found to be efficient workers as teachers or as preachers, as merchants or professional students. It became known that Acadia College, even in its crippled condition, and with all its drawbacks, was doing as thorough work as any similar institution in the land. The one thing that the faculty would not do, in order to gain numbers, was to lower the standard of admission or graduate classes for the sake of effect. Some contended that considering the state of education in the country, the college would better meet the wants and do more good by making the admission easier, and conferring degrees on those of smaller attainments. The President of the college took the opposite view. Advancement rather than retrogression must be the aim. We must not let the college down to the schools, but aim to bring the schools up to the college. Educate, stimulate, and fire our students with educational zeal. Keep the highest possible ideal before the minds of the young, and gradually they will come to appreciate progress and come up to the requirement. This was the principle acted upon in the low condition of the college. It was pressed on the attention of the Governors. It was exemplified in the lessons of the class-room. It was popularly proclaimed in many an able platform address. And the young men who had the germs of the student nature in them, caught the spirit of progress, and the results are manifest to-day in many of the callings of life.

In 1854 there was one graduate, the first since the appointment of the new President. In 1855, the Rev. A. W. Sawyer, was appointed to fill the chair of classics. For four years, he continued to fill that position with eminent success. The internal working of the college was now deemed very satisfactory. The various classes were well provided for, and the President could give more attention to theology, his own favourite work. But if there was a deficiency in any department, he never hesitated to fill the gap. Except in the mathematical department, which he never had occasion to undertake, there was scarcely any study then pursued in the college in which he did not at some time, during his presidency, conduct classes.

In 1855 there was a graduating class of four, all of whom have been eminently successful as preachers of the Gospel. One is a highly esteemed professor of Hebrew etc., in a theological college. He took his entire classical course, and his first instruction in Hebrew at Acadia College, much of it under the instruction of Dr. Cramp, and every lesson he received only intensified his thirst and fired his zeal for more.

Much has been said and written upon the various methods of imparting instruction. Some contending for one plan and some for another.

But the plan, whatever it may be, that fires the zeal of the student, giving him an intense desire for knowledge, is the only successful method of teaching. Inducing habits of observation, strengthening the memory, and developing the reasoning powers are all useful, nay essential, to make a man able to grapple with the problems of learning or of life. But the one thing that stands above all these put together, in order to constitute one a lifelong and successful student, is to enkindle in the heart a burning and quenchless desire to know. This was eminently the result of Dr. Cramp's instruction. Not that every student who attended his classes was so fired; but that a fair proportion of them were, became manifestly evident by the courses pursued and the success attained in after life. Although some of them, perhaps, never knew where they derived their inspiration.

In 1856 there was a graduating class of three. All of whom became efficient and successful men. One as a physician, who died early. One as a preacher, and one as a teacher and afterwards as inspector of schools.

In 1857, there was only one graduate who became a successful preacher of the Gospel.

(1). The small number of graduates during these years may be accounted for in various ways. The standard for matriculation had been raised. So that entering college was becoming more difficult year by year. The tests of scholarship were being more vigorously applied after entering. So that those who valued play more than work, found themselves falling below the standard, and turned off to other pursuits. While many, no doubt, who were valuable students, were compelled from various causes, to relinquish their studies and engage in the duties of life. And these were greatly helped by even the partial course which they took.

(2). The college had not yet risen above the depressing effects of the loss of funds by the injudicious investment already referred to. This not only took away the means which were needed for repairing and improving the buildings, and thus increasing the comforts of the students, but it resulted in giving things generally the appearance of decay. For many, attracted by the reputation of the college abroad, when they came to make arrangements for their sons, judging from the external appearance, returned disheartened, and sent their sons elsewhere, or perhaps worse, kept them at home. It is difficult, now that things are different, to realize how keenly all the teachers, but especially the President, felt this, and how he suffered under it year after year. Nothing but his own buoyant and hopeful disposition, together with his active and ever busy life, prevented him from sinking beneath these depressing influences.

The loss of money had also alienated some former friends. They, of course, would have counselled differently. And so would everybody, after the mistake was discovered. It is so easy to see that the tree is bad, when the bitter fruit is eaten. Not always quite so easy when the tree is being planted. It is much safer to give the probabilities of to-morrow's weather alter to-morrow has come. But, unfortunately, there is a class who always know what is right and safe, although that knowledge is most loudly proclaimed after the result of the wrong step is manifest. There were many such in the days to which we refer. Their declarations of the want of prudence and business capacity, upon the part of the college authorities, not only obstructed the agents in collecting funds but kept alive many weak prejudices and hindered students from coming, All of which was very annoying and disheartening to those who knew the possibilities of the school, and set their hearts upon making it worthy of the devoted men who had founded it, and the denomination, with whose growth and prosperity it was so intimately connected. But, inspired by the indefatigable energy and hopeful spirit of the President, they worked on in faith and prayer, and finally, saw the old prejudices giving way, and new friends coming forward to help bear the burdens.

A very wrong estimate, however, of the real value of the work done at Acadia during the first five years of Dr. Cramp's presidency would be made, were the graduates only to be reckoned. The large majority of those seeking instruction at Horton, in those days, both in academy and college, were young men who did not plan to go through the entire course. Some preparing for business pursuits. Some for the work of teachers in the common schools. Some to get enough knowledge of science and classics to enter upon professional studies, and many that they might better understand the Gospel of Christ, and how to make it known. And it would not be difficult to select many from among these, whose success in all the pursuits and professions of life has been so great, that some would say, a partial course student may succeed as well as one who has taken the full course. So he may, if he has more in him to begin with. Otherwise, he may not.

In 1858, there was a graduating class of six, one of whom became the President of a theological institute in the United States, and professor of theology and Biblical interpretation in the same. One occupies a prominent position as a judge in the Supreme Court of N.S., his native province. Almost all the members of the entire class have distinguished themselves as men of rare ability.

At this time, the college was largely attended, and everything seemed in a most hopeful condition, so far as spirit, energy and work were concerned. But the Board and the President were overburdened with anxiety.

We quote here from the Vaughan Prize Essay:—

"The internal history of the institution was eminently satisfactory. The academy had over 100 students; and with classes of eleven, twelve and fifteen successively matriculating, and such scholarly instructors as Dr. Cramp, Professor Sawyer and Professor Stuart, the college was, in everything but income, far in advance, at that time, of any other in the Lower Provinces. The unfortunate investment already referred to, seriously crippled the resources. About £8,000 of endowment was left, and this would barely support two professors. Various attempts were made to increase this amount, but with very discouraging results."

It may be added here that, at this time, professors' salaries, as the institution was then being conducted, were by no means the only urgent claim. Repair of buildings, apparatus, books, increased accommodations, were all loudly called for by the general advancement of education in the country.

"A crisis came in 1858, the most serious one in the whole history of the institutions. For once during the financial struggle, the friends of Acadia lost heart. All sources of additional income seemed dried up. To carry on the college with a reduced number of instructors, would be suicidal; to retain the present staff, with no prospect of paying their salaries, would be dishonest; there seemed, therefore, no alternative for the governors, but to take the decisive step of notifying the Faculty that, after January, 1858, their services would not be required."

Various reflections naturally spring up here. (1.) As to the source of this action. (2.) As to the wisdom of it. (3.) As to the result.

1. The source. — The President was *ex-officio* member of the Board. Action was generally taken upon his advice, never in opposition to it. Then the President either first recommended this course, or at the least heartily agreed with it when proposed by some other member. What he had passed through, before he could have reached that point,

was known only to himself and God. The Governors did not know, the students never suspected it, his own family were not aware. For he was so active and busy and cheerful, that many thought all was prosperity. And yet here, already far advanced in years, and therefore too late to set out on some new course, his position was about slipping away from him, and the work to which he had consecrated, all his energies and talents, nay his life, was about to fail. To be placed in a similar position may be needful in order fully to realize what it cost Dr. Cramp to recommend or agree to such a measure.

2. The wisdom of the action taken.—If it were the only course, the wisdom can hardly be doubted. But there were others. To go on with a reduced staff would have been one. To borrow money, another. And still a third remained ; to use up the endowment fund as far as it would go, and let the future provide for itself. The first would have been giving up all the advantages gained, and going back twenty years. The second would have been entailing burdens which the next twenty years might not remove. The third would have been thoroughly to destroy all confidence in college endowments and thus dry up perhaps forever all sources of future growth. Then with the prospect of scattering the professors, and upsetting the plans of students, some midway in the course, and others preparing to enter, the terrible resolve was reached, the doors of the college must be closed. And we can easily imagine that when

12

those grave men, after long deliberation, were required by the chairman of the meeting, probably Dr. Cramp himself, to cast their votes, it was with trembling of hearts, and great misgiving, whether they were not about, by this action, to sacrifice the growth and prosperity of the things which lay so near their hearts. And we do not refer here to Acadia College, simply as a seat of learning, but to those principles of personal piety, the rights of the individual conscience in things sacred, the supremacy of the law of the Lord, religious liberty and equality, which the rising ministry could better defend, with intellects fully trained, under the warming and restraining influences of a school not supported and governed by the State, but the outcome of earnest prayers, and managed by men of deep piety. This was the peril that seemed pending, and a stern necessity must have urged them on before they could hazard it. But the vote was taken, and we presume, that the notice implied in the resolution was forwarded to the parties concerned.

3. The result of the action.—They were perhaps what many hoped, perhaps what some foresaw.

The churches were awakened. The appeals for funds had become an old story. The college had lived so long with inadequate support, that many supposed it would continue to do this. That it should proclaim itself closed, was a new and startling disclosure. The writer will not soon forget the consternation manifested in Liverpool N. S., where he was located at the time. Dr. Cramp had been there a few years before, in the interests of the endowment fund. He had been very successful, and made many warm friends both for himself personally and for the college. Many scholarships had been taken, and smaller sums had been given. Nobly they had contributed and about all was done that could have been expected.

When the report of the terrible resolve to close the college reached the town, the pastor made no move, and but few comments. He knew not what to say, and far less what to do. But the members of the church would not let the matter rest. One especially, long since gone to his reward, became terribly restless. " I got no sleep last night," he said one morning. "What was the matter?" "Why this strange news from Wolfville. This cannot be. It must not be. They surely do not mean it." "It looks bad," said the pastor, "but I suppose there was no alternative." "Alternative!" he shouted; "there is, we must go to work and stop this calamity." And very soon a paper was drawn up, handsomely headed, pledging the Liverpool church for a large sum to be paid in yearly instalments for a number of years. Similar results followed in other places. Vigorous protests came in from all quarters. A special meeting of convention was called, and the humbled Governors were compelled to go back on their own action, and rescind the obnoxious resolution. This was the result. It was a fearful experiment, and might have turned otherwise. And probably would, had not the Spirit of God moved in many hearts, and a Divine voice said to the people. " Go forward."

The college moved on with unabated vigor. The President, relieved from a great load of anxiety, but not from any of his work or responsibility, addressed himself with new heart to the many duties of his office. Many of his lectures about, and after this season, were masterpieces, both in thought and delivery. His manner of conducting anniversary exercises was unique, and a great treat to spectators. Addresses to graduating classes were replete with wisdom, and full of paternal affection. "The right man, and surely in the right place," was the utterance of many as they walked out from the exercises.

In 1859, there was a graduating class of four. One became an efficient physician; one an able lawyer ; one a mathematical professor, and one a teacher.

The class of 1860 numbered eleven. The distinguished ability of this class, has been so frequently referred to, and is so well known, that further comment is needless. It is sufficient to say, that almost every profession has been enriched, and every good cause promoted by their endeavours. And most of them are still reflecting honor on their Alma Mater.

In 1861 there was only one graduate, who, however, became a very zealous preacher of the Gospel, and has been honored by winning many souls to Christ. His entire theological training was under the instruction of Dr. Cramp. And judging from the positions he has filled in the ministry, and the success of his work, we should judge that the theological course at Acadia College, with all the other duties pressing upon the President, was no mean preparation. Although the graduate of '61 was by no means the only one who went from Acadia direct to the onerous duties of the pastorate, and succeeded therein. There were many of them, and the churches have not suffered under their ministrations.

In 1862, there were ten graduates, which class has produced merchants, doctors, pastors and an editor. All of them among the first in ability and usefulness.

1863 turned out only two, but one became a physician in the United States, and one a leading lawyer in Halifax, N. S.

In 1864, there were only two. One became a lawyer of marked ability, and one a teacher.

The class of 1865, numbered sixteen, although there were nearly double that number, when the class entered college.

Men of marked ability, almost all of them. Quoting from a very interesting sketch of the class, by one of the number :—

"An important innovation in the internal work of the college was the introduction of studies, additional to the regular course, for those students of first-class standing, who desired to take the extra work. Of my class, five read the additional classics required, in 1863, '64 and '65, and the last named individual happened to be the first student who received from the President (Dr. Cramp) an honor certificate, when they were given for the first time at the anniversary in June, 1864.

Among the events worthy to be recorded, the same report states :—

"In the history of the college and in which we (the class) were prominent actors, was the addition of Dr. Cramp's portrait to those of "the Fathers" which then adorned the walls of the college library. Wishing to give tangible expression to their respect for the venerable President, the students, iu their associated capacity as members of the Acadia Athenæum, obtained the Doctor's consent to have his portrait painted. An excellent picture was at length obtained, the work of Mr. T. C. Doane, of Montreal. The expenses were defrayed by contributions from the undergraduates, and from many graduates who had studied under Dr. Cramp's instruction, as well as from others who generously assisted."

It was, of course, designed as a mark of respect to the President, and was very highly appreciated by him. But it reflects equal honor upon the students who erected it.

The addresses to the graduating classes were always appropriate, sometimes beautiful and eloquent. Only one of these has been found. It happens to be the one addressed to this class, of 1865. It is by no means one of the best. But it will probably call up some pleasing reminiscences to some of the members of that class, and also furnish a sample of Dr. Cramp's manner of closing his instructions to the various classes.

"ADDRESS TO THE GRADUATING CLASS, AT THE ANNIVER-
SARY, JUNE 6, 1865.

"The long toil is over! Your four year's course is
ended. You have been nestling together for the appointed
time under the wings of your Alma Mater, and now you
are about to take your flight, not indeed to unknown
lands, but to engage in untried duties. We cherish the
hope that you will be found much better fitted for those
duties, in consequence of your residence here, than if you
had contented yourselves with a meagre and insufficient
preparation. Money spent in mental culture is like the
bread cast upon the waters which is 'seen after many
days.'

"We live, gentlemen, in a very remarkable period.
The domains of knowledge are extending every day, and
new acquisitions are constantly made. Scarcely a year
passes without the inauguration of some society for the
purpose of pushing inquiries in unexplored regions.
Sciences, whose very names were unknown fifty years
ago, are cultivated with all the ardour of youthful zeal,
and already yield abundant harvests. Things knowable
are divided and subdivided, and so parcelled out as to
favour minuteness of investigation and accuracy of results.

"Novel applications of principles and facts in the
various branches of art, whether useful or ornamental,
attest the growing ingenuity of the age.

"Conclusions, which, to those who preceded us, appeared to be firmly established, have been first doubted
and then dismissed to oblivion; and new laws, or rather
laws as old as the creation, but which have been hitherto
hidden from human view, have been brought to light.

So vast and boundless, so infinitely diversified is the
prospect, that the mind is bewildered by the marvellous

complexity of the phenomena, and the untold numbers of objects that present themselves for review and examination.

"It is true that only a small minority, even of the well-instructed, can engage in critical pursuits, or track science to its remote and unfrequented haunts. Nevertheless, the influences of advancing knowledge cannot but be generally felt; wherever it plants its foot, the tone of intelligence will be elevated ; honourable ambition will be excited ; and there will be an up-rising of society to a higher-level.

"In this march of improvement, Nova Scotia has taken her part, and shares in the advantages.

"You will find a very different state of things from that which existed when this institution first began to send forth her sons. There is far more knowledge in the country, and it is more widely diffused. Efficient school-teaching has borne good fruit.

"The colporteur has circulated useful literature. The educated men of '65 know more, and know it better than the men of '45. Youthful intellect is subjected to more vigorous training, and demands a supply of mental aliment adapted to the altered circumstances.

"The improving process is still going on, exerting everywhere a healthy influence, and promising to leaven the whole mass.

"We are doing what we can to keep pace with the times. We shall do it better, especially with regard to the scientific and theological departments, when the people furnish us with the means, as we cannot but believe that they will, when they see the necessity of the case, and participate in the ambition to excel, which is gradually pervading the public mind.

"I call your attention to these facts for the purpose of impressing your minds with the importance of aiming at

continual progress.  This will be required of you, whatever course of life you may adopt.

"As Alumnæ of Acadia College, you will be expected
to stand in the first rank of the intelligent, and you will
find that it will task your utmost energies to maintain
that position. You will act accordingly.  Studies will be
reviewed.  Inquiries that have been commenced here
will be continued.  You will apply your powers to the
further and more extended consideration of many topics,
which have been, as yet, only glanced at, and await the
application of matured thought.  You will preserve mental health and strength by appropriate exercise. 'You
will 'forget the things that are behind,' and reaching
forth unto those things which are before, press towards
the mark."

Lest we occupy too much space with these details, we must group from 1866 to 1869, which
brings us to the close of Dr. Cramp's official connection with the institutions.

There were twenty-two graduates..  These, as
well as those before them, have engaged in
the various pursuits of life.  But nearly all have
devoted themselves to the work of the ministry,
to teaching, or to one of the "learned professions,"
so called, and have distinguished themselves in
their several pursuits.  And taking them all together, from 1851 to 1869, a period of nearly
twenty years, and including with them an equal
number who, for various reasons, were compelled
to be satisfied with only a partial course, we may
venture to invite comparison with any other institution on this Continent.  Not as to actual, but
comparative results.  We do not claim that Aca-

dia's sons have reached as high as the highest. How could they, under all the depressing influences, with which many of them have been surrounded? But we claim that as large a proportion of them have become able, honorable, and efficient workers in their various spheres, as any other college can claim.

The result may be confidently appealed to, in proof of the wisdom of the late President in standing firm for denominational colleges. Many efforts were made during the time of his presidency to swamp the college, and swallow it up in some imposing provincial university. All the arguments and eloquence of some of the ablest men in the Provinces have been employed in this behalf. The pulpit and the press have been employed. Legislators and governments have sympathized with this movement. The arguments employed often seemed unanswerable. A large, full, and well equipped college, with ample provision for every branch of learning, surely is better than a poor and feeble one. And with the long and almost ineffectual struggles Acadia was making, there were even not a few of her own friends who sometimes doubted the wisdom of the course. If with less cost and less care, our young men can get all the learning they need, why continue to bear burdens too heavy for us? And many could see no reason. And there were times when the danger of yielding the point was very great. But Dr. Cramp continued firm. He clearly saw that education without religion might be a curse to the church, and of doubtful good to the world. Education and religion must go hand in hand, in order to work out the best results in either department.

Shortly after Dalhousie College was revived in 1865, or thereabouts, and all denominations were so *kindly* invited to give up their little schools and establish chairs in Dalhousie, and thus become the joint owners of one grand establishment, a number of gentlemen from Halifax attended the anniversary exercises of Acadia College in Wolfville. The day was fine, and a great gathering as usual on such occasions was present. The " Alumni Dinner " had come at that time, to form an important part of the day's exercises. The after-dinner speeches were looked forward to with great interest. For the leaders of both political parties were there, and it was suspected that there would be a measuring of swords on some subject. Political feelings were running' high, and education had been a fruitful topic for discussion. The toast, " Our Sister Colleges," opened the way. The then leader of the Government, than whom no man was supposed to be a better authority on all matters pertaining to general prosperity, but especially in reference to education, saw, or thought he saw an opportunity which might not occur again very soon. He embraced it. If at the very heart of Acadia, in the presence of her warmest friends, her professors and students, the citadel could be taken, then the victory was secured. So the confederation of all the sister colleges was the theme. If this small one could gather around it such enthusiasm, and exhibit such results, what may we not expect to see when the forces of them all are centred into one? It was made to appear as very grand. It required a bold man to take up the position. For the views of the denomination were already before the public in many an able article from the pen of the President and others. But there was a bold man there. He had already fought and won many a hard battle, and the grandeur of the object aimed at was sufficient to drive away all fear. And eloquence worthy of the occasion was called forth. The one, unsectarian, grand central university of the Provinces, if not of the Dominion, was pictured out in glowing colours. Such a noble rivalry would thus be enkindled among all the students and their teachers, as had been unknown hitherto. Great progress and prosperity the necessary result. "And if not," asked the orator, "why not? Who can show any just reason why this should not be an accomplished fact in the very near future?"

He paused for a reply. Many thought that there was no reply to be given. Acadia is as good as closed. She may continue to do the work of an academy, and then forward her students to the central university, and perhaps give some assistance to a few ministerial students, but her Arts course is now nearly ended.

The President of the college, however, was not thoroughly convinced. He rose to offer a few observations. And never perhaps did an audience look with more interest, and in some cases, intense anxiety to see if anything could be offered, as an offset to the powerful arguments advanced. The arguments were reviewed. The false data of one overturned; the doubtful conclusions of another exposed; the difficulties here and the.insuperable obstacles there; the pledges made to the people in asking them to help to endow; the hopes and expectations centering in Acadia; the object in view when, by the fathers, her foundations were laid; the sympathies and prayers which had gathered around her, and through which she still expected to live and to grow, and concluded a most powerful exposure of this Utopian scheme by saying, " Whoever may favor the merging of denominational colleges into one grand central provincial university,—' My voice is still for war.' "

The Halifax friends went home gratified with the kind reception given them in Wolfville, but saying, " The time is not yet ripe for college confederation." And the prospect has not matured much since. Nor is it likely to, so long as the views entertained by Dr. Cramp, and so ably expounded on that occasion continue to prevail, viz., religion and education, the two elevating forces of the world, but only when they join hands and walk together, can they meet the world's great need—enlightenment and redemption.

From the records of the action of the Board of Governors of Acadia College, April 21, 1866, we take the following :—

"The Secretary read a communication from the Rev. J. M. Cramp D.D., tendering his resignation of the office of President of the college.

"This resignation was accepted. Voted that the Rev. D. M. Welton, and the Secretary, be a committee, to prepare and present at the next meeting, a resolution expressive of the sentiments of the Board, on the occasion of the resignation of the Rev. Dr. Cramp."

At the next meeting the following resolution was presented and passed unanimously:—

"Whereas the Rev. J. M. Cramp, D.D., from a desire of getting relieved from his onerous duties and responsibilities as President of Acadia College, has tendered his resignation of that office.

"Therefore resolved that this Board do not feel that it would consist with their deep regard for Dr. Cramp, and heir warm and undiminished interest in his personal comfort, longer to press upon him at his present advanced time of life, a further resumption of those duties and responsibilities.

"And be it further resolved, that this Board, in reluctantly accepting Dr. Cramp's resignation, do express, and hereby permanently record their high and grateful appreciation of his long and faithful labors as a president and professor of the college, and a minister of the denomination, and the marked success which has crowned those labors.

"Also that they express the great satisfaction with which they have learned, that while asking to be relieved from his present labors, he has been pleased to couple his resignation with an expressed willingness to continue in office until his successor is appointed and enters upon his duties.

"Voted that the above resolution be accepted as the

expression of this body. That it be recorded, and that a copy thereof be forwarded to the Rev. J. M. Cramp, D.D."

In accordance with this action, he continued to discharge the duties of the office until his successor was appointed and duly installed. .

His interest in the work did not cease with this retirement. For at almost every meeting of the Board of Governors for some years after this, he is reported in the records as being present and aiding in all the deliberations of the body.

The following is an expression of regard from the Hon. Dr. Parker of Halifax, one of the most efficient members of the Board of Governors during Dr. Cramp's connection with the college :—

"My first meeting with Dr. Cramp was on the occasion of his preaching in Granville Street Church, a short time before he entered upon his duties at Acadia College. I was impressed both with the matter of the sermon, and with the manner in which it was delivered. The fundamental truths of the Gospel were proclaimed with ability, and power, and I left the house, feeling that a scholarly man, an experienced Christian, and an able preacher, was about to be added to the Baptist ministry of our Province.

"Immediately after my connection with the Denomination, I became interested in our educational institutions at Wolfville, and subsequently, was placed on the Board of Governors of the college. Here my relations with Dr. Cramp were, at first, of a business character, but I very soon learned to appreciate his ability and worth, and to entertain a warm friendship for him, which continued until his removal by death.

"The work in which he was engaged, and to which he was devoting the energies of the best years of life, giving to our institutions his matured thought, his time, and his money, was the connecting link that brought us very often together, and cemented our friendship. During the earlier years of his connexion with Acadia, his trials were many. Apart from those incidental to the educational and general management of a college, inadequately equipped with a teaching staff, there were financial difficulties almost continually present, and few were the men, who, surrounded by such circumstances as he had to contend with, would have continued the struggle and retained the position. Yet, through all and every difficulty, while others were depressed, faint-hearted, and often lacking in faith, he was buoyant, cheerful, fertile in resources, and always relying faithfully on the strong arm of the Lord.

"When he announced, by telegram, to his brethren in Halifax, that his faithful colleague and 'right-hand man' Isaac Chipman, was buried beneath the waters of Minas Basin, our hearts failed us, and our first thoughts were: can our institutions survive the shock? Will Dr. Cramp not be disheartened, and relinquish the contest? But no such thoughts found a lodgment in his mind. His motto had been and was, 'Trust ye in the Lord forever.' He trusted, laboured, and conquered; and as a result of his 'faith and works,' Acadia lives, and will continue to live, sending forth from her halls, young men mentally qualified to fight the battle of life; many of them, to contend against the common enemy of mankind—to fight the battles of the Lord—thus imparting annually, additional vigor and strength to our denomination, and increased stability to the moral and social structure of our country.

"His versatility of talent was only equalled by his

untiring industry. The governing board ever found him, although always burdened with work, ready and willing to assume additional duties, when emergencies arose, and the necessities of the hour called for such extra labor."

"Notwithstanding his many and varied engagements as professor, president, and *ex-officio* Governor of the college, he *made the time* to perform the arduous duties of corresponding secretary of the Foreign Missionary Board of the Convention of the Maritime Provinces— and dearly he loved the work—for he was imbued with the missionary spirit, and with the desire that God's Word should be carried, by those, whom, he himself had educated, to the far-off lands of the heathen.

"His facile pen was constantly engaged in advancing our educational, denominational, and general interests ; and when necessary, in defending and upholding our doctrinal views—as Baptists.

"The familiar initials ' J. M. C.' were noticed in the *Christian Messenger* with great frequency, and I am free to say that the subjects then discussed by him, always attracted marked attention, and the articles of no correspondent of that denominational journal were more gladly welcomed by its readers than those which emanated from his pen.

"When physically able, his familiar face was always seen at our associations and conventions, where, as the head of our most important organization (Acadia College) and as the result of his ability and practical experience, he very early came to be acknowledged a leader in all departments of our denominational work.

"With voice and pen he was always ready to aid the cause of temperance, and never lost an opportunity of assisting its advancement. In this all-important moral reform, also, he became an active leader. Few men's minds were stored as his was with historic facts, whether

13

these had relation to Biblical, ancient or modern secular history, or to the origin and growth of the different denominations of the world. Hence his companionship was additionally interesting to those who were fortunate enough to claim him as a friend.

"His work, entitled 'Baptist History' has had a wide circulation, and will long keep his name prominently before our denomination.

" Let me briefly narrate an incident which will show how highly it is appreciated by those who dwell beyond our borders :

" Returning from Western Canada a dozen or more years ago, I spent a Sunday in Albany, the capital of New York State, and by accident was directed to the church then presided over by Dr. Lorimer. After the morning service, I had some conversation with him, and on learning that I was from Nova Scotia, he asked if I knew Dr. Cramp, to which question I replied affirmatively, when he continued in words to this effect: 'What a grand work his " Baptist History" is ! It should be in the house of every Baptist family. So highly do I, and my church value it, that we have supplied our colporteur or colporteurs with two hundred volumes, that it may be spread over this section of our land, and be made the means of educating our people in the history, and principles of our denomination.'

"Dr. Cramp has, by precept and example, left his impress on the minds and lives of a large number of young men, who were educated mentally and spiritually, under his supervision. These, or many of them, went forth from him, into the world, bearing in mind, and in their hearts, his teachings. Numbers of them engaged in secular occupations ; happily many more went throughout our own country, and to other lands, to preach the Gospel to their fellowmen, in heathen as well as in Christian communities; but wherever they went, they carried with them this 'impress,' and also, a great respect, and admiration for the life and character of him who had been their instructor and friend. Those who, like myself, were present, year after year, at the anniversary meetings of Acadia, will long remember his addresses to the graduating classes. They were so happily expressed, with pathos and power so appropriate to the occasions, and the circumstances, that I feel assured none could have listened to them without emotion. Let me say in conclusion, that Dr. Cramp came to us—I speak of the Denomination—a stranger, in whom very many of our number had no special interest, but as time passed, and we were brought into contact with him, his genial, companionable nature, his mental and moral characteristics, his love for our people, his long years of able and untiring labor for our best interests, together with his great generosity in contributing annually four hundred dollars ($400) to the funds of the college, from a very limited professional income connected with the presidential office, gave him a home in the denominational heart, and now that he has gone from us, we, who were his contemporaries, and in a limited sense, his co-laborers, as we think of him and the great work he accomplished, will ever hold his memory in affectionate remembrance.

"D. McN. Parker."

" Address from the Alumni of Acadia College.

" To the Rev. Dr. J. M. Cramp, D.D.

"The Alumni of Acadia College cannot allow the occasion of your resignation of the Presidency of that University to pass without attempting to express some of the feelings which they entertain towards you.

"Many of us have been your students—indeed most of

us; for, of the 108 students who have graduated since 1838, when the college was founded, eighty-three have graduated since you commenced your labours in the Institution.

"But all of us, as well those who were before your time, as those who had the privilege of attending your lecture-room, join in this expression of regard.

"Acadia College was fortunate in securing the services of one who brought to his work a large mind and attainments and ripe experience, and one whose fame as a historian, and a scholar had gone before him.

"We review with gratitude your eighteen years of abundant and useful labour. In the college, we all know with what unceasing activity and ability you have toiled, how you have fired lagging students with enthusiasm, and engendered love of study and thirst for knowledge, and with what pleasure and kindness you have dealt with the rough materials put into your hands.

"Be assured the Alumni speak from the heart, when they thank you for all the past.

"We thank you too, for the part you have taken outside of the college. In many of the great questions which have come up for discussion and settlement, you have contributed your wisdom in guiding public opinion to right issues.

"You have united the parts of a professor and a public man in happy proportion. You have not allowed your interest in public matters to interfere with the important duties which your profession required, nor, on the other hand, have you permitted your devotion to literary pursuits, to so engross your energies as to keep you aloof from the discussion of the important topics of the day.

"In thus uniting the public, with the professional, you have done inestimable service to all, and have contributed much to foster sympathy between the people and the college. With such presidency as yours, the college could never become isolated or alienated from the affections of the people.

"Though now resigning your presidency, we sincerely hope that during the years which may yet be given you, you may be permitted to aid in still further promoting the welfare of the institution, which has so grown in favor and efficiency under your hand.

"On behalf of the Alumni,

"E. M. SAUNDERS, President.

"EDWIN D. KING, Secretary."

Comparison of the condition of the institution at Wolfville, and also the state of the denomination in 1851, with the present, would afford some idea of the benefits arising from the efforts of these years. That education alone accomplished these results we do not claim. But all acknowledge that among the factors of progress, Acadia College stands in the first rank. That all the good accomplished by the college was due to its late president, we do not claim. He was only one among a host of intelligent men, who clearly saw their duty and were willing to do it. But if, on reviewing the past, and rejoicing in the signs of growth and the indications of a prosperous future, he should have said, " *Et quorum pars magna fui,*" there were few indeed who would have challenged the justice of the claim.

The following addresses, delivered at the memorial service in Wolfville, May 31st, 1883, are worthy of perusal in this connection. Other valuable addresses were delivered at the same time, all of which are well worth preserving. These are selected as representations of the whole. One from the successor of Dr. Cramp in the presidency of the college, the other from one who, for the four years of college life, occupied the position of pupil, and so well improved his opportunities of culture, that he has been, and is still, filling a large place in the education of the Dominion of Canada.

## THE LIFE AND LABORS OF DR. CRAMP.

Rev. A. W. Sawyer, D.D., President of Acadia College, delivered the principal address of the evening as follows :—

*"Mr. President and Gentlemen of the Associated Alumni :—*

"Your invitation to me to bear a part in the duties of this hour, meets a response of mingled hesitancy and willingness. These feelings arise from the nature of the event which has led to these services. It is remarkable that so large a number of those who have held the place of teachers in Horton Academy, or in Acadia College, are yet numbered among the living, and it is still more remarkable that, with a single exception, so far as I can learn, no one of those who have been thus connected, has died while in the relation of active service in either of these institutions. The two first teachers in the college are still living and the weight of their years seems to lie lightly on them. Of those who at later years have received appointments as instructors in the College, so far as is now known, all are still alive, excepting three. One of these, after he had become connected with another college, was removed by death not a long time since, while in the midst of a useful and honorable career. It is now thirty years, lacking a few days, since the first of these three was swept from life by that memorable calamity on the Basin of Minas. So deep was the affliction that then fell on some of the friends of this college, that they have scarcely been able at any time since to look out on that expanse of water, even when gleaming in its brightest hues, without feeling that a shade was over it. He, who a few days after that catastrophe stood in the presence of a stricken audience in this village to speak of the loss and its lessons, has been, after the lapse of so long a time, the third to be summoned away. The infrequency, therefore, of such an event as this, which has been the occasion of your meeting at the present time, might well lead one who is to take part in these services, to approach them with some degree of solicitude. Another reason for hesitancy appears in the condition of the minds of my audience. Your estimation of the worth of him whose name is foremost in your memories at this hour, your judgment of his character as a man, his worth as a friend, his usefulness as a teacher, his service of the public in every good cause, his devotion to the institution of learning in which you are so much interested, will naturally be taken as the measure of your expectations in regard to what should be said at such a time. If one must fill the measure of such expectations or come short of his duty in speaking, then it becomes me to be silent. But it is evident that while you have assembled in part to hear something concerning the chief characteristics and ruling principles of an excellent life, nevertheless your presence here and the distinctness of the appointments of this hour are the most emphatic expression of respect and affection for him whose life and character we are to contemplate. We come together in the exercise of common sympathies. It is because the tribute which we bring to the worth of a departed friend is the product of the heart as well as of the mind, that I am encouraged to feel that my words will not be out of harmony with the conceptions and feelings of the audience. A cherished memory is embalmed in the sensibilities of the heart. These will always respond to any genuine expression of esteem or affection for one whose memory is thus cherished. As we have these common sympathies, I shall trust that I have one qualification for speaking to you of him whom we have all so long known and honored.

"John Mockett Cramp was born in St. Peter's, Isle of Thanet, July 25, 1796. His father was pastor of the Baptist Church in that place. The son received such privileges of education in his earlier years as the locality permitted. On the 13th of September, 1812, he was received by baptism into the membership of the church of which his father was pastor. He soon after began to make public addresses on religious subjects. In September 1814, being then eighteen years of age, he entered Stepney, now known as Regent's Park College. After the completion of his studies there, he was ordained as pastor of the Dean Street Baptist Church, in London, May 7, 1818. He subsequently returned to his native place and was associated with his father in pastoral labors for thirteen years. In 1840, he became pastor of a church in Hastings, Sussex, being then in the maturity of his strength and displaying marked abilities as a preacher. A large amount of valuable work in the department of authorship had been accomplished by him before this time of his life. In 1844, an invitation was given him to accept the Presidency of the Baptist College in Montreal, from which the Rev. Dr. Davies had been called the year before to the Presidency of Stepney College. For several years Dr. Cramp discharged the duties of this new position in an efficient and honorable manner, laboring in the midst of adverse circumstances to make the College permanently successful. After a time, the financial difficulties seeming to be insuperable, he withdrew, and in February of 1851 he accepted an invitation to the Presidency of Acadia College. In his letter of acceptance he says: 'Henceforth I devote myself to the cause of education and religion in Nova Scotia, especially in connection with Acadia College.' To his fidelity to this devotion, the succeeding years bore ample testimony. His laborious and useful services in this College continued till June, 1869. After his retirement from official responsibilities and service in connection with the College, he continued to reside in Wolfville, in the midst of familiar scenes and surrounded by friends, occupied as his strength would permit in literary pursuits, and watching with hearty interest the events of the passing days, to note the effect they might have on the moral and religious condition of men, until his peaceful departure from this life on the sixth of December, 1881, in the 86th year of his age. Thus briefly are the more noticeable events of a long and useful life related.

"But it is hardly necessary to remark that the life of a true man is not measured or described by such a recital of facts. It is a development, a growth, marked by its own principles, and deserving of commendation according to the nature of those principles.

"It will be my purpose to lead you to consider somewhat the spirit and meaning of this long and active life, endeavouring at the same time, as far as possible, to abstain from trespassing on the special topics which have been assigned to others who are expected to address you.

"It is somewhat difficult to bring clearly before our view the condition of life in England, at the close of the last, and in the opening years of the present century. It was a time when men's minds were stirred by great questions. The old order of things was passing away, a new order was introduced. The principles of religious liberty were coming to be more legitimately applied. The great revival under Wesley was still felt. The great leader in that wonderful movement left the stage only just before the close of the last century. Men were beginning to enquire concerning their obligations to carry the Gospel to the destitute in various parts of the earth. In 1787, William Carey, who was afterwards acknowledged to be one of the foremost linguists of his day, was a pastor at Moulton, with a salary of $80 a year. In 1792, the Baptist Missionary Society of England was formed at Kettering, and soon after this, Carey and his companions were sent to India. Andrew Fuller, who was acknowledged by all who knew him, to be one of the ablest theologians of that period, did not die until 1815. John Ryland, Robert Hall and John Foster lived to a still later date. These were household names among the Baptists in England in the first quarter of this century. To know such men, to hear them, to live in a society quickened by their thoughts, stimulated by their purposes and moulded by their culture, was of itself a valuable education. John Howard died in 1790, Burke in 1797. In the same year, appeared Wilberforce's Practical View of Christianity, which passed through fifty editions in about fifty years. The society for the suppression of the slave trade was organized in London in 1787. After repeated attempts and failures on the part of the friends of the measure, the bill for the suppression of the slave trade, having passed both the houses of Parliament, received the royal assent on the 25th of March, 1807. It was not till August 28, 1833, that slavery in the British colonies was abolished by Act of Parliament; and in the same year, Wilberforce, the great advocate of this reform, died. Pitt and Fox closed their labors in the first years of the century, but Canning and Brougham were positive forces in the direction of public affairs to a much later date. The period before us was marked by genuine power and honorable achievement in literature. It displays a large number of names, famous in the realm of science. At that time the applications of the principles of science to the practical arts of life was successfully cultivated. Great political questions were then discussed with an earnestness and directness seldom surpassed in any age. After the fearful scenes of the French Revolutions and political re-adjustments consequent on the battle of Water-loo, men in England, and on the continent, felt that they had lived on into a new era. The future was bright and they were full of hope and courage. It could not be otherwise than that the active, intelligent, and observant young man, who went in 1814 from St. Peter's to Step-ney to begin his professional studies, and who was or-dained in London in 1818, should have been strongly influenced by the spirit of such a time, and by the know-ledge, which he could not fail to have, of such renowned leaders of thought and action. We should be led by the nature of the case to conclude, even if we did not know the fact from other sources, that such an individual in such circumstances must have felt the movement of the time, and have been himself prompted to take part in the discussions of great topics that were occupy-ing men's minds in those years. You who have sustained to Dr. Cramp the relation of pupil to teacher, have wit-nessed the pleasure with which he referred to memorable scenes in which some of these great men bore a promi-nent part, and have heard him describe the effects of their eloquence, and express his admiration of the abilities by which they commanded success in the various departments of public life. And if he sometimes permitted himself to reveal his feeling, Nestor-like, that men were men when he was young, we were not disposed to dispute the claim, remembering of what men he was thinking. He had been associated with some of them in the societies for important objects, which then had their origin. He had seen them at their best in their public labors, and their spirit, example and abilities had left an impress on his spirit, which he bore to the last.

"It was probably in part owing to the events that were transpiring in the early years of Dr. Cramp's life, but also quite as much to the natural tendency of his mind, that he belonged through life to the party of progress. He did not regard an existing order of things as right, merely because it existed. Having accepted certain principles, he expected them to be wrought out in practice. Reference has already been made to the fact that the first third of this century presented many vital questions on which the English people were divided, some holding with the past, others pressing on to a different and, as they hoped, a better future. Only the most general reference to these could now be permitted. It will be enough simply to name Catholic emancipation, the suppression of the slave trade, slavery in the British colonies, the monopoly of the East India Company, the rights of missionaries in the British provinces of Asia, the removal of the restrictions on trade and commerce, separation of the Church from the State, the right of Dissenters to University degress, and other civil privileges in regard to which the laws discriminated against them, the advancement of national education, the circulation of the Bible and of a religious literature. Few generations have been called to act on so large a number of important subjects. On most of these Dr. Cramp developed strong convictions early in life, and afterwards labored most

earnestly and untiringly to carry them into effect. His
interest in the extension of education among the people,
and in the promotion of Christian missions, and his
spirited advocacy of the principles of religious liberty,
deserve special mention. He desired " the greatest good
of the greatest number,' with a broader and truer view of
things than that political philosopher, to whom this
maxim is ascribed, possessed. These early preferences
and convictions he cherished to the last, and rejoiced in
the successive stages through which the labors in behalf
of these various objects were caried forward towards a
successful issue, In regard to some of them, he was permitted to share in the exultation of victory. In respect
to a few, the contest still continues; but he never lost hope
in regard to the result, and died believing that others
would ere long see what he had desired. The great
questions of public interest that arose with the passing
years, Dr. Cramp met with the same spirit that distinguished his early life. During the revolutions that con-
vulsed Europe in the middle of this century, his sympathies were with all who desired to enlarge the freedom
and improve the civil condition of the people. To the
close of his life, he was a thoughtful student of the various
problems growing out of the relations of the colonies to
the mother country. He was jealous of anything that
might tend to weaken at any point the integrity of the
Empire, and yet he believed that the strength and great-
ness of the Empire wonld be best promoted by a large
measure of freedom and self-regulation in the several
parts. He was among the first to discern the benefits of
a union of the British Provinces of North America, and
the development of the new Dominion was watched by
him with the affectionate interest and hopefulness of true
patriotism. Very soon after his removal to Montreal, he
declared himself in sympathy with the purpose of the

various organizations which were designed to prevent intemperance. He labored perseveringly to bring the communities in which he lived to a clear perception of the dangers that constantly rise from this great source of disorder and crime, and his voice and pen contributed not a little to the force of argument and appeal by which so marked a change has been produced in public opinion in regard to the physical and moral evils of intemperance. As Dr. Cramp was greatly interested in his earlier years in the success of the societies that had been formed in England for the wider circulation of the Bible and the production of a sound religious literature, so when in subsequent years the question of the revision of the translation of the Bible began to be agitated, he at once declared himself favorable to the project. He connected himself with the American Bible Union when its supporters were few, and for a long term of years was a regular contributor to its funds, believing that the immediate as well as the more remote consequences of its efforts for a clearer translation would be a wider diffusion of the knowledge of the Bible and a more abiding interest in its truths. And when, more recently, revision was undertaken by the English Commission, again his sympathies and hopes were wakened. He watched the events that indicated the progress of the work with constant interest, and when the fruit of so much patient study appeared, he received it with thankfulness. Many of the changes introduced by the revisers he had anticipated. There were others which surprised him. We accepted his expression of dissatisfaction with these, not as the complaints of an old man looking to the past for his ideal of wisdom or goodness, but as the utterances of a life-long habit of mind according to which he judged that no human work was to be accepted as ultimate, but that the best of to-day must be improved in the days to come.

He was not blindly optimistic, but, believing that all things are directed by a beneficent providence, he found strength and comfort in constant labors for the good as yet unattained. His eye turned naturally to the future, and for him, memory was the servant of hope.

" But while the natural impulses and settled purposes of his mind were in the line of new acquisitions of knowledge and a higher development of human institutions, in one department of thought and belief he held by the past. In his view, the best fruits of the civilization and culture of the last eighteen centuries were to be traced to the principles on which the church has rested. His hope for the future was based on the truths which, as he believed, had thus quickened thought and directed life in the past. He accepted in the main what has been called the Theology of the Reformation, and found constant delight in following the labors of the strong men who wrought and suffered for these doctrines. His early life fell at a time when the influence of such men as Leigh Richmond, Henry Martyn, Simeon and Cecil was felt as an inspiring power,—names which a generation ago were pronounced in the church with reverent affection, but which seem to be now almost unknown in the rush of new events. His sympathy with the spirit and methods of these devoted laborers continued through life. The writings of Cecil were especially valued by him, and some of them were for many years a handbook of private comfort and edification. The nature and tendency of the Tractarian movement he discerned at its beginning. Its later development had been but the unfolding of what he saw in the germ. Though he found little in rites and ceremonies to satisfy his soul, he was not inclined, on the other hand, to mystical or quietistic notions of religion. A theology developed from metaphysics he disliked. As an interpreter of the Scriptures, he sought the grammatical and logical meaning, rather than some occult doctrine which must be evolved by a spiritualizing or allegorizing process. He was satisfied with the plain statements of the Scriptures, and believed that these should be preached, not to please a philosophical curiosity, but to produce the proper fruits in the practical life. His active mind followed closely the efforts of the noted men of culture and learning who are attempting to show how the wisdom of the present must dispel the most cherished beliefs of the past. But their methods of reasoning brought no conviction to his mind. He gratefully acknowledged that the critical studies on the Scripture, by which the century has been distinguished, had shed light on some portions of the written Word. But notwithstanding all these criticisms, the Word remained unchanged for him in its essential character. It was to him something more than the voice of a dead past speaking to an age that could not comprehend it; it was rather the voice of the living Spirit from whom all truth proceeds, speaking to the heart of man for all time. He found great pleasure in tracing the marvellous researches of modern science. The learning and the patient industry by which such valuable accumulations of facts have been made, and so many scientific principles elucidated, evoked from him admiration and gratitude; but when these explorers amidst the mysteries of nature permitted themselves to speak as if they had discovered the secret of the universe, they lost their hold on his mind. To account for this wondrous sum of things about us and the relations of part to part, something more seemed to him to be necessary than could be expressed by the terms force, environment, heredity and luck. The new cosmology was to him a dreary desert. The new theology was only an ingenious effort to turn the world upside down and put the last first. In the midst of a generation,

many of whose wise men declare that in all their search-
ings they cannot find God, that in all the realm of nature
they can see no trace of His hand, nor in all the course
of human history, discover any indications of His will, he
was ready to stand in his place and avow his faith: I
believe in God, the maker of heaven and earth; I believe
in His revealed word, spoken by holy men as they were
moved by the Holy Ghost; I believe in the Gospel of His
Son, the power of God leading men unto eternal life.
Most of us will say that such a faith was the manifestation of true wisdom. Some may say that such expressions indicate a type of mind that is passing away. The
future will determine which is right. But we remember
the words which our departed friend occasionally quoted
in his expressive style of utterance: 'Sire, the church of
God is an anvil that hath worn out many a hammer.'

" It was not necessary that one should remain long in
Dr. Cramp's presence in order to learn to what denomination of Christians he belonged. Acknowledgment of
the revealed Word as the rule of faith in distinction from
ecclesiastical traditions and decrees,—the preservation
of the constitution and ordinances of the church after the
type which the Apostles had given to it,—the manifestation of the faith of the individual as the condition of
membership in the church,—the acknowledgment of the
invisible and spiritual Head of the church as the source
of life and authority,—the independence of each community of believers in applying for itself the principles
of church organization and church discipline, while
bound to kindred communities by the duties and the ties
of a common fellowship,—the insistence on the fruits of
faith manifested in a high morality, as distinguishing the
believer from those who have not the faith,—dependence
on an ever-present Spiritual Power to give efficacy to the
word and constantly renew the energy of the church,—
14

a vivid sense of personal responsibility, joined with a
freedom of thought and speech that reverently regards
the authority of the Scriptures and is chastened by the
heaven-born graces that accompany genuine faith,—these
were the notes by which he recognized the true church.
Wherever men appeared holding these principles, he regarded them as brethren.  His long and toilsome duties
in the records of the past were, for the most part, a labor
of love, since he desired to bring into the light, as far as
possible, the fidelity of all who had been true to such
principles, however humble may have been their station,
or however few or dishonored they may have been at
times when the majority of the church had a name that
they lived and were dead.  But while he was clear and
decided in his convictions and beliefs, his eye was quick
to discover the manifestation of the love of truth.
Wherever this might appear it commanded his sympathy.
He was willing to learn of any, no matter of what name.
It did not concern him whether one had been pronounced
orthodox or heterodox. The chief points with him were,
what is the spirit, what the life, what the affections which
one bears to the unseen Head of the church.  He had
learned from the study of the past, that often the streams
of true doctrine and life have come down through devious
channels.  The lessons of experience combined with his
natural hopefulness to make him feel that a leaven of
truth might be at work in forms of thought that might
be disturbing the placidity of many good men.  He believed that it was well to have a form of sound words,
but he always remembered that the spirit giveth life.

"All who became acquainted with Dr. Cramp, very
soon knew of what nationality he was.  He never had
any inclination to conceal the fact that he was an Englishman.  The vast accumulations of wealth and consequent increase of power, together with the wonderful

development of the practical arts in England, the achievements of British arms in all parts of the world, the lists of English names famous in science, literature and statesmanship, the development of a system of constitutional government which, by the experience of centuries, has been shaped to guard the rights and freedom of the humblest as well as the highest in the land,—all this he contemplated with genuine satisfaction, and he firmly believed that a people who were made illustrious by such achievements in the past, were destined to a more glorious future. But he claimed the privilege of expressing his opinions on any action of the government of the day; and we all know that he was able to express these opinions in terms that could be easily understood and remembered. But these criticisms did not lessen his attachment to the great name of England with all that term conveys of proud remembrance of the past or hopeful promise for the future. But while he was so attached to his native land and the realm of which it is the heart, his thoughts and desires for the welfare of mankind were not bound by national limits. Love for his own country made him none the less interested in the prosperity of others. The unity of Italy, the changing phases of the Eastern question, the condition of Russia, the political changes in Central Europe,—these were frequently, with him, subjects of earnest and anxious study. He always rejoiced in seeing the condition of the degraded improved, and the yoke of oppression removed. He spoke with pleasure of the fact that he had been permitted to take in his the hand of the man who signed the proclamation of freedom for four millions of slaves. In truth it could be said of him, that whatever concerned man interested him.

But time will permit me only to mention some other points in the character of which a sketch has been attempted. The extraordinary diligence and industry which distinguish the life we have been reviewing, deserve a moment's attention. Dr. Cramp believed that in all the callings of life, labor is the price of success. Idleness was a burden to him. His recreation was found in change of occupation. For a large part of his life, the time which he spent in the class-room would have been enough to exhaust the energies of most men, but, in addition to this, he was at the same time carrying on original and prolonged historical investigations which of themselves were enough to distinguish his life. Besides this, understanding as he did the power of the press to guide public opinion, he was a constant contributor of articles on the leading topics of the times. As he was ready to meet calls to public service, he always had in hand some special business which had been committed to him, and which called for energy and tact. He enjoyed preaching, and his hearers would have been led by his manner to conclude that had been his chief employment. His familiarity with the principal events, and the lives of the leading men of the time was such that the casual visitor would judge that the larger portion of his time had been spent in reading the news of the day. His resentments faded away, but he cherished old friendships and found time for an extensive correspondence. By constant and methodical studies, his knowledge of the Scriptures and his large stores of learning were kept under easy control. Thus his life was a life of labor and consequently of growth, and as this labor proceeded from benevolent motives, the result was a prolonged course of usefulness."

"I shall ask you to note but one other characteristic of him whose life we are reviewing—that was, his abiding conviction that Christianity and intelligence are not antagonistic, but, on the contrary, that the latter is

properly the servant of the former; and hence his abiding
desire to see an intelligent and comprehensive application
of the principles of Christianity. He believed in the
equality of the members of the church, and in the responsibility of the entire membership; but he also believed
that gifts of teaching and of government were bestowed
on some for the good of all, and that these gifts should
be exercised in such a manner that the church should
appear as a well-ordered and thriving community, showing how diversity of gifts contribute to perpetuate unity
of life. Intelligent laymen are in the church to lead it
forward in every cause. The duty, the privilege, is theirs.
Their call will be manifest in the wisdom of their work.
It follows from this that the ministry is the highest of
all offices. Hence it is necessary that this office should
be held by men who are able to meet its responsibilities.
They may be great classical scholars and philosophers or
they may not, but they must be men who know the
people and whom the people can know,—men who understand the doctrines of the Book they are sent to teach,
who understand the spirit of the times and can adapt
their methods to it, men who in general intelligence and
culture can win the respect of the communities they are
to lead, men who can speak a word in season to the timid
Nicodemus, and the alarmed jailer, and the enquiring
eunuch, but who can also comprehend the meaning of
the fact that the last chapters of the Epistle to the Romans are the bloom and the fruitage of the earlier portion,
that herein is the type of the development of the church,
that, if it does not perpetually show the corresponding
bloom and fruitage, it is because there is no life, or, at
best, but a feeble life in the stock. You may question
whether it is possible to realize such an ideal in this imperfect world, but we must admit that the presence of it
in one's mind is an inspiration. Probably Dr. Cramp's

greatest work was in the line of his efforts to train such a ministry for such churches. He sometimes grieved that the people were not more eager to give all the assistance that is needed in maintaining a school for such an object. Some of you will remember the tone of sadness with which he closed an address at the laying of the corner stone of the new College, when he said (to give the substance of his words) that he hoped that when, after the lapse of a century, the people should be gathered on those grounds in 1978 to lay the foundation of a more spacious and costly building, they might say, 'At length the Baptists of these Provinces have a theological department such as they need.' But though he would have done much more in this part of his labors, he effected a great good, and his works do follow him to testify to his faithfulness.

"But these observations must not be prolonged. A useful life has become a memory for us. If we look into the heavens on a clear night, it may seem to us a small thing that one of those points of light should be put out; but when we consider how much of life and hope, of strength and effort, of pleasure and sorrow, can be concentrated on one such sphere, its importance is enhanced beyond our powers of imagination. So, when we look on the multitude of lives about us, one may ask, of what significance is it if one of them goes out? But when we think how much of love and hope, joy and energy, noble purpose and successful accomplishment, has been concentrated within the life that we have been considering, its value grows in our estimation as we contemplate it. While we honor the memory of the dead with the tribute that is its due, we are gaining deeper and truer views of the possible dignity and value of every human life, and so the good who have left us, live again with us in the better lives of those who remember them."

## DR. CRAMP AS A TEACHER.

Theodore H. Rand, D.C.L., Chief Superinten-
dent of Education, N.B., and one of the Governors
of Acadia College, spoke as follows :—

"Although, Mr. President, I have been unable to command either my time or my thoughts in any adequate
degree for this service, I should be unfaithful to a great
and revered memory, and untrue to my own feelings,
did I not say a few words on this occasion. The shock
of that stroke of death which, on the 6th of December
last, removed John Mockett Cramp, the second founder
of Acadia, and the beloved and revered teacher of so many
of us, was felt wherever in the wide world a scholar of
Acadia happened to be. When I bade him farewell in
his study one sunny day last September, he spoke words
which cheered me in my work, as he had so often done
before, and added with resignation and hope, ' I am now
only waiting for the great change.' That was the last
time I saw him. I cannot now recall the time when I
first saw him. It seems to me as if I had always known
him, so early and so large a place does he fill in my present recollection.

"It was in 1854 or 1855 that I took residence on this
hill as a pupil in Horton Academy. Dr. Cramp had then
been connected with Acadia some three or four years.
He had left England in 1844 to take charge of the Baptist Theological College, Montreal, of which institution he
was President till 1849. This was his first public educational labor. While in the pastoral office in England,
however, as early as his pastorate in London, he gave
private instructions to occasional students. I have recently read a letter written to one of his pupils in 1819,
in which I instantly recognized ' the touch of a vanished
hand and the sound of a voice that is still.'

"When Dr. Cramp came to Acadia there were few students at the College. With the aid of Professor Chipman, he carried on the Arts department and the department of Theology. This was a courageous undertaking; but the following summer, Professor Chipman and four students of promise were suddenly removed by the appalling disaster in yonder Basin. That was an overwhelming event to Dr. Cramp, but his brave heart rose above it, and his trust in God inspired him to do great things for the salvation of the College. During this period of intensified trial, his labours were prodigious, disclosing a depth of resource, a breadth of attainment, and a range of acquisition which were fortunate indeed for the future of this institution. At one time or another he here taught Latin, Greek, history, mental philosophy, moral philosophy, evidences of Christianity, rhetoric, logic, political economy, and geology, besides the various branches of theological department, including Hebrew and Greek exegesis; and he was almost equally successful as a teacher in each of these subjects.

"The wide range of scholastic attainments doubtless had much to do with his marked freedom from old-time prejudices respecting the subjects which should find a place in the undergraduate course. He attached much importance to a study of those branches of knowledge which the experience of the world had proved to be fit instruments of culture, being himself undoubtedly the best patristic scholar in the Dominion; but his mind was always open to considerations designed to adapt the curriculum to the progress of knowledge and the currents of modern thought.

"Dr. Cramp believed that right conduct and capacity for effective work were the objects of education. There were ever present to him the practical relations subsisting between a sound body, a pure heart, and a clear head.

Physical, intellectual, and spiritual health, certifying its existence in conduct and labor, was, in his view, a preparation for independent life, and ensured self-direction and progress. Worthy and purposeful activity, which brought the energies of the whole man into play, was to him the chief end of knowledge and discipline. He reversed the saying of Bacon, and affirmed with the emphasis of his own example that ' light is not only a good thing to see, but to see by.' The result which he desired to see in the course of hopeful accomplishment in the case of every student who came within these walls, was the producing of a Christian man, standing four square to all evil in his own heart, in society, in church and in state, with sympathies as broad as humanity, and with skilled energies for doing abundant work.

" His old scholars present in this great assembly will readily recall his paternal interest in their physical health, his practical hints on food, clothing, and daily exercise, and the encouragement he always gave to manly sports, though looking with disfavour on violent exertion and feats of strength. He took note of physical training only so far as it is a necessary condition of perfect health. The doctrine of Pascal, that ' disease is the natural state of Christians,' was abhorrent to him.

" As I call up before me the every day conduct of students with him in College work, I feel afresh the inspiration of his intense personality. Dignified in mien and bearing, with an eye to command, his presence in the lecture room was stimulating in a high degree. Every student instantly recognized in him a man of original force and skilled equipment In his teaching, all truth rested on facts, and reputed facts must be verified before serving as a ground of induction. He taught that lesson with as much persistency as the leaders in modern physics, but unlike many of them, he set his face steadfastly against every phase of mere speculative knowledge. Clearness and realness were essentials with him. The over-wise student found himself put suddenly and severely on the defensive, and felt the thrust of a Damascus blade. He had a rare gift, which he used in a rare way, of humbling self-conceit, and giving pride a fall. He made his students feel the immense superiority of intellectual honesty to intellectual power. Accuracy was demanded as a quality of prime importance. He believed with Arthur Helps, that the man who is to succeed must have an almost ignominious love of details. His own knowledge was wonderfully minute and exact, and once acquired, seemed to be always at the command of his will. His extraordinary memory was his right arm in the presence of his class. His criticisms and comments were keen and incisive, cleaving error to the bone with the inevitableness of fate. His students were made alive to the truth that correspondence between the thing thought, the thing done, and the thing said, is a test of consistent and noble type of life. Every recitation was a discipline in veracity, in careful statement, in thinking before speaking. Desultory reading was seen to be of little avail, and wide reading—that it tended to confusion, unless care was had to read first the latest standard works in any department of knowledge.

"There was always a breezy and stimulating freshness in the atmosphere of his lecture. It was no cloister dim. The shoutings from the fields of victory in the outside world, whether of peace or war, resounded within its doors, and were turned to swift account in animating the facts of history, in which he was so deeply and accurately versed, or in giving vividness and reality to some practical truth of science or philosophy. It was his practice to use the latest discoveries of science for the purpose of emphasizing the limitations of existing knowledge, and the vastness of the domains awaiting exploration. He kept the windows of his lecture-room wide open to the world of action, and trained his students to share, in thought and feeling, the struggles of the men of this age the world over in establishing or defending the principles of political or religious liberty. As an extreme illustration of the freedom with which he handled before his classes subjects which were not set down in the printed course, but which he knew were really there, I may instance his exhibition of righteous indignation when the facts in connexion with the so-called Jamaica rebellion were laid before the world. Rising in the lecture-room, (to the stature of a giant, as it seemed), the lightning flashing from his eyes, he denounced the hanging of men, the flogging of women, and the burning of houses, as the acts of a weak and cowardly tyrant, who was a shocking disgrace to the English name, and worthy of death. It was nothing to him that Kingsley, Tennyson, Ruskin and Carlyle lent the weight of their great names in defence of Governor Eyre. The inviolable rights of citizens of the Empire, and the rights of humanity itself, had been outraged. It was therefore, he said, of concern to the students of Acadia, and demanded their execration. Intelligent but downright hatred of oppression and tyranny, in every form and in every clime, and glowing yet intelligent sympathy with freedom and constitutional liberty, were aims most surely accomplished by him in all his students. A loyal Englishman himself, his students learned from him the force and power of a discriminating and ardent Christian patriotism. They not only gathered new love for their native land, but felt the noble reverence of his spirit for the institutions of England—reverence not so much for any special forms which they had assumed, as that their existence testified historically to the courage, endurance, and moral stamina of the race, and thus gave assurance of stability and progress in personal liberty and free government. By means such as these he sought to lift his students out of the isolation and poverty of mere provincial life, and enrich and ennoble them by a consciousness of vital relations as wide as humanity. Within the range of my experience, his educative force in this direction was unique, and altogether remarkable and immeasurable.

" Associated with the earnestness of which I have spoken and penetrating it through and through, was the not less striking characteristic of his cheerfulness. He was habitually cheerful, and his spirit, like that of all earnest souls, was contagious. The discontented, gloomy student was lifted out of himself by the buoyancy and stimulating quality of Dr. Cramp's animal spirits. There was perpetual sunshine in him, whose warmth revealed the singular youthfulness of his sympathies. Students divined at a glance, and proved through long years the correctness of their first impression, that he had never lost the boy's heart. His freshness and spontaneity; his interest in comparative trifles when these were of interest or profit to his students; his swift transition from mirthfulness to gravity; his purity of heart; his gentleness and tenderness—these and such as these, so obvious to all, and so perennial in their manifestation, attested the childlike nature which dwelt at the very centre of his being. Every one who knew him as a teacher will say that he was, of all men, a stranger to

'The hardening of the heart, that brings
Irreverence for the dreams of youth.'

" In College discipline, Dr. Cramp was considerate, but firm and decided. He knew well the virtue of Arnold's maxim, ' A teacher must not see everything.' He expected, and secured in a very high degree the conduct of

Christian gentlemen on the part of all. He largely relied on healthy activity, manliness, the sense of honor, and the feeling of moral obligation. He desired to train every student, not merely to obey when the pressure of authority was upon him, but also to use freedom aright when he became a law unto himself.

" He was interested in the spiritual welfare of his students. His public sermons seemed to be largely prepared under a sense of their needs, and were full of the helpfulness of the Gospel. My mind reverts, however, with special interest to his Sunday afternoon addresses in the old Academy Hall. Who that heard them can forget how his words revealed a strength and ardency of loyalty to a personal Christ, hardly inferior, as it seemed to that of Paul's ; an intelligent reverence for the Bible as ' the great text-book '—' the Magna Charta of soul-liberty,' ' the manual of conduct,' and ' the final authority' in this world in all matters between man and his God. There must always be a large percentage of college students whose moral and spiritual Rubicon is passed before their arts course is completed—sensitive spirits who, as their outlook grows more and more elevated, are overwhelmed with a consciousness of what it means to live loyally to all that is noblest in them and above them, and do a righteous man's work in the struggling, roaring world for whose contests they are preparing. Such spirits are oppressed in secret under a sense of the awful solitude that encompasses personal responsibility, and yearn for the sympathy of strong and tried souls. I know that I speak to the hearts of many when I say that they recall with grateful emotions the affectionate and helpful sympathy with which Dr. Cramp was wont to receive them under such circumstances, when sought in his private study. The solemnity of life was no new thought to him. He did not argue with one who thus approached him, but gently drew aside the almost transparent covering of his own inner life, disclosing its undergirding and overarching faith in the crucified and risen Christ. That was the citadel of his confidence, and his repose was a great testimony to doubting and perplexed hearts of the sustaining power of religious faith.

"Beyond all verbal instruction and conscious aid rendered to his students in the capacity of stimulator, helper, and director, Dr. Cramp taught very powerfully by the force of his own example. In this way, more continuously and perhaps even more successfully than in any other, he appealed to his students to regard time as a priceless gift, to adopt regular and orderly methods of work; to cultivate intellectual thrift; and to labor with fidelity and conscientiousness. In the same forceful way he was ever giving emphasis to promptness and despatch, and reading out to his students in cheerful and earnest tones the practical truths that they must be self-instructors; that they must not only be good, but good for something; that the battle of life is not fought by proxy; that nothing has been done by man that cannot be better done; that every one should be occupied, and die with the consciousness that he had done his best; and that humility is

'—— the root
From which all heavenly virtues shoot.'

"We Alumni, to whom he addressed such stirring words at graduation, saying 'Quit you like men' have known the perfection of his professional courtesy since we left the precincts of Alma Mater, now doubly endeared to us by his precious memory. He followed us all into the wide world with a watchful eye and the deepest interest. He was always open to our confidences, and never violated them. He rejoiced in our success and

sympathized with us in our misfortunes and trials.  The
gifts from his splendid library to his old students, as a
last act of tender remembrance, have touched many of us
to tears.  Alas! the grave has shut him from our sight;
but we trust his freed spirit drinks in all knowledge as
it flows from the lips of the Great Teacher, his and ours.
Let me apply to him the words so recently, but more
fittingly, uttered of another :—

> 'Strong for the right;
> Stern against every wrong;
> His large heart could feel for human pain.
> Through youth's dark night
> Of doubts and fears that throng,
> His silent deeds were potent to sustain.
>
> 'Yea, though we miss
> His steadfast, helpful glance;
> Hear not again the rugged Saxon speech;
> Death leaves us this,
> Through failure and mischance—
> Pride in the man; the loyal friend to each.
>
> 'Warm human heart!
> Upright thyself, to be
> Pillar and prop for feebler steps that trod.
> Yea, though we part,
> It must fare well with thee,
> Victor of death, immortal soul with God.' "

# CHAPTER XII.

*LITERARY LABORS IN ENGLAND.*

"As on, the teachers after truth are moving,
They may look backward with deep thanks to thee."
ALEXANDER.

1818–1844.

These were abundant, and long continued. Dr. Cramp was emphatically a student. There were some favorite pursuits, such as ecclesiastical history, and general literature. It would be difficult to exaggerate, in speaking of the amount of time, or the intensity of energy given to these matters. He loved learning for its own sake. For this reason he pursued it, but still more with practical aims in view, fully believing that it is for religion and learning united, to lift the world out of its degradation.

An extract from the preface of one of his published works, will show the secret of his active and laborious life. A reference had been made to error and the evil wrought by it. The question is asked :—

"How shall it be resisted? 'By universal and comprehensive education; by an energetic Gospel ministry; by the truth-proclaiming Press; by holy living; by active, watchful zeal, providing for the wants of the masses; by fervent, persevering, believing prayer.' The weapons of our warfare are not carnal, but mighty, through God, to the pulling down of strongholds."

In the true spirit of this answer he, who gave it, spent the years of his life.

An extract from his journal of the year 1862, will show how intensely this course was pursued. He was still filling the responsible position of President of Acadia College, and probably spending nearly as much time in the class-room as the other professors :—

"During the year 1862, I have read 47 volumes containing 21,655 pages. Have preached 41 times. Have written 11 letters on 'The Baptists of N.S.' as 'Menno.' Have written and published 'A Portraiture from Life,' a 'Lecture on the Great Ejectment of 1662.' Have written 266 letters. Have written several articles for the *Christian Messenger* and the *Baptist Magazine*. Have read the English Bible throughout, as last year.

"I have been visited with the greatest affliction of my life in the removal of my dear Anne. May I, by divine grace, rejoin her in the blessed, holy world, Amen."

It was indeed, a year of great anxiety, but there was no abatement in the persistency of work.

So large a proportion of Dr. Cramp's literary labor was of the class referred to in this extract, that is, articles for papers and magazines, and often without signature, or appearing as editorials, that it is impossible now to form an accurate estimate

15

of the amount of matter which went forth to the world from his pen.

It was, however, very great. And as Dr. Angus, of Regent's Park College, says of it : " Nearly always discussions on live questions, vigorous and helpful."

His first publication was a sermon on St. Bartholomew's Day, in 1818, delivered in Dean Street Church, Southwark, Aug 24th. Published and sold at one shilling. A note on the title-page of that tract is illustrative of all that Dr. Cramp wrote and did through his life. It was this :—

"The profits (if any) will be given to the Protestant Society for the Protection of Religious Liberty."

The idea of pecuniary returns never seemed to enter in, even as a partial motive, for action, in anything that he undertook. To be able to help the world on towards what he believed was its ultimate destiny, liberty, light and life, was all the reward he asked for.

This first pamphlet was followed by many more of the same general description. In 1820, a sermon on the Inspiration of the Scriptures. In the same year, one on the death of King George III., both preached in London. A copy of this sermon, beautifully bound, was sent to Her Majesty the Queen, and the following acknowledgment received from her secretary :—

" Sir :—

"I am commanded by the Queen to thank you for your most elegant book, which her Majesty is graciously pleased to accept as a mark of that attachment which is always grateful to her feelings, and I have the honor to subscribe myself,

"Your most obedient,

&c., &c.,

"A. HAMILTON.

" Brandenburgh House,

" February 16, 1821."

---

" SIR :—

"Allow me to say, without flattery, that *superior merit* is always diffident. Else, why should you, sir, *shrink back from observation,*—or, suppose it *presumptuous* to ask for an acknowledgment of so handsome a present, and so flattering a letter. I am proud to thank you for the same, but still more for your approbation of my conduct towards her Majesty, who, from her own virtues, merits any attention that can be paid to her Majesty.

"Again I thank you, and shall be happy to make any personal acknowledgments at some future opportunity, should the occasion present itself.

" I remain your

" obliged and obdt.

"A. HAMILTON.

" Feb. 16, 1821."

In 1822, the substance of two sermons on " The Scripture Doctrine of the Person of Christ." In 1823, "A memoir of Mrs. Maria Cramp." In 1824, " An Essay on the obligation to the weekly observance of the Lord's Supper." In 1829, a circular letter "On the Signs of the Times."

During these years, the " Tract Society " of London was constantly publishing and sending out religious books on a great variety of subjects. The names of authors were not given. Many of the books were simply abridgments of larger and more expensive works. But it is within the knowledge of some still living, that a great amount of this work was done by Dr. Cramp. Among other abridgments, Barnes' Notes on the New Testament were revised by him, and prepared for publication.

In 1831, "The Text-book of Popery" was published. A second edition was called for, and appeared in 1839. The third and final edition of this work was published in 1851.

The whole ground was gone over afresh ; improvements and additions were made as each new edition was demanded. This is, doubtless, Dr. Cramp's greatest literary work. Including the appendix and index, it is a book of 568 pages. But these figures give a small idea of the work itself. The reading and research necessary for its production were very great. It professes to be an accurate description of the leading views and doctrines of the Roman Catholic Church, drawn from the accredited writers of that body. The author shows how, step by step, the ancient churches wandered away from the simplicity of the Gospel. Appealing to historical records, he points out the place and the date when many innovations crept in. The Eclectics appeared. An endeavour was made to improve upon the divine plan of redemption, by adorning it with the more showy rituals of heathen worship. Sincere and earnest Christians protested against this mixture of the human and the divine. They began to draw off from these churches. Disputes were referred to the Church of Rome, until, little by little, her Bishop came to regard himself as the head of Christ's people on earth. Strife and conflict followed. Diets and Councils innumerable were called. From these Councils, the last and most important of which was the Council of Trent, having had many sessions and continued for eighteen years, came forth the things to be believed by the church, the anathemas and penalties of refusing to believe, and a long succession of sufferings inflicted upon those who dared to worship God in any other than the way prescribed. The calling of these Councils, the innumerable difficulties in getting them together, the opposing views advanced during the discussions, the decisions reached, the plottings and counter-plottings, to bring all into harmony with the views of the Pope, constitute a most interesting history. The story is told with such clearness, and so many historical sketches interwoven as so make it almost like a romance. No one could have done it, except one of extensive reading, most thorough and persistent investigation, and with great power to seize the main points of an intricate system, and put them in such coloring as to be clearly seen.

The book attracted much attention in England, when it first appeared. It was regarded as thorough and reliable, and was used as a text-book in several of the English colleges. It is still regarded as an authority on the matters discussed.

Probably the two religious systems, Popery and
Protestantism can be studied, compared, contrasted
and understood better from a careful perusal of
the Text-book of Popery than in any other way.

The author of the "Text-book" regarded the
Church of Rome as full of error. But he gave many
of her adherents credit for ability, honesty, sincerity and piety. He was not so blinded by sectarian zeal as to suppose that there could be no good
found among so much that was evil, or that all the
churches which separated from Rome were pure
and perfect. He insists, however, upon the sufficiency of the sacred Scriptures, when rightly interpreted, to settle all religious disputes; the Divine
Word as competent to guide every sincere en-
quirer into the truth.

The concluding observations of the book are
very beautiful and very suggestive. They show
what the Gospel is in its influences upon the
heart and life, under the following heads :—

" 1. Christianity is a system of grace.

" 2. Christianity is a system of spiritual worship.

" 3. Christianity is a system of holiness.

" 4. Christianity is a system of benevolence.

" 5. Christianity is a system of happiness.

" 6. Finally, Christianity is peculiarly the religion of
Christ. He is the 'Alpha and Omega, the first and the
last.' And then closes thus: 'Inquiry into religious
truth is the most important of all inquiries. Pray for
divine instruction and grace. Opposing systems cannot
both be right; neither ought it to be regarded as a matter of indifference, whether we serve God according to
His revealed will or not. Be open to conviction; search

with impartiality; seek wisdom from above. Every one of us shall give account of himself to God.'

" Let us hold fast our profession. ' Buy the truth and sell it not.' And especially, let us honor the sufficiency of Scripture. Are there among us no practices unwarranted by the word of God ? Is no further reformation necessary? Have we no human traditions, no corruptions or abuses, to be disavowed and removed? Let us institute rigid examination. We live in eventful times. All religious peculiarities are about to undergo a severe ordeal. God is saying to his church, ' Arise, shine; for thy light is come and the glory of the Lord is risen upon thee.' Let us hear His voice betimes, lest if we slumber, ruin overtake us; for the judgments that shall befall Anti-christ in the latter days, will not leave unpunished the popery of Protestantism."

In 1832, " An address to British Christians on the ' Importance and Necessity of a Revival of Religion,' with an appendix containing hints on the formation of Revival Unions."

In those times, revivals of religion, as experienced in the churches in the United States, were almost unknown in England. The additions were more gradual, one by one, or two or three at a time, as the truth was brought home to the individual heart. Any special religious excitement was not expected, and would, in fact, have been discouraged. Dr. Cramp's eyes then, as ever, were open to what was going on all over the world. The account of the displays of divine grace in America, aroused his interest. He was impressed with the importance of the subject, and set himself to work to find out from the Bible and other sources of information, whether these special awakenings were a part of the Divine plan in spreading the Gospel in the world.

The result of the enquiry was that "special revivals" are scriptural, needful, and therefore earnestly to be looked for and sought after. The " Address to British Christians " is all aglow with the zeal enkindled by the investigation. They are reminded of their vast opportunities for usefulness, the blessed privileges they enjoy, and also of the coldness and formality prevalent, of the infidelity and lawlessness abounding, and in view of it all, they are called upon to ask for the old paths and seek reviving showers from on high. A plan was proposed for the formation of revival unions, which, had it been adopted, would, doubtless, have resulted in great good.

In 1835, a pamphlet entitled " The Just Cause." This tract was issued by the Committee of a Protestant Dissenters' Association, in one of the southern counties of England. It showed by facts drawn from actual life, the grounds upon which Dissenters justly complained, and asked for such changes in the laws of the land as would give equal rights and privileges to all classes.

In 1837, five letters of Dr. Cramp's appeared in the *Kentish Chronicle* in reply to letters of the Rev. J. E. N. Molesworth to the " People of England on the iniquity of resistance to Church Rates." These of Dr. Cramp were afterwards collected and published in pamphlet form, and they are admirable in many ways. More keen and cutting and conclusive they could hardly be made. They show that upon the teachings of the New Testament, church rates, as then levied in England, were unjust to a large class of the people, un-Christian in spirit, and a great injury to the religious body, for whose maintenance they are expended.

The spirit of them may be gathered from an extract or two :—

"Before I commence, however, I will take this opportunity to observe that I see no reason why we should not maintain our respective opinions without losing temper. Nothing is gained by anger and vituperation. Our sentiments, it is true, materially differ. . . . . . But I do not see why we should not differ amicably. Hard arguments, if you please, let hard words be used by those who have nothing else to offer. . . . I must confess, too, that I am as disinclined to ridicule as I am to passion. It is very easy to make the multitude laugh at distortions and caricature; but ridicule is not reasoning. The questions at issue between us are of too grave a cast to be settled by witticisms. I shall write in sober seriousness, remembering that we are not only commanded to put away all bitterness, and wrath, and anger, and malice, but also to repudiate filthiness and foolish talking and jesting, which are not convenient."

The letters go on in this spirit of candor and honesty, showing that the writer had a far more extensive knowledge of church rates, their origin and history, than most churchmen themselves, and conclusively proving that the Gospel, as a system, must be sustained by love to Christ, and not by Acts of Parliament. The conclusion is admirable. After showing that it is neither the destruction nor the injury of the Church of England that is aimed at. but its liberation from fetters that are binding her, and common justice to all other sects, the writer closes thus :—

" After all, Sir, you and I have something more important to do, than to quarrel about pounds, shillings and pence. How much is it to be lamented that the state of things in this professedly Protestant country should be such as to render necessary the employment of so much time and effort on such subjects. May the desired change quickly take place, that we may all retire from the arena of conflict, and address ourselves to the work of God in our respective spheres, with renewed and undiverted zeal ! While *you* labor in ' the poor man's church ' and I in the poor man's chapel, let us both remember that we are best fulfilling the high duties of our calling, when, eschewing all merely sectarian purposes, we spend our energies in the advancement of personal religion among those who are committed to our care,—cultivate Christian principles and love with all that call upon the name of Jesus Christ our Lord—exhibit the holy influence of the Gospel in our temper and lives, and thus—

    ' Allure to brighter worlds, and lead the way.' "

These concluding remarks admirably illustrate the character of the writer. Great principles he held with tenacious grasp. Defend them he must, when they were imperilled or ignored. But he was by no means sectarian in his views or feelings. Upon the contrary, he was exceedingly broad and liberal. He frequently gave utterance to his feelings of admiration and esteem for the great and the good in the churches, some of whose principles and practices he contested with all his energy. He would have done the same, only more severely, if he had discovered these errors in the body to which he belonged.

In 1839, "The Council of Trent," comprising an account of the proceedings of that body. This volume, the preface states, contains the historical portion of the work, entitled "A Text-book of Popery." The matter was re-arranged and abridged by the author. This was the second edition of the work; the date of the first edition has not been discovered by the writer.

In 1840, "Testimony of History against the Church of Rome," issued by the Tract Society. Facts are drawn from a wide range of records of the past, and they are marshalled in such order as to be impregnable.

"The Reformation in Europe," a work full of information and of interest to every lover of truth. Published in 1840, by the Tract Society of London. Beginning with the rise and progress of the corruptions of Christianity in the third century, it carries the reader through the various stages of the conflict,—giving the names of the heroic men engaged in it, till a large portion of Europe was set at liberty, and the word of the Lord once more free to speak to the hearts of the people. A chronological table of the period adds much value to the work.

In 1844, a work of 308 pages was published, entitled " Lectures for these times." It contains fourteen lectures which had been delivered at Hastings, in the winter of 1842–1843.

From the Preface we read :—

" The author has aimed to furnish a brief, but accurate statement of facts and principles, with which all professing Christians, and especially the younger members of our churches, should be familiarly acquainted. He ventures to indulge the hope that the volume will be serviceable, as an introduction to argumentative treatises on the works of ecclesiastical historians."

It was an effort to set forth the grand fundamentals of our faith in strong contrast with all anti-Christian assumptions. While everything on the one hand favored an onward movement all along the line, Dr. Cramp thought that on the other hand, "the signs of of the times" indicated danger abroad. He saw and lamented the fact that a large portion of the Christian world was clinging to forms not warranted by the word of the Lord. He believed that the "Reformation in Europe," grand as it was, needed to be reformed afresh, before simple faith in Christ would be universally recognized as the world's only hope. All tendency towards ritualism was deplored by him, and in this book, as in many of his other sermons, he labored hard to separate the chaff from the wheat, and warn the people of the dangers to which they were exposed.

More than forty years have passed away since "Lectures for these times" were published. And developments have proved that the fears of the author were not groundless. Nor has the danger referred to, all disappeared yet. "Justification by faith" alone needs still to be placed in strong contrast with every delusive hope.

## 2. LITERARY LABORS IN CANADA.

As the President of the Montreal Baptist College, and then of Acadia College, Wolfville, there was certainly work enough for any one man. The office was no sinecure. It was not only the direction of the literary work of these institutions, but a large portion of the teaching fell upon the President. Not only general management and teaching, but the securing funds to pay off old indebtedness and provide for the annual outlay. Not one man in a thousand would have found either time or energy for anything beyond the actual, pressing calls of the hour. And yet the active pen could not rest, so long as truth called for defense, or progress needed a fresh stimulus. The religious papers on this side of the Atlantic were frequently enriched by readable and racy articles, no one, except editors, knowing whence they came.

In 1845—A sermon, Nehemiah, vi. 15, 16, preached at a general meeting of the Canada Baptist Union, held at Beamsville. The condition and work of the Christian church are ably set forth, and the duty of the hour enforced. An Appendix is attached, giving the names, statistics and pastors of all the churches in Canada at the time, so far as could be discovered. A note states:—

" There are other churches in the Province. but particulars have not been ascertained. Imperfect as this table is, it has required much time and labor to gather the materials together."

In 1846—" The Prominent Doctrines of the Gospel." The circular letter of the Montreal Baptist Association.

In 1850—A lecture delivered in Montreal. A vivid description of the changes and improvements of the last fifty years, 1800–1850. During some portion of these last few years, Dr. Cramp's chief literary labors appeared in the shape of editorials in the papers which he conducted.

In 1851—" Inaugural Address at Acadia College." Some extracts from this able address have already been given.

In 1852—" The Future of the Baptists." A lecture delivered in Wolfville, at a meeting called for the purpose of considering the propriety of undertaking to raise an endowment fund for Acadia College.

The denomination was well nigh disheartened at the time. The ringing words and conclusive paragraphs of the new President inspired fresh courage and hope. The college was saved; and the impetus given has not yet died out.

We give one extract from this lecture, simply as an illustration of Dr. Cramp's familiarity with facts, and his ability to use them when needed :—

" The Baptists of the North American continent have, for the most part, evinced a praiseworthy zeal in the cause of education. In the United States, besides academies and literary institutions in great numbers, there are twenty colleges owned by them or under their control, in which about one thousand young men are now pursuing their studies. There are also Theological schools, wherein nearly three hundred candidates for the

ministry are under preparation for that great work. . . .
New enterprises of this kind, involving large outlays, are
entered upon nearly every year. For Rochester University, for instance, the sum of nearly $200,000 has been sub-
scribed within the last two years. An addition to the
former endowment of Brown University, amounting to
$125,000, was raised without difficulty, a year or two
ago. The respective sums of $75,000 and $50,000, are
now in course of collection for Madison University and
Newton Theological Institution respectively; three pro-
fessorships in the University of Lewisburg, are about to
be endowed at an expense of $55,000; and a proposal has
been recently issued, to create an endowment of $100,000
for a college on the Mississippi. These are gratifying indications of enlightened zeal. How much it is to be re-
gretted that in these respects, the Baptists of the British
colonies of North America are so far behind."

Nothing very remarkable certainly that a college
President should be able to collect such facts as
these, and use them to stimulate to like endeavour.
But the thing worthy of remark is this. It was the
same on every subject. Whatever matter, pertaining to human welfare, was up for discussion, the
leading facts, in relation to it, appeared to be
either in his possession, or so near at hand that
they could soon be there.

In 1859—A sermon preached at one of the Associations, entitled " The succession of martyrs."

The same year—" Scripture and Tradition." A
masterly reply to a letter of Mr. Maturin, on " The
claims of the Catholic church."

In 1860—A sermon preached at Hillsburgh, N.S.,
and published at the request of the Western Bap-

tist Association, "The Centenary of the Baptists." Text, Ps. cxxvi. 3. "The Lord has done great things for us." This sermon is full of information and inspiration. It contains a sketch of the history of the denomination in these provinces for one hundred years, the names of the ministers who had passed away, the dates of their ordination and death, the origin of the Home and Foreign Missionary enterprise, and many other facts, that he only knew how to ferret out and bring to the light. Honorable mention is made of many men whose record is on high :—

" They did not enter the regular ministry, but engaged in itinerating labours, and were gladly welcomed by the people, to whom they declared the Gospel with much acceptance and blessing. Among the men of our own times, Professor Chipman holds the first place. Snatched from us at the early age of thirty-five, and in the prime of his vigor, he has left an enduring monument of his worth in our institutions at Horton. . . . . To promote our educational schemes, and advance the general interests of the denomination, in all their varied aspects, he tasked his powers to the extremity of endurance, and devoted his whole life—a life, alas! far too short in the estimation of Christian friendship, and as unbelief would say, prematurely cut off. Sad was the day when he and our beloved brother Very and the four young brethren who accompanied them (W. E. Grant, W. H. King, A. Phalen and B. Rand) sank in the waters of the Basin of Minas. . . . A hundred years ago, a solitary minister landed on these shores. There are now upwards of fifty pastors presiding over churches, besides other ministering brethren, variously engaged in the work of the Lord—an increasing number of candidates for the holy office—and a host of active servants of Christ, co-operating with the ministry in carrying into effect the purposes of Christian benevolence. Well may we say "What hath God wrought?" "The Lord hath done great things for us."

In 1860—"What will become of the wicked?" A lecture before the Ministerial Conference of King's Co., N.S. Published by request of the Conference.

In 1862—"The Great Ejectment of 1662." A lecture before the Acadia Athenæum, and published at the request of the students.

The same year—"A Portraiture from Life." A loving tribute to the memory of Mrs. Cramp, who had been the companion of Dr. Cramp for thirty-six years, and died July 26 ; held in the highest esteem by all who enjoyed her acquaintance.

In 1866—"Catechism of Christian Baptism." A masterly work, establishing, on the authority of Scripture, the principles upon this subject, which are beginning to be acknowledged the world over.

Dr. Cramp's next published work was "Baptist History, from the foundation of the Christian Church to the close of the eighteenth century."

This work was published in 1868. It contains 559 pages. Great labor, research, candor and fairness, are manifest. There is an "Introductory Notice" by Dr. Angus, of London, from which we take the following extract :—

"Though I have undertaken to say a few words on behalf of this volume of Dr. Cramp's, it really needs no introduction. He himself is well known in both hemis-

16

pheres, and has labored in both. He has been a student of ecclesiastical history from his youth. Nor has he studied in vain. His work on the 'Council of Trent' is still a standard book on all questions connected with the doctrines and policy of the Church of Rome. His candor and intelligence, his love of good men, and appreciation of great principles, have won the esteem and affection of all who know him. These qualities will be found to distinguish the volume which is now introduced for the first time to English readers. The volume deserves and will repay careful study, and I very heartily commend it."

Among the numerous questions asked and answered in the New York *Examiner*, a very widely circulated paper, was one in reference to the most reliable history of the Baptists. This volume of Dr. Cramp's was referred to as the only one covering the whole ground. Other works of the kind are more limited either in the time or extent of country embraced. Dr. Cramp's extensive library put him in possession of the facts from all quarters. Knowing how few there are who have time or opportunity to go through large and expensive works, he undertook the laborious task of bringing the materials into small space, and placing them within the reach of all.

The contents are divided into eight chapters, headed :—

"The Primitive Period," from A.D. 31 to A.D. 254.
" The Transition Period," from 254 to 604.
" The Obscure period," from 604 to 1073.
" The Revival Period," from 1073 to 1517.
"The Reformation Period," from 1517 to 1567.
" The Troublous Period," from 1567 to 1688.

" The Quiet Period," from 1688 to 1800.

" Statistics and Reflections."

The information furnished under these heads is very extensive. The privations, sufferings, fines, imprisonments and martyrdoms through which the denomination had passed, are described without malice or party feelings. It is the work of a historian and not that of a partizan. Leading men in other denominations have frequently expressed their admiration of the ability and candor manifested in this history. In fact there is so much in the book, of general interest, that it might well find a place in any library. The historical references, apart from denominational information, are very numerous and important. The Apostolic Fathers; the date and place of their birth; the position they occupied ; their writings ; their general character, are described. The rise of different sects in Europe and elsewhere ; the names of kings, and other prominent individuals, from the early days of Christianity down, and their connection with the history of the church; the men of eminent ability and piety ; and the part they took in the movements of the times, make the work especially valuable as a book of reference. There is a page of " Chronological Notes " attached to each chapter. In this department of general literature, Dr. Cramp especially excelled. By some mysterious method of his own, the dates of important events in religious or secular history, and of the lives of prominent men, also all great changes, were labelled and put away in some appropriate

place in the memory, and once there, they seemed
to remain. The arrival of new ones never displaced
the old; it was in fact like his own library. Long
after we thought it was full, and could contain no
more, many valuable additions were made, and
yet a place would be found for each; and the
owner knew where to find both the old and the
new.

These "Chronological Notes" are worth more
than double the cost of the book to any one engaged in literary work. They begin at the year
"A.D., The Christian Church founded," and following through all the centuries and struggles, end at
" 1799, The death of Samuel Pearce, the Religious
Tract Society founded."

In addition to these " Notes," the time is given
when the leading colleges and universities, such
as Oxford and Cambridge in England, came into
existence. All the colleges and theological schools
in the United States and Canada, founded by the
Baptists, with the president or principal of each,
at the time ; the denominational organs, magazines
and papers on both sides of the water, and the
editor of each ; the statistics, general condition and
growth of the body, together with the names of
the leaders through all the struggles of the past,
and many anecdotes connected with them, constitute a work of great interest, and invaluable to
those who wish to know for what the denomination has been contending, and how far success has
crowned the efforts. Whatever other histories may
hereafter be written upon the same subject, it will

remain true, that the Baptist denomination owe a large debt of gratitude to God, for the special gifts and persevering research of the author of the work we have been reviewing.

Nothing but the fear of extending this part of our work beyond the limits of prudence, could prevent us from giving extensive extracts from the work; for there are many passages of rare excellence. Energy of style, candor in judgment, and impartiality in criticism, mark the book throughout. Superior attainments and devotion to Christ are acknowledged and praised, in whatever class they were found. Error in doctrine, or in the life, is deplored and condemned, as readily when found among the Baptists, as elsewhere. The following extract will illustrate; the reference is to the condition of religion in England after the persecuting Acts of Parliament were repealed :—

"I have remarked that the denomination had evidently fallen into a state of religious declension, almost immediately after the restoration of freedom. The statistics prove this. To whatever other causes the condition of affairs may be ascribed, there can be little doubt that the paralyzing influence of the doctrinal sentiments, entertained by many of the ministers, must be regarded as mainly contributing to the result. John Brine and Dr. Gill were chief men in the denomination for nearly half a century. They were Superlapsarians, holding that God's election was irrespective of the fall of many. They taught eternal justification. Undue prominence was given in their discourses to the teachings of Scripture respecting the Divine purposes. Although they themselves inculcated practical godliness, and so were not justly liable to the charge of Antinomianism, there is reason to fear that numbers of those who imbibed their doctrinal views, kept out of sight or but feebly urged the obligation of believers to personal holiness; and this is certain, that those eminent men, and all their followers went far astray from the course marked out by our Lord and His Apostles. They were satisfied with stating men's danger, and assuring them that they were on the high road to perdition. But they did not call upon them to 'repent and believe the Gospel;' they did not entreat them to be 'reconciled unto God;' they did not 'warn every man and teach every man in all wisdom;' and the churches did not, could not, under their instruction, engage in efforts for the conversion of souls. . . . . . The backsliding and coldness had affected all religious communities in England. Had it not been for the merciful revival which accompanied the labors of Whitfield and the Wesleys, evangelical truth would have well nigh died out. Those extraordinary men were raised up for a glorious purpose; the effects of their ministry were felt in all denominations; the churches began to arise and shake themselves from the dust. A new order of things may be dated from the commencement of their itinerancy, indicating a gradual return to Apostolic simplicity and fervour; Christian ministers preached differently; if they uttered the same truths, there was more affection and power in the utterances. Some of them found that an addition to their creeds was necessary, to bring them into accordance with the heavenly standard, and Christian churches saw that there were duties incumbent on them, which they could not neglect without incurring 'guilt.'"

This, and many other passages, prove that while the "History of the Baptists" was being written, and their principles defended, the author of the book was in no mood to champion their cause, when they swerved from the truth ; or to detract one iota from the good found in other Christians. The wrong he attacked, wherever seen, the right he applauded, whoever held it.

An earnest effort to stimulate the people, whose history he had given, to greater zeal in the work of the Lord, closes the book thus :—

" There is a future for the Baptists, and it is our duty to prepare for it. Thousands of souls, just looking out of obscurity and feeling after God, ask our guidance in the search for truth and life. Freedom, outraged and down-trodden by earthly tyrants, calls upon us to assert the rights of conscience, and its entire immunity from human control; and while it beckons us to the holy war, reminds us that it is our glory to wield the sword of the Spirit, with hands that have never been reddened by a brother's blood. Our martyrs—burnt, beheaded, strangled or drowned, in every European country, at the era of the Reformation, and as yet unknown to fame, although their Christian heroism was right noble,—expect that in the diffusion and defense of the truths for which they suffered, we will display a zeal befitting our privileged lot. A great work is before us, both at home and abroad, de-manding ardent love, enterprising boldness, and indom-itable perseverance."

In 1871—" The Lamb of God." An extract from the preface may explain the feelings and motives of the author :—

" In other works, historical and controversial, I have endeavoured to set forth, clearly and impartially, the course of events, and to defend truth. . . . I am now in the seventy-fifth year of my age, and cannot expect to render much more service to the church of God. The days of the years of my pilgrimage are drawing to a close.

" This little book, containing the substance of several sermons, is designed as a final testimony on behalf of those precious truths, which constitute the Gospel of Christ. As it is not sensational or fictitious, which classes of writing are all the rage in these times, I could not expect to gain anything by publishing it in the usual way. I send it among you, therefore, in this private manner, trusting that some souls will be profited, and the Great Master honored."

With ripened experience and mellowed hope, the great doctrines of the Son of God, which had been his solace in many a trial, are in this little volume set forth with great clearness and beauty. And thus, being dead, he " yet speaketh."

In 1873—" Paul and Christ." Paul's early life, his conversion, his abundant labors, his success and Epistles are described, as affording proofs of the grace of God in Christ Jesus our Lord, and the power of the Gospel to change the heart and purify the motives of men.

During the same year, a small pamphlet, entitled " The Case of the Baptists, stated and explained ; addressed to all whom it may concern."

There was a cause, and Dr. Cramp, although at that time of life much disinclined to controversial subjects, could not suffer the occasion to pass misimproved. Certain writers, finding no arguments against something he had written in defense of the truth, hit upon the happy expedient of sweeping all claims of our body out of existence till the sixteenth century. Dr. Cramp was too thoroughly informed in the history and growth of all the denominations, to allow such statements to pass for sound reasoning.

The little pamphlet referred to went forth. And if the writers spoken of above took the trouble to read it, they were probably convinced that however commendable their courage might be, their wisdom might be improved by fuller investigation.

In 1875—"A Memoir of Madame Feller, with an account of the origin and progress of the Grande Ligne Mission." A note in the preface, similar to one that appeared on the first publication from the same author, states, "should any profits be derived from this publication, the amount will be appropriated to the Feller Institute."

The life of Madame Feller was one of great consecration and usefulness. The record of it has been the means of doing much good. By its perusal, all unprejudiced readers are convinced that the work of the "Grande Ligne Mission" in Canada is of the Lord. New friends have been raised up, both to pray for and give support to that good cause. All the reward that he asked, who spent some of the last days of a busy, useful life, in hunting up reports, and ferreting out the meaning of letters and papers, usually in the French language, and often very difficult to decipher at all, because of their age or hasty composition.

In 1876—"The Realities of Religion;" being the circular letter of one of the associations. In

this letter, one who has been nearly sixty years
trusting in the promises of Christ, and finding
them more and more precious as the years have
passed away, endeavours to convince his younger
brethren, that their hope is neither a myth nor a
fable, that the unseen is the real, the Eternal God
in Christ, the Rock of their defense. Glowing
with the prospect of the glory, he exclaims,—
" Worthy is the Lamb that was slain, to receive
power, and riches and wisdom and strength and
honor and glory and blessing." Brethren, shall we
be there? shall we join in that song? shall we
take part in the triumph of the glorified and dwell
with them in the presence of the Lord for ever?

" For ever with the Lord,
　　Amen: so let it be,
Life from the dead is in that word,
　　'Tis immortality."

And it was an inspiring sight ;—Jacob leaning
on the top of his staff, or Moses uttering his farewell blessing, was scarcely more imposing. The
snow-white locks and yet erect form, the beaming
countenance, notwithstanding the eighty years of
life, the ringing words of assurance and hope, all
conspired to drive despondency from the hearts of
the doubting ones, and gird them afresh for the
toil.

One more published work, so far as we are aware,
completes the list :—

" The Second Coming of our Lord," an essay delivered before the King's County Ministerial Conference, in 1879, and published at the request of

that body. The fact of the Second Coming is established by many Scripture declarations. The various views held since the days of Christ are explained, with the errors fallen into, and the brethren are cautioned not to be dogmatic on matters which lie beyond our grasp, but to be humble, active and hopeful, fully assured that in due time, the Lord will come to take vengeance on the ungodly, and to be admired by all his saints. But that day and hour are, as yet, with the Lord.

This completed list, beginning at 1818 and ending at 1879, sixty-one years, with the imperfect references we have made to some of the works, affords after all but a faint idea of the fruitfulness of the life. The unwritten was vastly more than the written. Putting together the long years of active service, the unending persistency in work, the methodical employment of time, and the unusual rapidity with which work was accomplished, we may venture to claim that the life we are reviewing, was one of the most fruitful of any, at least, connected with the body for which Dr. Cramp labored.

Had a little more strength been allowed, there would probably have been additions to the long list. The history of the Baptists of the Maritime Provinces was written and published in a series of letters in the *Christian Messenger*, over the signature of "Menno." These were collected and revised. It was the intention of the author to publish the history in a separate volume, but difficulties presented themselves, and before these were all removed, the hand became too weak and trembling to guide the pen, either to conduct correspondence or correct proof, and so the work was left unfinished. The manuscript was left to the Baptist Convention for any use that may be made of it.

Another small volume was designed, entitled, "The last things." The manuscript was prepared. In it are many reflections on the close of life, and the end of all, beautiful and touching, coming as they do from one who had lived so long and so worthily, but fully realizing that his own last day was near.

# CHAPTER XIII.

## THE LIBRARY.

" The library was like a tree which he had himself planted, of which he had nurtured the growth, which spread its branches far and wide over his dwelling, and in the shade of which he delighted."—DEAN STANLEY.

It has already been stated that the remark was frequently made at the close of an "Anniversary exercise," conducted by Dr. Cramp—"the right man in the right place."

The president's address was always so animated and timely, so in harmony with the spirit of the occasion, that it was looked forward to as a special feature in the day's proceedings; and the expectations were generally more than realized. A similar remark was often made at public meetings of the denomination. For when vexed questions came up for settlement, and long, excited discussions, seemed only to be making things worse, the mists and fogs becoming denser all the while, it often happened that a few clear, but forcible words from the Doctor, or a resolution moved by him, would end the disputes, and open the way for united action. Then it was felt, how good it is to have a man among us of ripened age, extensive reading and experience. It was "the right man in the right place."

The younger brethren in remote parts of the Provinces, contending against error, often found themselves in difficulty. They would be required to meet arguments which they knew were groundless, and yet sustained by great profession of wisdom. Not always having the means at hand to refute these statements, they would send to Wolfville for information. And when the return mail would inform them, that such a book, (name, date, and place of author given) contains such and such statements, the page and paragraph marked, they too, would thankfully exclaim—"the right man in the right place."

If there was, however, any one place having a pre-eminence in the adaptations, the man fitted to the place and the place to the man, Dr. Cramp's own library was the spot. It belonged to him and he belonged to it. He nursed it with an affectionate care, and it returned him large rewards.

As far back as any member of the family can recollect, "the library" received more attention, money, and time, than all the other rooms; more thought perhaps than all other household demands put together. And so completely was Dr. Cramp at home, in every sense when seated among his books, that the record of his life would be incomplete and altogether inadequate, unless this book passion of the man were referred to. It would be like describing Milton, without referring to "Paradise Lost," or some eminent artist, forgetting every picture that his skilful hand produced.

Every home of Dr. Cramp had its library. For he commenced to collect as soon as he began to read. The more he collected, the stronger the passion grew. He never ceased, so long as pleasure or profit could be derived from the matured thoughts of the wise and the good.

The following extract from a letter to a member of the family, early in 1871, will give some idea of the work performed in this place of his resort:—

" On Saturday evening I placed in my book, as usual, a note of the work of the year, it is as follows :—

" During the year, I have read fifty-nine volumes containing 27,032 pages. I preached very little, only twenty sermons. I wrote 303 letters. I prepared twenty-eight articles for the press, twenty-four of which appeared in the *Christian Messenger.* I revised for the press my letter on 'Church Development,' which has appeared in the *Baptist Quarterly.* I wrote a small treatise, entitled 'The Lamb of God,' which is yet in manuscript. Whether it will see the light of day, I cannot say.

" It was one symptom of advancing years, that on Saturday night I retired to rest at the usual hour, instead of waiting to welcome the New Year."

But we have wandered from the room to the work performed in it. We now return to Dr. Cramp's library. We take his last one as a sample. The place where the last twelve years of his busy life were spent ; and it was a rich treat for many of his old students to spend an hour with him there. A treat for them, and equally enjoyed by himself. For it revived old memories, and brought in a little news from the pastors and churches, for which he greatly longed, when he could no longer gather information for himself.

The room was of fair average size, enlarged by himself to make room for the constant arrivals.

There were originally two fair sized windows, one on the east, the other on the north.

The eastern window, however, was soon sacrificed to make more room for books. It was boarded over on the inside and the space filled in with shelves.

The Doctor's chair always stood in the same place, at the side of the table, and there, in the one spot, he himself was to be found from about an hour before breakfast until ten o'clock at night, except the time necessary for taking meals. For the last two or three years, he would occasionally sit for an hour or so, just after dinner, in an easy chair which stood at his left, while he finished glancing over the various papers and magazines which the morning mail had brought in. Otherwise he was, pen in hand, at the desk, the table so completely buried up with books, papers, letters and magazines, that no one could tell of what it was made, or where anything was to be found. And yet, if the doctor wanted a special paper or book, he knew very nearly where, among the confused mass, to put his hand upon it. On his left, or at the south-east corner of the room, were the various biographical works so arranged and placed that at a moment's notice he could take down the one wanted.

The following additional remarks are furnished by a member of the family :—

" The library was a room apart ; and family traditions trace its history through many changes ; the earliest recollection of each member having some special connection with it. Not that it was ever a gathering place for family enjoyment ; something of mystery and awe, seeming, in earlier years, to invest precincts into which childish footsteps seldom strayed. Order was observed in each of the rooms that, through many changes, in turn held the books. Theological works, commentaries, &c., had their appointed compartments, where also were to be found a collection of Bibles in various languages. Some of them curious editions, valuable for age and rarity, and handled with the pleasure only experienced by the true book-lover. The Latin Fathers, in stately folios, filled a large space undisturbed by the neighborhood of more modern authorities.

" Histories, ancient and modern, science, geology,— each branch of thought finding its accustomed niche, familiar only to the occupant. Good editions of standard works were indispensable,—type, paper, binding,—all must be of the best, and, as books were felt to be the most valuable possession, when gifts were thought of, their form was invariable.

" Some well-known, and well-loved author's productions, were sure to be forth-coming, enhanced in value, by carefully selected binding, as a gem receives an added touch in the setting. There was no room for decoration in the library. Two or three portraits of old and valued friends found a place, and one of the Rev. R. Cecil was never missing. An engraved copy of a pencil sketch of the old 'Baptist meeting house, Shallow's, Isle of Thanet ;' done by fair hands, in youthful days, could not be dis-

17

placed, but any additions to these were inadmissible.

"In later years, the epergne, presented to Dr. Cramp, on retiring from the college, placed on a stand in one corner, was an object on which he liked to look, reminding him of the appreciation felt and expressed for the work which had been so dear to him."

The shelves all round on every hand, right, left, behind, and before, reaching from the floor to the ceiling, with every nook and corner over the doors and windows utilized, to find a place for books.

The fact is, that the doctor, sitting in the centre was literally walled in with books. And there he was, emphatically,—"the right man in the right place." No one who knew him could feel that there was any incongruity there. The *nouveaux riches* sometimes surround themselves with all that is beautiful and luxurious, and their own habits of life, and uncultivated natures are such, that the polished furniture loses half its charm for the want of a corresponding polish in the owner; the adaptation is incomplete. The same applies to literary decorations. A house adorned with valuable and costly books, but no one within able to appreciate the contents, has so much of the mere exhibition about it, that the books themselves lose half their value, so long as they display themselves there.

There was no approximation to this condition of things in the library now under consideration. For if ever a man appreciated and enjoyed a good book, Dr. Cramp did. He had some favorites among them. These were read many times over. The Bible always took the first place. For many years, about fifty, if memory serves us aright, his rule was to go through the Bible course, from beginning to end, once a year. But this formed the smallest portion of his Bible reading. There was a chapter or so of the New Testament in the Greek every day, and various psalms· and New Testament portions for devotional purposes.

The works of Richard Cecil were first met by him when a student at Stepney. These were gone over once a year, and as he himself often remarked, with increasing pleasure and profit as the years passed away. The works of such men as Foster, Hall, Fuller, Baxter, Bunyan, *et al.*, all, in fact, of the distinguished divines, were very familiar to him. The latest books on theological subjects, commentaries, and especially the lives and labors of the missionaries, as fast as they appeared, were found on his table and eagerly devoured.

He lived so completely among the books that his knowledge of them was very extensive and accurate. There were about 3,000 in his own library, besides the 1,500 that were destroyed in the burning of his house in 1856, and many in other parts of the house. He not only knew what was in his own library, but he had extensive knowledge of what was not there. It was, indeed, a rare thing for one to refer to any English author, from Chaucer down, without finding that Dr. Cramp knew something about the book. The name and date, the subject matter and the general value of the work, seemed to be in his possession.

Some books he read and re-read and reviewed

for the press, or for his own profit. But he had a marvellous facility for finding out and remembering what was in a book, in a general way, without reading it. A very few pages glanced over, (and from long practice, this could be done very hastily) were quite sufficient to convince him, whether there were anything there to repay a careful perusal. If not, the table of contents and a magazine review, if there were such, would suffice, And still he would know enough to discuss the merits of the author.

The old standard authors in history, science, poetry and theology, etc., occupied a prominent place in his regard. He revered many of these men, and placed a very high estimate on their productions. And yet, he was intensely eager to get the latest thoughts on all important matters. Nothing, in his estimation, was finished. Growth and improvement were to be expected in every department of thought. Improved methods of research should be continually revealing new truth. And he was ever on the alert to catch the new, when it came. Even theology was, to him, a grand science in the course of development. The Bible was finished, revelation completed, but the interpretations, the applications, the relations to human life and history, these were all in a course of constant unfolding. More was to be expected, and he was as one eagerly looking for the next development.

His library, extensive and complete as it was, did not go far enough. It was always a little behind the time. The history, written twenty years ago, needed a supplement to bring it up to date. How is this blank to be filled in ? It was done by the daily mail.

The arrival of the mail was the signal for laying down the pen, or rather for placing it with two or three quick thrusts into a box of small shot on the corner of the desk. And if the mail were half an hour behind the time, that was a season of unrest. The work would go on, but with a good deal of uneasiness. When, occasionally, trains were snowed up, and no mail for two or three days, then the doctor was greatly disconcerted. A whole week without contact with the mind and thought outside, appeared like falling behind the world's movements and progress.

The papers usually came every day, and at about the same time. And they were from all quarters. The dailies, the tri-weeklies from Halifax, St. John, Boston, New York. The quarterlies, and illustrated papers, and magazines from every direction. If a week's mail should come at once, after a storm, no wonder the bag was long in coming, for its load was heavy. Then the dailies are glanced at. A few minutes would decide whether there were anything worth reading. If so, they are carefully laid aside ; then the letters opened and read or laid by, according to the circumstances. Then the wrappers torn from the magazines. A glance at the contents, writers, etc., and put in positions for future perusal. All of which is done quickly, and yet methodically, and Dr. Cramp has a general idea of all that the mail has brought him. He is at rest, and the reading will come in at intervals till the next mail arrives.

The large daily mail, perhaps, was nothing uncommon. But the eagerness for the contents was very uncommon. And the rapidity with which all the leading events of the world's history were gathered up, was perfectly astonishing.

As public duties, one after another, were dropped, the library, of course, became more and more the one place where Dr. Cramp was to be seen. He was greatly missed from the church, and other meetings, where even his presence, in other days, added so much of interest. But the intimate friends were glad to know that there was a place where he could be found, and that a visit from any of them was always welcomed. And for any one with an eye to see the beauty of perfect adaptation, the harmony of fair proportions, it was a sight worth going some distance to see Dr. Cramp in his library. There are many who will not soon forget the impressions made upon their minds in visiting him there. The dignified and yet wasting form; the snow-white locks reaching down nearly to the shoulders; the genial and beaming countenance, even to the last; the mellowed manner; the gentler and softer bearing; the maturing faith and brightening prospects, were all visible to those who had an eye to mark the changes that time and Divine grace united, can produce. Many a day must pass before such a man will sit again in such a library.

The following is clipped from the *Christian Visitor* of Aug., 1883. Dr. E. M. Saunders, of Halifax, N. S., was one of the editors at the time, and furnished jottings of visits to the country :—

### "A CALL AT WOLFVILLE.

" It would be very difficult to find words to express the impression made by entering the library of the late, venerable Dr. Cramp. So accustomed have we become for many years past, to drop into that library and have a few moments with its genial occupant, who always extended a hearty and cheerful welcome, that it seems difficult to discontinue the practice, although the facile and active pen waits in vain for the vanished hand, and the empty chair for the vanished form. The books are on the shelves, as if still ready to serve a faithful and appreciative master, but the familiar hand is not laid upon them. No, all the books are not there ; for parcels of them, valuable indeed for their intrinsic worth, but much more so for the love and esteem cherished for the father in Israel, who, while living, arranged for their distribution, after his own departure for the rest he ever held in view, sure to follow his long and active life, are now on the shelves of ministers and other students, who in the happy days of the past sat at this good and great man's feet.

" Still the shelves seem full. The venerable form is not there ; but the room, the books and every object in that sacred spot seem instinct with the learning and spirit which ever animated the very surroundings of that man, whose rest seemed to be hard labor. All this appeared more real, we suppose, because of a likeness exquisitely executed in oil and of perfect resemblance to the original which overlooks this room in which Dr. Cramp spent a cheerful old age. No father could be more affectionately and worshipfully remembered than is Dr. Cramp, both by those who, from natural and spiritual relations, will ever esteem him their father. 'The lips of the righteous feed many.' 'The pens of the righteous feed many.' If in the audience of all the people we, who knew him, should say, 'Thank God for Dr. Cramp,' every one of these thousands of hearts would send up a hearty, Amen!"

Dr. Cramp's library was always available when truth needed defense, and he was not afraid to defend the truth, however wise and good those might be who were discovered in any error.

This disposition led him in the course of his life into correspondence, sometimes of a controversial character. Not because he loved controversy, but because he loved the truth, and could not rest when it was assailed.

Sometimes he had the happiness of coming into contact with men of broad and liberal views. Like himself, they were free from all bigotry, and only needed to have their attention called to any misconception of theirs, in order to have justice done, so far as that could be accomplished.

The following letters, one written in the library described above, near the close of the year 1870, and the other at the Deanery, Westminster, early in 1871, will afford an illustration of the characteristics of two honorable men :—

"WOLFVILLE, N.S., Dec. 28, 1870.
"*To the Rev. A. P. Stanley, D.D., Dean of Westminster,*
"REV. SIR:—

· "Glancing into your volume of 'Essays' just received

from England, I noticed at p. 36, this phrase: "the insignificant sect of Baptists." You will allow me to say, (I am a Baptist minister of fifty-two years standing), that I was grieved and pained. I did not think that the denomination which has produced John Bunyan, William Carey, Robert Hall, and John Foster, besides many living men of eminence, one of whom is a member of the 'New Testament Company,' should be stigmatized as an 'insignificant sect,' and I am especially sorry for the appearance of the expression *now*, because you have reprinted it, after the lapse of twenty years, as if to intimate that you justify its original use.

"I send you by this mail a copy of 'Baptist History,' and also some documents relating to our denomination in this part of the world. If you can find time to read them, I hope you will be prepared to acknowledge that the Baptists are not an 'insignificant sect.'

"Allow me to express the indebtedness which I feel to you for great pleasure and profit derived from the perusal of your works. Your 'Lectures on the Jewish and Eastern Churches,' your 'Sinai and Palestine,' your 'Memorials of Westminster Abbey,' and your 'Historical Memorials of Canterbury,' were placed on my library shelves as they were successively published: the 'Essays' have just reached me.

"I was particularly interested in the perusal of the volume on Canterbury, because I was two years at school in that city, and frequently visited the cathedral.

"I am,

"Rev. sir,

"Yours respectfully,

"J. M. CRAMP."

### Reply from Dean Stanley.

" Dear Sir :—

" I have just received your kind letter and your valuable work, for which I beg to return my sincere thanks.

"Your criticism on the phrase, ' the *insignificant* sect of Baptists ' is most just. It was, perhaps, excusable in an essay, written twenty years ago; but it was inexcusable to have left it uncorrected. I can only account for it by the natural inadvertance with which one corrects statements printed long ago. If you will do me the honor of looking at a somewhat parallel passage in my lectures on the Eastern Church (p. 29, 2nd ed.) you will see that the offensive phrase is there omitted. I can assure you that in my lectures at Oxford, I have often spoken of the Baptists as being numbered amongst Honorables in our day. ' The most beloved of English soldiers, (Havelock) the most popular of English preachers, (Spurgeon), and the most celebrated of English travellers, (Livingston),' thus adding three more to the departed glories that you commemorate, and whose history you trace in the volume which I shall hope to read. Pray, therefore, erase from the copy of my essays, which has been honoured by a place on your shelves, an epithet so inaccurate and inappropriate.

"With all good wishes to you in the coming year,

" Believe me to be

" Yours faithfully,

" A. P. Stanley.

"Deanery, Westminster,
" Jan. 10, 1871."

# CHAPTER XIV.

" The boundary of man is moderation. When once we pass
that pale, our guardian angel quits his charge of us."—*Feltham.*

It would be an injustice to the memory of Dr.
Cramp to make no mention of his efforts in behalf
of the great Temperance reform. During his early
years, clergymen in England were not generally
total abstainers ; the moderate use of wine was
not deemed improper. In fact, by many it was
regarded as absolutely essential to continued
vigor of body and mind ; ale and porter were the
common beverages of the country.

As already stated, it was during the pastorate
at Hastings that Dr. Cramp changed his views on
this subject. It is hardly necessary to state that,
when the views were changed, the habit of life
was brought into harmony with the new principle. From that time till the end of life, the
Temperance cause had no warmer friend. Both
by precept and example, he inculcated the principles of temperance, and often spoke of his own
continued health, and ability to work as resulting,

in no small degree, from his avoidance of stimulating beverages. During the last half of his life, he never touched even the weakest wines, except on the recommendation of a physician.

One of the papers presented at the memorial service in May, 1882, was by Avard Longly, Esq., M.P., since deceased. He had been an active worker in the Temperance cause for many years. As a member of the Sons of Temperance, he had been much in contact with all the leaders of the movement, and was well qualified to speak of the service rendered by Dr. Cramp. We will, therefore, in lieu of further remarks on the subject, give the substance of that paper.

### DR. CRAMP AS A TEMPERANCE WORKER.

"Dr. Cramp came to Acadia in 1851—just 31 years ago. He immediately identified himself with the temperance movement, then already recognized as a potent agent for good within this province. Almost at once, the Doctor became a standard-bearer in this great reform, in connexion with the Order of the Sons of Temperance. In October 1852 he was initiated into the Grand Division of Nova Scotia, and at the same session was elected Grand Chaplain—an office to which he was called a second time in 1871. A year later—in 1853—he was elected to the office of Grand Worthy Patriarch, and in 1855 he was again called upon to preside over the Grand Division. In 1866 he attended a session of the National Division,—an assembly representing the Sons of Temperance of the United States and Canada—convened that year at Montreal, as a delegate from the Grand

Division of Nova Scotia. He at once gained a position in that large and influential body as one of its leading men, and, on the ballot for officers being taken, was elected Most Worthy Associate—the highest place, but one, in the gift of the order. He continued his connexion with the Sons of Temperance up to the time of his death, but of late years, through feeble health, was unable to meet with the brethren. He was greatly missed. The last session of the Grand Division attended by him, was held at Wolfville in 1878. I well remember the occasion. As Dr. Cramp entered the division room, the members of the body instantly and spontaneously rose to receive him. It was a touching tribute of affection, and betokened, in some small degree, the high veneration and respect with which all who knew him regarded him.

"In connexion with this great reform, Dr. Cramp was ever ready to work in any way most likely to do good He never shrank from any task where, by the pen or the voice, he could help forward the good work to which he had set his hand. He was a frequent contributor to the *Athenæum*, a most able temperance and literary paper, formerly published in this province; and the ripe productions of his skilful pen often found a place also in temperance periodicals published in other parts of this continent and in Great Britain. He kept himself posted in respect to the progress of temperance reforms throughout the world, and in the counsels of his brethren, where he was ever heartily welcomed, he was able to render most valuable and efficient service. Among Dr. Cramp's contemporaries in temperance work were many gentlemen of ability and power. Hon. Messrs. J. W. Johnston and Creelman; Messrs. W. M. Brown, J. S. Thompson, Noble, Taylor, Scott, Monaghan and Redding; Revs. Messrs. McMurray, Christie, McArthur and Temple, were among the leaders in this movement. Some of these, although among the oldest members of the order, were much younger men than Dr. Cramp, but none excelled him in devotion to the cause, nor yet in the amount or efficient character of the work accomplished.

"To the Order of the Sons of Temperance, the credit is due very largely of having moulded public sentiment in respect to prohibition. Dr. Cramp was an unswerving advocate of this policy; and he permitted no opportunity for giving expression to his views to pass unimproved. In 1854, during his first term as Grand Worthy Patriarch, the question was forced upon the attention of the Provincial Legislature, by numerous petitions, emanating from all sections of the province, and signed by persons from all ranks and professions of the people, including not a few of the victims of the intoxicating bowl. At this crisis, Dr. Cramp came boldly forward to champion the good cause, and delivered an address at Temperance Hall, Halifax, before members of the Legislature, bristling with facts and arguments, and distinguished by more than ordinary power and eloquence. He portrayed with great ability the baneful effects flowing to society from the use of intoxicating liquors, and contended that prohibition was the only remedy. He denounced the absurd system of 'Liquor Licenses' in the strongest language. The peroration to Dr. Cramp's address was most eloquent and effective, and will bear repetition.

"Our friend and brother has passed to his reward; who will fill his place as a temperance worker? Others, good men and true, seem ever to have more work in connexion with their ordinary avocations than they can well accomplish. Not to the censure of these, but to the praise of our departed brother, be it said, he, although

ofttimes burdened with double and treble the work of
ordinary men, could always find time for temperance
work. We would not unduly exalt him, but his brethren of the Order fondly and gratefully cherish his memory, and years ago promoted him to an equality with
the best of their number. No doubt, they would have
cheerfully given him the very first place. ·

"Eighty and six years, nearly, he numbered. His
was a long and eminently useful life. Serenely he
passed away, surrounded by loving friends. His departure suggests to our minds most forcibly the beautiful
lines of Dr. Bonar:—

"Fading away like the stars of the morning,
  Losing their light in the glorious sun;
  So let me steal away, gently and lovingly,
  Only remembered by what I have done.

"Needs there the praise of the love-written record?
  The name and the epitaph graved on the stone?
  The things that he lived for, let them be his story,
  Only remembered by what he has done."

"A Prohibitory Liquor Law was passed by the Nova
Scotia House of Assembly in 1885—the year following."

The paper from which these extracts are taken,
refers to an address delivered in the presence of
the members of the Nova Scotia Legislature in
Halifax in 1854. As that address contains
thoughts worth remembering, and also illustrates
Dr. Cramp's earnest and practical manner of dealing with the vital questions of the day, we give
it entire:—

## " PROHIBITORY LIQUOR LAW.

"Address delivered in the Temperance Hall, Halifax, on Thursday, February 23, 1854, by Rev. J. M. CRAMP, D.D., G. W. P. of the Sons of Temperance of the Province of Nova Scotia.

" GENTLEMEN,—The delegates composing the Temperance Convention, who have been sent to this city from every part of the province, in order to adopt such measures as shall tend to secure the enactment of a Prohibitory Liquor Law, have unanimously resolved that the law required must prohibit the importation, manufacture and sale of intoxicating liquors of all kinds, except for certain purposes, to be distinctly provided for. It is now my duty to present to you a statement of the principles on which this demand is founded, and of the reasoning by which it is sustained.

" I observe, in the first place, that *the use of intoxicating liquors is extensively injurious to society.*

"Thirty years ago, it would have been necessary to argue the point. It is not necessary now. It is now universally acknowledged that no healthy man stands in need of these liquors—that they stimulate, but do not nourish—that their habitual use produces many diseases, aggravates all diseases, and, in innumerable instances, prevents the possibility of cure—and that tens of thousands die every year in consequence. It is now universally confessed that the habitual use of these liquors stupifies the intellect, destroys all delicacy of feeling, and reduces the victim below the level of the brute.

"Take a single case. Yonder goes a miserable man, besotted, befooled by strong diink. Listen to his incoherent ravings. See the children mocking him as he attempts to thread his crooked course along, or struggles ineffectually in his kindred gutter. What sight so melancholy, so humiliating?

"That man has children at home—and a wife, whom long ago he promised to love and to cherish. Why does that wife now shudder at his approach? Why do his children run and hide themselves? It was not so once. Strong drink has done the mischief. It has turned the husband and father into a demon. He is a man no more. Natural affection has died out of him. The lion will provide for its mate; the tiger will take care of its young; but the drunkard abandons both, and gives the price of their bread to the rumseller, while the wife pines away in wretchedness, and the children, half-clad, squalid, dirty, ignorant and uncontrolled, are rising up to be outcasts and pests in society, and probably future inmates of the jail.

"That man had character; it is lost. He had friends; they disown him. He enjoyed comforts; they are handed over to the keeper of the groggery. He possessed health; it is fast failing. He was once happy; happiness has long since fled. Hope then encouraged him; but all now is a cheerless blank. His body is corrupted; his mind is a wreck; he is hasting down to ruin—a lost man—lost in both worlds.

"This is the case of myriads of the human race in all countries. Wherever we turn our eyes, we see strong drink in connection with misery, suffering, and evil of every kind. What is it that sinks the proprietor into a tenant? What is it that sinks the tenant into a laborer? What is it that sinks the laborer into a pauper? What is it that cheats children out of their inheritances? What is it that dashes many a noble ship against the rocks, hurling passengers and crew into eternity? Perhaps some of yourselves remember the officer who left this harbor in charge of a government vessel, and never

18

returned to it, he and all his crew—*they were all drunk*—being lost with the vessel within a few hours after their departure. How many similar losses, involving the destruction of an immense amount of property, are continually occurring from the same cause—justifying the observation made some years ago by Capt. Brenton, when giving his evidence before the Committee on Drunkenness, that 'spirits are more dangerous than gunpowder!' From what quarter may we not summon witnesses? Are they military or naval officers? They assure us that, in almost every instance, the disorderly conduct which renders punishment necessary is traceable to the use of intoxicating liquors? Are they merchants, or manufacturers, or builders of palaces or railroads? They tell us of losses continually sustained by the unsteadiness, negligence and insubordination of drunken clerks and workmen. Are they physicians? They describe horrifying cases of delirium tremens, and show us how the cholera, as it passes along from town to town, always sweeps off the drunkards. Are they lawyers? They point to the strong boxes on their shelves, containing title-deeds which once belonged to sober men, and now belong to those whose fire-water maddened them on to ruin. Are they clergymen? They refer to death-beds of anguish and horror inexpressible, and the bitter wailings of penniless widows and orphans —made penniless by the intemperance of their natural protectors. Are they judges? Every charge complains of the increase of crime. Are they juries? Their presentments, year after year, give the same unvarying testimony. Are they officers of police, jailors, governors of lunatic asylums and penitentiaries? They bear witness, as with one voice, that three-fourths of the crime committed in every country, and three fourths of the pauperism, and consequently of the expenditure incurred by society to punish the one and sustain the other, must be laid to the charge of the bottle and the glass. You build prisons—and intemperance fills them. You establish poorhouses—and they are occupied by the families of inebriates. You erect lunatic asylums—and one-half of their inmates have been prepared for those melancholy abodes by the use of strong drink. What is worse, you license men to sell the brandy, the whiskey, and the rum, and thus secure a continual succession of inhabitants for the prisons, the poorhouses, and the lunatic asylums.

"Crime has been mentioned. The worst of all crimes —those springing from the fiercest passions of human nature—and perpetrated in the most horrible manner, are the fruits of intoxication. Is it an atrocious highway robbery? or the murder of a father by his son—of a son by his father—of a husband or a wife ? A thousand to one, but alcohol is the exciting cause. It is estimated that in the United States one murder, at least, is committed every day under the influence of intoxicating drinks.

"Government, as the organ of society, cares for the health, the property, the life of every member of the community, and plans and strives to build up a prosperous people. But strong drink is the great obstruction. It stands in the way of all patriotism. It thwarts the best intentions, blasts the brightest hopes, mocks and balks the wisest efforts, and spreads desolation all around. I do not wonder that a German author, writing recently on this subject, has given to his work this title, ' *Alcohol is Satan's blood.*' I do not wonder at the expression used by the Swedish peasantry, who, as they go from distillery to distillery, putting out the fires and stopping the work, say to the owners, ' You shall make no more *hell-broth.*' ' A touching incident,' says a Swedish clergyman, in a letter written about four months ago, ' has taken place in my neighborhood. Some poor country people have determined to go on foot to the King (360 miles). 'We must beg him,' they say, 'to take away the brandy; we are most of us lost drunkards, and when the rich proprietors and farmers force upon us brandy, as payment for our labour, then we have not strength to withstand the temptation.' This thought has occurred to the poor men themselves. Their words seem to me inexpressibly affecting. It is an awakened conscience which cries out loudly during the intervals between the fits of intoxication. It begs for mercy and deliverance from the evil. I could weep to hear them.'

"Let me now proceed to observe, that *legislative enactments for the regulation and control of the sale of intoxicating liquors have proved an entire failure.*

"Before entering on this part of the discussion, I will briefly advert to the Temperance reform. The agitation commenced about twenty-nine years ago, and quickly spread through the United States,—thence to Great Britain and her colonies,—and afterwards to almost every part of the civilized world. Beginning with a pledge of abstinence from ardent spirits, the pledge was afterwards extended—and that is its present form—to every kind of intoxicating drink. We bind ourselves by a promise of total abstinence; we labour to induce others to do so—especially those who have fallen under temptation; and we combine for mutual encouragement and aid, and the effective employment of effort. Such is our simple plan of operation.

"The object obtained at once the advocacy of a large number of the wise and good, of all classes, and of every variety of thought and profession. Talent, learning, benevolence, and piety, consecrated their energies to the cause, with zeal and perseverance unexampled. True, there has been opposition—for everything good, especially if it wears the appearance of novelty, is sure to be opposed. Ridicule, sarcasm, and argument have been by turns employed. Many have stood aloof, who ought to have given in their adhesion, and the friends of temperance have been sometimes taunted with the quixotic and hopeless nature of the enterprise. But they have held on. And now the Temperance reform is a 'great fact,' and the Temperance power in the community is a power that cannot be safely slighted. We have been accustomed to hear of the 'three Estates' of the realm—the Queen, the Lords, and the Commons; our brethren of the press contend that they constitute a 'fourth Estate'—and truly great is the power of the press—its claims may be conceded. The Temperance power may as reasonably be called the 'fifth Estate'; it will influence the rest, and ultimately leaven all society.

"The success of our endeavours has greatly encouraged us. How many have been restored to themselves—to their families—to their social position? How many more have been turned back, even when they had reached the very edge of the precipice!—How many have been preserved, who would have otherwise fallen! and how delightful is the union of men of all parties, sinking for the time their differences, in order to promote the common good! In our Temperance organizations, we admit no recognition of each other's religious or political opinions; but as our respective principles and objects, tend to promote the further development of talent and power in various forms, we avail ourselves of the advantage, and secure the results. The characteristics of differing, and opposite parties are harmoniously united in this glorious cause. The prudence and caution of one—the dashing energy of another—the business tact of a third, are happily combined. Logic comes from this side, rhetoric from that; here, is enthusiasm; there, is persevering diligence. This honest fellowship is doubtless the great secret of our success. May it ever remain unbroken !

" But we are checked, if not disheartened, by the appalling extension of the traffic. We reclaim one, and the drunkard-manufactories send out two in his place. So powerful is the temptation, and so contagious is the habit, that the establishment of a groggery is inevitably followed by the slaughter of its victims, and the consequent wretchedness of those who are dependent on them.

" Contemplating these effects, we cannot but wonder that men bearing the Christian name should engage in the traffic—and that they should continue in it after the effects have been ascertained. For those effects are not occasional. They are not accidents, which may or may not occur. They are the natural and necessary results of the traffic in intoxicating drinks. Plant a grog-shop anywhere, and you have founded a nursery of poverty and a school for crime.

"All this has long been mournfully evident. What is the proposed remedy ? It is license! The sale shall be regulated, controlled, placed under supervision ! Now what is this but legalising it—giving it a place and a standing—making it form part of the government arrangements of the country? And be it borne in mind that it is legalizing that which is sure to produce poverty and crime, and to demoralize society. Was it imaginable that by this means the traffic would be lessened ? Was this the way to put down drunkenness ? As well might you attempt to tie up the whirlwind with a thread, or to put out the light of the sun with an extinguisher ! The history of the license system speaks volumes. It demonstrates most clearly and convincingly the futility and folly of the attempt.

"No ! *The suppression of the traffic in intoxicating liquors, except for manufacturing, mechanical, or medicinal purposes, and for the services of religion, is the only sure remedy for the evils with which society is afflicted through the use of those liquors.*

"If the question of revenue be mooted, it is sufficient to reply, that in this country the amount (from twelve to fifteen thousand pounds annually,) is too small to deserve consideration. But were it ten times as much, the argument would not be affected. A heathen monarch may instruct us. When the late Emperor of China was solicited to legalize the sale of opium, and it was suggested that a large revenue would accrue therefrom, he said—'It is true, I cannot prevent the introduction of the flowing poison; gain-seeking and corrupt men will, for profit and sensuality, defeat my wishes; *but nothing will induce me to derive a revenue from the vices and misery of my people.*' It may be further observed, that in the event of prohibition, there will be an increase of revenue from other quarters, as more money will be spent on necessary and useful articles, the introduction of which into the country is one of the sources of public income.

"In asking for the prohibition of the traffic, we are not bringing forward a new thought. It is no modern innovation. At the settlement of Georgia, nearly 120 years ago, the importation of rum was prohibited, and in order to secure obedience, trade with the West Indies was forbidden. Negro slavery was forbidden at the same time. They were classed together.

"In the course of the debates on the Gin Act, 1743, when the distillers flooded London with their poison, drunkards lay in heaps in the streets, and Government was defied by the mob, the celebrated Lord Chesterfield addressed the House of Lords in the following terms:—

"*Luxury*, my Lords, is to be taxed, but *vice* PROHIBITED, let the difficulty in the law be what it will. Would you lay a tax upon a breach of the *ten commandments?* Would not such a tax be wicked and scandalous ? Would it not *imply* an *indulgence* to all those who could pay the tax? *Vice*, my lords, is not properly to be taxed, but SUP-PRESSED ; and heavy taxes are sometimes the only means by which that suppression can be attained. *Luxury*, or that which is only pernicious by its *excess*, may very properly be taxed,—that such excess, though not strictly unlawful, may be made more difficult. But the use of those things which are simply *hurtful* in their own nature, and in every degree, is to be PROHIBITED. None, my lords, ever heard, in any nation, of a tax upon *theft* or *adultery*, because a tax implies a *license* granted for the use of that which is taxed, to all who are willing to pay for it. Drunkenness, my lords, is universally, and in all circum-stances, an EVIL, and therefore ought not to be taxed, but *punished.* The noble lord has been pleased kindly to in-form us, that the trade of *distilling* is very extensive—that it employs great numbers—and they have arrived at exquisite skill—and therefore the trade of distilling is not to be discouraged ! Once more, my lords, allow me to wonder at the different conceptions of different under-standings. It appears to me that since the spirits which distillers produce are allowed to *enfeeble the limbs, vitiate the blood, pervert the heart,* and *obscure the intellect,* that the *number* of distillers should be no argument in their favor,—for I never heard that a law against *theft* was re-pealed or delayed, because thieves were numerous ! It appears to me, my lords, that really, if so formidable a body are confederate against the *virtue* or the *lives* of their fellow-citizens, it is time to put an end to the *havoc,* and to interpose, whilst it is yet in our power, to stop the *destruction.* So little, my lords, am I affected with the merit of that wonderful skill which distillers are said to have attained, that it is, in my opinion, no faculty of great use to mankind to prepare PALATABLE POISON; nor shall I ever contribute my interest for the reprieve of a *murderer*, because he has, by long practice, obtained great dexterity in his trade. If their liquors are so delicious that the people are tempted to their own destruction, let us, at least, my lords, SECURE them from their *fatal* draught, by *bursting the vials that contain them.* LET US CRUSH AT ONCE THESE ARTISTS IN HUMAN SLAUGHTER, WHO HAVE RECONCILED THEIR COUNTRYMEN TO SICKNESS AND RUIN, AND SPREAD OVER THE PITFALLS OF DE- BAUCHERY SUCH BAIT AS CANNOT BE RESISTED!'

" In 1833, it was resolved by the American Union— and the resolution was adopted in various parts of the United States—' that the traffic in ardent spirits is mor- ally wrong, and ought to be abandoned throughout the world.'

" A select committee was appointed by the House of Commons on the 3rd of June, 1834, on the motion of J. S. Buckingham, Esq., ' to inquire into the extent, causes, and consequences of the prevailing vice of intoxication among the labouring classes of the United Kingdom, in order to ascertain whether any legislative measures can be devised to prevent the further spread of so great a national evil.' The following passages are extracted from the Report of that Committee:—

" The ultimate and prospective remedies which have been strongly urged by several witnesses, and which *they* think, when public opinion shall be sufficiently awakened to the great national importance of the subject, may be safely recommended, include the following :—

" The absolute prohibition of the importation from any foreign country, or from our own colonies, of distilled spirits in any shape.

" The equally absolute prohibition of all distillation of ardent spirits from grain, the most important part of the food of man in our own country.

" The restriction of distillation from all other materials, to the purposes of the arts, manufactures and medicine; and the confining the wholesale and retail dealing in such articles to chemists, druggists, and dispensaries alone."

" Sufficient evidence has now been produced to show that, in asking for a prohibitory liquor law, we are not bringing forward a novel and unheard-of project.

"But it will be asked, *'Is it right to enact a law that will interfere to so great an extent with property?'* Let that question be met by another—*'Is the traffic right?'* Is it right to sell, for drinking purposes, an article, the use of which is followed by such destruction? Is it right for a man to derive his living from that which spreads disease, poverty, and death? Is it right for a man to derive his living from that which debases men's minds and ruins men's souls? Is it right for a man to derive his living from that which destroys for ever the happiness of the domestic circle? Is it right for a man to derive his living from that which brings upon society three-fourths of the crime and pauperism which distress it? Is it right for a man to derive his living from that which does all this at once, and does it continually?

"I have quoted, in substance, the language of Dr. Wayland, President of Brown University. He adds—'If any man think otherwise, and choose to continue it, I have but one word to say. My brother, when you order a cargo of intoxicating drink, think how much misery you are importing into the community. As you store it up, think how many curses you are heaping together against yourself. As you roll it out of your warehouse, think of how many families each cask will ruin. Let your thoughts then revert to your own fire-side, your wife and your little ones; look upward to Him who judgeth righteously, and ask yourself, my brother, IS THIS RIGHT?'

" Nearly a century ago, the great John Wesley, whose authority is justly held in high esteem by many in this assembly, wrote these words :—' The men who traffic in ardent spirit, and sell to all who buy, are poisoners generally; they murder his majesty's subjects by wholesale ; neither doth their eye pity or spare. And what is their gain? Is it not the blood of these men ? Who would envy their large estates and sumptuous palaces? A curse is in the midst of them. The curse of God is on their gardens, their walks, their groves ; a fire that burns to the nethermost hell. Blood, blood, is there; the foundation, the floor, the walls, the roof, are stained with blood.'

" This is strong language. But it may not be reasonably diluted, unless it can be shown that the facts are not as they are alleged. And that cannot be. The facts are not to be denied. Admit them, and the conclusion follows. That conclusion is, that the traffic, except for the purposes which have been mentioned, is morally wrong. Now, that cannot be politically expedient or right, which is morally wrong. Consequently, it becomes the duty of the State to interfere and remove the evil.

" The right of the State to interfere cannot be fairly questioned. ' The right,' say the Committee of the House of Commons to whose Report I have already referred, ' The right to exercise legislative interference for the correction of any evil which affects the public weal cannot be questioned without dissolving society into its primitive elements, and going back from the combined and co-operative state of civilization, with all its wholesome and lawfully-imposed restraints, to the isolated and lawless condition of savage and solitary nature.'

" Nor can it be fairly alleged that the State has no right to interfere with a man's use of his property. He may use it as he pleases, most certainly, but not so as to injure his neighbour or prejudice the interests of society at large. When that use becomes an injury, a mischief, a nuisance, society interferes and puts a stop to it. This is done continually. Lotteries have been abolished, though once they yielded considerable revenue to the Government: they were found injurious to society, and were put down. Gambling houses are declared nuisances. An unwholesome manufacture, established in an inhabited place, is held to be a nuisance, and the proprietor may be compelled to remove it, at whatever inconvenience and cost. Intra-mural cemeteries are now regarded as nuisances, and the State shuts them up. Whatever a man does, that is proved to be annoying to his neighbours, or detrimental to their property or health, he may be forcibly prevented from continuing to do, by the strong arm of the law. When the cholera was raging in the city of Washington, the authorities passed the following resolution :—' *Resolved,* That the vending of ardent spirits, in whatever quantity, is considered a *nuisance,* and, as such, is hereby directed to be discontinued for the space of ninety days from this date.' In the opinion of some, this was a high-handed interference with private rights; but the necessity of the case justified it, for the authorities had discovered that ardent spirits were to the cholera as fuel to the fire.' The only wonder is, that they were not induced, by the good effects of the measure, to declare the vending of ardent spirits a perpetual nuisance. Their successors, I am happy to say, are preparing to do it now.'

"The following decision of the Chief Justice of the State of Maine, which was concurred in by the full bench, places the matter in a clear and satisfactory point of view :—

" 'The State, by its legislative enactments, operating prospectively, may determine that articles injurious to the public health or morals shall not constitute property, within its jurisdiction. It may come to the conclusion that spirituous liquors, when used as a beverage, are productive of a great variety of ills and evils to the people, both in their individual and social relations. That the least use of them for such a purpose is injurious, and suited to produce, by a greater use, serious injury to the comfort, morals, and health; that the common use of them for such a purpose, operates to diminish the productiveness of labor; to injure the health; to impose upon the people additional and unnecessary burdens; to produce waste of time and property; to introduce disorder and disobedience to law; to disturb the peace, and to multiply crimes of every grade. Such conclusions would be justified by the experience and history of man. *If a Legislature should declare that no person should acquire any property in them, for such a purpose,* THERE WOULD BE NO OCCASION FOR ANY COMPLAINT THAT IT HAD VIOLATED ANY PROVISION OF THE CONSTITUTION.'

"Another question is anxiously asked—*Is it practicable?* It may be answered by an appeal to facts. In the youngest-born of civilized nations (the Sandwich Islands) the manufacture and sale of ardent spirits were prohibited by law more than twenty years ago, under a heavy penalty, and the prohibition remains in full force. When permission was asked to sell to foreigners only, not to natives, the Governor's reply was, 'To horses, cattle, and hogs you may sell rum, but to real men you must not on these shores.'

"The sale of intoxicating liquors is prohibited in Vermont. It is prohibited in Rhode Island. It is prohibited in Massachusetts. It is prohibited in the Territory of Minnesota. It will soon be prohibited in the State of New York, in Pennsylvania, and in New Jersey. The Southern States are waking up. The

Western States are roused. In a few years' time, the ' Maine Liquor Law ''will become a ' United States Liquor Law,'' and that vast country will be delivered from the abomination of the traffic. The deliverance will be shortly accomplished in Canada (I know some of the Temperance men of that Province—they are resolute, persevering men—and they will not be balked), and in New Brunswick. Shall it not be simultaneously accomplished here?

" As to the practicability and effect of the measure, take the Hon. Neil Dow's testimony, given at the last Annual Meeting of the American Temperance Union.

" You may go up and down the State of Maine, and not find a place where liquors are exposed for sale. The wholesale trade in Maine stopped instantly, upon the passage of this law."

" I may remark here, that one of the distillers, whose establishment was thus closed, was afterwards so pleased with the beneficial operation of the law, that he declared, if he had ten distilleries, each worth $10,000, he would willingly give them, to secure such excellent results. That man deserves a niche in the temple of Fame !

" Let us hear Mr. Dow further. ' *The retail trade is now as disreputable as picking pockets or stealing sheep.* An action for libel would lie against a man for calling another ' rumseller,' as quickly as for the other. Intemperance ceased almost immediately, and the begging and wretchedness consequent upon it. They fined the rumseller instead of the drunkard, and filled the lockups, of which there are eighteen in Portland, which were full under the old law, with barrels and demijohns, instead of men. Every respectable man quitted the business when it became unlawful.'

" It may be said that Mr. Dow is a partisan, and that

he will necessarily speak in favour of his own scheme. We can obtain information from other quarters.

" Do you ask, what have been the effects of the law in reference to *crime?* Crime has been reduced 38 per cent. in Lowell, 30 per cent. in Springfield, and even three-fourths in some other places. At Burlington, and other places in Vermont, the jails have been emptied.

" Does your inquiry relate to *pauperism?* At Portland, the amount levied for the relief of the poor has been lowered from five dollars to one—or in that proportion.

" Do you ask about *industry?* The contractors on the St. Lawrence and Atlantic Railroad inform us that whereas before the passing of the law they could not rely on more than two-thirds of any given number of men, because the remainder would be away drinking, they can now depend on from forty-five to forty-eight out of fifty.

" Is *taxation* the object of inquiry? At Fairfield, Maine, a town of 2400 inhabitants, there were eighteen dram-shops. Fourteen of them were closed as soon as the law went into operation; the constables used their peculiar methods of persuasion in closing the others. And now for the fruits. The pauper-tax has been reduced from $1100 to $300. And what have the men of Fairfield done with this saving? They have added $600 to their school-fund. The people of Fairfield are ' wise in their generation.'

" Once more. Is it asked, what have been the effects on *peace* and *order?* The experience of the town of Augusta may be adduced. The police of that town used to be called out a hundred nights in the year. In six months after the law taking effect, they had not been called out once.

" At Agricultural Associations, and public gatherings in general, intemperance formerly prevailed to a great extent. Governor Wright of Indiana attended the last State Fair in Vermont, and expressed his great surprise that during the two days of the fair he had not seen one man drunk. How was that? The Vermont Liquor Law had recently taken effect.

" These few cases are specimens of hundreds of the like kind that might have been produced.

" We do not say that the race of drunkards will be altogether abolished by a prohibitory liquor law. We do not say that there will not be found men determined to perpetuate that race, at all risk, whatever it may cost, and whatever ruin it may bring down upon their fellow creatures. We do not say that rum will not find its way into certain holes and corners, and that depraved beings will not creep into those holes and corners to drink it— even as thieves and murderers perpetrate their deeds of infamy under cover of the darkness. But we do say that, it will be a great thing to drive intoxicating liquors into concealment, and to make it disgraceful to use them. As one has justly remarked—

" Take away the lawfulness of the traffic, and that moment its respectability goes along with it.

" Take away the lawfulness of the traffic, and that moment its morality deserts it.

" Take away the lawfulness of the traffic, and that instant its guilt and criminality become strangely apparent.

" Take away the lawfulness of the traffic, and the outlawed vendor holds rank with the smuggler in an illicit trade."

"It has been said that we are not prepared for the law, and that, if passed, it will not be kept. I deny the fact— and I repel the insinuation. Temperance men have been long prepared, and, as has been already observed, they are no insignificant power in the community. Pass the law, and you will at once find a people prepared to carry it out through all its issues. Those who are indifferent now will take their stand by the law then, because *it is* law. A bad law cannot be sustained : but who will dare to say that Prohibitory Liquor Law is a bad law ? Who will venture to plead for drunkard-manufactories ? Who will be so far forgetful of himself, and so lost to all sense of honor and right as to maintain that it is a violation of freedom to deprive a man of the power of impoverishing and ruining his neighbour—body and goods—mind and heart—for time and eternity ? No ! All honourable and true-hearted men will proclaim it a good law, and will watch over it and secure its observance. I have not so mean an opinion of the people of Nova Scotia as to fear a contrary result.

" This, Gentlemen, is our case. We maintain, that the use of intoxicating liquors is extensively injurious to society—that the attempt to regulate and control the sale of those liquors by legislative enactments has proved an utter failure—and that the suppression of the traffic, except for certain specified purposes, is the only sure remedy.

" Gentlemen of the Legislature,—Petitions for the suppression of this traffic are about to be presented to you, containing upwards of thirty thousand signatures of the people of Nova Scotia ; and we could tell you of many thousands more, who, though their names are not appended to the petitions, desire from their inmost souls the success of the cause. The petitioners are of all ranks, and of every profession, calling, and religious denomination in the province. Among them are many drunkards, who, while they confess their inability to resist the temptation, will hail the passage of the law as the harbinger of their deliverance. Some of them are actually engaged in the traffic. So general is the desire for a prohibitory

19

law, that in some places only one in ten, in others only one in twenty-five have declined to sign the petitions. There has not been shown such unanimity before in this country, on any subject whatever. These, then, are the petitions of *the people*—not of a few, nor of the minority. We are assured that nine-tenths of the adult population of Nova Scotia are in favour of the proposed law. Public opinion was never so loudly, so generally expressed. Surely, the old adage is now verified—*vox populi, vox Dei :*—we trust that you will reverently obey.

"This is not the first time your interference has been sought. Again and again have the friends of Temperance entreated you to interpose—though as yet without success. We approach you once more—in greater numbers—and in full confidence that we shall at length prevail. The request we prefer is no selfish one. We ask for no grant of public money ;—we ask for no favour—no monopoly—no exclusive rights—no preference over others. But we ask you to do a patriotic deed ;—to free your country from an intolerable nuisance ;—to hear the prayers of the wretched ones who implore your aid ;—and to promote the health and happiness of the people, the general prosperity of the country, and the interests of knowledge, morality, and religion, by giving the sanction of law to a measure which is as just as it is generous,—which will benefit all, and do harm to none.

" What is our desire for Nova Scotia and its inhabitants ? We long to see our country freed, wholly freed from the bondage and curse of intemperance :—her statesmen and judges, and magistrates, free—her halls of legislation and her civic councils, free—her clergy, and physicians, and lawyers, free—her merchants, free—her yeomen, and all the people, free—all free !

" And that this our desire may be accomplished, we ask you, Gentlemen, to grant the prayer of the petitions which will be presented to you, and to give the country a *sound, unmistakeable, efficacious* PROHIBITORY LIQUOR LAW."

To show the kindly feeling toward him by the other active workers in the same good cause, a resolution passed at a meeting of the Grand Division in 1866 is also added. And it is worthy of note that those noble men, banded together to overthrow the common enemy of the common country, did not allow any difference in politics or creeds to stand in the way of kindly regard, or harmonious action for the common weal.

" *To the Most Worthy Associate, Rev. Dr. Cramp.*

"WORTHY BRO.:—

" Your brothers of this Grand Division, in Grand Division assembled, beg to congratulate you on your elevation to the office of Most Worthy Associate of the National Division of North America; and would express our pleasure that to you has been committed the supervision of the several Grand Divisions of the British American Provinces during the divisional term.

" We would embrace the opportunity, while thus tendering to you our congratulations, to give expression to our admiration of your wisdom and ability evinced in advancing the interests of our Order, and of your zeal and devotion in the cause of Temperance.

" We cannot overlook the fact that, notwithstanding the multitudinous duties of your profession, your venerable presence has frequently graced the sessions of this Grand Division, guiding us in our deliberations with words of wisdom.

" That you may long continue ' a live member of our

Order, wearing the honors and performing the duties of the several branches with which your name has been so long and so honorably associated,' is our sincere prayer.

" Be pleased, therefore, to receive our hearty congratulations, in Love, Purity, and Fidelity.

"HENRY A. TAYLOR,
"Grand Worthy Patriarch.

"PATRICK MONAGHAN,
" Grand Scribe.

"North Sydney, C.B., 25th July, 1866."

# CHAPTER XV.

*SERVICES RENDERED IN AID OF THE MISSIONARY CAUSE.*

" With others, he held one end of the rope by which the Missionaries descended the shaft, to work the gold mine that had been opened in the distant East."—KIRTLAND.

Missionary effort, in all its branches, always received a large share of attention and interest from Dr. Cramp, but perhaps his greatest enthusiasm on this subject, was reserved for the Foreign Missionary enterprise. This can be traced back to a very early period in his history, as, in the year 1819, we find the young pastor of Dean Street Church seriously weighing the important question of personal consecration to that department of labor in the Redeemer's Kingdom.

A visit from Mr. Ward, of Serampore, one of "The Immortal Three,"—Carey, Marshman and Ward—seems to have been the means of arousing greater earnestness, and awakening feelings on this subject of which he had hitherto been unconscious.

The occasion was the week of Missionary Anniversaries, held in London, and the record of each

day, in the journal of that period, is of special interest, as affording some insight into motives and
desires that had much influence all through life.

On June 25, 1819, he writes :—

"This has been indeed a glorious week, which, I trust,
I shall long remember with gratitude. . . On Wednesday morning we met in the City of London Tavern,
to hold the Anniversary of the Baptist Missionary Society.
It was, on the whole, a pleasing time. At eleven o'clock
we met at Great Queen Street Chapel, Lincoln's Inn
Fields. Mr. Edmonds preached from Rom. xvi., 14, 15.
The sermon was too argumentative and too long, extending to an hour and three quarters. But the crowning
part was the presence of Mr. Ward, one of our missionaries from Serampore. I cannot describe my feelings
when I saw him ascend the pulpit stairs after the sermon.
There is so much Apostolic simplicity in his countenance,
and so much seriousness and fervor in his address, that
one cannot but be interested in him. He delivered a
short address after the sermon, and concluded in prayer.
In the evening, we met at Zion Chapel, which was completely filled by six o'clock. Mr. Ward preached from
Acts xxvi., 18. 'From the power of Satan unto God.' It
was rather an address than a sermon, describing the influences of Satan on the principles and practices of the
heathen world, in a strain of animated and pathetic eloquence, which affected the audience in a manner which I
never saw equalled before. £330 were collected in the
day for the mission. Thursday evening, at six o'clock, we
met at Albion Chapel, Moorfields, when an encouraging
report was read on the state of the Mission. Prayers
were offered, and a Missionary address delivered by Mr.
Ward. This also was a delightful time, and £60 were
collected. This morning I reached the tavern between

five and six o'clock, where we breakfasted, and held the meeting of the Irish Society, which lasted till between eleven and twelve o'clock. A very interesting report was read, and excellent speeches delivered ; among them was one from Mr. Ward. Some thoughts I must notice. The chief thing insisted on by Mr. Ward, in his addresses, has been the necessity of Divine influence; he has been to India, and seen the necessity, and seems, indeed, full of the subject. Many of us will have learned an important lesson from this. Again, at these meetings my mind has been more affected than it ever has been before. I seem to have attained a greater degree of spiritual sensibility. God be praised for it.

" Once more ; my Missionary feelings are more roused ; I cannot tell how I feel, but it is very sensibly for the salvation of the heathen. Sixty millions of British subjects in Bengal, perishing in idolatry—what a thought! If I love Christ, and the souls of men, what can I say but ' Here am I, send me. ' My mind is all confusion. I am looking up to the Lord,—many difficulties stand in the way : He will direct me."

Returning to his own quiet field, ministerial engagements seem again wholly to engross every hour, but thought was busy, as the following reference to the subject reveals :—

" My mind is still incessantly occupied with thoughts on the heathen. A pamphlet, written by Messrs. Hall and Newell, American Missionaries, has increased the flame. I desire to give myself up to God ; for His work, whether at home or abroad. I am utterly insufficient. The importance of my office sometimes presses on me with great weight, and if it has no other effect, I trust this will result, that I am made more prayerful. When I think on the heathen, their wretched condition, and the small number of Christian missionaries (494 among 600,000,000 immortal souls) my soul is all on fire, and I long to be the instrument, in the hands of God, of rescuing them from their degraded condition. I flatter myself that I could be of some use in forwarding the translations, and seem quite ready to go as soon as Providence opens the way. On the other hand, I consider my situation at Dean Street, the manner in which the Great Head of the Church is blessing my labors, and the attachment that exists between the people and myself. To this I add my endearing connections at home, and the difficulties and dangers of a missionary life. Putting these things together, I scarcely know what to do, and yet I trust I have so learned Christ, that whatever may prove evidently to be His will, will also be mine, whether it be to stay or go: for the indications of His will, I am seeking, and shall say nothing to anyone for sometime. It may be only a momentary excitement; if so, it will, in time, subside.

" I wish my motives to be pure, whatever my final determination. In order to possess myself fully with every view of the subject, I am reading the periodical accounts, in which I find much instruction and profit."

Though so evidently his heart's desire at this time, the guidance thus earnestly sought, did not point to foreign service.

He was to influence others, and impart much of the eager enthusiasm that in after life glowed as fervently as in these early days, but the Master had chosen other portions of His vineyard for him to cultivate, and the servant had only one wish—to do his appointed work wherever placed Many circumstances combined to strengthen and perpetuate the deep interest always felt.

Mrs. Cramp's father, Mr. Burls, was for a long period closely identified with the Baptist Missionary Society, and the following record taken from a Memorial published at the time of his death, shows the extent of services rendered by him, which, doubtless, brought the subject into constant prominence among his family connections :—

" At an early period of the history of the Baptist Mission, Mr. Burls' name appears as a member of its committee. He was, in fact, for some time the only member resident in London, the affairs of the society being then managed by brethren in the country, and chiefly by the ministers composing the Northamptonshire Association. Having become acquainted with Mr. Fuller, a very affectionate friendship was soon formed between them, which was productive of much advantage to the mission.

" Mr. Burls' services were many and great. His extensive knowledge of business, his prudence and sound judgment, qualified him for great usefulness to the society.

" Acting for many years as agent for the mission in London (and he held the office of treasurer in the years 1819 and 1820), its pecuniary concerns were much benefitted by his activity and wise management. By allowing the missionaries in India to draw their bills upon him, and thus becoming personally responsible in their respective amounts ; by receiving at his house the ministers who, at that time, annually visited the Metropolis to collect subscriptions, and by various other acts of generous hospitality and zeal, he evinced the lively interest which he felt in the society, and his concern to consecrate to the Lord his talents and substance. On the occasion of the fire at Serampore, he collected in London nearly one thousand pounds towards repairing the loss ;

such efforts procured for him the confidence and esteem of his associates in this good work.

" Sutcliff, Ryland, and others, whose memory is blessed, were his fellow-laborers and friends, and Fuller said of him, 'Mr. Burls is himself a host.' His exertions on behalf of the society were continued with unabated zeal till his retirement from active life, and he manifested to the last a deep concern for its success."

Such an example could not but enlist the ardent sympathy of one so like-minded as Mr. Cramp, and, doubtless, added another link to the chain of influences that became stronger as years passed on. A visit from Rev. W. Knibb (called " the friend of the enslaved"), while residing at Thanet, and, later on, during the pastorate at Hastings, an interview with Rev. J. M. Philippo, aroused interest in another branch—the Jamaica Mission—a correspondence being maintained with the last named missionary till the close of Mr. Phillippo's long and useful life.

Missionary literature always occupied a large department in the library ; every available source of information being carefully consulted, when new fields were opened up, and, as in turn the toiling heralds passed on to their reward, the records of their lives added fresh inspiration. During many changes, at each successive stage of his history, an unvarying attachment to the cause led to constant effort in its behalf, combined with endeavors to arouse the same interest in others. Shortly after coming to reside in Wolfville, the monthly missionary meeting came under Dr. Cramp's direction, and was conducted by him until his retirement from public labor. To maintain and increase the interest of these services, (held on the first Sunday evening of each month) became an object of constant endeavor.

Numerous were the publications laid under tribute for this purpose, and very wide-spread, and unsectarian the information presented to the large and appreciative congregation that usually assembled. Many will remember the enthusiasm with which the attention of the hearers was directed to whitening harvest-fields, and the persuasive eloquence employed to enforce the need of more laborers. Some, now bearing the burden and heat of the day,—successful workers in far distant India and China,—attribute their first determination to enter on this course to the unanswerable arguments and earnest pleading then used to enforce the great commission.

After his resignation of the presidency of Acadia College, having more leisure at his command, Dr. Cramp devoted much time to missionary correspondence, especially after the formation of an independent mission by the Baptists of the Maritime Provinces. From the beginning of that enterprise, he entered into its details with characteristic ardor.

When the band of missionaries first left in 1873, he went with them to New York, finding great satisfaction in rendering such assistance and comfort as his presence afforded, "accompanying them to the ship" with cheerful words of encouragement.

He then undertook the office of foreign secretary, but apart from the necessary correspondence of a business nature, his letters, expressive of personal sympathy in their work, were numerous and much valued.

Writing shortly after their departure, he thus addresses Rev. R. Sanford :—

"WOLFVILLE, Dec. 1, 1873.

" I suppose that you are now on the ocean, proceeding, under God's care, to your destination. Few missionaries sail under such pleasing auspices. You have not only a pleasant company of your own, but a duplicate in that of your American friends, and there is no reason why you should not become for the time being, a united, happy family. I trust that your highest wishes in this respect will be realized, so that it may not be unlikely that you will be almost sorry when the voyage is ended, because parting-time will come. I shall rejoice to hear also that there has been a commencement of missionary work on board, and that, at any rate, you have been able to keep up worship and ' edify one another.' Be assured that you are remembered, all of you, in many a church, and at many a family altar. God forbid that we should cease to pray for you."

Also, to Rev. G. Churchill,—

" This will find you at Rangoon, in the first bustle of inquiry and preparation. All is new, but it does not follow that ' all is beautiful.' Strange it may be, and awkward, perhaps repulsive; but all that is expected. You have not gone to Burmah or to Siam to be pleased— but to be profited, and to be useful.

" The preparatory work is rather a long process, and in some respects it is dull; but all work for God is good,

and our translators, who must have had many a dull
season in the search for proper words and phrases, could
only be helped on by that thought. Cheer up, therefore,
and believe that 'grace sufficient' will be ready at hand,
as new cares and trials present themselves."

Again, to Mr. C., on the subject of Preparation.

" . . . Perhaps you are sometimes depressed on
account of slow progress. It takes so much time to get
ready for actual work. There is so little that can be
really done during this preparatory process. That is
true; but the time spent in preparation is not lost time;
it is the Master's time, and spent in His service. It is
necessarily so employed, because there is now no miraculous fitness to be attained. The Apostles were under
preparation during the whole period of the Saviour's
public life; and, even then, they had to 'tarry at Jeru-
salem' till they should be 'endued with power from on
high.' Paul had to spend three years, or thereabouts,
in Arabia, where he went to school to the Saviour
Himself, and proved a remarkably apt scholar.

"Under some circumstances, God's servants have to
occupy situations not at all pleasant or agreeable, in
order that they may attain the knowledge and experience which their actual life's labour requires. It is
enough, however, if fitness be realized, whatever may
be the cost."

The country of Siam had been at first thought
of as the probable field for the establishment of
the new mission, and a long time was spent in
exploring several districts before any decision
could be arrived at. Much difficulty and perplexity had to be encountered, under which the
missionaries are thus encouraged:—

" You are now engaged, I presume, in exploration.

You will probably meet with questions difficult of solution, and may be embarrassed by perplexities which will be puzzling to human wisdom. But there are two considerations of a relieving character. One is, there are four of you, each possessing a peculiarity of talent and qualification, and all bringing what they have into the common stock. The darkness that appals one, may be looked at hopefully by a second, and penetrated by a third, and contemplated at last by all four with gratitude and joy and united 'Ebenezers.' The second consideration is that God Himself is your friend, by His Word, which is a lamp to your feet at all times, casting light on all subjects,—and, by His gracious permission, to carry all doubts to the throne of grace, where they may be dissolved much more easily and quickly than had been feared. . . . There are, no doubt, special difficulties connected with the enterprise, for Siam is one of the devil's strongholds; but it has to be undermined or stormed, as the Lord shall direct, and perhaps our detachment is to be the forlorn hope. Be it so, I trust you are all prepared to take your stations, relying on the power and faithfulness of the Great Captain of our salvation. Some may fall in this war; but dying in Christ's work is an honourable death, which will be followed by 'glory and honour' in the next world—not as the rewards of merit, but as the gracious bestowment of Him whose 'Well done, good and faithful servant' is the highest distinction that man can receive. . . . We are waiting now for the results of your exploration. The hardness of the task should not deter us,—God's grace and spirit will be as mighty there as elsewhere, but always by the *preaching of the Gospel;* the cross of Christ is the only medicine for human disease in all lands; it is unpalatable to depraved taste, but it must be taken, and nothing else will cure."

To Mrs. Churchill.

"We have entered on another year, the events of which are all unknown to us. Offering you the usual salutations of the season, I conjoin with them the expression of hope that it may be an active and useful year in a missionary point of view. What may be the year's developments, we cannot tell, but, standing ready to follow the Lord's guidance, we may feel confident of a favourable issue. No doubt, you are desirous of direct missionary effort. May you not begin, as soon as your knowledge of the language will allow, with individuals, after the pattern of the Zenana work in India? So that, before your husband shall be able to preach to a congregation, you may talk to the women. If you get the ear of one only, it will be a blessed thing. The work is hard and difficult, I know, and Buddhism is like the Chinese great wall, an effectual barrier—yet not effectual against the power of the Lord. As soon as possible, it will be desirable to talk the Gospel by the narration of its main facts. Why did the Son of God become a man and die? Let some curiosity be excited. Genuine enquiry may follow, and the usual process of conviction take place. What a joy it will be to have a Siamese woman exclaim, 'What must I do to be saved?' and then to guide her to the Cross! I hope you will have many experiences of that gladness."

Again :—

"I shall hope to hear favourable accounts when the brethren return. But we must be prepared for difficulties, discouragements, and temporary failures. Such has been the history of the Church in all ages. Can we wonder at it? Our object is to turn men from darkness to light, from the power of Satan to God. It is not to be supposed that we shall have a smooth and easy time of it, or that the enemy will allow us to go wholly unmolested. He is a very dull scholar, or he would have learned by this time that the Church is always a gainer by trials, and that if he wished her to be useless it would be wise to let her alone. To the individual Christian,

'Trials make the promise sweet.'

And Churches often find that God has chosen them in the furnace of affliction. These remarks will not have a disheartening effect upon you, but they may possibly help you to look forward to Assher's blessing—Deut. xxxiii., 25. It comes to all God's servants, and suits all their circumstances."

"July 23, 1875.

"The hospitable reception you met with at St. Thomas must have been doubly cheering under your circumstances. How easy it is for the Lord to touch the hearts of those to whom He has given the means, so that His children may be well provided for. Abraham did well to call the name of the place Jehovah-Jireh, 'The Lord will see, or will provide;' it matters not which translation is taken, for with Him to *see* is to *provide*. Our God bears the name still, and we do well to trust Him. 'I will trust and not be afraid,' said one of the good men of olden time. Adopt it as your motto—not in word only, but in act and habit, and yours will be the experience of Phil. iv., 6-7.

" . . . So various are God's dispensations, yet always just and wise and good,—and the good exists, though we do not always see it. The Hebrew choir in the Temple was continually singing, 'Praise the Lord, for He is good, and His mercy endureth forever.' Let us always believe it."

Some disappointment was felt by Dr. Cramp

when the enterprise, as far as Siam was concerned, seemed hopeless, and had to be abandoned, the mission being finally established
among the Telugus. He thus expresses his
unabated interest in their surroundings:—

To Rev. R. Sanford.

"Nov. 15, 1875.

" . . . I shall be glad to receive any remarks or
information respecting the structure of the Telugu language. I wish to become as well acquainted as possible
with everything *Indian*. In my early years, I read all
that was published by our English Baptist Missionary
Society in their 'Periodical Accounts,' and gained a
pretty accurate knowledge of Hinduism and its effects.
I am revising and correcting that knowledge by the
perusal of modern publications. You will find that
Hinduism produces as deep moral debasement as
Buddhism, and that the system of *caste* is a diabolical
obstruction to improvement and freedom. When the
first convert was baptized, one of the missionaries
exclaimed, 'The chain of *caste* is broken! Who can
mend it?' Alas! the breakage is very slight and local.
Nothing but the power of God can destroy that institution. Meanwhile, it is our duty to promote intellectual
improvement, and to seek the emancipation of our
fellow-men from slavery of all kinds."

Writing to a member of his family on this subject, about the same time, events transpiring in
India are thus referred to :—

" . . . The native Christians of Calcutta, of all
denominations, held a meeting the other day, and
formed a plan of a *United Church*—government Episcopal, modified by Presbyterianism and Congregational-

20

ism; the Bishop to have about the same power as the Moderator of a Presbytery; baptism *to be by immersion*, and infant baptism *optional*. *This is progress!*

"I take the *Friend of India*, from which I gather a large amount of information respecting that part of the world."

The following words of counsel, as regards theological training among the new converts, may not be without interest:—

". . . You have some young men under tuition. I may remind you of two points of importance—

"1. Teach the laws of Scripture interpretation. The Bible is a peculiar book in contents, style and manner; its figurative language requires special attention. . . . I dare say the Easterns think us Westerns rather dull and cold; on the other hand, we Westerns deem the Easterns somewhat wild, luscious and fiery. We need the old motto, '*Medio tutissimus ibis.*' 2. It will be very useful to initiate the young men into the exposition of Scripture by giving examples of running commentaries, and showing them how to find out the meaning of the sacred writers, and the truths taught by them. A concordance is almost necessary to success in this exercise, and it is not likely that you have one yet in Telugu. But you can help them by using your English book. The object of theological instruction is to teach the student how to ascertain *for himself* the truths inculcated by Paul, Peter and John.

" . . . The theological system you introduce must be thoroughly *biblical*. The question is not what *we think*, but what *God teaches*,—and to that teaching there must be absolute submission; it is not ours to *reason*, but to *believe* and *obey*. The importance of a right beginning in this matter cannot be over-estimated.

"   .   .   .   This reminds me of a duty which ought to be regarded by missionaries, and which is better attended to now than it was in the early years of missionary effort. I refer to the training of converts in benevolence and activity. Formerly, they were expecting to have everything done for them ; but a gratifying change has been accomplished, particularly in the American missions, and the liberality of many of their Churches is very exemplary. In new missions, it is exceedingly desirable to begin well. I would not import into them the plans and usages of our Churches, and expect them to be adopted as authoritative. I would rather join them in an independent inquiry into New Testament order, both in regard to belief and practice, and advise the adoption of such methods as should be found to come nearest to the Divine pattern.

"Converts should be taught how to manage church affairs for themselves."

Towards the close of the year 1876, the sad intelligence of the death of the Rev. A. R. Crawley was received, and is thus referred to :—

"WOLFVILLE, Oct. 15, 1876.

"The first thought is *death. Brother Crawley is dead.* He died at Liverpool, England, on Monday last, the 9th inst. He was one of the best missionaries that America has produced. Born in 1830 ; graduated, 1849 ; ordained, 1853. I gave him the charge at his ordination. The Churches in Burmah will mourn greatly. Brother Crawley entered the college in April, 1844, being then fourteen years of age, so that he was only forty-six when he died " in the midst of his days."

"We might have reasonably hoped for fifteen or twenty years more of work, that is, for a person of ordinary strength of constitution. All we can say is, It was the will of God.     .

"There are ulterior purposes to be wrought out by this dispensation which will be developed years hence, though *when* and *how* we know not. Yet those purposes are 'unfolding every hour,' and is it not a marvellous thing that the great God overrules all mortal things and manages our mean affairs? To think that our insignificant lives and histories form part in the grand schemes of Heaven, and are known and calculated on, and planned out, so that every event occurs at the fixed time, and falls into its proper place, and accomplishes its pre-ordained purpose—bringing us worms of the earth into fellowship with the 'High and exalted One,' gives dignity to man, and invests the Redemption with glory unspeakable. Perhaps you sometimes feel a sense of isolation and loneliness, as though you were away and forgotten. Do not dwell on it. The Churches here remember you constantly,—at family altars, and social gatherings, and public assemblies—and you can say of the Father in Heaven, 'The Lord thinketh upon me.' We cannot understand it, but we are assured of the fact. Comprehended or not, we have a place in the mind and heart of God, and he never forgets any one! Therefore, "comfort one another with these words." I do not feel inclined to write on any other subject. This death reminds us of first principles; we have an interest in God—God has an interest in us. Let us cleave to Him 'with purpose of heart,' and 'work while it is called to-day.' "

## Rev. R. Sanford (Later).

"I was getting anxious about you, fearing that you might be attacked by the Jeypore fever, and was very thankful to hear of your safety. You live in a country of perils, and may be stricken down any day; and yet, on the other hand, some men live to be old in India.

Dr. Carey left England in 1793, and never revisited it. He died in 1834, in his 73rd year. Dr. Marshman was within a few months of 70 when he died. The servant of God is 'immortal till his work is done.' We need not trouble ourselves about the length of life, or the time and manner of death, ' my times are in Thy hand.' We shall work for God as long as He pleases to employ us, and He will not dismiss us before that time."

## Rev. R. Sanford.

" Nov. 6, 1876.

" Mr. T., I observe, dwells at length on the desirableness of preventing the native preachers from becoming spoiled by association with white men. Let them be enlightened, and suitably qualified for their work, but let them retain their native simplicity—habits—mode of life, let them live among the people, and be especially careful to shun everything like a professional air. The Gospel is plain and powerful, so must its preachers be."

## To the same.

" Nov. 10, 1877.

"The last point referred to in your latest communication was the famine. The telegraphic reports from India on that subject are more favourable, a fruitful rain-fall having taken place, insomuch that contributions to the fund at the Mansion House (now amounting to £450,000 sterling) are no more called for; but it may be expected that individual cases of great distress may still continue to occur, and it is very desirable that ministers should be able to administer relief in instances coming under their own notice. The Baptist Missionary Society recently remitted £300 to their missionaries for this purpose, and other societies have taken similar step. I sent a letter to the *Christian Messenger*, recommending the Churches to take collections for this object, and that the proceeds be remitted to our missionaries, to be applied at their discretion. Something will be done. The treasurer will send to you whatever amounts he may receive, and it will be gratifying if, thereby, you should be able to render assistance to some who might be overlooked in the formal distribution."

Some plans for increased liberality are adverted to in the following letter to Rev. G. C. Churchill:

" . . . It is difficult to invent any plan by which all the membership of our Churches should be brought into simultaneous and voluntary action. If a government determines to procure 5000 dollars in a district, it levies a tax on the several properties, sufficient for the purpose, and the thing is done; but we have no power to levy a tax, and a voluntary tax is a kind of anomaly. There is a general impression that we are *able* to raise the money needed, but many persons are much more willing to 'believe that others have the requisite ability, than that they themselves have it;' nevertheless, it may be surely hoped that there will be found religion enough in the churches to furnish the money called for. Revived godliness, made permanent, would meet the case,—for christians would be ' willing of themselves,' as they were in Apostolic times. So it must be the Lord's work, after all, and that means that we must be brought into a state of preparedness to do whatever the Master bids, to give whatever He requires, to go wherever He directs, and to suffer whatever He may lay upon us ; that is, whenever all believers are really willing that the Lord shall do as He pleases with them and theirs, things will be well in Zion; but it must come to that, *all* have to come to it, at home and abroad. We are living in the dispensation of the Spirit, and it will appear that the Spirit has *power*."

"Aug. 7, 1876.
" *To the same.*

"When I read your last letter and noted what vexations you endured through the laziness of your workmen, and how you felt it necessary to take up the tools and use your own energies and skill, I found myself pursuing a train of reflections on the duty and pleasnre of employing in the Lord's cause all the opportunities and acquirements we may possess. They are all entrusted to us, and may some day come into use. You little thought, when you learned the use of tools, that the time would come when the Master would call for the employment of your skill, individually, for the promotion of His cause. Yet so it was, and when you handled the plane, the hammer, the chisel, etc., on that occasion, you really handled them for Christ, and did missionary work. It is pleasant and profitable to bear in mind that we are trustees for the Lord, in regard to whatever gratification or power He may have bestowed upon us. All is ' by Him,' and all is ' for Him ;' and it is condescension in Him to make any use of us and ours for the advancement of His interests. So let us ever be watching for opportunities of doing something for the Lord. A rich man one day said to me, ' Mine is the meanest of talents,—only gold and silver dust—yet the Saviour condescends to use it, and I am thankful that it shonld be so employed ;' you may say the same of your tools."

Under the pressure of severe illness, Mr. and Mrs. Churchill are addressed in a joint letter, as follows :—

"WOLFVILLE, Jan. 11, 1880.

" I had intended to write to you in the first week of the year, but was hindered. It is not, however, too late to express the usual wish of ' many happy returns.' And how are they to be obtained? God knows *how*. Perhaps the sharp afflictions you have been called to endure, have something to do with it. You remember the text ' Every branch that beareth fruit, He purgeth it,' and you may possibly remember Cecil's anecdote of the tree *cut almost through*, which, before the cutting, bore leaves only,— afterwards it bore fruit. The pruning is followed by the fruit-bearing. Such is the Lord's method—and it is as kind as it is *wise*. You will know how to apply all this to your individual cases.

"I hope to hear soon that a physician has been found, and that his prescriptions and treatment have proved success- . ful by God's blessing. I was told that your particular want was a skilled physician, but that for a time there was none at hand. But our Heavenly Helper is always at hand. He said, ' I am with you always." Do we heartily be-lieve it? And does our belief show itself in confiding expectant prayer.' Surely the Apostles expressed the need of every day, and every place, when they said, increase our faith.' Let us not forget that the Lord He means all says—all He promises—and always keeps His word, *according to our faith*, as Jesus often said when they went to Him to be healed,—He is ready, whether we are, or not.

. . . "We, none of us, aim high enough, or draw large enough drafts on the Divine Bank. There, as Montgomery says, is ' enough for all, enough for each, enough for evermore.,

" But we don't seem to think so ; we are familiar with *peradventures*, and forget the *shalls* and *wills* of our God, and His ever-abounding graciousness in regard to prayer.

"I am glad to hear from the reports of some who have visited Bobbilli, that your town is a healthy, well-built place, and that your compound is in a good spot. I trust you will both be spared by the Lord's mercy, to occupy it, with renovated health, and with increasing usefulness. May it be the birthplace of many souls."

"WOLFVILLE, Oct. 31, 1881.

"Your last was very acceptable. I would advise you to keep your eye on those men of different tribes to whom you refer. Your further acquaintance with them may lead to interesting developments respecting Indian religion and morals. If any further information is obtained, favour me with the particulars. I believe that we are still very ignorant of much of the interior of the Brahminical religion, and its influence on character. The Hindoos have the credit of a philosophical turn of mind; but I should judge that their lower classes are at a considerable remove from anything that can be truly called philosophy. You are not likely to gain further insight into their arcana. · · · "You have had trials in many forms, and if the Lord keeps you still in the valley of humiliation, it will be for good issues. See Rom. viii., 28. · · · "My own health is as good as can be expected by a man who is between eighty and ninety. I am getting weaker daily, and have ceased to go up and down stairs, my library and bed-room being on the same floor. The grave will be lower still. I shall soon be there. Let us all ' lay hold on eternal life,' and seek daily to be better prepared for it!

"Grace and peace be with you, and with the dear children.

"Yours faithfully,

"J. M. CRAMP."

The time was drawing very near when these expectations were to be realized. A few sentences expressing the writer's views with regard to future knowledge and service, taken from a letter on this subject, may suitably close this series of extracts :—

"We are accustomed to speak of Heaven as a state of rest. It is rather a changed state of work. 'His servants serve Him' there. *Here*, we do not understand the nature of heavenly work, only that it is doing something for God. Still it is action. We are living in wonderful times. There will be re-actions and struggles—for error, and evil die hard; but we are on the eve of still greater events, and those who reach Heaven, will not be ignorant of them, for the branch of the Church in Heaven is acquainted with the general history of the branch on earth, and celebrates its triumphs in hymns of joy."

The Rev. W. B. Boggs, now Principal of the Theological Institution at Ramapatam, India, was associated with this mission in its early history. Many letters of this period were addressed to him, chiefly occupied with the special characteristics of the efforts then contemplated in Siam, one of which offers the following suggestions:—

"WOLFVILLE, Nov. 30, 1874.

. . · "Although I know not where you are, I take it for granted that the quickest way to find you is to send this to Bangkok.

"I take this first opportunity of writing to place before you some facts and considerations.

"It appears that the Karens in Siam are not more than 50,000 in number.

It further appears that they are scattered over a wide extent of country, reaching to some hundreds of miles.

"It also appears that they are very wandering in their habits, and indisposed to settled abodes. Their villages are very few.

"All this being assured, the inference is, that it would be unwise and useless to expend all our missionary strength on the Karens. The proper policy, I think, will be to select a spot where a sufficient number of them may be found, to warrant the establishment of a school, and which may be near enough to other collections of Karens, to furnish employment for the native preachers, who are intending to pass into Siam with our missionaries. *They may be immediately engaged in the work.* .

" I would suggest that the brethren and sisters now in Savoy and Rangoon, might undertake the *Karen department.*

" With regard to brother and sister Churchill, yourself, and Mrs. Boggs, I think that a *Siamese Department* should be established, and that it should be located at Bangkok, or its vicinity. That city must be the base of operations and the source of supplies.

"I would say, therefore, settle there, learn the languages, acquaint yourselves with the people, study Buddhism in its effects, and prepare to show the blinded ones the 'more excellent way of the Gospel.'

"I would advise, if this course be adopted, that you establish yourselves where you may form your own plans and carry them out according to your own judgments."

" I greatly long to see a successful attack on Buddhism in Siam; far be it from us to dream of Buddhism being impregnable. The Lord be with you."

Long after, when the busy pen was laid aside, Mr. Boggs thus refers to Dr. Cramp in the *Christian Messenger* of March 8, 1882 : —

" Dr. Cramp, my reverend and beloved father, instructor, and benefactor, he also has fallen asleep in Christ. What a full, and rich, and beautiful life of Christian faith and Christian service! Truly, ' the memory of the just is blessed.'

" The steady, well-directed, indefatigable labors of a

long period; the rich productiveness of his earnest efforts; the eminently evangelical, scriptural character of his ministry; his genuine, living piety; the genialness of his social life, and the calm lustre of his closing years, leave behind them a pathway of light, like the setting sun, where he sinks beyond a cloudless horizon.

"I cannot here express the high esteem, the reverence and the love with which I regarded Dr. Cramp.

"His instructions were eminently practical and useful. I have lately been looking over, with deeper interest than ever, the course of lectures which he delivered to the ministerial students in the college and academy twenty years ago.

"I never went to him without being received with the kindness of a father, and with just the wise counsel and encouragement that I needed.

"When my desire to obtain an education became known to him, and also the fact that the question of pecuniary means was one that caused some hesitation, he wrote to my parents, saying, 'If you send your son to college, I will supply him with all the text-books he requires.' That promise was fulfilled with unchanging kindness during the five and a half years that I spent at Wolfville.

"It was the monthly missionary concert, conducted by Dr. Cramp during all the time that I was at Horton, which, more than anything else, stirred up in me that desire to engage in Foreign Missionary service which has since been realized. These meetings always made a deep impression on me, and many a Sunday evening his earnest words concerning the Redeemer's last command, and the appalling spiritual wants of the heathen nations, followed me to 'the Hill,' and kept me thinking till late at night.

'He possessed, in large measure, the true missionary

spirit. Being intimately acquainted with that apostolic missionary movement, which was represented in India by such men as the 'Immortal Three of Serampore,' and in England by such grand leaders as Fuller, Ryland, Sutcliff, and others, he was ever ready to advocate and labor for this greatest of all Christian enterprises. His hearty sympathy with the cause of missions finds appropriate expression in his beautiful 'Memoir of Madame Feller.'

"I am about to translate into Telugu, for the use of our native ministers, his lectures on 'Ministerial and Pastoral Duties,' which we took in the old college library in 1861, and thus his instructions will go on blessing men of another tongue, and, through them, thousands more.

"By the present prosperous condition of Acadia College, by the labors of many of his students, and in many other ways, he 'being dead yet speaketh,' and his influence will continue to be felt through long succeeding years.

"'Mark the perfect man and behold the upright, for the end of that man is peace.'"

"IN MEMORIAM.

"At a meeting of the Foreign Mission Board of the Baptist Convention of Nova Scotia, New Brunswick and Prince Edward Island, held at St. John, N.B., 9th Dec., 1881, the following preamble and resolutions were passed :—

"*Whereas*,—It has pleased God, the Creator of all, the All-wise Disposer of events, to remove from us by death our venerable and honored brother, the Rev. J. M. Cramp, D.D., for many years a highly esteemed and useful member, as well as an efficient officer of our Board ;

"*Be it Resolved*,—That, while we bow ourselves lowly before this afflictive dispensation and acknowledge the wisdom and righteousness of the Judge of all the earth, yet we are fully conscious that our Board and the Denomination at large sustain a severe loss in the demise of Dr. Cramp, who, by his wise and judicious counsels to his brethren at home, and also to the missionary corps abroad, and by his persistent and zealous advocacy of the claims of the heathen, had rendered himself conspicuous as a friend of the Foreign Mission enterprise.

" The services he rendered to our infant missions were invaluable, and his paternal instruction to our missionaries on the field in his correspondence with them, was weighty, inspiring, and fully appreciated by those addressed.

" His views on matters of business claiming the attention and action of our Board, were characterized by clearness, Christian manliness and admirable good sense. We therefore mourn our brother's removal as a most serious bereavement, and an almost irreparable loss.

"We would also desire to convey our expression of sympathy and condolence to the family of our dear brother, in this hour of their overwhelming sorrow.

"We can only commend them to resort to their fathers' God and Saviour, in whom he trusted for so many years, and who has received him to that presence in which there is fulness of joy forever;

*Resolved,*—That a copy of the foregoing preamble and resolutions be forwarded to the family of the deceased."

# CHAPTER XVI.

## DR. CRAMP AS A PREACHER.

"We must combine Luther with St. Paul. '*Bene orare est bene studuisse*' must be united with St. Paul's 'Meditate upon these things : give thyself wholly to them, that they profiting may appear to all.'"—CECIL.

Our first remark under this head is that he *was* a preacher. If long tenure of office strengthens the claim to a position ; if ability and willingness to discharge the duties incumbent; if love for a work and success therein afford any proof of a divine appointment to a calling, then Dr. Cramp was emphatically a preacher of the Gospel. He began to preach, in the way of exhortation, in 1814, a little over a year after his baptism. His first sermon was at St. Peters, from Eph. iii., 19, when about 18 years of age. He was ordained to the work of the Gospel ministry in May, 1818, as the pastor of Dean street Baptist church, London. From that time till his decease in December, 1881, he continued to magnify his office as a preacher. Whatever other business may have been under-taken or thrust upon him, however pressing other claims, or burdensome other duties, he never found or sought for an excuse for not preaching, when called upon to do it. Whether from a sense of duty in his high calling, or from a hope of accomplishing some good, or from the pleasure which the exercise afforded, or from a mingling of all these motives, the subject of this memoir dearly loved to stand before an audience and proclaim the way of life.

That he made thorough preparation for pulpit exercises, no one who had the opportunity of hearing him frequently could doubt. And yet he was ready, almost at a moment's notice, to enter the pulpit and give an instructive discourse. His familiarity with the Bible, in its historical, devotional and doctrinal aspects, was so great and accurate, that he was never at a loss. His memory, so quick in action and so tenacious in its grasp, that a skeleton of a sermon, once prepared, was ready again for use when the occasion demanded. This readiness was often made available in cases of emergency. At public gatherings, for instance, when the appointed preacher failed through some unexpected event, all anxiety was soon allayed if it was found that Dr. Cramp was present. He was pretty certain to be the one selected to fill the gap, and the service would go on as though no interruption had occurred.

Dr. Cramp's pastoral labors extended over twenty-six years,—from 1818 to 1844—with a short break for rest and the recovery of health between the first and second pastorates. There were nearly three years, beginning in 1824, during which his principal work was of a literary character, in connection with a publishing company in London. The only thing that reconciled him to this change, was the fact that his medical advisers regarded it as necessary on the score of health. The six years of his first pastorate at Dean street, with all the extra work he was performing, had greatly undermined his constitution. Both he and his intimate friends, at that time, feared that his strength was exhausted, and that his working days were few. And yet, during these three years, much preaching was done. For calls to supply vacant pulpits in and around the city were very frequent. But this period of his life was never reviewed with much pleasure. The business of the company with which he was connected became too engrossing, and turned him away too much from the work congenial to his feelings. Some entries in the journal of those days indicate that there was deep regret that the associations, as well as the work, were all tending towards loss of spiritual fervor and zeal for God. It was, however, only a temporary arrangement, and by the time he was again prepared for pastoral labors, the way was opened for another settlement.

From 1827 to 1842 he was co-partner with his father, Rev. Thomas Cramp, at St. Peters, Isle of Thanet. The father was already advanced in years, and the burden of the work rested on the son. The preaching was constant, and greatly appreciated by the people. The time, however, which under the circumstances would have been

21

given to pastoral work, was spent in literary labor. It was during this pastorate that the first edition of the "Text-book of Popery" was published.

Some entries in the journal of this period show how intently the young pastor was longing for more spiritual life in his own soul, and in the Church for which he was laboring. Such, for instance, as the following :—

"July, 1831.—I have been spending some time this morning in self-enquiry, self-examination and prayer. Here I am laboring among the people in conjunction with my father, but there seems to be no good doing. . . . I have recently been much affected by this thought, and my impressions were deepened at our late missionary meeting in London, where we had the pleasure of Mr. Malcolm's company, an American minister, pastor of the Fourth Baptist Church in Boston, U.S. He gave us some cheering and remarkable intelligence respecting the progress of the word of God in that country. Why is not similar progress witnessed here? The enquiry is interesting and important.

"My own impression is that we shall never witness a revival of religion in this land till our Churches themselves are reformed, and that the Churches will not be reformed until their ministers are brought into a state of more lively piety. For myself, I see abundant cause for humiliation. I do not wonder that they (the people) have not been blessed. I only wonder that I am permitted to live and am invited to return to God. What coldness! What omissions! What neglect! How little private and personal godliness! On every hand I discern reasons for God's anger and my own abasement before Him. . . . No wonder that I have been useless, an encumbrance to the ground. Why have I not been rooted up? Adored be the long-suffering of an injured God! I have endeavored to humble myself before Him this morning, confessing my sins. I have asked forgiveness, with grace to reform, and the influences of the Holy Spirit. I trust I do desire to live a different life, to live for God, to realize the truths of the Gospel for myself, to be prepared for usefulness by the teachings and discipline of the Holy Spirit. I wish to surrender myself to God, and to be dealt with as He shall see good. . . . What cause shall I have to bless the Lord if, from this time, a new era should begin of humble and spiritual walking, devotedness, zeal and efficiency!"

Following this, there is a plan laid down, prayerfully made, and carefully drawn up, for the use of means every day to bring about a better state of things both in his own heart and in the community. The above is only a specimen. The diary of those days abounds with them. Honest, intensely earnest, through and through heart-searchings, that every lurking evil might be searched out and rooted up, that nothing might be left, however dear, to stand in the way of progress and usefulness.

This is one phase of the life of Dr. Cramp as a preacher. For it was the contemplation of the solemn and responsible work of the pastor that led to this train of thought. Every Christian ought, indeed, to enquire frequently into the state of his own heart. But he, whose business it is to "feed the flock of God," is under a double obligation to see to it that his own soul is fed,—and the

journal, from which the extract above is taken,
affords convincing proof that the subject of this
memoir attended to that duty, as to all others,
with the intensity of his whole nature. Very few
men have gone through greater struggles of heart,
alone with God, than he. And yet it was so completely " alone with God," that, so far as others
were concerned, it was unnoticed and unknown,
except in its results. And many who, perhaps,
saw the fruit, did not know whence it came. Dr.
Cramp's step was quick, his movements elastic,
his whole bearing, even in the pulpit, cheerful ;
his countenance often beaming with hopefulness ;
his voice ringing, as though there were a great
fund of assurance behind it all. There was very
little, indeed, in any of the externals to give the
impression of one with intense inward struggles.
And yet they were gone through. The battle was
often long and fierce, but, like Jacob with the
angel, he prevailed, and seemed so to come out of
the conflict, that very few even knew that he had
been in it. Not one in a hundred, perhaps, of his
hearers was aware that he chided his own unbelief much more severely than he censured theirs.;
or that it was the deeply-felt want of more warmth
and life in his own soul that prompted his most
earnest words to others as to their formality and
coldness. But his own recorded resolutions and
prayers, that no one ever saw, while he lived,
prove that this was the case ; and these struggles
through which he passed, qualified him all the
better for the positions which he afterwards

filled, as the teacher and guide of young men preparing for the responsible work of preaching Christ, for by his own experience he had found out the difficulties in their way, and what would be the most effectual means of removing them. "Carefully, young brethren," he would say, "watch your own hearts if you would have success in the work of the Lord."

From 1842 to 1844 he was pastor of the church in Hastings, Sussex, during which time, in addition to his ordinary services, he delivered a course of lectures, afterwards published in a book, headed "Lectures for These Times." Here his pastorate labor ended.

### His Style or Manner as a Preacher.

1. It was intensely earnest. His was no mere official discharge of a duty imposed. His effort was not to find something to say which would occupy about the reasonable time of a sermon. It was not an effort, by sounding out platitudes with holy intonations, to delude easy-going piety into the belief that it was being fed with angels' food. There was no priestly mystery in tone or in manner ; no chanting of musical melodies to drive away evil spirits ; no assumption of any special sacredness in the earthen vessel that bore the treasure. The preacher was a man, standing in the presence of men of like passions as his own, and needing the same pardon and grace which he had found. He relied solely upon the power of truth, truth made efficacious by the Spirit of God, and not by thea-

trical performances or human inventions. The truths of the Gospel were, therefore, brought forth and marshalled in order, and put into the simplest language possible, the plainest Saxon speech, uttered in all sober earnestness of one who fully believed God, and designed that others should do the same, if he could persuade them to this course. But the persuasion must come from the truth; not the truth and human emotions accompanying it, but truth and the Spirit of God attending it.

2. The preaching was eminently Scriptural, sometimes doctrinal; the great principles of truth had taken firm hold of his mind. The doctrines, so-called, were dearly loved and strongly held. They had not been received from any human authority. However deeply the works of the old divines had been studied, the "law of the Lord" had been perused still more thoroughly. His intimate acquaintance with the Bible was a source of wonder to many. He strongly recommended the constant use of a concordance to all Bible students, but during the last half of his life, he seldom had occasion to refer to one himself. The Bible, in his hands, seemed almost of itself to open to the passage wanted. He never confounded the language of Isaiah with that of Ezekiel, Matthew with Luke, or Paul with Peter. His quotations, which were frequent, were not only true to the exact meaning of the author, but to the words by which the meaning was expressed.

The fundamental doctrines of the Gospel filled a large place in his thoughts. Man's utter ruin and helplessness ; salvation by grace, through faith in Christ ; the absolute need of regeneration, and that the work of the Spirit of God ; the vicarious sufferings of the Saviour ; a life of entire surrender and consecration, following the acceptance of Christ ; the ultimate triumph of the Gospel ; the absolute safety of all who are in Christ Jesus ; the Church a voluntary union of converted persons and none besides ; the spread of the Gospel to be secured by the voluntary offerings and prayers of the redeemed ; the second coming of Christ ; the resurrection of all the dead ; the eternal blessedness of those who die in the Lord, and the eternal condemnation of those who neglect the great salvation.

These were themes often dwelt upon, and sometimes with great feeling and power ; but there was no human speculation ; there was no attempt at any " philosophy of the plan of salvation "; no logical reasonings as to the Divine scheme of redemption. It was simply—" Thus saith the Lord." He hath spoken, and He will do it. Shall the thing formed say, " Why hast thou made me thus ?" " God is not a man that He should lie, neither the son of man that He should repent," hath He said ; and shall He not do it ? Or hath He spoken, and shall not He make it good? This was the style of Dr. Cramp's preaching. What the Word of the Lord declared, that was ultimate. Man's ability or inability to comprehend or receive it, made no difference with the truth, that liveth and abideth forever.

The effects were, of course, various, according to the state of feeling of the hearer. One personal experience may suffice as an illustration. The sermon was preached in the old Baptist church of Wolfville, in the year 1854. The listener may explain in his own language :—

"I sat in the gallery. I cannot recollect the text. I had long, as I thought, desired to be a Christian. I was walking about Zion and telling the towers thereof, but I could not see the place to enter. There was not to me a logical connection between the different doctrines. I was longing for some system that would take me on from simple axioms to fixed and undeniable conclusions. The preacher held me up as a helpless and guilty sinner, and then declared that my condemnation was certain, and would be just. Here my heart rebelled. ' Helplessness ' and ' just condemnation ' seemed to lack the logical connection,—I became very angry. From an ignorant preacher I could have borne it; but from a learned divine, not so patiently. I rebelled against the doctrines, and thought the preacher very unsympathetic, unfeeling, unkind, and in my heart despaired of ever becoming a Christian. Further on in the discourse, the fullness and the freeness of the great salvation were dwelt upon. In gentle tones, and with sweet, persuasive eloquence, all sinners were invited to come to the fountain. Before the close, a strange and unaccountable tenderness of heart came over me. It was with great difficulty that I controlled my emotions, and then hurried alone to ' my room, to pour out such a flood of penitential tears as never before or since gave vent to my hitherto pent-up feelings.' "

It was *practical* ; even when it was doctrinal, the practical bearing of the doctrines was not forgotten. If these things are so, "what manner of persons ought ye to be in all holy conversation and godliness?" This was the question which sprang naturally out of every great doctrine. To believe the truth aright was to live; and to live was to bring forth all the fruits of holiness. Dr. Cramp was no visionary or sentimental dreamer; the ecstacy that some professed to have experienced was not regarded as of much value, unless the life was moulded into the likeness of the life of Christ. Great doctrines believed, implied great duties discharged; great joy in the salvation, implied great toil in the service,—and it was an abiding grief in his heart that the fruits of holiness, in the lives of professing Christians, did not more fully correspond with the transports talked of. He fully believed that those "called to be saints," were just as loudly called to be workers in the vineyard of the Lord. That all the members of the Church, with their varied gifts and qualifications, were needed for the work, and that if any one of the number failed to perform his part, the whole body must suffer in consequence. As an example of his earnest and practical manner of enforcing the truth, take the following extract:

"Let us, therefore, brethren, humble ourselves before God, confess our sins, mourn over our 'low estate,' and be abashed and weep for the affecting contrast between our privileges and our attainments. Regard Christianity as the religion of the heart, and yield yourselves unhesitatingly to its full influence, to be sanctified in spirit, soul and body. Aim at an elevated standard of piety. Converse often and much with your best friend, through the Word of God and prayer. Recognize the special claims which Jesus has upon you; cheerfully admit His rights as Master and Lord, and 'thus judge, that if He died for all, then were all dead, and that He died for all, that they which live should not, henceforth, live unto themselves, but unto Him which died for them and rose again.' Let the awful condition of the ungodly be constantly before your eyes. Think of all the sinners you see as destined to everlasting burnings, unless they repent and return to God; hasten, oh hasten, to warn them, if by any means you may save some."

## ORIGINALITY.

Dr. Cramp was eminently original in his style of preaching. He had his own way of putting things, and could employ that of no one else. He admired the Apostle Paul, and was not ashamed to quote his language. He had read the Psalms devotionally, and his own devotions were often guided by expressions found therein. He loved the Saviour, and was willing to acknowledge Him as the purest, highest and best of all models. But so far as any literature or preachers were concerned, outside of the Bible, he copied no man. He thought for himself, and put his thoughts into expressions of his own, and delivered them entirely in his own way. His illustrations were apt and telling, usually drawn from the Bible itself, and employed in a happy manner. His sermons on special occasions were frequently far beyond the range of average preaching. The anniversaries of great events in history were sometimes made the occasion of a review of the past, and a cheerful setting forth of the improvements of the times and hopeful indications for the future. It was a rich treat, on such occasions, to listen to the ringing tones of one who believed in the complete triumph of the right, partly because there were indications of progress, but much more because the mouth of the Lord hath spoken it.

As already stated, Dr. Cramp's pastoral labors ended in 1844, when he resigned the charge of the church at Hastings. The farewell services were affecting, both pastor and people feeling that the separation was final, so far as Christian fellowship in this world is concerned. And so it proved to be, for he never found the time to recross the Atlantic and visit the scenes of his childhood and early efforts for God. But how inspiring the thought, and what unbounded thanksgiving to God should accompany it, that those who, amid blinding tears in April, 1844, said their farewells, were doubtless permitted to greet each other again, in December, 1881, in the presence of Him who had given strength for the journey and grace to its end.

The preaching, however, did not end with the pastorate at Hastings. During the seven weeks' voyage in the "Prince George," religious services were kept up each Lord's day, as far as the weather permitted. When Montreal was reached, and the work of the college taken up, there was constant preaching, either in the city or out among the churches. When Dr. Cramp came to

Nova Scotia in 1851, he was warmly welcomed by those who were then the pastors of the churches, and by none more warmly than by those who were still left of " the fathers " in the ministry. To the praise of those veterans of the faith, or rather to the praise of divine grace, it may be said that they were above all petty jealousy. They were " unlearned," and yet not " ignorant " men; the cause to which they had given their lives was dearer to them than the thoughts of any personal preëminence. They welcomed the man who came to them with the reputation of an earnest worker for Christ, both in his study and in the pulpit. As their hearts were open, so their churches were thrown open. He soon learned to love and trust these men. He admired their faith, love and zeal, quite as much as they admired his learning and ability. To them he was no rival, but a fellow-helper in the truth. To him they were no disbanded soldiers, to be pushed aside, but heroes in the conflict, worthy of all honor and esteem. Among the foremost of these was Rev. Theodore S. Harding, the pastor of the First Horton Baptist Church. He was then in the 79th year of his age. He had been ordained as pastor of the church, July 31, 1786, just six days after Dr. Cramp was born. Who would have dreamed that on the day of the ordination of a pastor over the first Baptist church organized in these provinces, there was an infant of six days in St. Peters, Isle of Thanet, who would come to cheer this pastor in his old age and take up the armor that he was about to lay down? But so it was, and it was not in the nature of the child of '86, now a man of vigor, to see the " old man eloquent" bearing burdens "too grievous to be borne." So he took a large portion of the work. One service every Sunday was provided for by Dr. Cramp, and frequently more. In June, 1855, Father Harding died, and then the entire work of the Church, so far as the pulpit was concerned, was undertaken by him, till another pastor was secured. And all this was done without any expectation of pecuniary reward. To help on the cause of truth was all the recompense he sought. That "the workman was worthy of his hire," he often taught; but seemed to suppose that the principle was applicable to other laborers rather than to himself. After a successor to Mr. Harding was secured, in December, 1855, Dr. Cramp still continued to preach every Sunday evening, thus allowing the pastor, the late Dr. de Blois, to supply the stations outside.

As a token of esteem a present was made to him by the First Horton Baptist Church, in June, 1863. The following, to his son, refers to this subject :—

"July 13, 1863.

"  . . . Two days before I went to Prince Edward Island, two gentlemen waited on me, and presented to me a handsome gold watch, in the name of the congregation, as a testimonial of their satisfaction and esteem, with special reference to my ministerial services on Lord's Day evenings. This was very gratifying, and was altogether a surprise to me; for, though contributions for the object were made throughout the congregation, the secret was so well kept, that not the least inkling of it reached me.

"The gift was remarkably appropriate, as my old watch, bought in 1812, was so thoroughly worn out, that the watch doctors had given it up ! "

A record was made of all the sermons preached. Some of these have disappeared ; but enough has been retained to show how abundant the labors were. From such records as we have, the number of sermons preached in England was about 3,840. In Canada, about 336. There are no records for this period ; the amount is made up from a general average of other years. In Nova Scotia, not less than 1,000, making in all, 5,176 sermons.

This, with lectures and addresses on all religious, moral and philanthropic subjects, as they came up, with professional and literary burdens continually pressing, constitutes an amount of work performed that, certainly, not one man in a thousand could undertake. How it was accomplished we know not, only we know that it was done.

The following resolution will explain itself ; it was received by Dr. Cramp's family after his decease :—

REV. J. M. CRAMP, D.D.

" It having pleased the wise Disposer of events, to remove by death on the 6th inst., our beloved brother, the Rev. J. M. Cramp, D. D., this church, at its first conference meeting thereafter, desires to record its sense of the great loss it has sustained by this event.

" The late Dr. Cramp came to Wolfville from Montreal, in the spring of 1851, to take the oversight of Acadia College. On arrival, he connected himself with this church, of which he remained a most faithful and useful member till his death.

" During the last few years of our late pastor, Rev. T. S. Harding, he was not able to perform his duties so effectually as formerly, owing to age and growing infirmities. Dr. Cramp then came to his aid. and rendered the church most essential service in the pulpit and otherwise, till the time of the said pastor's death. This occurring some six months before our present pastor (Dr. de Blois) took charge, Dr. Cramp most kindly supplied the pastor's place during this vacancy, rendering his services most cheerfully, without expecting or receiving any pecuniary consideration.

" After the settlement of our present pastor, Dr. Cramp continued to benefit the church by taking charge of the Sunday evening services for many years, till infirmities and advancing age rendered such efforts impracticable. By this means, he enabled our pastor to bestow labor on other portions of the Church which he could not have done under other circumstances.

" Dr. Cramp ever manifested a strong interest in the welfare of this church in her various enterprises,—and when unable to be present at prayer and conference meetings, anxiously sought information of what took place on such occasions.

" He was jealously desirous for the welfare of the pastor of the church, and anxious that he should be upheld and supported by its members, both by their prayers and their contributions, to which his share was added with cheerful promptness.

" The benevolent schemes of the Church received his hearty coöperation. No one was more ready to urge to duty in this matter than he was, both by precept and example; this was not with him a fitful emotion, but a steady, active principle, ruling his whole life, and continuing up to the time of his death.

"In a word, from his entering this Church, over thirty years ago, till the time of his death, he ceased not to labor by every means in his power for its welfare and spiritual advancement.

"Whilst reviewing our loss, we can but feel thankful in being able to refer to his holy life, most useful counsels, and faithful example; whilst we shall miss his prayers and devoted labors, may we feel that though dead he 'yet speaketh;' and may this Church ever gratefully remember him as one long connected with it, and one fervently and justly beloved in all the relations he sustained to it during his long membership.

"To the family of our late brother, Rev. Dr. Cramp, this Church would tender its heartfelt sympathy in their heavy bereavement, and prays that they may be sustained under their affliction by the same grace which upheld their beloved parent during his long and useful life, and which, in the hour of death, did not fail to sustain and comfort him.

"The above passed unanimously at conference meeting this day, and was ordered to be copied on the book of church records, and a copy of the same to be forwarded to the family of the late Dr. Cramp.

"BURPEE WITTER,

"Church Clerk.

"Wolfville, Dec. 31, 1881."

The resolution above shows in what estimation Dr. Cramp was held as a preacher, a Christian and a man in the Church, where, without fee or reward, he had labored longer than in any other place. His last sermon in Wolfville was in the summer of 1878,—and, taking the 27 years from 1851 up to that time, he had averaged about 35 sermons a year. In addition to this, he was seldom absent from prayer and conference meetings, on which occasions his voice was always heard with profit.

His preaching was spiritual in its character. He could say, "I have believed and, therefore, I speak." He believed in vital godliness, in experimental religion. The necessity for conversion, an entire, radical change of heart and life, was with him no mere theory; it was a most serious fact ; he so treated it. The "fall " and the " ruin " of the race were no figurative expressions to be explained away, but solemn truths to be accepted and mourned over. He fully believed that no power less than the Divine could remedy the evil wrought. This he persistently taught.

His Christian sympathy was deep and abiding. Those in sorrow had his words of condolence, either spoken or written, as opportunity offered. His prayers for the bereaved in their times of grief were often most tender and affecting. It was no official discharge of duty, but rather the pleadings of a heart, that had often been smitten, in behalf of those who were then under the rod. On such occasions, no one could doubt the genuineness of the piety which prompted the prayer. The college professor, the learned author, the earnest preacher, were all lost sight of, as at the common mercy-seat ; many hearts, following the

22

one voice, were "letting their requests be made known to God." Experimental religion was to him as far superior to all professions and forms of service as the light is superior to the darkness. The deeper the experience, the more he enjoyed it. And yet, Dr. Cramp was not a man of an emotional nature. His feelings were deep and quiet, rather than noisy and manifest. He seldom, we might almost say never, in the pulpit, gave any expression to his own feelings, either of a joyous or a painful kind. The truths of the Gospel were declared, and the hearer was left to draw his own conclusions as to what special effects were being produced in the preacher's own heart by them. That wonderful results were produced in transforming, purifying, and mellowing power, became more and more manifest as the years passed by. And yet it may be frankly owned that it was, in part, left for those who have had access to his private papers, since he has gone, to know the depth of his piety, or the struggles he passed through to get a firm hold on God. The Gospel he preached became to himself the power of God unto salvation, and he loved to preach it, that others might believe and be saved. "He rests from his labors, and his works do follow him."

Reference has been made to the system of shorthand used by Dr. Cramp all through his life. It was adopted by him before the present methods were employed, and consists of a mingling of characters with ordinary words. We furnish on the following page, as a sample, a fac-simile of one page of the notes of a sermon, the whole occupying four such pages.

This, in ordinary English, is as follows:—

"Heb. xi., 13. Annual commemoration of the dead by the Moravians. Many have died in the past year: it has been a busy year with the king of terrors. The Church, too, has lost some bright ornaments. Very probable that the ravages of the destroyer will be great in the present year. How important to be prepared!

" 1. *An interesting fact* :

" Death ought never to be contemplated but with great seriousness; it is the most momentous change of all. How differently men die: Some stupidly, like the beast, without thought or care; some with affected calmness, while the dart rankles in the conscience. Hume. Some boastingly, cherishing to the last a conviction of their superiority to others, and their consequent safety; some despairingly.

"Some few die 'in faith:' Jacob, Joseph, David, Stephen, Paul. 'I know whom I have believed,' 'I am about to be offered,' &c., &c. What is included in this? *Rejection of all self-confidence.* This is involved in the very nature of faith, which means simply resting on another. His insufficiency, his unworthiness, &c., never so felt by the Christian as when death is approaching. He may have been exemplary, active, devoted, but now he sees things as they are, and must judge, not by the flattery of partial friends, but by the unerring Word of God. He cannot but say, 'Enter not into judgment,' &c. The holiest man that ever lived, with nothing but his holiness to confide in, would be covered with confusion."

It will be observed that these are only heads of a discussion, which would be filled in by the preacher as he proceeded with his theme.

# CHAPTER XVII.

## YEARS OF QUIET AND REST.

" Remember that some of the brightest drops in the chalice of
life may still remain for us in old age. The last draught which
a kind Providence gives us to drink, though near the bottom
of the cup, may, as is said of the draught of the Romans of old,
have, at that very bottom, instead of dregs, most costly pearls."

—W. A. NEWMAN.

### 1869–1881.

And yet it would require some skill in writing
to produce a chapter under this heading which
would be both true to the life, and at the same
time such as the words "quiet and rest" would
suggest to many minds.

What some would regard as a season of rest,
would be a complete giving up of all labor; working not at all with the hands; making no plans for
further improvement; carrying no anxieties for
the condition of things; quietly leaving everything to be done by others, or to be left undone,
and settling down into undisturbed repose, as
though all were now finished, and the end of the
existence completely secured. To all who would
love to see a truthful picture of such a period in

human history, we would say,—you must look at
the biography of some one very different from him
whose life we are considering. There was no such
period in Dr. Cramp's life; and the biographer cannot produce it, except he make it fiction rather
than fact. And yet there was a period of rest. His
own advice to the students may illustrate :—
" Gentlemen," he would say, " when you are tired
of studying mathematics, turn to the classics ;
and when you have exhausted your strength on the
Latin, take up the Greek." And sometimes this
was said with a significant smile, as though he
would delude them into the belief, that they
would find " Demosthenes de Corona " mere play,
after " Cicero de Officiis " had baffled all their
efforts. If they were so deluded, the delusion
probably vanished in due time. The true philosophy of the advice, however, will be recognized by
all adepts in mental philosophy. A change of
labor is often tantamount to rest.

In this sense, we find materials for twelve years
of " quiet and rest." Acadia College, whose condition he found very low in 1851, had been greatly
revived. The finances had been improved. Many
prejudices had yielded before the logic of undeniable facts ; the number of students had greatly
increased ; some of them had already grown and
developed into able professors in Acadia and other
similar institutions. A competent man had been
found and installed into the office of president.
Instead of one professor there were six. The future
existence and continued growth of the college was

believed to be assured ; there was not a whisper to be heard throughout the Maritime Provinces that education, either denominational or general, might have been in a healthier condition, if some other man had been our leader for the last eighteen years. Few men, indeed, have ever retired from a post of responsibility and toil, with better reasons for believing that his labors had been appreciated and successful. So, when the president's position, influence, work and reponsibility, were transferred to him who now so worthily fills the office, there was a sense of relief, and a feeling of complete rest. Henceforth, all efforts in 'this direction could be of a voluntary kind, and put forth as inclination might direct. As the warrior lays his armor by, when the field is won, Dr. Cramp laid the old class-books and manuscripts of the lecture-room aside with the feeling,—this conflict is ended, and I may rest.

He had earned a good rest, if any man ever had. The friends of the college gave an expression of their feelings, in the presentation of a beautiful epergne, and the address accompanying it will show their appreciation of the work which had been done. This token of esteem was highly valued by the recipient. It had cost $500, but was worth ten times that amount to him :—

" *To the Rev. Dr. Cramp:*

" DEAR SIR,—

" A number of your many friends are happy to embrace the opportunity offered by your retirement from the presidency of Acadia College, to express their high appreciation of your successful and laborious services, rendered for a period of eighteen years, in connection with the Baptist Denomination in these Provinces.

"They beg also to state that your personal intercourse with the churches has won general esteem and love.

"You will call to mind that when you entered upon your labors in Acadia College, the institution was not only without endowment, but was seriously embarrassed by debt.

"You found the students reduced to a very small number, and but a single professor—the lamented Isaac Chipman—to share with you the labors of the institution.

"The debt has been paid, and an endowment of between $30,000 and $40,000 secured.

"The students in annual attendance have been increased from year to year, till they now number upwards of forty, and there is now a Faculty of *six* professors.

"For this measure of prosperity the friends of the college feel that to *you* they are largely indebted.

"The pains which you have taken to examine the history of Baptist principles, and the successful efforts which you have made to place before the public the biographies of the worthy men whose labors preceded yours in these Provinces, have been sources of much profit and gratification to the body generally.

"The interest which you have ever manifested in social reforms, and especially in the promotion of free common school education, has contributed in no small degree to the success which has attended the efforts of those especially employed in these departments of moral and intellectual labor.

"As a token of esteem and regard, your acceptance of this epergne of pure silver is requested.

"May your health be continued and your life prolonged, and, having accepted the position of " professor emeritus," may you long continue to sustain this relation to Acadia College."

We said the class books were laid aside, but the new appointment of "professor emeritus," referred to in this address, opened the way for pleasant recreation, in meeting college classes still, as opportunity offered. Twice a week, for some years, this exercise was kept up. To give some instruction in ecclesiastical history, could hardly be called work to Dr. Cramp. Help was also afforded to ministerial students in their study of Hebrew. But this was given in his own room, occasionally, and helped more than it hindered the rest.

A house was purchased in the west end of the village of Wolfville. It was pleasantly situated, with ample grounds in the rear for cultivation or ornamentation. Some changes and improvements were made in the house, the room designed for the library being considerably enlarged. A magnificent elm stands in the field, the admiration of all who visit it. It was a source of pleasure to the doctor to spend a half hour, occasionally, under the shadow of this fine tree. It was considerably older than its owner, yet there was a resemblance between them ; the tree had stood through many storms, its roots penetrated farther through the soil, and its great branches covered a broader space, than those of any other tree for many miles around. Truer still of him who rested in its shade. His mental and spiritual growth had

been the work of long years ; the fibres of his
being had reached out far for their nourishment,
and the influence of his life, like the branches of
the tree, covered a wide space.

In August, 1869, Dr. Cramp removed from his
former residence in the college buildings to this
retreat of his old age. Some time before, his
family had been so reduced, that there was but
one daughter to occupy the new home with him.
She was the constant companion of her father in
all the later years of his life, and he frequently
acknowledged his debt of gratitude to God for
such a support and solace as she proved to be. Of
course, the actual resting could not commence till
the needful changes are made both outside and
in ; and especially the large collection of books
have found their appropriate places. But in due
time the arrangements are completed, and the last
stage of the journey is entered upon—the period of
"quiet and rest."

In some respects, this may be regarded as the
most instructive period of Dr. Cramp's life. The
heading of the chapter is a misnomer, unless the
sense in which the words are used is remembered.
Some one has said that every man is naturally
lazy, and that it is only when heavy pressure is
on that the greatest possibilities can ever be realized. In each of the preceding stages, the subject
of this memoir has been under heavy pressure.
As the pastor of three different churches in England, weak and struggling interests, as compared
with the national churches alongside of them,

there was absolute necessity for constant work. Responsible for the literary matter of a publishing company in London, he must work. As the president of two colleges on this side, one in Montreal and one in Wolfville, both low in finances and weak in teaching facilities, he must work or go under.

We have reached the period when all this is gone. He is the editor of no paper, responsible to no Board. No type-setter is calling for " copy ;" no church is expecting three or four sermons a week; no university is looking to him for instruction or guidance ; the pressure is gone, and the man, for the first time in his life, is free to rest,—and no one will say that he has not earned this brief respite from toil.

An extract or two from his own journal, for one of these years, will show us how he rested. Those we give are a fair sample of them all, only shortening a little the last two or three years, especially in the number of sermons preached :—

" Dec. 31, 1870.—During this year I have read 59 volumes, preached 20 times, written 303 letters ; I have written 28 articles, which have been published in the *Christian Messenger, Christian Visitor, Canadian Baptist* or *Baptist Magazine ;* my lecture on ' Church Development ' has been published in the *Baptist Quarterly ;* I have written a small volume, entitled ' The Lamb of God,' which has not yet been published ; I have read through the English Bible ; have read the prophets Jeremiah, Ezekiel and all the minor prophets in Hebrew."

This record would not contain more than half

the reading, for the dailies, tri-weeklies and various magazines are not included,—and when Dr. Ciamp says, "I have read a volume," it means not that the words were glanced over, but that every thought contained in it was weighed and the full measure of the author taken.

Some of the letters referred to were letters of friendship to members of the family; some were official letters to the missionaries in India, requiring much thought and precision; some were letters on the various questions of public interest in the Provinces, in England, or in the United States, showing how wonderfully the writer was awake and concerned in everything, everywhere, which touched human well-being and progress. As a man, he cared for everything that pertains to man; as a Christian, he cared for everything touching Christianity, In this phase of his character, we believe that very few men have ever surpassed him.

The following, as letters, may illustrate the style of his communications; some of them date a little farther back than the period of this chapter:

To his daughter, Mrs. Muir:—

"Dec. 30, 1864.

" . . . This is the anniversary of my baptism, fifty-two years ago. I have done very little for God, and that little very imperfectly; but I have received many and great mercies. May the short remnant of my life be spent more in harmony with principles and obligations. Three were baptized on that occasion—one is dead; the other, an old servant, at home, still survives.

" . . . I have just finished a sketch of a sermon for to-morrow evening from Deut. vii : 2. I intend it to be a plain exhortation in this wise :—

" 1. *What* we should remember :—God's ways towards us—in mercies, privileges, exemptions, and in sorrows ; noting their connections and causes, and our deportment under them. Our ways towards Him—the state of our hearts, our general conduct in regard to His will, the manner and degree in which we have served Him, seeking to save souls and to benefit the Church.

" 2. *Why* we should remember :—Generally, because God commands it. Specially : it is suitable—a proper, reasonable exercise—we should stop and think. It is salutary—it promotes self-knowledge—produces humility—excites thankfulness.

" 3. *When* we should remember :—Habitually, Ps. xxxiv. 1-2 : ciii. 1-2. Particularly on Lord's days : the resting day should be a thoughtful, examining day—on memorial days, such as anniversaries of events in our lives—at the close of the year. God remembers—Mal. iii. 16-17. Ps. l. 21. Memory will be quickened in the next world— 'Son, remember.'

"I think that the perusal of that sketch may do you as much good as if I had retailed to you abundance of news."

" July 25, 1875.

" . . . I have entered on my eightieth year this morning. It is marvellous, remembering what a feeble person I was fifty years ago. No one could have imagined it possible that I should reach this date : yet, here I am, and during those fifty years I have performed a considerable amount of work, mostly with my pen ; nor am I without some assurance that good has been effected by that pen. Our gifts vary, as well as our opportunities, and it is a merciful arrangement that they may be employed in the Great Master's service. At present you are withdrawn from activity, but rest, as well as work, is useful. Milton says, 'They also serve, who only stand and wait.'

"Sanctified affliction is a good preparation for labour."

"Nov. 21, 1876.

" . . . Who can imagine the difference between the modes of existence here and in the heavenly world, and how useless are our speculations? I wonder whether they smile in Heaven; if they do, it will surely turn to a downright laugh, when they compare the realities of that blessed state with our blundering guesses on earth. And we, too, will be apt to quote Paul's words, 'I spake as a child.' John Foster used expressive phraseology when he said, a short time before his death, 'I shall soon know the great secret.' But we must die to know it, and what is death, but a change in the mode of life—living without the body for a few ages or a few milleniums, to receive it back again, or what will be equivalent to it, in a new, improved and perfected form —needing no food, no medicine, but existing in, and of, and by itself—without dependence on any other thing or being, except the great God, who could annihilate it, but will not, because the aggregate of redeemed humanity forms, in an exalted sense, the 'glorious body' of the Lord Jesus! It is His—and it is Himself. See Eph. ii. 23 and xxvii. 30; Phil. iii. 21; 1 Cor. xv. 49. Now do not pretend to say, after this, that an old man cannot speculate."

To his daughter :—

"June 12, 1877.

" . . . God has not told us when we shall die, but those who have reached four-score know that the final close cannot be far off, and may occur at any moment.

How necessary that they should 'die daily' in the best sense, by living to God and keeping eternity in view— 'laying hold on eternal life.'

And if we entertain the hope of being 'forever with the Lord,' we must be like Him now in 'going about doing good.' The Church is sadly defective in this matter. She does not do half enough for her Redeemer and Lord. 'Awake, thou that sleepest'—to each one I would say, 'This matter belongeth unto thee. Realize it and act accordingly.

" . . . For my part I am an optimist, that is, I hold to the creed of the good woman, of whom we had an account in one of the early tracts of the Tract Society, and who was accustomed to say, when disasters were reported, and people were groaning and weeping over them—' 'Tis all for the best.' The practical application is very desirable and important, and the occasions for it are very often occurring. Only we must bear in mind that it is not a *notion* but a *reality*—a plain fact, and we can verify it by many a reminiscence. In cases where the verification is doubtful, we can believe, and that act of faith gives quietness to the soul, as Isaiah says, 'Thou wilt keep him in perfect peace whose mind is staid on Thee, because he trusteth in Thee.' Verily, the Bible contains the best ethics as well as the best theology. Implicit confidence in it is becoming unfashionable in certain quarters, but the old book will live, when others are forgotten.

" . . . I am disgusted at the arrogance of some thinkers. They dare to tell God what He may or may not do, and that if He should fail to accomplish certain results which they think He ought to bring to pass, they will not respect Him. Now, I think that we ought to be very, very careful how we pass a verdict on God's proceedings. His Bible tells us that He is 'holy in all

His ways, and righteous in all His works.' So it will be in the issue, whatever may be the amount of calamity or the number of the lost, the fact of the existence of God settles the whole matter. I wish that some men who set a high value on their own thinking powers, would study 'Butler's Analogy' a little more closely, as well as Paul's epistle to the Romans, chapters viii. to xi."

To his daughter, Mrs. Muir :—

"Dec. 9, 1878.

". . . If Mr. G. had asked me to speak on the last Lord's day I joined you at the 'Olivet,' I should have taken for a text Eph. iii. 19, for a reason which will be assigned before I close. The course of remarks would have been to this effect : — 'Our Lord's demeanour during His sojourn on earth was marked by benevolence of the highest order, both spiritual and temporal ; He went about doing good. When He left this world, and assumed the mediatorial throne, *love* was still the guiding, controlling principle, and so .it is still.' He manages all affairs— supplies all wants, listens to all requests soothes all sorrows, cares for every member of the family. At the same time He governs the universe, and attends to the cares of individual saints. Such loving grace passeth knowledge, and is as truly incomprehensible as the Divine omniscience itself. See Ps. cxxxix.

" This practical manifestation of the great Intercessor's love may be satisfactorily illustrated by reference to special instances. We may take the cases of three Apostles :—

" *Peter* :— No sooner was He risen from the dead, than He said to the women, 'Go, tell my disciples; *and Peter* ' — mark the special message. When the Apostle was imprisoned, and about to be led out to execution, the Saviour sent a messenger to effect his deliverance, and Peter acknowledged that 'the Lord had sent His angel ' on this merciful errand.

" *Paul*:—Passing by his wonderful conversion, which was the Lord's own work, the following facts deserve notice:—

" 1. The difficulties and dangers encountered at Corinth had produced great depression. The Saviour appeared to him by night with a comforting assurance of deliverance and success. See Acts xviii.

" 2. The trouble of the thorn in the flesh, about which he prayed to Christ, and received a gracious answer, which abundantly relieved him. See 2 Cor. xii.

" 3. During his voyage to Rome an angel was sent to guarantee the safety of all who were in the ship Acts xxvii.

" At his trial in Rome, all the Roman Christians forsook him, ' but the Lord stood with me and strengthened me,' he says. 2 Tim. iv. 17.

" *John :* — Banished to the wild island of Patmos, the Lord's day came round, and found him alone. No meeting of the brethren—and he is the last of the Apostles ! He was broken-hearted. The Lord knew it, and a merciful manifestation followed. Rev. i. 9–18.

" These are facts, and the intercession is not so much a doctrine as a *fact*, and ought to be so regarded by us. The Lord Jesus is acting on our behalf; we may claim the benefit.

"The reason for preferring to take that text was, that it was the first text on which I ventured to speak in public. *Time*—Jan. 31, 1814. *Place*—Baptist Chapel, St. Peters. I have often preached from the text since then, and have thought much of the subject it treats of; but still it ' passeth knowledge;' and it will do so as long as we are here, and thousands of years afterwards; for—' Who by searching can find out God ?' "

23

Dec., 1879.

" . . . The stealing of ministers from churches is a common offence ; but it *is* an offence, and sometimes is followed by punishment. So, do not steal ; do not tempt a man to come to Olivet, who is not otherwise known to be desiring a change. If *sheep*-stealers are condemned, surely *shepherd*-stealers cannot be innocent. Therefore, let the Olivet Church be careful. Do not seek the *great*, the *flashy*, or the *odd ;* be content with the *good*, the *sound* and the *active*—more especially if the man of your choice not only works for the church, but keeps the church in action ; for the great fault of many of our churches is that the members are not personally active."

To his daughter :—

Feb. 22, 1879.

" These alternations are like human life ;—now joyous —now sorrowful—now prosperous—now adverse—now sickness—now health. So one thing is set over against another, and there is a mingling together of opposites which promotes the general good, and subserves the gracious and wise designs of our God, who, ' like as a father pitieth his children, pitieth them that fear Him,' knowing, (that is, considering) their frame, and remembering that they are dust.' Merciful words ! and as marvellous as they are merciful ! We are so accustomed to the Divine style, that we fail to wonder as we ought. If our feelings were rightly affected and governed, we should be in a state of constant ecstasy, and singing 'Hallelujah' all the day long. They seem to be perpetually so engaged in Heaven, but they are never weary of it ; they do not complain of monotony. Those who sang ' Worthy is the Lamb that was slain,' when John wrote the book of Revelation, have continued singing the same song ever since, and are singing it now, without weariness, and will never cease. It will be the same with ourselves. Sameness is irksome on earth; it is delightful in Heaven; probably, because the blessed above know what it is to enjoy variety in *feeling* in connection with or without the continuousness of matter and mode. We do not know much about Heaven, but one description (Rev. vii. 14–17) will bear deep study, and when we have exhausted all thought, we shall still confess that we 'know in part,' and that Christ's riches are unsearchable."

"Oct. 11, 1881.

" . . . The sovereignty of God is freely admitted. He does as it pleases Him, and all He does is wisely, and righteously, yea, and kindly done, as it will one day appear even to those most deeply interested. Blessed are all that 'wait for Him.' That blesssedness, however, is reserved for those who wait on Him in trust and hope and quiet submission. 'I know,' said one of God's ancient saints, 'that Thy judgments are righteous,' and so it is, although the prospects are shrouded in gloom. It is famine time in the deceased brother's family, but Gospel truths and covenant promises are the food provided for sufferers, and in partaking of it they receive help and strength in time of need. All God's promises are full of meaning, and are *kept in their full meaning*, because He is God, and always keeps His word."

To his son :—

"Our Province is in a state of some excitement at the present time, on account of a new franchise bill brought in by the Government. We have had universal suffrage for a number of years, and it is now found not to work well. All parties are dissatisfied with it, and desire some change. It is proposed to introduce a property qualification made manifest by assessment, so as to restrict the franchise to persons who are assessed for $300, and upwards, either real or personal estate. The general scheme is reasonable enough, but so many persons will be disfranchised by it—many of whom are men of influence—that much feeling is evinced. Certain classes—such as ministers, teachers, &c., are exempt from assessment; they will, therefore, be disfranchised.

"I shall lose *my* vote; but that is of no consequence, as I abstain from the exercise of the privilege.

"The tariff was 12½ per cent. The revenue is in so good a state that it is now reduced to ten per cent."

"April 11, 1873.

" . . . I am hardly sorry that Mr. Gladstone's university bill was defeated. It would have been lost in the Lords, anyhow. He attempted an impossibility. Romanists are not to be conciliated. Education is now free to all, but they will not take it. They must have an education of their own—provided and paid for at the public expense. That ought never to be granted. Let them educate their own people in their own way, but at their own cost. We must have liberty and equality, pure and simple. But the Province of Quebec stands in the way in this Dominion."

To his son :—

"June 17, 1873.

" . . . The Roman Catholics, or at any rate the priests, hold that education without religion is worthless, and, therefore, protest against being taxed for the common schools, and demand separate schools. The answer is two-fold :—

"1. The Roman Catholics themselves are not agreed on the subject. A majority of them in Ontario send their children to the common schools, avowedly preferring them to their own separate schools, and being untroubled by any conscientious convictions.

"2. The separate schools must, of necessity, in any

scattered population, be partly dependent on the public fund, and so the evil against which we protest comes into operation, the general taxation being charged with the support of Roman Catholic instruction.

" I fear that the dissentient schools in the Province of Quebec, are similarly circumstanced, and that they also are partly chargeable to the common fund, so that Roman Catholics are taxed for *them* indirectly.

"The whole question is beset with difficulties, the only fair solution is the establishment of general education at the public expense, leaving religious instruction to be supplemented by each denomination out of school hours.

" One mode of getting out of the difficulty might be the establishment of two funds, one Catholic, the other Protestant, each made up of the amount of taxation on those parties respectively, and the application of the funds restricted to them. In that case, the deficiencies of the poor districts would be supplied by the rich ones, and neither party would be taxed for the religion of the other."

To his son :—

"WOLFVILLE, Oct. 22, 1873.

" . . . I found such an amount of arrears on my return home that my time has been entirely occupied in clearing them off, which must account for my seeming delay in writing to you.

"Access to the Alliance meetings was obtained, and I attended some of them with very great pleasure. It was certainly a noble assembly, and the proceedings were of the deepest interest.

"I spent Sunday, the 5th, at Brooklyn, where I preached for Dr. Sarles, who has been twenty-six years minister of one of our churches there.

"On Wednesday following, I left New York for Boston, and next day left Boston for St. John, by steamer, thinking to have a quiet and easy trip. But I was disappointed. There had been a heavy fall of rain the day before, and the sea was still so rough that we were compelled to take refuge in Gloucester harbour, where we remained all day. Everything was so rough and uncomfortable on board the steamer, that when we reached Portland on Friday morning, I went ashore, and performed the remainder of the journey by railway, arriving at St. John on Saturday morning.

"I preached twice at St. John the next day, and attended a meeting of our Missionary Board on Monday. On Tuesday, I travelled from St. John to Halifax by the Intercolonial Railway, which is well constructed, and well managed."

To his son :—

"July 15, 1878.

"I sent you, the other day, a copy of the *Chronicle* containing an account of the laying the corner-stones of our college and seminary. It was an exceedingly hot day, which somewhat marred our enjoyment, for we had no awning over our heads. Our convention meets this year at Fredericton, N.B., Aug. 25. It is a very hot place, and Dr. Parker thinks it would be unwise to expose myself to the heat. He dissuades me also from attempting a journey to Montreal, even if it were broken up into three days. You will conclude from this that I am in a feeble state. Nevertheless, if the weather should become cool about the beginning of September, I might possibly venture on a short trip from home, but cannot form any plans at present; an old man of eighty-two cannot plan, and that will be my age on the 25th inst."

The journey to Montreal was taken contrary to expectation, and the following refers to the return trip :—

"Nov. 8, 1878.

" The journey was performed, after we left you, with comparative ease. . . .

" To-morrow I must get to work. Opportunity and strength will fail as time passes on, but we must work, as the Lord said, ' while it is day.' The resting-time is not far off."

"Dec. 4, 1879.

" . . . My health continues about the same as usual. I suffer some annoyance from trifling causes, but they are *bagatelles* which need not be much regarded. I soon get weary, and my eyesight is failing. This troubles me much in writing, so that the pen sometimes seems to slip out of straightness. What little work I do must be done before nine o'clock, and I retire at ten.

" . . . I have been greatly interested lately in the study of Farrar's ' Life and Work of St. Paul.' It is a splendid performance. All clergymen should read it. But my reading days are nearly ended. I cannot sit long at the desk. But *I have sat* there a good many hours in time past, and have reason to be very thankful for the benefit received.

" It may seem strange to a younger man, but the fact is, I am tired by writing this note ! So must lay down the pen, with love to all of you. I think I will write oftener in future."

"Jan. 27, 1880.

" . . . The outlook abroad is very gloomy. The cartoon in *Punch*, representing the British lion ' at bay,' is, I fear, a true representation of the actual state of affairs. Gladstone has made a triumphal progress through Scotland, but there is a hard fight before him."

"May 14, 1880.

" . . . I have had a somewhat trying indisposition in the shape of influenza. . . .

"Now I am recovered, and am about as usual, but the general weakness is doubtless increasing, as must be expected, and, as the Apostle Peter says, I may expect 'shortly to put off this tabernacle.' It is a merciful and wise arrangement that the *time* of future events is hidden from us. Hezekiah had his life lengthened for fifteen years, and therefore knew, generally, how long he had to stay in the world; though it is not likely that his knowledge was more particular, including *month* and *day*, as well as *year*—for that would not have been merciful. As it was, he probably watched the flight of time very anxiously, and felt unusual emotion when the fourteenth year ended. Christians are better circumstanced."

To his son :—

"Aug. 24, 1880.

"I have bought a lot in our new cemetery, and intend removing your mother's remains, that I may rest in the same place till the day of rising again. It will come, for 'the dead shall be raised incorruptible.' I do not trouble myself with modern speculations on that subject, but am content with the facts and promises of Scripture. God is true, and His word will not fail, although the *end* is unknown.

"I have read the Greek New Testament *sixty-six* times—

> 'And still new beauties do I see,
> And still increasing light.'"

To his daughter, Mrs. Muir :—

"Aug. 30, 1880.

" . . . Your visit was like an oasis in a desert—supremely welcome and gratefully remembered. I may not hope for a repetition of it, and have only need to think of 'the land of silence and of death,' which certainly will be 'my next remove.' We cannot defer it.

When the Lord turns the key, the door will open. May it be our unspeakable bliss to 'enter into the joy of the Lord.'

"Your affectionate father,

"J. M. CRAMP."

To his son :—

"Feb. 3, 1881.

" . . . These checks and hindrances to our comforts make up the history of each person, and a moral lesson is no doubt derivable from them. David could say, 'It is good for me that I have been afflicted,' and many a man has traced his greatest blessings to his sharpest pains, and clearly discerned the connection, acknowledging the righteousness of the Divine government. There are many mysteries in God's dispensations; but the answer in all cases is, '*It is God*,"—and that will satisfy a reasonable man, who does not want to know all the ins and outs of affairs, but says, '*I can wait*,' 'Thy will be done.' Let us be willing to learn in that school.

" . . . I was sorry to hear of the death of Senator P. I knew his father, who was a worthy deacon of the Baptist church in Eagle Street, London, and also treasurer of the *Baptist Magazine*. Mr. M.'s death was very painful, a great loss to the 'Olivet' Church.

"God's dispensations are sometimes charged by us as mysterious, which is but another name for our ignorance. The Divine plans are good, and wise and right, but the complete understanding of them is reserved for another world, where, as the Apostle Paul says, 'We shall know as we are known.' "

These are only extracts from the letters, the portions relating to family matters being omitted. But they are enough to show the channel in which the thoughts were running. They also show that when the writer recorded, "I have written during the year 240 letters," and again, "380 or 420 letters," these figures represent no small amount of work.

For several years after Dr. Cramp retired from public life, he kept up the habit of attending associations and conventions as heretofore. His interest in public matters suffered no abatement. He watched educational and political movements as closely as ever. Wherever he saw danger of retrogression, he raised a warning note. His motto was "Progress," and his brain and pen were both busy, in order to promote it His chief care, however, was towards the kingdom of Christ in the world. If he took less part in the discussions of important questions at public gatherings, it was only because he felt less able to do it. But he had a feeling of great satisfaction in knowing that one result of his long labors was, that many men were raised up who could seize the helm when his own grasp of it was loosening. This thought gave him rest. "Instead of the fathers shall be the children," he would say, "and the succession is sure to be kept up." "When David failed, Solomon was on hand," "When Paul was 'ready to be offered,' Timothy was ready for the service."

More frequent visits were made during these latter years to the members of his family in Montreal and elsewhere. These were greatly enjoyed both by himself and them ; and they were always found to be beneficial to his health and stimulating to his general activity. Their earnest solicitations might frequently have induced him to prolong the time of these visits, only, whatever comforts their homes could offer, his own library was not there. And without his large daily mail, by which he was brought into contact with the world's movements, he was never quite at rest. No business or professional man on his return from a furlough, met greater arrears of work than he did after a few days' absence. It would sometimes take him a full week to open, examine, read and make up for the lost time. If this was not rest, it was to him far more restful than the torture of feeling that he was by any neglect falling behind the movements of the age. The pastors and the churches were constantly on his thoughts. He never failed, as opportunity offered, to make enquiry as to their welfare. Difficulty with any of them was a source of grief. Their prosperity was his joy. That the college, during his presidency, had sent out a number of young men, who were becoming efficient workers in the vineyard of the Lord, was a source of special gratification to him. He followed, with his sympathies and prayers, each and all. A tender, paternal regard for them was in his heart continually. And it is within the knowledge of the writer, that, only a year or so before his departure, he was endeavouring to mature plans for the assistance of some of them, who were either overworked or not meeting with the desired success. Failing powers probably prevented the execution of many of those, but, like David with the Temple, it was in his heart to do it, and doubtless was accepted of the Lord as service rendered.

It was in many senses a season of rest. For it was far more restful to Dr. Cramp to feel that he was still doing something for humanity and God, than to believe that he was entirely dismissed from the service.

These years of respite from public responsibilities produced a great change in Dr. Cramp in the direction of developing the social qualities of his nature. He had always loved intercourse with friends, and visits from members of the family were highly prized, but in former years he was so completely engrossed with work, that there was hardly an hour to be spared for domestic or social comforts. A little impatience was keenly felt, though seldom manifested, when interruptions occurred.

During these latter years there was a marked change. He welcomed and even hungered sometimes for intercourse with friends. The visits of children and grandchildren were seasons of special delight. He looked forward to them with pleasure, and thoroughly enjoyed every hour while they lasted. He entered also into everything pertaining to home life as never before. There were frequent walks, as long as strength permitted, in the garden; vegetation was noticed, the flowers were admired, and he entered with real zest into many small matters of daily life, in which formerly he seemed to feel no interest whatever. The natural buoyancy of his heart asserted itself as soon as the burdens which seem sometimes to turn even young people into old ones were removed. His season of rest became, therefore, a season of cheerfulness.

Among the pleasant reminiscences of this period, a short visit from his friend and countryman, the late Rev. Dr. Spurden, with Mrs. Spurden, was often referred to with great satisfaction.

The opportunity thus afforded of recalling many mutually interesting events of earlier life in their native land, and discussing the changes that had transpired among friends, and scenes connected with those days, was one seldom enjoyed, and therefore specially welcome.

Amid it all he could frequently say : " Return unto thy rest, O my soul, for the Lord hath dealt bountifully with thee." There was much satisfaction to him in reviewing the past, which he often did with heartfelt thankfulness ; but there was much more in anticipating the future, that became brighter and more glorious as the. hasty months sped away. There were many sweet foretastes of "the rest remaining." He may have had doubts as others do ; if so. he seldom gave an expression to them, for he fully believed that the promises of God are " yea and amen " in Christ Jesus our Lord. It cannot be doubted that the partial rest of those last twelve years of a busy life is now lost and swallowed up in the unbroken repose of the heavenly home.

# CHAPTER XVIII.

### " THE LAST THINGS."

" Last words are sacred treasures laid up in the casket of memory,—echoes that repeat themselves till recollection fails. But the life is a more reliable witness."

Among the MSS. papers written by Dr. Cramp, during the quiet years that followed more active labours, one, bearing the title given above, contains a full expression of many thoughts connected with the close of life here, carried forward also to the bright future prospects that to him always included its continuance and perfection when " absent from the body.'

Referring to the uncertainty connected with the time of death, and consequent need of a watchful readiness for the summons, the following sentences occur :—

" There is one thing that is satisfying to the Christian. His Saviour has the charge of the whole affair. He employs His servants as He pleases. He calls them home when their work is done. He has the keys of the invisible world, and of death.

"When He turns the key, the door opens, and the believer enters the invisible abode.

"Till then, he is a stranger and pilgrim on earth. He is contented with this arrangement; he emulates Paul, being ready to go, but willing to stay, though the staying may involve toil and sorrow, if so be, it may be ' more needful ' for the work of God."

Possessed of this calm confidence, his entrance upon what proved to be the last year on earth, seemed marked by even an accession of cheerful interest in all that surrounded life here, and evening shadows were so brightened by the setting sun, that they gathered imperceptibly. A frequent reference to the near approach of death, observed formerly, was less noticed, though the thought might have been more constantly dwelt upon, it seldom found expression. In the month of February, the unexpected arrival of his eldest son was a great gratification, and the few days spent together were often referred to as having afforded an especial pleasure.

Thomas Cramp was, indeed, a son of whom his father might well be proud. In the city of Montreal, and to those interested in its commerce, and to the public men of Canada generally, he was as well known and equally respected as Dr. Cramp by the Baptist denomination; and his unusual abilities, which early led to his occupying important positions in connection with Canadian trade and navigation, were joined to a most amiable disposition, and a constant readiness to spend himself to save others, promote public objects, or aid in good works. He was not destined long to survive his father, and his unexpected and premature death was mourned by all who knew him. (See Appendix.)

His coming had always brought comfort and satisfaction to his father, who relied with implicit confidence in his calm, wise judgment and tender consideration. Through many years of a busy life, devoted largely to important public affairs of widening interest and responsibility, no detail that could minister to his father's gratification had ever been forgotten. To him he was frequently indebted for the ability to exercise the benevolence that was truly part of his nature, a generosity fully shared by the one who often quietly made it possible.

This characteristic finds a description in a favourite line, bearing the mark of approval, in Dr. Cramp's copy of *The Christian Year.*

> " He only, who forgets to hoard,
> Has learned to live."

Greatly in sympathy as regarded literary tastes, their discussions on new books, periodicals, and topics of the times, were reviewed with keen pleasure whenever opportunity offered. On this occasion, a recent visit to his native land afforded fresh interest. Reminiscences of Thanet and old friends in England—the political horizon, with descriptions of many public men of the day—filled up the fast fleeting hours.

" My father is a most remarkable man," said his son, on regretfully closing their conversation when about to leave.

Frequent visits from members of his family and

friends, during this last year, were a source of
comfort ; nor was there much diminution in the
satisfaction afforded by reading and writing,
though failing strength did not permit prolonged
efforts. Among letters written at this period, one,
on the subject of " Weekly Communion," may be
inserted here. It is addressed to his son-in-law,
G. B. Muir, Esq., who had requested a statement
of his views on that point :—

" Feb. 28, 1881.

" . . . The principal argument in favour of the practice is derived from the history of the Lord's day. The
setting apart of the first day of the week, as a day of
rest and worship, took place very early; and the history
of the worship then celebrated shows that a component
part of it was the Communion ; it was the crowning act
of the day, which was spent as we spend it now. *Every*
Lord's day was so spent. We have no authority to
separate one Lord's day from others, as though it was
holier than the rest; that would be a Jewish practice,
for they ' observed days,' etc. All Lord's days are alike
holy. Monthly or quarterly Communion wants New
Testament precedent, and can only plead tradition and
human custom in their favour. I think the evening is
the best time for the celebration. It should be the
closing service of the day, and there should be sufficient
time allowed to render it efficient and impressive, which
cannot be when it is a hurried appendage to the morning
service.

" Put these scattered hints together and think them
over, and plead primitive practice. Weekly Communion is regularly observed in all English cathedrals.
Our Baptist brethren in Scotland, and the Independents
there, keep up the same practice. It will universally

24

prevail, I feel assured, when 'the Spirit is poured out from on high.'

"I must close. The Lord guide, guard, and bless you all!"

Many instances of keen sympathy in affairs of the outer world, recur to those who were familiar with his daily life. Well do they remember the eagerness with which he awaited the appearance of the revised version of the New Testament, and the pleasure manifested when the first copy, sent by Dr. Angus, was placed in his hands ; then the writing an article for the Press with reference to it, difficult and painful though the effort had now become.

During the summer of 1881, frequent attempts were made to continue his usual contributions to the *Christian Messenger*, and several short reviews of new books and memorial notices of deceased friends, appeared from time to time.

Writing to his eldest son, July 9, 1881, he thus describes his manner of life :—

" As to myself, I am seldom able to walk about without the aid of a stick. I can read pretty much as usual, but in writing am apt to exhibit the defects of decaying eyesight. When Moses says that the man who reaches eighty, does it 'by reason of strength,' he lays down a great principle, which admits of many exceptions. In my case, it is quietness and regularity of life, not 'strength.' I have opened a vein of moralising, but must desist."

Again—

"Nov. 2, 1881.

"Yours of the 8th inst. reached me yesterday, and I

take the earliest opportunity of sitting down to pen a few lines in reply. They can be but few, however, for I am not competent to much work. I seem to be in fair spirits, and can enjoy reading and pleasant conversation, but application to anything soon tires me. Nevertheless, I have much to be thankful for. I am free from pain, I can enjoy food, my daily Bible readings contribute to comfort and pleasure, and, though I cannot walk far, I can sit an indefinite time in my library and amuse myself with the papers; while, in their columns, I am furnished with sad records of crime and suffering, which, fifty years ago, would have produced melancholy, but now pass by unheeded, as constituting the general news of the day, which I can receive without being affected by it—not that I am destitute of feeling, but I am not troubled or worried as I used to be, and can be indifferent on occasions which formerly produced vexation, or even anger. Old age has its chills and fogs, before it settles down in frost.

" You remember the spot where we left the remains of your dear mother. I had it enclosed with an iron railing, which has since been removed to our new cemetery, and another grave prepared, alongside of which my resting-place will be. I hope you will be able to accomplish your purpose of returning via Halifax. We long to see you.

" I am,

" Your affectionate father,

" J. M. CRAMP."

His daily journal, a brief record of books read, letters written, etc., contains the following entry for Nov. 23, 1881 :—" Finished Greek Testament for the 68th time." The words " Laus Deo " usually follow this statement in previous years, but writing had become too difficult to admit additions to the fact, eloquent in its simplicity.

A ready sympathy with those suffering under bereavement was a well-known characteristic. It was his invariable custom to write at once on hearing of the presence of affliction, and many letters of this nature attest the tenderness and sincerity of his feelings at such times. One of the last efforts of his pen was called forth by the intelligence of a sad loss sustained by our missionary friends, Rev. G. Churchill and Mrs. Churchill.

The following words of consolation were sent without delay :—

" Wolfville, Nov. 6, 1881.

" . . . I read yesterday, in one of our local papers, a statement that made my heart ache. It was to the effect that you had both been down with fever, and that your little boy had been carried away by it.

" . . . And now, what is to be done? You may copy Job, and say, ' The Lord gave, and the Lord hath taken away.' You know the rest; you may copy Eli, and exclaim, 'It is the Lord, let Him do what seemeth Him good;' you may imitate the friends of Paul (Acts xxi., 14), and whisper, ' The will of the Lord be done.' I think I hear you say, ' How can this be done ?' Turn to Heb. iv., 15-16. *Put it in practice ;* it will be a healing balm to your wounded spirits.

" I am a very old man, and this effort has wearied me, but it may possibly do you good, and that will be an ample reward. One of the good old Puritans had a customary form of salute when he met a friend. It was ' *God is good,*' and that is true still.

" Yours faithfully,

" J. M. Cramp."

Looking back upon the last few weeks of the life so soon to close, brings only the remembrance of a quiet waiting-time undisturbed by the pain of illness, and often brightened by intercourse with friends and the visits of his family. Towards the end of October, his younger son, G. B. Cramp, spent some days with him, and was impressed by his vigor of mind and the happiness of his daily life, restricted as it had now become, being chiefly spent in his library and adjoining room. It was observed that in saying " good-bye," instead of referring to the unlikelihood of again meeting, he seemed able to look forward to the possibility of extending another welcome ere long.

But this was not to be. The few days preceding the last brief illness were not marked by any special circumstances, shewing that he felt premonitions of the approaching event. A slight accession of weakness on Friday, Dec. 2, obliged him to call in medical aid, but he soon recovered his wonted vivacity.

The arrival of the English mail, with its welcome variety of news, aroused unfailing interest, and, seated in his easy chair, surrounded by the *Times*, *Illustrated News*, etc., he seemed as well as usual.

The funeral of a friend had taken place that day, and on his enquiring about the service, reference was made to the hymns used, when he said, "There is one that I consider specially suitable for such an occasion, particularly this verse," repeating—

> " Far from this world of toil and strife,
> They're present with the Lord.
> The labors of this mortal life
> End in a large reward."

A somewhat restless night was followed by a day of weakness, without pain, but, towards its close, increasing prostration obliged him to give up the effort of rising, a most unusual circumstance. Alluding to this, when a friend called in, he said, in a cheerful manner, " I don't like staying in bed, but am obliged ;" then added, with seriousness, " It is all right." Towards evening, every alarming symptom increased ; but a heavenly calm rested on his spirit. After listening to the 40th Psalm, he said, with solemnity, " It is time for prayer," offering up a most earnest and comprehensive petition, committing himself, and those dear to him, with the Church of God, to the Divine compassion. During that night of restlessness, and rapid sinking of the mortal powers, one subject only occupied his thoughts, even in the occasional wanderings that were observed. Then it was that he asked for the hymn, " All hail the power of Jesus' name ;" seeming disappointed that no one could sing it. After the last verse had been repeated, he raised his now faltering voice, and sang it through, saying, at the close, " That's it !" " Crown Him, Lord of all," dwelling with evident delight on the sentiments expressed in the concluding lines.

He was to see another " Lord's day," but its dawning found him very near the eternal Sabbath, " quite on the verge of Heaven," and resting calmly on the promises,—manifesting pleasure as they were occasionally repeated, especially the words contained in John xvii., 24.

He spoke of having " given a text " (John iii., 16) to one present, hoping he would "remember it; " and was able to see several friends as the day passed on.

One theme alone was present to his mind, even during the partial cloud of unconscious wandering, and the work and service in which his life had been so happily and usefully spent, formed the subject of constant reference. Scenes in the life of the Apostle Paul were re-called, then the class-room re-visited, while almost the wonted fervor and energy could be traced in his occasional utterances. The arrival, on the following day, of those members of his family who were able to reach him in time for a last interview, seemed to revive the fast-failing powers, other friends also obtaining a word or look of recognition. The pastor, the late Dr. de Blois, paid a farewell visit, and offered prayer, in the afternoon. Mr. Selden, his son-in-law, who had been with him during the day, being about to leave, was requested to sing the hymn, "All hail the power of Jesus' name!" which afforded evident pleasure.

His old friend, Mr. Barss, who had hastened from a long journey to see him, came in a little later.

To his question, "Is it peace?" the reply, "Happy, happy, happy!" was uttered with difficulty, but abundantly confirmed by the peaceful expression

resting upon his countenance. These words were
the last that could be understood; consciousness
continued through the evening, but the power of
utterance was gone. He still evinced his pleasure
in sacred themes, assenting to the words of Scripture as repeated to him, and waited, evidently
resting on the Rock of Ages . . . At length, "The
weary wheels of life stood still;" and on the morning of Tuesday, Dec. 6, "He was not, for God
took him."

> "Servant of God: well done!
> Rest from thy loved employ,
> The battle fought, the victory won,
> Enter thy Master's joy."

The following account of the funeral services is
taken from one of the Halifax daily papers :—

"WOLFVILLE, Dec. 8.

"The funeral of the late Rev. J. M. Cramp, D.D., took
place from his late residence this afternoon. During the
day, many callers were admitted to see the remains. As
he lay in his library, surrounded by the thousands of
volumes he had prized, he suggested the poem composed
on the death of Bryant :

> ' Dead among his books he lay.'

"A number of clergymen of different denominations
were present. The funeral services were conducted by
the pastor of the Wolfville Church, Rev. Dr. de Blois.
After a short service at the house, the procession was
formed, including the Sons of Temperance, members of
the Grand and Sub-Division, the Faculty and students of
Acadia College, in addition to large numbers of friends.
The casket was carried into the church, and remained

there during the services. These consisted of anthem by the choir:

'Blessed are the dead.'

"The hymn—

'Asleep in Jesus,'

read by Rev. S. B. Kempton, was sung, after which Rev. Dr. Welton read the 90th Psalm, and the Rev. Dr. Sawyer offered prayer. The hymn—

'Servant of God, well done!'

was read by Rev. Thos. Rogers, after which the pastor preached a very appropriate discourse from 2 Tim. 4; 7, 'I have fought a good fight.' Dr. de Blois gave a brief, but very clear exhibit of the labors and character of the deceased. Having been intimate with him for thirty years, no one was better prepared to render this last tribute to his memory.

"At the close of this address the hymn, read by the Rev. J. B. Logan, 'Hear what the voice from Heaven proclaims,' was sung, and prayer offered by the Rev. Dr. Crawley. The large congregation were then permitted to file by the body and look their last look upon one who has been a conspicuous public man for over sixty years.

"After the procession had re-formed, the remains were taken to the new cemetery, and deposited by the side of his wife. The burial service was pronounced by pastor de Blois, and the Rev. Dr. Saunders closed the proceedings by prayer and benediction. The church was appropriately draped for the occasion, and all the Faculty and students of the college wore mourning."

The following expression from the Board of Governors of Acadia College, will show the kindly relations existing between that body and deceased:

## "Rev. Dr. Cramp.

" Ed. Visitor.—Please insert the following resolution of condolence passed at a meeting of the Board of Governors of Acadia College, Dec. 15th, 1881 :—

" 'Our Heavenly Father in his wise Providence has taken home to himself our beloved brother in Christ, Rev. Dr. Cramp. The event, though not unexpected, for he had reached a ripe age, fills us with a sense of personal and public bereavement. This Board, and our whole Denomination has sustained a great loss, for though removed from active service through the weight of years for some time past, his sympathies were with us and his prayers unceasing in our behalf.

" ' Of the work performed for Acadia College by our deceased brother it is needless, if it were not impossible, for us to speak particularly. For his labors were incessant and abundant, and such as only a Christian man endowed with his great qualities of mind and heart, assisted by his wonderful and varied learning, could perform. They were labors for which Acadia College owes the most profound thanks to the Giver of all good.

" ' When Dr. Cramp came to take charge of our institutions of learning, great difficulties lay in our way, great discouragement was upon the hearts of its friends and patrons, and since then our way at times has been through serious trials.

" ' But from the first he manifested, and he ever maintained, a cheerful manly courage, and a truly Christian faith. To this spirit, as well as to the great efforts he put forth, is due, in great measure, the success that Acadia College has enjoyed.

" ' Our remembrance of the zeal of Dr. Cramp, in all our denominational enterprises, is grateful and will long be cherished. He sought to inspire all around him with zeal for Christ and his cause.

" 'By his pen he not only defended the truth, but he sought to comfort his brethren and to confirm their faith.

" 'The pastors of our churches, our home and foreign missionaries, will greatly miss his kind and wise counsel and sympathy.

" 'With the Board of Governors Dr. Cramp ever sustained kind and pleasant relationship. Before the Board he brought wise and generous measures of usefulness ; to the Board he looked for co-operation and support ; and with the Board, through all the changes and events of its official history, he maintained the most amicable relations.

" 'We have lost a dear friend, but our Lord has taken him from us. He rests from his labors and his 'works follow ' him.

" 'To his family in their bereavement we tender our sincere sympathy. May the God of their honored father grant to them abundantly the consolations of his grace.'

" By order of the Board,

" S. W. DE BLOIS, Sec'y.

" Wolfville, Dec. 15, 1881."

In addition to other expressions of regard from former students of Acadia College, the Alumni Association placed a Tablet in the library bearing the following inscription :—

IN MEMORIAM.

JOHN MOCKETT CRAMP, D.D.,

PRESIDENT OF ACADIA COLLEGE FOR MANY YEARS,

DIED AT WOLFVILLE, DEC. 6, 1881,

AGED 84 YEARS.

"THE SECOND FOUNDER OF ACADIA,"

FIRST ELECTED PRESIDENT IN 1851.

HE CONTINUED HIS CONNECTION WITH THIS COLLEGE UPWARDS OF 30 YEARS.

---

ERECTED BY THE ALUMNI OF THE COLLEGE.

# APPENDIX.

## THOMAS CRAMP.

Reference has been made, in the foregoing volume, to this eldest son of Dr. Cramp. A somewhat more extended notice will not be unacceptable to the reader. If he has taken an interest in Dr. Cramp's parents and forefathers, in their worth and works, he will be pleased to learn that one of his children should have so spent his time, and employed his talents in the service of his fellows and the commonwealth, that, on his premature decease, his fellow-citizens deemed no marks of honour and respect too great to pay to his memory.

A constant resident in Montreal from the year 1844, date of the arrival there of the Cramp family, he early took a prominent position and held a leading place in the commercial, political and social life of his adopted land. He survived his father scarcely more than three years; dying on 18th February, 1885, Æt 57; meeting his death, as will be seen, through exposure, in the service of a philanthropic institution.

The following extracts from newspapers published at the time, in the city of Montreal, will give a short sketch of his life, and some idea of the universal esteem in which he was held. Every periodical in that city contained leading articles in reference to him, with an account of his life and works, and expressions of the highest appreciation of the worth of the deceased, and the general grief at his loss—but space will not permit of their entire production :—

(*The Times*, Montreal, Feb. 18, 1885.)

"Thomas Cramp.

———

"Nothing could have been more surprising or startling to our business men and fellow-citizens generally than the news which, this morning, circulated through the city that Mr. Thomas Cramp was no more. The feeling was intensified from the knowledge conveyed by the public press that, almost the day before, he had attended to his business affairs apparently in his ordinary health and spirits, and, in response to the calls upon his noble spirit of philanthropy, had, in the evening, taken a prominent part at a meeting of the Boys' Home, when he availed himself of the opportunity of addressing to them and for them timely words of counsel and encouragement. We learn that on Saturday Mr. Cramp had experienced a slight pain and soreness in his throat, to which he paid no attention; but which on Sunday became greater, particularly on his way home from church. Feeling no worse, and attaching no importance to the affection, he went down to business as usual on Monday, not leaving his office until half-past six. He attended the meeting we have referred to in the evening, because he considered it a duty incumbent upon him, although he was somewhat out of sorts, and the weather more than ordinarily tempestuous. On Tuesday he became seriously ill, and early in the day grave doubts were expressed as to the possibility of his recovery. In the afternoon, the symptoms became so alarming that, after consultations between Drs. Howard, Roddick and Bell, it was determined to perform an operation upon the throat. This afforded temporary relief, but it soon became apparent that Mr. Cramp's case was hopeless, and he passed away this morning at four o'clock. To say that the life of the deceased had been an active and a useful one, that he had a bright and keen intellect, that he was esteemed for his many excellent qualities, not only by the mercantile community, but in social circles and benevolent efforts, would scarcely describe his nature, for his was a more than ordinarily noble character. In everything which tended to promote the best interests of Montreal, and indeed, the whole country, he was—to say the least of it—foremost. Those who knew him best have in every sense lost a wise and kindly counsellor. Indeed, Montreal has not, for a long time, experienced so great a loss by the death of one of her inhabitants.

"Mr. Cramp was born in April, 1827, in London, England, and came to this country in 1844 with his father, the late Rev. Dr. Cramp, who had been appointed President of the Canadian Baptist College in this city. Shortly after his arrival here he entered the office of Messrs. John Leeming & Co., then one of the leading auction and commission houses in Canada. Soon after, he obtained a position with the old and influential firm of John Torrance & Co., this firm being succeeded by that of David Torrance & Co., in which Mr. Cramp was a partner for about thirty-five years, becoming head of the establishment on the demise of Mr. David Torrance. His business career has been a most stirring one, the firm being at one time the largest exporters and importers in the St. Lawrence trade; and to this Mr. Cramp materially contributed. He was considered, in fact, so experienced and reliable an authority on commercial matters that, as an adviser, he was largely sought after. Among many positions which he filled, have been that of Director in the Liverpool, London & Globe Insurance Company, the Molsons and Union Banks, the Canada Guarantee Company, and a host of other positions of responsibility and usefulness. He had filled the office, several times, of President of the Board of Trade, and, during his whole life, was one of its most active members, taking part in all the deliberations which affected the trade of the country. While at the head of the Board, in 1860, it will be remembered that the Norwegian corvette Ornen arrived in port, the event being appropriately celebrated. For the interest which he took in this affair the King of Sweden and Norway invested him with the order of St. Olaf.

"Among the very last compliments paid to the deceased by the merchants of Montreal was his election, the other day, to the Presidency of the Corn Exchange; and he had just begun to introduce some much needed reforms in the government of that body. But it was in matters connected with the port of Montreal, that Mr. Cramp's great ability and far-sightedness were best manifested, especially in connection with the harbor, he having, for many years, been a member of the Commission, succeeding the late Hon. John Young as Chairman. There are few, if any, matters which directly affected the shipping interests of the St. Lawrence, which did not engage his serious consideration, and his name will long be remembered in connection with those important concerns.

"Of late years Mr. Cramp had devoted himself almost exclusively to the ocean carrying trade. In 1872, the line of steamships known in England as 'The Liverpool and Mississippi,' of which Captain Flynn was the head, was induced, through the exertions of Mr. Cramp, to trade with the St. Lawrence, the name of the line being changed at that date to 'the Mississippi and Dominion Steamship Company,' Messrs. David Torrance & Co., being then appointed the agents. At that date the gross tonnage of the vessels supplying the service was 9,072, the vessels being the Mississippi, Captain Bouchette; the Vicksburg, Captain Pearson; the Memphis, Captain Weeks, now the Company's agent in New Orleans; and the St. Louis, Captain Roberts. The energy with which the line has been managed since the time of its organization is abundantly shown by the increase in its tonnage to 38,910 and the improved class of vessels which it now owns. We may add that during the writer's residence in Montreal, about thirty years, Mr. Cramp had always been a prominent member of every delegation seeking concession or redress at the hands of the Government. In politics, Mr. Cramp was a staunch Liberal, and never swerved from the political principles which he held. This much can be said of him, that he never was known to offend a single member of the party to which he was opposed. In temper, in fact, he was, perhaps, the most calm man we have known, even in the discussion of the most burning questions, and was personally held in the highest esteem by every member of the Conservative Party.

"The late Mr. Cramp leaves a widow, to whom he was married in 1866, and had two children, a boy and a girl. Among those who specially mourn his loss are his four sisters, Mrs. G. B. Muir, of this city; Mrs. T. A. Higgins of Wolfville, Nova Scotia; Mrs. Stephen Selden, of Halifax; and one unmarried. Mr. G. B. Cramp, the well-known advocate, of this city, is his brother. Mr. Cramp will be sadly missed in every circle

25

of life, particularly by the inmates of the Deaf and
Dumb Institute, the Boys' Home, Ladies' Benevolent
Institution and many kindred establishments. The
funeral will take place on Saturday afternoon, at two
o'clock, from his residence, St. Urbain street."

———

(*Montreal Herald*, Feb. 19, 1885.)

## "THE LATE MR. THOMAS CRAMP.

### "A VOID LEFT IN COMMERCIAL CIRCLES THAT CANNOT BE ADEQUATELY FILLED — DECEASED'S CAREER IN MONTREAL FOR FORTY YEARS.

"It is a long time in the history of Montreal since
any local event or calamity has happened that awakened
so much surprise and profound regret and sympathy as
the announcement yesterday morning of the entire unexpected death of the late Mr. Thomas Cramp. Those
who knew deceased intimately felt the blow as a personal affliction, and all who had met him in life were
bowed down with grief and emotion for his loss. His
presence in his daily haunts here was so recent, and
nothing being known of his illness, every one expressed
a hope the report was untrue, but on proceeding to the
office of D. Torrance & Son, the sight of the sad emblem
of mortality left no longer room to doubt that their
former friend's spirit had taken flight from earth. The
fatal news becoming current early in the morning,
nothing else was thought of, and as friend met friend
the absorbing subject was the irreparable loss that had
fallen upon the city. Everyone who had known the
man whose prominence as a citizen has been long admitted, had nothing upon their lips to say of the deceased but to praise his merits and extol his genial
manner.

"That he had rare gifts of intellect, of oratory, not, however, of the ornate style, and persuasive eloquence in public all acknowledged. His great services in behalf of the city and port, as well as all our public benevolent institutions, were recognized in the most complimentary terms. Who will fill his place? was repeatedly asked. But no one would venture to answer, and no wonder; for the deceased was no ordinary man in any respect, as those who have measured his mental calibre can testify. There was probably no commercial man in this great city, who had only received a practical business education like deceased, who was his peer in having such a well-stored mind from extensive reading of the highest literature of every description. His rich fund of information, particularly on local and national questions, was well known to all members of the Press who had the pleasure of knowing him. The writer has had much personal experience in drawing upon the never-failing stores of valuable information which the subject of this obituary notice possessed. It was like a fountain that never ceased to flow, and it always came with such geniality and facility of expression that captivated the listener, and made the most abstruse subject clear and simple. . . . . .

"Deceased's business instincts and training gave him a methodical system of conducting all assemblies he presided over. He had a difficult function to perform when appointed to take up the important work of the harbor and river, left unfinished by his accomplished predecessor, the Hon. John Young. How well he succeeded is known by the thanks he received from the Board when the exigencies of politics obliged him to retire from the office. The most striking testimony to his merits in the office of President is the fact that his successor has followed on the lines laid down by the late Messrs.

Cramp and Honorable John Young. Ever since his retirement, the late Mr. Cramp has taken as deep an interest as previously in promoting every well-devised scheme to improve the port and increase its supremacy on this continent. His views were often deferred to, and he was looked upon as an authority on all projects connected with the harbor. Deceased's advice was equally sought and valued in connection with commercial troubles or intricacies arising in public bodies, that his clear judgment and preciseness soon settled. One of his greatest achievements has been the successful founding of a fleet of magnificent steamships which are not surpassed in any part of the world, with a tonnage of nearly 40,000 tons, and all accomplished in a few years.

"The deceased inherited from his father that love of freedom which the old English Whigs were so conspicuous for. He was not extreme in his political views, and like many other intellectual Liberals, here and throughout Canada, espoused the National Policy. He was not an office-seeker, and never deserted the principles he set out on. Probably no citizen in any station had such a placid and kindly disposition as deceased. Even in the heat of debate he never wounded the feelings of the most sensitive of his opponents, and it is a proverb that he never made an enemy. In his long career in commerce his credit and integrity were unimpeached and unimpeachable. He was universally respected and esteemed for every good quality that adorns an honorable, upright and honest man. . . The deceased identified himself both by his purse and public advocacy with all our benevolent institutions, and will be sadly missed in the sphere of doing good in an unpretentious way. The inscrutable hand of death has been severe in Montreal of late, many of its most estimable and honored citizens having fallen before the scythe of time, but the memories of none will remain longer engraven on the hearts of friends than those of noble Thomas Cramp. . . . "

———

(*Montreal Daily Witness*, Feb. 18th, 1885.)

"THE CORN EXCHANGE SORROWS FOR ITS PRESIDENT'S DEATH.

"A meeting of the members of the Corn Exchange was held to-day at twelve o'clock, to express their sense of the loss sustained in the sudden death of Mr. Cramp, President of the association. Amongst those present were:—Messrs. James Allen, Robert Archer, John Baird, John Brodie, Charles Drummond, R. W. Esdaile, W. J. Fairbairn, Charles H. Gould, Robert Hampson, J. G. Hunsicker, W. F. Johnston, Edgar Judge, II. Labelle, John Magor, James Macdougall, Alexander McFee, J. B. McLea, D. A. McPherson, John Ogilvie, W. W. Ogilvie, R. Reddie, D. G. Rees, David Robertson, R. T. Routh, S. St. Onge, W. Stewart, D. A. P. Watt, John M. Young and others.

"Mr. Magor, acting president, said they had just sustained a great loss in the sudden death of their president, Mr. Thomas Cramp. The calamity was so unexpected that it almost took their breath away, and rendered it difficult to say all that might well be said. When asked to accept the office of president, Mr. Cramp's modesty rather inclined him to shrink from the honor, and he stated to him, the speaker, that he had not taken sufficient interest in the association, or made sufficient effort to merit such a distinction. One of the projects which he had in contemplation was the establishment of a reading room and mercantile association, with the object of infusing new life and vigor into their body.

He was sure every member present deplored the loss
which had been sustained. Among other qualities Mr.
Cramp bore a warmth and goodness of heart, for which,
perhaps, he did not always get sufficient credit. The
following resolutions have been drawn up for the acceptance of the meeting :—

'That the members of the Montreal Corn Exchange Association have heard with the deepest sorrow of the sudden decease
of their president, Thomas Cramp, Esq., who had been associated with this Association from its organization, and has also
been prominently identified for the past thirty years with the
mercantile and shipping interests of this port.'

'That the acting-president and committee are hereby desired to convey to the bereaved family the heartfelt sympathy
of this Association.'

'That to mark their respect for the memory of the deceased
the Board do now adjourn till Monday, the 23rd inst., and that
the acting-president, the committee of management, and the
Board of Review, with the members of the Association generally, attend the funeral on Saturday next.'

"The Acting-president formally proposed the foregoing
resolutions, which

"Mr. Edgar Judge seconded in a few well-chosen and
feeling remarks. He endorsed all that had been said by
the chairman, referred to the interest which the deceased had taken in the affairs of the associations, and
to the suddenness of the blow which left them unpre-
pared to adequately express all that was felt upon so
melancholy an occasion.

"Mr. Watt said that upon such an occasion silence was,
perhaps, more fitting and more eloquent than speech.
His intercourse with the deceased had been of long
duration, extending into the forties. He was in thorough
accord with the resolution of sympathy which was before the meeting, and endorsed all that had been said
regarding the estimable qualities of the deceased.

"The resolutions were put to the meeting and unanimously adopted.

"The meeting then adjourned.

"Much admiration has been expressed by many of Mr. Cramp's friends for what proved to be his last public act in life. For a citizen to leave upper St. Urbain street on such a night, and go down to the Boys' Home on Mountain street, was no ordinary act. It is generally believed that the over-exertion thus made in the interest of these boys was the exciting cause of the trouble which carried him off."

---

(*Montreal Daily Witness*, Feb. 21st, 1885.)

## "AN HONORED GENTLEMAN.

### " FUNERAL OBSEQUIES OF THE LATE MR. THOMAS CRAMP.

" Seldom has there ever assembled in Montreal such a large and representative gathering of citizens, mourning for the loss of a departed friend and *confrère*, as that which gathered this afternoon to pay the last tribute of respect to the late Mr. Thomas Cramp, whose lamented death has caused so much sorrow in the community. The funeral took place from the late residence of the deceased, No. 70 St. Urbain street, at two o'clock, and at that hour the street was thronged, sleighs bringing to the house Montreal's most prominent citizens, the majority of whom took occasion to take a last look at the face of him who in his lifetime had been such a genial companion and true friend. The mournful *cortège* formed shortly after two o'clock, and proceedad by way of St. Urbain street to St. Martin's Church.

" Among the last number of prominent citizens noticed in the procession were Messrs. Thomas Workman, Hec-

tor Mackenzie, Lieut.-Col. Fletcher, Ald. Donovan, John
Torrance, William Weir, F. W. Henshaw, Henry Lyman,
S. Bethune, Q.C., George Hague, William Angus, Joseph
Hickson, L. J. Sargeant, M. P. Ryan, T. B. Hawson,
Hon. Justice Cross, Hon. Henry Starnes, Rev. J. Edgar
Hill, E. K. Greene, Henry Bulmer, John Molson, Andrew
Robertson, President of the Harbor Commissioners; John
Kerry, President of the Board of Trade; John Magor,
Acting-President of the Corn Exchange, of which the
deceased gentleman was only recently elected Presi-
dent; W. J. Patterson, Secretary of the Board of Trade
and Corn Exchange; Capt. Morrison and Mr. Shaw,
representing the Port Warden's Office; Capt. Howard,
Harbor Master; Edgar Judge, F. W. Matthews, D. J.
Rees, Lieut.-Col. Crawford, D. A. P. Watt, Mr. J. F. D.
Black, City Treasurer; H. R. Ives, H. W. Whitney, Sec-
retary of the Harbor Commissioners; the Rev. Canon
Ellegood, the Hon. Judge Monk, Thomas White, M.P.,
ex-Ald. Hagar, Capt. Shepherd, S. Waddell, John Baird,
J. K. Ward, Guillaume Boivin, ex-Ald. Proctor, W. H.
Munderloh, H. Blaiklock, M. M. Tait, Q.C., Edward
Murphy, Richard White, J. C. Baker, R. J. Routh, —
Benson, — St. Onge, Ald. Stroud, — Kinghorn, R. D.
Haig, Joseph Doutre, Q.C., Ald. Laurent, James Stewart,
Dr. Bell, C. R. Hosmer, Charles Drinkwater, Hon. Donald
A. Smith, D. A. Macmaster, Q.C., James Darling, J. C.
Gilman, Ald. McShane, — McIntosh, William Murray,
Hon. Judge Loranger, J. N. Loranger, Q.C., W. H.
Kerr, Q.C., James Popham, Alexander Gowdey, F. L.
Beique, John Crawford, the Hon. Judge Mathieu, the Hon.
Judge Sicotte, Hollis Shorey, Henry Hogan, Charles Alex-
ander, Capt. Ritchie, William Clendinneng, S. P. Starnes,
United States Consul-General; L. Armstrong,—Grant, L.
Sutherland, Hugh Patton, W. H. Arnton, the Hon. J. S. C.
Würtele, A. B. Chaffee, Louis Lesage, Edward Holton, M.

P., John Lewis, William Norris, J. Kennedy, Harbor Engineer ; Alexander Walker, J. Ross,—Forsythe,—Law, J. M. Duff, F. N. Boxer,—Peddie, Selkirk Cross, A. W. Hadrill,—McEwen, Learmonth, W. M. Ramsay, Hugh Mackay, E. Stewart, J. F. Wulff, Robert W. Tyre, R. W. Shepherd, James Gilmour, Hon. J. R. Thibaudeau, C. A. Geoffrion, Q.C., and many others. The *cortège* was followed by numerous private sleighs, and the unanimous opinion was that it was the largest funeral seen in Montreal for a long time, the gathering showing in what universal esteem and regard the deceased gentleman was held.

"The pall-bearers were Sir Francis Hincks, Messrs. A. Allan, A. M. Forbes, J. Torrance, J. Molson, F. W. Henshaw, F. W. Thomas, and the Hon. H. Starnes. Immediately after the hearse came the chief mourners, consisting of the son of the deceased, Mr. Martin B. Cramp; his brother, Mr. George B. Cramp; his nephews, Messrs. Frank Muir and H. B. Muir ; his brothers-in-law, Messrs. G. B. Muir, W. Dunn and J. Dunn, and his nephew, Mr. G. Dunn.

"Previous to the formation of the procession, a private service for the widow and other relatives of the deceased was conducted at the house by the Rev. J. S. Stone, B.D., pastor of St. Martin's Church.

"St. Martin's Church was filled to overflowing. The coffin was met at the entrance, amidst solemn silence (except for the tolling of the funeral bell), by the Rev. Canon Ellegoode, who preceded the remains, reading the first portion of the Church of England service for the burial of the dead; the organist, Mr. Taylor, at the same time rendering 'The Dead March in Saul.' The hymn, ' When our heads are bowed with woe,' was then sung, and the Thirty-ninth Psalm followed, together with the Ninetieth Psalm (*Domine, refugium*). The Rev. Canon Mulloch then proceeded to the centre aisle and read, in

26

a most solemn voice, the beautiful words of the fifteenth chapter of the First Epistle to the Corinthians, beginning at verse 20, 'Now hath Christ risen from the dead.' Hymn 105, 'In the Lord's atoning grief,' was next sung, and the Rev. J. S. Stone, the rector, read the concluding portions of the service. Hymn 140, 'Jesus lives,' having been admirably rendered by the choir, the service closed with the benediction.

"The funeral *cortège* again formed, and the mortal remains were conveyed to the Mount Royal Cemetery.

"The deceased lay in a handsome coffin in the room wherein he died, and appeared very life-like. The coffin was covered with beautiful floral trophies from sympathising friends—one, a sheaf of corn resting on a floral sickle, being extremely nice. The largest and most noticeable tribute was the one from the Boys' Home, Mountain Street, consisting of a cross and anchor. The letter sent with this trophy, Mrs. Cramp desired our reporter to state publicly, was, she considered, an extremely kind one, and nothing could have been sent more acceptable to herself and family than the letter and tribute, especially as her late husband had often expressed his belief that no institution existed of a more deserving nature than that of the Boys' Home. Mrs. Cramp has received very many sympathetic letters from kind friends, all of whom she also desired to thank.

"Other floral trophies were a beautiful cushion composed of camelias, roses, smilax, etc., from the Liverpool, London & Globe Insurance Company; a magnificent anchor from the employés of the Portland office of the Dominion Steamship Company; a very large and costly wreath from the members of the Corn Exchange, etc.

"The inmates of the Boys' Home sent a beautiful floral tribute in the shape of an anchor interwoven with beautiful flowers, bearing the inscription, 'Boys' Home.' The tribute was arranged by Mr. Bain, florist. The following letter accompanied it:—

" 'Boys' Home,

" 'Montreal, 19th Feb., 1885.

"'Dear Lady,—Our hearts have been saddened by the loss we boys of the Home have sustained through the death of our friend, your husband, Mr. Thomas Cramp. Throughout the past year his interest in the Home has been steadily increasing, and at our annual meeting he expressed himself so warmly attached to us, that he would in the future, if spared, advocate our cause among the commercial community, of which he was so prominent a member. This providence of our Heavenly Father has cast a gloom over all our spirits, and we will not soon forget him, who sacrificed his comfort on that stormy night, and no doubt aggravated the disease which prematurely shortened his life.

"'Dear Mrs. Cramp, please accept this wreath from us boys, our humble and only way of conveying to you and family our earnest sympathy. Our prayer is that the Great Friend, our Heavenly Father, who has been, according to His promise, a husband to many of our mothers in a similar position, and a father to us also, who has always gone before and guided our footsteps until to-day, may be thy husband and father,—and though to-day the darkness seems impenetrable, rest assured He will not leave you comfortless, but will send his light and life into your heart and mind.

"'We will try and imitate his example in his self-sacrifice, for the good of others in need, and we are confident this is only our Lord's way of raising up for us many friends, who will carry on the work he desired should be done on behalf of the boys.

" 'Yours, in sympathy, One of the Boys,

" 'Horace Davis.

·" 'Mrs. Thomas Cramp.'"

"The boys of the Boys' Home, under Mr. Dick, attended the funeral in a body."

# A PASTOR'S NOTICE.

The Sunday following the funeral, the Rev. J. S. Stone, vicar of St. Martin's Church, at the close of an eloquent and earnest sermon on the text, "Who then can be saved," in which he pointed out the self-sacrifice necessary in a truly Christian life, referred in touching terms to the decease of Mr. Cramp. He said that his loss was terribly sudden, as only a week ago he was worshipping with them in that church, and now he was dead and buried. As a business man, as an active member of philanthropic movements, as a member of that church which he loved so well, the deceased gentleman stood high in public estimation. His activity in every good work, and his sympathy with every benevolent movement were well known; and the loss caused by his death would be widely and generally felt. Although Mr. Cramp was very fond of music and singing, he very rarely joined in the singing, so far as he himself had observed, and yet he had noticed, he could not tell why, that at the last service which he attended, the deceased gentleman joined most heartily in singing the hymn, "Just as I am without one plea," while his face seemed lit up with joy and happiness. That was the last time that he saw him in church; the last time he saw his face in this world it wore the same happy and peaceful expression. "And the next time," said the preacher, "that I see him—may God have mercy upon my own soul—I shall see him before the Throne, singing the song which only the redeemed know."—G. B. C.